D0207795

Praise for
the Ladies of
St. Jude's Abbey Series

A Moonlit Knight

"*A Moonlit Knight* is . . . lively . . . full of exciting action and adventure." —Roberta Gellis

"Exciting, thrilling, and very romantic! Jocelyn Kelley has renewed my love of medieval romance with her unusual, but brilliant, perspective." —JoyfullyReviewed.com

One Knight Stands

"A splendid read." —Virginia Henley

"Exhilarating . . . an action-packed tale of honor, courage, and spirit that never strays from its wonderful romance. I'm hooked on this series!" —Susan Grant

continued . . .

A Knight Like No Other

"A fresh approach to a medieval romance."
—*Romantic Times*

"A wondrous tale of love and honor set among one of the most troubling times of the past."
—Huntress Book Reviews

"Kelley brings new excitement to medieval romance with a powerful swordswoman heroine, a stubborn knightly hero, and a nonstop adventure that draws them together in a passion like no other." —Mary Jo Putney

"Historical romance at its best!" —May McGoldrick

"Jocelyn Kelley is an engaging storyteller with extraordinary skill . . . lively and entertaining!"
—Margaret Evans Porter

**The Ladies of
St. Jude's Abbey Series
by Jocelyn Kelley**

A Knight Like No Other

One Knight Stands

A Moonlit Knight

My Lady Knight

Jocelyn Kelley

A SIGNET ECLIPSE BOOK

SIGNET ECLIPSE
Published by New American Library, a division of
Penguin Group (USA) Inc., 375 Hudson Street,
New York, New York 10014, USA
Penguin Group (Canada), 90 Eglinton Avenue East, Suite 700, Toronto,
Ontario M4P 2Y3, Canada (a division of Pearson Penguin Canada Inc.)
Penguin Books Ltd., 80 Strand, London WC2R 0RL, England
Penguin Ireland, 25 St. Stephen's Green, Dublin 2,
Ireland (a division of Penguin Books Ltd.)
Penguin Group (Australia), 250 Camberwell Road, Camberwell, Victoria 3124,
Australia (a division of Pearson Australia Group Pty. Ltd.)
Penguin Books India Pvt. Ltd., 11 Community Centre, Panchsheel Park,
New Delhi - 110 017, India
Penguin Group (NZ), cnr Airborne and Rosedale Roads, Albany,
Auckland 1310, New Zealand (a division of Pearson New Zealand Ltd.)
Penguin Books (South Africa) (Pty.) Ltd., 24 Sturdee Avenue,
Rosebank, Johannesburg 2196, South Africa

Penguin Books Ltd., Registered Offices:
80 Strand, London WC2R 0RL, England

First published by Signet Eclipse, an imprint of New American Library,
a division of Penguin Group (USA) Inc.

First Printing, January 2007
10　9　8　7　6　5　4　3　2　1

Copyright © Jo Ann Ferguson, 2007
All rights reserved

SIGNET ECLIPSE and logo are trademarks of Penguin Group (USA) Inc.

Printed in the United States of America

PUBLISHER'S NOTE
This is a work of fiction. Names, characters, places, and incidents either are the product
of the author's imagination or are used fictitiously, and any resemblance to actual per-
sons, living or dead, business establishments, events, or locales is entirely coincidental.
　　The publisher does not have any control over and does not assume any responsibility for author or third-party Web sites or their content.

For James Jones
Thanks for all the information you shared.
Sometimes what happens in Vegas doesn't stay in Vegas.

Chapter 1

A single mistake could be disastrous.

Isabella de Montfort repeated those words over and over to herself, not that she needed to. Whenever she worked with dangerous elements, she was aware of how unforgiving they could be. It was not like when she blended herbs or used polished healing stones. Then, a single mistake only meant starting over. A misstep with elements could do far more damage.

She held her breath as she raised the glass bottle over the dish set on the table in the center of the stone barn. She watched a drop slide down the glass toward the opening. Only a single drop must be allowed to fall into the dish. More would be unsafe. The strong, bitter odor of the elements scratched her throat as she stirred them together.

With a satisfied smile as the elements blended correctly, she carried the bottle to the shelves where she stored her supplies. She kept them behind a locked door because she did not want anyone else in St. Jude's Abbey moving them and causing an accident. Closing the door, she secured it with the key she wore on the end of a string around her neck.

Isabella went back to the table as she wiped her hands on the leather apron she wore over her simple gray gown. She opened one of the half dozen pouches she wore on her waist sash and drew out a slip of smooth hide. For the past few years, she had kept her most frequently used materials in small pouches. She needed to make notes about the experiment, for she must be able to repeat the process with the same result to prove it was not a fluke. Sitting on a stool by the table, she tapped the quill against her chin as she considered the next step.

She did not have much time before vespers. The rest of the experiment would have to wait until tomorrow. Nobody else should be nearby because she was never certain what the results of her mixtures might be. During the afternoon, being alone was not difficult. Each day after the midday meal, the other sisters of St. Jude's Abbey practiced their skills with Nariko and her fellow instructors who taught swordsmanship and other defensive arts in the cleared areas within the Abbey and in the fields beyond its walls.

Isabella always took advantage of the hours when the cloister was quiet. Unlike most of her sisters, she enjoyed the silence. It offered her an opportunity to think without intrusion.

And just now she was thinking if she added a bit more salt water to the mixture . . .

Jumping to her feet, she went to the storage cupboard, unlocked the door, and took out a bottle. Once she finished this test, she wanted to turn her attention to the experiment she never had been able to make work. A fantastic tale from beyond Outremer spoke of a compound that, when properly mixed and lit with a brand, created a controlled explosion. She had been trying for the past six years to devise the proper formula. She was getting closer to the solution, knowing it contained both sulfur and charcoal because of the description of its residual odor, but she had not solved it.

For now, she must concentrate on her current project. She bent over the bowl and prepared to pour more water into it.

"Sister Isabella, are you here?" came a call from the other side of the barn.

Isabella set the bottle down, then moved it away from the dish, as she looked past stacks of empty barrels in the barn. She recognized the youthful voice. "What are you doing here at this hour, Zuki?"

A girl, who had celebrated the twelfth anniversary of her

birth a few weeks ago, stepped out from the shadows. Mikazuki was the only child born to Nariko and her husband, George, who oversaw the Abbey's gardens and fields. Born in the second year of Queen Eleanor's imprisonment, Zuki—as she was called by the sisters—had inherited her mother's tilted eyes and ebony hair. She had dark green eyes like her father and his ability to make anything sprout, which was why she often spent time with Isabella. She had endless questions about the herbs Isabella grew for the stillroom.

"I am avoiding *Kāchan*," Zuki said as she shut the door before inching closer to where Isabella was working. She wore the short tunic donned for practicing with the instructors.

"Your mother will be vexed," Isabella replied, knowing that the word meant "mother" in Nariko's native language. It was of the far distant land from where her mother's father had traveled west to Persia and the Holy Land. There, Queen Eleanor first encountered him and his daughter, Nariko, and invited them to return with her to England.

"She knows I do not like to practice with a bow and arrow." She slashed the air with an imaginary blade. "I prefer something sharper. Or maybe you can teach me to use a whip as you do." She pointed to the leather coiled over Isabella's right hip.

With a frown, Isabella walked around the table to keep the girl from coming nearer. Zuki was all elbows and knees as she seemed taller each morning. If she bumped something . . . Isabella did not even want to think of that. Folding her arms in front of her, she said, "You cannot hide here today."

"But, Sister Isabella, you said I could always come and learn from you."

"Not today. What I am doing is dangerous, and I will not put you in jeopardy."

Zuki crossed her arms over her narrow chest, copying Isabella's pose as she stamped her foot against the stone floor. "You said—"

"*Ame futte ji katamaru* is what your mother says."

The girl rolled her eyes. "Sister Isabella! Don't use that old saying! *Kāchan* speaks in her father's tongue only when she wants to teach me a lesson."

"Do you remember what those words mean? 'Rain firms the ground.'"

"I know it is supposed to caution a young person that challenges make one stronger." She let her arms fall to her sides. "Please don't lecture me, too."

"Too?"

"Sister Dominique insists I study all sorts of weapons."

"As everyone else does."

"You don't."

Isabella forced her lips to remain in a smile. "Not now, but I have. You know it is the abbess's wish that each of us find the path that brings us the most joy and offers us a purpose. I found my path when I was close to your age. You need to continue studying until you find yours."

Muttering something, Zuki went to look out the window. She did that, Isabella had learned, when she had no argument left, but was unwilling to concede. That stubborn nature was the very thing that would compel Zuki to keep at her studies.

It was unfortunate that Isabella had not learned that lesson herself. She admired the sisters who could command a sword. She had seen Sister Fayette swing a sword through a stack of onions in a single blow, slicing them in equal halves. The sisters who controlled the flight of an arrow with ease awed her. Sister Dominique was equally skilled with a quarterstaff and a short blade, sometimes combining the two, and Isabella was breathless watching her.

But working with herbs and science was the way Isabella had chosen. She had read every manuscript she could find about elements and humors that could bring health or sickness. During a hard winter almost five years ago, she had saved the abbess when a vile fever had taken several lives within the Abbey. She had been commended, but she wondered if everything she learned really mattered when she was not as skilled as her sisters. If she could create the compound from the bits of information she had garnered from torn pages and discussions with Nariko, she would prove she was as capable of serving the Abbey as anyone else within its walls.

"Sister Isabella!" came a shout from beyond the barn.

"It is Sister Charlotta," Zuki said, pushing away from the window. "Running!"

"Sister Charlotta is running?" Isabella was shocked. The stout sister seldom moved faster than a snail, even when going into the chapel. Sister Charlotta had been the cause for many sisters getting soaked in a sudden shower outside the church door.

Going to the door, she opened it. "I am in here, Sister Charlotta. Is something amiss?"

"Thank goodness you are here." The rotund sister stumbled into the barn. "The abbess— Let me catch my breath." She put her hand out to steady herself against a barrel as she sucked in air. The barrels rocked; then one tumbled onto another. With a loud thump, one fell onto the table. It collapsed. The bowl and bottle flew, smashing against a wall. A barrel bounced toward Zuki.

Loosening the whip from her belt, Isabella snaked it out. It wrapped around the girl's waist. She tugged hard. Zuki stumbled toward her. The barrel struck the wall near the window. Another rolled across the barn, hitting beneath the other window and shattering. The wooden hoops holding it together bounced across the floor to land atop the broken table.

"Oh my!" choked Sister Charlotta. "I did not mean to ruin your barn, Sister Isabella."

"Are you all right?" She looked at Sister Charlotta and then at Zuki, who was loosening the whip from around her.

"That was amazing!" Zuki cried. "I did not realize you could do that with your whip, Sister Isabella. Will you teach me how to capture someone with a whip?"

"Maybe later." As she coiled her whip once more, she stared around at what was left of her work area. It would take days to clean the mess.

"I never guessed," Zuki continued, too excited to stand still, "that barrels could bounce so high. Did you see the one that hit the ceiling?"

Isabella was about to reply when a motion caught her eye. Something liquid was running along the wall. She gasped in horror. The door on her storage cabinet was open. Bottles were broken or tipped over. Liquids and powders were mixing together. A finger of smoke came from beneath the cracked table.

It was the only warning she needed. She shoved Zuki toward the door. It was too far.

"Get behind the barrels!" she ordered.

"Barrels? Which ones?"

"Any one!" She grabbed Sister Charlotta's arm. She pushed the shocked woman next to Zuki and threw herself over another barrel to kneel behind it.

"Cover your ears!" she shouted. "It is going to explode."

Sister Charlotta stared in horror. Zuki's eyes were wide with excitement and fear.

"Cover your ears!" She put her hands up over her own ears. "Now!"

The explosion rocked the building. Flames erupted toward the thatched roof. Shards of stone and wood crashed into the walls. Pain rammed her left shoulder. Hearing a cry, she could not tell if it came from Zuki or Sister Charlotta. The sound was everywhere, inside her as well as outside. Was the whole world blowing up?

Then it was silent.

Dust and thatch and slivers of wood tumbled around her. She coughed as she waved aside the cloud jabbing invisible needles into her eyes. Its acrid stench burned her throat, and she tried to see through the tears cascading down her cheeks.

They had to get out of the barn. She could not be certain what the cloud might contain, but as each breath seared through her, she knew it was dangerous.

Shaking Zuki's shoulder, she got no response. She rolled her over onto her back. The girl's eyes were closed, but she was breathing.

Isabella drew the girl over her shoulder and struggled to come to her feet. She should not have any trouble lifting someone as slight as Zuki, but her knees seemed unable to function. Forcing them to lock in place, she stood. Her head rang as if the chapel bell were inside it.

"Sister Charlotta?" She tried to shout the name. Only a raspy whisper emerged.

It was enough, because Sister Charlotta raised her head, shaking pieces of thatch and daub out of her dark hair.

"We have to get fresh air!" Isabella poked her with a toe when the sister let her head fall back on her hands. "Hurry!"

Sister Charlotta came to her feet, weaving as if she had swallowed all the wine in the undercroft. Somehow, Isabella was able to steer her out the door, which thankfully had not collapsed.

Shouts came from every direction, and the sisters ran toward them from the cloisters and the stables and the falconry mews and through the gate. Isabella motioned for them to stay back. Her raspy warning vanished as another explosion ripped through the building. Oddly colored flames rose through what was left of the roof.

The concussion knocked Isabella to her knees. She struggled to stand. Hands came from everywhere, guiding her to her feet and away from the fire. She heard her own voice— as if from the depths of the Abbey's well—ordering the others to flee. Then she heard nothing, save the endless ringing, as she sank into darkness.

As she stood in the abbess's office, Isabella adjusted the sling around her left arm and tried not to wince. She was lucky to be alive. As were Sister Charlotta and Zuki. Both were in the infirmary overseen by Isabella's assistant, Sister Marthe. Sister Charlotta had burns on her left arm as well as a broken wrist. Zuki had been hurt worst, for she had a lump the size of a fist on her forehead. The girl had been senseless for more than an hour, but was now conscious and able to identify herself and others.

Wanting to remain by their bedsides, Isabella had not

been able to ignore the abbess's request to come to her office. It had been a terse repetition of what Sister Charlotta had intended to tell her. The abbess of St. Jude's Abbey wished to see her, and no sister kept the abbess waiting. Yet, when Isabella had arrived, the abbess's office was empty.

The room was the grandest in the abbess's house because she received visitors in it. By the broad hearth was a table with a pair of benches, but Isabella had never seen anyone but the abbess sit there. A prie-dieu was placed by the window offering a view of the cloister where the sisters would soon be gathering after the evening meal. A portrait of Queen Eleanor graced one wall and a crucifix the other.

The abbess came into the room. She was short and as round as Sister Charlotta. Unlike Sister Charlotta, she always traveled around the Abbey at a speed that would be the envy of a woman half her age. As she crossed the room, Isabella felt as if she were shrinking. She towered over the abbess, but she always felt small in the abbess's presence.

"I am pleased to see you here," the abbess said, her clear voice cutting through the ringing that remained in Isabella's ears. "At last."

Isabella gulped hard. The abbess asked nothing less from the sisters than what she asked of herself. Perfection. "It was an accident. It will not happen again. I—"

"Sister Isabella, I understand that the injuries are minor."

"Yes." She did not admit that her shoulder ached fiercely.

"You told me that you would not attempt inside the Abbey to create the dangerous powder that Nariko told you about."

The abbess had stopped short of forbidding Isabella's trying to discover the formula for the powdery mix. She had, however, insisted the experiments not endanger anyone or the sacred parts of the Abbey.

Not that the restriction had mattered. Isabella's mixtures, made in the fields beyond the Abbey, had sputtered or hissed. Nothing more.

"Abbess," Isabella hurried to add, "the explosion in the barn was an accident. I did not gainsay your orders."

"I am pleased to hear that." She frowned. "We shall speak more about this after you have returned."

"Returned? From where?" Her stomach twisted with anxiety. The sisters of St. Jude's Abbey left the Abbey for only one reason: when Queen Eleanor requested a sister's help. But wasn't that impossible? The queen had been imprisoned by her husband almost a dozen years ago, and in all that time, there had been no communication between her and St. Jude's Abbey.

She looked at the portrait of the queen. Queen Eleanor, wife of King Henry II, mother of Prince Richard—the king's heir—and his brother, Prince John, had established St. Jude's Abbey. Named for the patron saint of hopeless causes, the Abbey served the queen as a source of highly trained women who could be called forth to serve the queen with amazing skills.

But Isabella de Montfort did not have amazing skills. She had excused herself from too many classes and avoided too many practices to experiment with herbs and elements. Her stomach cramped more. Was the queen ill? Queen Eleanor was no longer a young woman, and evil humors preyed on those who had left their youth behind. No, that made no sense. The queen had physicians and surgeons to tend to her. She had no need to call forth the Abbey's healer.

"When you return from where you are being sent," the abbess replied with a hint of reproof in her voice. St. Jude's Abbey might not be exactly like other religious houses, but the abbess demanded the absolute sense of duty that was present in any abbey.

"I see," Isabella said, because she thought she should reply.

"And what do you see, Sister Isabella?" The abbess scowled as she sat at her table. "Have you been studying the dark arts of divination along with healing?"

"No, no. I meant—that is, I should have said . . ." She paused and took a deep breath. The motion sent a whetted pang across her aching shoulder. She was not sure if she had banged it against a barrel or hurt it while carrying Zuki's limp body from the burning barn. "Forgive me for speaking when I should have been listening."

The abbess's face eased from her frown. "Now that sounds like the Sister Isabella I know well. You depend on logic rather than emotion, and you will be well served by that skill on the errand I have for you."

Errand? Disappointment welled up, even though, moments ago, she had been overwhelmed at the idea of leaving the Abbey. She had been certain she was about to be tapped to go on a glorious adventure in the service of Queen Eleanor. It seemed the abbess was aware of Isabella's lack of skills. Another twinge swept over her, but it had nothing to do with her shoulder.

"What do you wish me to do?" she asked quietly. If she spoke more loudly, her jumbled feelings might come pouring out to humiliate her further.

"I have received a missive from the queen."

Shock made her blurt, "But I thought the king's favor remained with the Abbey as long as the queen did not contact you."

The abbess's lips twisted in a smile better suited to a thief than a churchwoman. "It was agreed, in the wake of the rebellion by the king's sons in 1173, that *I* would make no attempt to contact the queen. There was nothing to keep the queen from writing to me for guidance on her life."

Isabella bit her lower lip to keep from laughing. Anyone who believed the abbess was concerned only with her own soul and the souls of the residents of the Abbey was mistaken. If the abbess had been born a man, she surely would have been raised to the position of archbishop from where she could have advised both church leaders and the king.

"You may be curious how the queen sent a message past her jailers," the abbess continued. "The simple truth is that the king has agreed to allow her to travel with him to Normandy, where they are to meet Prince Richard."

"If she wishes me to travel with her—"

"No, she has another request. The queen wants you to retrieve documents left in Lincoln Cathedral and to bring them to her." She held out a small iron key. "They are in a small brass casket that can be opened with this key. They must not be destroyed and, more important, they must be delivered to no one other than the queen."

"What documents?" Isabella asked as she took the key.

The abbess stood and kneaded her hands, a sign she was distressed. "Queen Eleanor left the documents with Walter de Coutances when he was Bishop of Lincoln, but he was made Archbishop of Rouen last year. It is unlikely he took the pages with him, because he would not have moved them without the queen's permission."

"Why are the pages important?" Her shoulders tensed as she asked the question, and she was rewarded with another burst of pain across her left one.

"They contain information that Prince Richard tires of waiting for the throne and may rise again against his father."

"Again?" This time she could not restrain the laugh. "He and his brothers have been shown time and again that the king is their master when it comes to battle strategy."

"True." The abbess continued to rub her hands together. "And it is true, as well, that such battles have left fields and villages burned throughout the king's holdings on the Continent. I do not want that to happen in England. Nor does the queen. In addition, the queen has no wish for her beloved son Richard to be slain, for she fears for the future of England if John is crowned king."

"Tell me where the pages are, and I shall retrieve them and take them to the queen."

"*That* is the problem. No one seems to know where the casket is. The queen asked the archbishop to be certain it did not fall into her husband's hands. It may be in the cathedral or in his residence or maybe somewhere else in the city."

"If the archbishop were contacted—"

"That could make the king suspicious. You must find the pages and take them to the queen by month's end. I have given you all the information I have. Now you must do as the queen asks, Lady Isabella."

She flinched at the title that had become hers when she

accepted the task for the queen. It was one she had never heard connected with her name. Someone might have used it before she was sent to St. Jude's Abbey before her sixth birthday, shortly after her father died and her half brothers consigned her and her mother to a cloistered life. Her brothers then fought over their father's wealth, as they continued to do from what little she heard of her family. No one had been able to tell her where her mother had chosen—or been taken—to retire from the world far from the family's estates near a lake in the mountains to the north and west of England. Her mother, Gemma de Montfort, might be still alive or dead. Isabella had never been able to learn.

She should not be thinking of her mother. She should be considering how to do as the abbess bid. Uncertain how she could find the pages, she knew there was only one answer the abbess would want to hear. "I will depart for Lincoln at first light."

"You will depart for Kenwick Castle at first light." The familiar authority had returned to the abbess's voice.

Knowing that questioning the abbess when she used that tone was reckless, Isabella had to ask, "Why do you want me to go there? That takes me several leagues out of my way, and if the matter is urgent—"

"It is urgent, for you must reach the queen before the month of May begins. That is why I want you to have someone to assist you on your journey. He will help you traverse the city, which has many secrets that even the king has not uncovered." She walked to Isabella and reached up to put her hand on her shoulder. "I could not ask my nephew to come here, for we have secrets of our own. He is bound, I am told, for Kenwick Castle, and you can meet him there. Tell him that you are a healer who has studied here at the Abbey."

"He *knows* about the Abbey?" Isabella was astounded. Few beyond the Abbey's walls knew the truth of what was taught within it. King Henry did, she reminded herself, and he had no more trust of the Abbey than he did of his queen.

"My nephew knows little about the Abbey. He had great

curiosity as a child, and I doubt that trait has diminished. For all I know, he may already have guessed some of the truth about St. Jude's Abbey."

"What if he has more questions?"

"I trust you to reveal only what is necessary, Lady Isabella, about why you are there and why you seek his assistance. Tell him that you serve the queen and that you wish his help in retrieving some pages from Lincoln for her. Tell him no more."

"But why would he help me if I tell him no more?"

"He will help you. My nephew is a man of honor and will not hesitate to assist a woman serving the queen." The abbess smiled coolly. "As well, I believe both of you have strengths and weaknesses that will complement each other. There is much you can learn from him and much he can learn from you."

"Learn? What do you mean?"

"You, too, have a lively curiosity. Do not deny it, and you will garner much on your journey." She went back to the table. "You should seek your bed now, Lady Isabella, for dawn comes earlier as the days of Lent count down to Easter."

She nodded, her head spinning. From the explosion or from everything the abbess had told her? As she turned to leave, she paused and asked, "What is your nephew's name?"

"Jordan, Lord le Courtenay."

Again she nodded. She hoped Lord le Courtenay would have some idea where to begin their search in Lincoln. She had none.

Chapter 2

Jordan le Courtenay was not surprised it was raining as he emerged from the small wood. The drops appearing out of the mist provided the perfect weather for his horrendous errand.

He led his gray horse through the dead grass in the wake of Brother Maurice. The monk, who was so short the top of his tonsure barely reached Jordan's shoulder, had hefted his white robes out of the damp. Breeches that looked to have been made for a man of a much greater height and girth almost fell off him on every step.

But Jordan did not feel the least like laughing. He had come to Kenwick Priory to pay his respects to his friend Ryce de Dolan, who had died the previous fall. When he had searched the priory graveyard, he had found no resting place for his friend. A question to one of the brothers had sent him to Brother Maurice, who guided him through a copse and across a field. Kenwick Castle's massive keep dominated the horizon, even though it stood almost a league from the priory.

"Where are we going?" he called to the monk's back.

Brother Maurice looked over his shoulder, baffled. "I thought you wished to go to your friend's grave."

"I do, but why are we walking this way?"

The monk pointed at where, in the shadow of the outstretched branches of the wood, the outline of a mound could barely be seen. Weeds had claimed the raw earth and were sprouting wildly.

"Your friend is here," Brother Maurice said, tugging at his breeches to keep them from falling around his ankles. "Where he died, milord." A disapproving tone slipped into the monk's words. "No man who participates in tournaments can be given a Christian burial."

Jordan clamped his lips closed before the words burning on his tongue spewed out. King Henry's late heir, the young king, had spent his last years, when not rebelling against his father, riding from tournament to tournament. The young king was buried in a fine tomb in Rouen Cathedral. But Ryce de Dolan had been a knight, not the son of a king.

"He died here?" he asked when he realized the monk was waiting for him to respond. Lashing his horse's reins to a tree branch to keep the horse from grazing on the mound, he added, "We are far from Kenwick Castle."

"Not far for men on horses who are determined to defeat each other." Brother Maurice's face lost its practiced serenity. "It was a horrendous melee, milord. I was helping close our shutters so that none of the participants could seek shelter within our walls when I saw a quartet of men attack your friend. Even when he announced he was willing to surrender, they did not end their assault until he was dead." He closed his eyes and crossed himself. "I cannot get the memory of that moment out of my head."

"Who slew him? Did you see heraldry to identify the men?"

"I don't remember." His bottom lip trembled as tears filled his eyes. "I don't want to remember." Holding up his loose breeches and his cassock, the monk fled toward the priory.

Jordan continued to stare at the unmarked mound. He cursed the fate that had left Ryce de Dolan dead. No, he could not blame fate. He could not even blame the men who had killed Ryce at the tournament last fall. He blamed that she-devil who had enticed Ryce into risking everything to win her hand and, once he was dead, had gone readily to Sir Algernon Emmet's arms.

It had been stupid. If Jordan had been here, he would

have halted his friend from entering the tournament. Not because Ryce could not win prestige and horses in the mock battles that bored knights enjoyed. Ryce should have won. He had been one of the victors in every tournament he had entered before the fateful one. Yet, even with his skills, he could not fight off men who had abandoned the rules of a tournament and slain him after he offered his surrender.

What a waste of a good man!

Jordan swore again. There had been too much wasteful dying since the royal heirs grew old enough to demand a share of their father's power. Everyone had heard of the prophecy, supposedly first spoken by Merlin the Great Sage, that *"from him shall proceed a lynx penetrating all things, who shall be bent upon the ruin of his own nation."* It had been said the words spoke of the young king, Henry like his father, who had inspired in too many men—Jordan le Courtenay included—the need for honor gained only in battle.

Now the young king was dead, having died from a horrible flux in the wake of looting a pilgrim shrine not far north of the Pyrenees. King Henry continued to play one son against the others, both his legitimate sons and his illegitimate son, Geoffrey, who had not been content with the bishopric of Lincoln and left the church to participate in the war games the Plantagenets seemed doomed to play endlessly.

So the death continued. Death on the battlefield where men broke their vow of liege service to one king in order to fulfill their duty to another. Death in the sham battles fought between men who sought to hone their skills for the next war.

"I want no more of it," Jordan said as he put his hand on the hilt of his sword. "I vow to you, Ryce, that I want no more of the madness that brought you to lie in this low grave. After all we have endured, all we survived, why did you throw away your life for a woman who now shares the bed of another man while you sleep beneath the earth?"

Ryce de Dolan had not even spoken of the lady whose honor he had come to Kenwick Castle to defend. How could

Ryce have said nothing to him about a woman he wanted to wed? They had had no other secrets, so why had Ryce hidden his plans to marry? Maybe he had believed Jordan would be angry that their evenings with eager maids were coming to an end. Maybe he had thought Jordan would not approve of the match. Maybe . . .

He swore savagely. He would never know the answer because the truth had died with Ryce.

All that mattered now was that his friend was in an unmarked grave on unconsecrated ground. He must arrange for Ryce's body to be moved to La Tour du Courtenay. There, he could be interred, with the men who had fought and died beneath the le Courtenay banner. Father Eloi would not deny any friend of the le Courtenay family burial in sacred soil.

To disinter the body and move it should not be too difficult. Jordan paced around the mound as he made a list of what he needed to do: get a cart to carry the body; hire guards to make sure no thieves stole the clothes from Ryce's corpse; find sculptors to create a worthy tomb for the man who had saved Jordan's life more than once; engage a painter to give life to the angel who would look down upon the tomb as others did in the chapel. An angel who . . .

He paused in midstep and stared at the woman beside his horse. She stood in silhouette. The spring breeze toyed with her cloak, fluttering it about her. She was tall, almost his height, and wisps of angel gold hair fluttered from beneath the cloak's hood. For a moment, he wondered if wings were hidden beneath that dark wool; then he realized it was a only large wool sack.

"Why are you watching me?" he asked more crossly than he had intended. He was annoyed that he had been interrupted in the midst of making his pledge to Ryce. And he was irritated at himself for the silly thoughts. Having such thoughts about a woman—thinking she was somehow something magical and wondrous—was what had led his friend to that unmarked grave.

"I did not want to intrude," she replied.

He was amazed by her voice. It was feminine, but had a

depth that was intriguing. His sisters' voices were like
birds', chirping and twittering and pleasant. This woman's
voice was even more enticing to a man's ear, for it contained
a huskiness that he could easily imagine whispering against
him as he held her close.

Again he chided himself. She was only a woman, just
like all other women. Simply because her voice had a pleas-
ing timbre should mean nothing. He glanced down at Ryce's
grave. Had he, by coming to stand on the accursed field,
been tainted by the insanity, too?

"You are not intruding," he lied, eager to silence his disturbing thoughts. While pledging to give his friend a decent
burial, he should not be lusting after a woman, especially
one whose face he had yet to see.

She walked toward him. When she stepped into the dim
light sifting through thickening clouds, her hood continued
to shadow her face. She did not step gingerly through the
grass to protect her shoes, but walked with even, assured
paces. Her gray gown caught on a stone, and he was surprised to see, before she yanked her hem free and brushed it
down over her legs, that she wore boots much like his own.
And like his own, they bore signs of a long journey.

Pausing just beyond where he could reach with the tip of
his sword, she lifted back her hood and asked, "Are you
Lord le Courtenay?" Blond hair hung in raucous curls
around her heart-shaped face, which held no emotion he
could discern. Her gray-blue eyes were direct, not flirtatious
or frightened. He had never encountered a woman who was
so close to his height, and he found the idea both appealing
and unsettling.

"I am." He did not lower his own hood, not wanting to
see her reaction to what it hid. "Who are you?"

"I am Lady Isabella de Montfort, and I have traveled here
to speak with you."

His gaze swept along her again. More slowly, so he could
admire the curves shadowed by her dark cloak and simple
gray gown. He noticed, for the first time, that she wore sev-

eral pouches of varying sizes on a belt that emphasized her slender waist.

"Aren't you curious," she asked, "why I wish to speak with you?"

Jordan's brows lowered. She was unlike his sisters in other ways, obviously, for she spoke as if she and a man were equal instead of waiting for the man to take the lead in the conversation.

"I am more curious why you wish to speak to me by a grave." He did not keep the ice from his voice.

"Because I was told, upon my arrival at Kenwick Castle, that I could find you at Kenwick Priory. There, I was told to look for you here." She regarded him as if he were truly deranged. When she glanced at the mound of earth, dismay flickered across her face. "If I *am* intruding, milord, you need only say so, and I shall wait for you by the priory's gate."

"Please do."

Jordan watched as she walked away without another word. What a peculiar woman! And what an astonishing sway to her hips that set her cloak to a beguiling rhythm. He could not keep from wondering what she carried in that sack. Was she on a long journey and carried all she owned within it? That made no sense. She was Lady Isabella de Montfort. Why was a lady traveling alone on such a dreary day? He looked at his friend's grave, but his eyes were drawn again to the lady until she vanished from sight among the trees.

In his mind, as clearly as if Ryce de Dolan stood beside him, he heard his friend say, "Women! They are the bane and the boon of manhood." Ryce had said those words while they sat in the great hall of La Tour du Courtenay, each with a willing maid on his knee. There always had been willing maids, ready to trade an hour or two of pleasure in exchange for a trinket. That night had been followed by Jordan leaving the next morning to serve Prince Richard. He had almost died in battle, but recovered to discover Ryce was dead and the woman whose honor he had ridden for had quickly found comfort in the arms—and the bed—of another man.

Jordan frowned as a thick drop of rain struck him, quickly followed by another. Standing by Ryce's grave was silly. Standing in the rain was even more stupid. He loosened his horse's reins. He needed to make the proper arrangements for moving his friend to La Tour du Courtenay.

But first he owed Lady Isabella the duty of finding out why she was seeking him. As he walked amidst the trees on his way toward Kenwick Priory, he frowned.

De Montfort. Jordan knew the family by name, but had never met any of the family who held the title on lands near the border of wild Scotland. The family—a quartet of brothers—were rumored to be in constant battle with one another, each determined to be declared the holder of the family's baronage and the lands that went with the title. They stopped fighting each other only when the king or one of his sons called them to serve in war. He had met the brothers during the rebellion in 1173, but recalled little of them other than their aggressive arrogance. Lady Isabella had not displayed that same haughtiness, but she was a de Montfort.

Lady Isabella had four brothers, so why had the lady journeyed to Kenwick to find him? Journeyed *alone*? What was so urgent that she had not waited at La Tour—or even at Kenwick Castle—for him to return?

As he led his horse from beneath the trees' barely green branches into a downpour, Jordan saw the lady standing next to her sack within the arch of the priory's gatehouse. It was so shallow that it offered her little shelter from the rain. Again he was surprised.

"Why are you standing in the rain, milady?" he asked in lieu of a greeting.

She regarded him coolly. "I said I would wait here."

"That you did, but it was not raining then."

"I said I would wait here," she repeated as if he had no more sense than one of the spring blossoms bobbing beneath the rain along the priory's wall. "I need to obtain your assistance."

"Who sent you?"

"I am here on behalf of Queen Eleanor."

He frowned at her. "Do you expect me to believe that?"

"Yes."

"Why?"

When rain splattered on her face, she drew her hood up over her head. "Because I have just told you that I am here on behalf of Queen Eleanor. You have no reason to accuse me of lying."

"Nor do I have any reason to believe you."

"True." A hint of a smile tipped one corner of her expressive mouth. A very charming motion, he thought before he could halt himself. "However, milord, if I wanted to fill your head with lies, I could have done so in the shelter of the priory. I would not have waited in the rain."

"Unless you wanted me to believe you were being honest when you were not."

She laughed, and he wondered if the storm had been swept away by sunshine. Everything seemed abruptly alive with light.

"Lord le Courtenay, we can stand here for as long as you wish and debate what I might have done if I had come with lies. However, the truth is that I have been sent by Queen Eleanor to find you, and it would behoove you to believe the word of a lady in her service."

He had to admit she was right. Unless she made the queen appear out of thin air—an unlikely event—she could not prove she was speaking the truth . . . and he could not prove she was not. And she was kind not to remark on how he had been less than truthful when he first told her she was not interrupting him by Ryce's grave.

"If you are the queen's emissary, why do you come to speak with me?" he asked.

"Because you are the nephew of the abbess of St. Jude's Abbey."

He had not expected to hear her speak of his aunt. He had

seldom seen Aunt Heloïse, for she had been named as abbess of St. Jude's Abbey before he was born. Four times she had come to his father's estate of La Tour du Courtenay, staying less than a fortnight each time. He had enjoyed her visits because she spent time talking with him, answering questions no one else seemed to care about. Her interest in the world seemed out of place for a woman who had chosen a life within the church. He recalled her smile, because he had noticed, even as a child, that her eyes remained intense and gauging the reaction of everyone around her. When he had mentioned that to his father, he had been told that he should not expect an abbess to react as others did. But she had acted in a very familiar way. She had, at those moments, resembled his father when the earl had some important matter on his mind.

"Why did the queen send you?" Jordan asked. "Is something amiss with my aunt or her abbey?"

A faint smile eased the tension on Lady Isabella's face. "The abbess told me before I left the Abbey that you would be concerned, and she said as well that I should assure you that she is well."

"You were at St. Jude's Abbey?"

Her smile wavered, and she bent to pick up her satchel as she said, "I have studied with their healer before I came to serve the queen and to seek your help in that service."

"Mine? For what?"

She drew her cloak closer as the breeze freshened with a chill that had not been banished with winter. "Will you walk with me, milord? What I have to say should be heard by no other ears."

"Even monks?"

"No other ears." She went toward the trees.

Jordan pulled his own cloak more tightly to him as he turned into the wind and the driving rain. His horse whinnied a protest. Ahead of them, Lady Isabella had bent her head only slightly, as if she were indifferent to the storm's discomfort. As he caught up with her, matching her paces, he waited for her to speak.

Even though she did not glance in his direction, she clearly realized he walked beside her because she said, "The task I was given—and for which I need your help—sounds quite simple. Queen Eleanor entrusted some pages with the erstwhile Bishop of Lincoln, and she wishes to have the pages delivered to her."

A delicate fragrance drifted from her, tempting him to imagine what hid beneath her cloak instead of heeding her words. He forced himself to focus. "Why would the queen need us to retrieve pages from the cathedral? She could petition the bishop—"

"There is no bishop in Lincoln now."

He wanted to fire back that he knew there was no bishop and that she should not interrupt him when he was about to suggest the queen could petition whoever had served as the bishop's assistant at the cathedral. He swallowed his retort when they stepped out from beneath the trees. Ahead of him was the mound. It appeared even more pitiful and lonely in the downpour.

"Who lies there?" Lady Isabella asked, her voice gentling from its assertive tone.

"My most trusted friend."

"I am sorry." She was silent a moment as they paused by the grave; then she asked, "Why does he lie here?"

"The brothers within Kenwick Priory denied him burial inside their walls because he died during a tournament."

For the first time since they had walked away from the priory's gatehouse, she looked at him. Her eyes were narrowed, and he guessed she was appraising him anew. "During a tournament? What a shame for a man to lose his life so worthlessly!"

"It was a waste. If I had been here, I would have persuaded him not to accept the challenge to gain a woman's hand. No woman is worth a man's life."

Again she did not speak for a long minute as she stared at the grave. "I agree."

"You do?" He was astonished. His disparaging comment about a woman's value would have gained him rebukes from his sisters. And he could not imagine her brothers accepting such an implied insult without demanding a chance to regain their honor through personal combat.

"There are enough men dying in wars. More should not die simply to gain a woman's admiration." As she raised her head to meet his eyes, her hood slipped back to reveal her hair that framed her face in a golden cloud. He barely noticed that as she caught his gaze with her intense one. "What the queen has asked of us could prevent another war from erupting between King Henry and the princes."

"How?"

"That is all I was told. It was enough for me to offer my service. Is it enough for you, milord?"

He stared at the unmarked grave. An end to battles between the king and his sons? Was it possible? He had to find out. "It is more than enough. Tell me how I can help you, Lady Isabella."

Chapter 3

"Can we continue our talk under a roof?" Isabella asked with the best smile she could offer. Every drop falling on her shoulder hurt. Getting rid of the sling before she met Lord le Courtenay had seemed like a good idea, for she did not want anything to suggest she would be a burden on their journey to Lincoln. The decision had left her whole arm throbbing. "The rain is finding too many ways through my cloak."

Lord le Courtenay gave a half bow toward the priory. "You need not linger here, milady."

"Isabella," she said quietly as he walked around to the other side of the mound.

"Excuse me?" He faced her. His dark eyes glittered from beneath his hood like two jewels from deep beneath the ground. She was surprised he eclipsed her own height, because the abbess was not much taller than a child.

But there were so many ways he did not resemble the abbess, for mixed with his grief was an anger that surrounded him like an aura. It was powerful and dangerous and undeniably male. The abbess kept firm control of her emotions. Isabella wondered if Lord le Courtenay could do the same. Even though he tried to hide that rage, its savagery seeped into his every motion and honed every word.

"My name is Isabella." She wanted to avoid explaining how strange the title of lady felt. She would have preferred for him to address her as "Sister Isabella," but she could not—must not—explain why. With a quiet dignity she borrowed from the abbess, she added, "Please call me by my given name."

"Why?" he asked as he had before.

"We are both serving the queen," she answered, even though it was an insipid response. It was the best she could do when he was watching her intently.

Why had the abbess failed to tell her that Jordan le Courtenay was so compelling? Isabella had been prepared with everything she needed to say . . . and then he regarded her with those intense eyes. Even though the rest of his face was shadowed, she was flustered, struggling to meet his gaze but not becoming lost within it. She had thought she regained her equilibrium while she stood by the priory's gate, but she had been shown how silly that assumption was when he walked toward her with the fluid steps of a tested warrior. His cloak could not conceal his honed muscles. A scar across his left hand showed he had not emerged from battle unscathed.

Just as she had not escaped her fascination with his obvious strength. When she had tried to compose her thoughts, she failed. She almost had betrayed the connection between the queen and St. Jude's Abbey, as well as her place behind its walls. The abbess believed him trustworthy, but Isabella was not yet convinced.

Still, she had to be relieved that he had agreed to travel with her as the abbess suggested. Relieved? That was not the word to describe the tempest roiling within her.

"So you are not a nun at my aunt's abbey?" Lord le Courtenay asked.

"No." She must be on her guard and not reveal that no one within the Abbey's walls took a nun's vows, for their pledge of service was to Queen Eleanor.

"A novice?"

"No. I went to the Abbey to apprentice to the healer so I might learn about herbs and poultices and mending broken limbs."

"If using your name is what you wish, milady, I will comply." He gave a low chuckle, drawing her gaze back to his hood. She realized she had been staring at his strong legs encased in well-worn boots. "I mean, Isabella. But you know that you must use my given name as well, for it would not be appropriate for you to call me by my title when you have asked me not to use yours. Now if you will excuse me . . ."

"Excuse you?" Hadn't he just agreed to go with her?

As if she had asked that question aloud, he said, "I will help you after I arrange for my friend's eternal rest."

"You said the brothers within the priory would not—"

"I intend to take Ryce to La Tour du Courtenay, and then I will assist you in serving the queen."

"We need to go to Lincoln as soon as possible."

"La Tour is on our way." He gave her a wry grin. "I assure you that *I* am being honest with you."

"So I should not question you as you questioned me."

"I would hope not." He knelt and tugged at weeds growing over the mound.

She admired his loyalty to his friend, even in death. Yet the time they had was short. To make sure she had his help in time to get the pages for the queen, she must assist him in moving his friend to consecrated ground.

Ignoring the storm fading to a drizzle, she asked, "What can I do to help?"

"Help?" He looked up, and his hood fell back. Astonishment blazed in his earth brown eyes.

And in her own, she was sure, when she stared at him. His face was puckered near his right temple, appearing as if his skin had been stitched by a madwoman. When he reached to pull his hood over his head again, his left profile was heart-halting handsome. Sleek, dark hair brushed his shoulders and dropped over his eyes. His strong jaw was emphasized by a low mat of whiskers.

"How can *you* help me?" he asked sharply, and she knew he had seen her staring.

She had seen other scarred men on her journey to Kenwick. She had seen too many, a sure sign of the ongoing wars waged by the Plantagenets, both father and sons. None had startled her as much as seeing the ravages left on Jordan's face. Not just on his skin, but the pain in his eyes.

She shrugged off her pack, glad the motion gave her the chance to look away. She paid no attention to the twinge that swept along her left shoulder. Once she had fulfilled her duty to the queen, she would have plenty of time to rest it.

Surreptitiously, she put her fingers to the hollow between her breasts to make sure that she had not lost the key to the casket the queen had given to the bishop. She had slipped the key onto a ribbon and tied it around her neck before she left the Abbey. Each day, she found herself checking the key a half dozen times. To lose it would mean failing the queen. The very thought was horrific.

Opening her pack, she drew out a wooden shaft and handed it to Jordan. She reached more deeply to find the wooden shovel head she always carried, never certain when she might find an herb or a stone she wanted to study further. Another twinge swept through her. The barn would not be standing when she returned. The abbess had ordered it torn down because the sharply leaning walls might fall at any minute.

Jordan regarded her with amazement. "Pardon my curiosity, but why are you carrying such things?"

She started to explain, but he waved her to silence.

"You can enlighten me later," he said. "Now if you will take your leave . . ."

"My leave?" She looked at her empty hands. "I don't have a second shovel, so I cannot dig, but I can keep you company while you do."

"Leave. You cannot help."

Isabella did not like the tone of his voice which suggested she had no more wits than his horse. Maybe less. "Why can't I help?"

"A corpse is nothing a lady should handle."

She stood and started to wipe her hands down the front of herself. Then she realized she did not have her apron on, and she must not ruin her gown with filth. She had another dress in the pack, but she wanted to keep it for when she presented the pages to the queen.

"Who," she asked with every bit of indignity she could put in her voice, "do you think has prepared husbands and fathers and sons for burial all the centuries men have been waging war? Women have."

"But Ryce's body has been in the earth for months."

"Then there is probably little left but his bones." She knelt again and ran her fingers through the soil on top of the mound. "The weather has been very warm, and we have had regular storms. Heat and damp hasten the decomposition of anything buried so close to the surface."

He choked out something. When she raised her eyes from her examination of the soil, she discovered Jordan regarding her with as much shock and disgust as if she had just crawled out of a grave herself.

"How do you know that?" he asked.

"I have learned about such things from my studies."

"You *study* death?"

"I study nature. Death is a part of life." Sitting back on her heels, she added, "I enjoy working in the stillroom, and the changing processes of food and the study of healing herbs has led me to be curious about other things."

"Very well." Jamming the handle into the shovel's head, he dug into the mound. "Stay if you wish."

Isabella watched in silence. The only sounds were the shovel cutting into the mound, water falling off leaves as the rain stopped, and the shifting of the horse.

He dug with the smooth motions of a man accustomed to hard work. The scars on his hand and face had told her that he was unafraid of battle. Such a man would need to wear a full mail shirt as well as a coif and mail gloves to protect himself. The weight of such garments required powerful muscles.

Odors rose from the earth. Odors of damp and rot and death. Rising, she edged away from the stench. She knew he was watching her, because the rhythm of the shovel changed. Pausing beneath the trees, she reached down and pulled two handfuls of moss from the base of a trunk. More smells surrounded her, but these were of the fresh earth and the recent rain.

Pain resonated through her left arm, but she hoped ignoring it would make it disappear. She knew how ridiculous that was. Later, when they had Sir Ryce out of the ground, she would prepare a potion with thyme and strong ale to place on her shoulder. She must do that every evening for nine days to draw the pain out of her joint, and she had not taken the time to tend it during long days of travel and long nights with scanty sleep. With Jordan to help her watch for thieves, she would be able to heal her shoulder and sleep.

Carrying the moss to where Jordan was working, she opened one of the sacks tied to her belt. She sprinkled dried lavender on the moss before holding one handful out to him. He looked from it to her, confusion in his dark eyes.

"Hold it to your nose," she said. "It will help keep you from sickening at the reek from an open grave."

"I don't—"

"You don't need it?" She frowned, hoping she looked as vexed as the abbess did when someone said something foolish. "You have little color in your face, and what color there is varies between gray and green. If you do not want to be ill in your friend's grave, I suggest you use the moss."

He snatched it from her hand. When he lifted the velvety moss to his face and drew in a deep breath that sent dried bits of lavender floating about his head, he said, "If you would have let me finish, you would have known that I intended to say that I don't know how to thank you for your thoughtfulness."

"Oh." Isabella was seldom at a loss for words, and it was an uncomfortable feeling.

"You look less than hale yourself." He reached up and took her hand, gently raising the moss toward her face. "You look as if you could use some help, too."

With a choked gasp, she drew back, staring at him. How had such a simple touch sent a quiver rippling up her skin with such amazing warmth?

"Are you ill?" he asked.

She shook her head. Every word she had ever known had fled from her mind.

When Jordan bent once more to his task, she was glad. She did not want him to discover how his commonplace gesture had left her trembling. She had not expected his touch would unsettle her like *that*. Maybe, once she was accustomed to his company, the unnerving sensation would vanish. She hoped so.

"May I ask you something?" he asked, not pausing in his work. "Ah, I believe I just did." A hint of a smile fled across his lips so swiftly she doubted she had truly seen it. "So I shall ask something else, if you are agreeable."

"Of course." She knelt by the grave again. Was his jesting his way of submerging the grief of uncovering his friend's corpse?

"Why are you wearing a whip?"

"I find it useful."

"To protect yourself?"

Isabella smiled. "Quite to the contrary. I have not used it in that manner since I was a child. There are other ways to deal with troublesome people than snapping a whip at them."

"So other people are as troublesome to you as you are to them?"

She was shocked to silence. No one had ever described her that way. The sisters considered her too engrossed in her studies, as quiet as one of the rabbits hiding in the bushes by the Abbey walls.

He dug into the mound and tossed aside dirt and weeds. His face became bleaker with each shovelful he cast aside. Abruptly, he tossed the shovel away and knelt to use his hands to push the loosened earth out onto the grass. When she did the same on the other side of the grave, he glanced at her.

"Milady—Isabella, this is not your obligation." His jaw worked on every word, attempting to spit out each one without becoming ill as he uncovered his dead friend.

"We are allies in our service to the queen. Anything I can do to help you now will mean you helping me sooner."

"Are you always so logical?"

"Yes."

Again he regarded her, his forehead wrinkling as if he were trying to solve a puzzle.

She looked down at a whiteness in the dirt. It was, she knew, bone. Sympathy flooded her when she saw Jordan's grief. She wanted to tell him that she understood his pain, but she could not. She could only imagine what he must be feeling.

Silence settled on them as they lifted the last handfuls of dirt away from what remained of Jordan's friend. Her eyes filled with heated tears. Sir Ryce de Dolan had been reduced to bones. Gone were his flesh and his soul. Nothing remained of his clothing. The corpse pickers had been thorough. Had his enemies stolen his mail and his weapons after killing him?

She did not realize she had whispered that question aloud until Jordan replied, "A victor in a tournament has the right to take the loser's weapons as well as his horse, just as in real battle."

"So why would anyone participate?"

"For honor."

"Honor is worthless when a man is dead."

"It is."

At the regret in his voice, she wished once more for the right words to offer him comfort. Again they would not come.

"Do you have a blanket in your pack?" Jordan asked.

"Yes."

"Let me have it. I will replace it with another once we have reached La Tour du Courtenay."

She drew out a pale brown blanket and spread it across the ground at the foot of the grave. He started to protest when she reached in to help him lift out what remained of his friend, but said nothing when she frowned at him.

In spite of her avowal that she could help, her fingers

wanted to curl away from the bones. She had examined many bones during her studies, but those bones had belonged to animals. Setting a bone for a sister who had been injured during training was nothing like touching what was left of a once breathing man. She tried to swallow the acrid taste in her mouth, but her stomach was lurching like an unbroken horse.

"I have him," Jordan said, his voice as strained as hers would have been if she dared to speak.

Nodding, she scrambled to her feet as he gently placed the bones on the blanket. He wrapped them with as much care as if his friend could still be healed. She looked away. The power of his grief was too overwhelming.

A sparkle in the grave caught her eye. It was pale, and for a moment she thought a bone had been left behind. Ignoring the crunch in her stomach at the thought, she bent to see what it was. It was no bone. The light was playing off a knife with an ivory haft.

"Jordan, don't forget his knife." She stretched to pick it up.

His broader hand grasped her wrist. Reaching past her, he lifted the knife out of the grave as carefully as he had his friend's bones. He released her and peered at the haft.

"What is it?" she asked.

"This knife could not have belonged to Ryce." He ran his finger across the engraving on it. "This is not his family's crest."

She leaned forward to see an engraving of two men, one on a horse, the other leading it. "Then it must have belonged to one of the men who killed him. What does it say? *Semper minax, nunquam summissus?*"

"That is Latin for 'always defiant, never humble.' "

"I know. What else can you see?" Wanting to examine it more closely, she put her hand on his arm.

Dazzling sensation raced from her fingers up her arm and surged through her before she could draw another breath. It was like when, as a child, she had stood outside in a thunderstorm to view the lightning. A quiver rippled beneath her skin, exciting and frightening at the same time.

His hand covered hers, and she slowly lifted her gaze from

his broad fingers and across his chest covered with the simple wool tunic before rising up over his chin—which had a slight cleft she had not noticed before—to meet his dark eyes. Could he hear her heart? It was throbbing in her ears as it had been when the elements exploded in the Abbey's barn.

"Are you all right, Isabella?" His voice seemed to come from far away, even though he was standing so close.

"Yes," she said automatically.

"You look a bit flushed, and I was hoping you were not going to sicken." He gave her a smile, and her roiling stomach seemed to flip about like a fish on dry land.

Was she dying like a fish out of water? Why couldn't she catch her breath? If she had been able to endure the sight of a man's skeleton, why did a living man's touch unsettle her utterly?

"Are you certain you are not ill?" he asked again.

"Yes."

"Good." He lifted his hand off hers at the same time he slid his arm from beneath her fingertips.

Clasping her hands together, Isabella took a deep breath. She was letting her reaction to his grief distress her. There could be no other explanation for her silly reaction.

As she released the breath, she asked, "Do you recognize the crest on the haft?"

"No." His fingers curled tightly around the knife as if he intended to drive it into someone. "The monk who brought me here could not name Ryce's killers. He seemed afraid to speak their names."

"Afraid? Why?"

"I don't know." He shoved the dagger into his belt. Walking to the shrouded body, he asked, "Where is your horse, Isabella?"

"I don't have a horse."

"You walked from Kenwick Castle?"

"It is only a league or so."

A hint of a smile tipped one side of his mouth. "I cannot argue with that." His face became somber again. "If we don't have two horses to put a sling between them to carry Ryce, we will need a cart."

"Maybe the brothers would lend you one."

He laughed without humor. "They denied him a decent burial, so I doubt they would let his final ride be in one of their carts."

"If we ask—"

"No," he said firmly as he put his hand to his forehead and scanned the field and beyond. He pointed to a collection of buildings less than a half mile up the road. "Maybe someone there will be willing to exchange a cart and a horse for some coins."

Isabella did not want to disagree, even though she thought he was wrong. If there was a horse on the farm, she could not imagine a farmer parting with such a valuable creature for any amount of money. But if she expected Jordan to go with her to retrieve the pages, she had to help him take his friend to his final rest.

Wiping dirt from her hands, she said, "We will never know unless we ask."

Chapter 4

Pausing only long enough to place Sir Ryce's skeleton back in the grave so it would not draw attention, Isabella walked with Jordan and his horse along the pebble-strewn road. He said nothing, and anything she thought might break the silence seemed insipid, so the only sound was the screech of a hawk putting an end to a field mouse's life.

The farm was not inviting. Behind a low wall that may have been much higher at one time, large patches of thatch were missing from the house's roof. Another building was collapsing into itself. Broken pails and a few scrawny chickens littered the muddy yard.

"It certainly looks as if its owner could use a coin or two," mused Jordan.

Isabella wrapped her arms around herself, her fingers settling on the whip's handle, as a grimy man approached them. He wore just a tattered muddy tunic and a piece of string tied at his waist to hold his knife. He stopped an arm's length from them, on the opposite side of the broken wall. He scratched his ribs, which were visible through his torn tunic. A twisted brush of dark beard dropped around his face, obscuring some of the dirt crisscrossing his features.

"Begone," he growled. "No varlets wanted here."

Pointing to a rickety cart by the byre, Jordan said, "We wish to speak to the owner of that wagon. Is that you?"

"Maybe." The man spat on the ground and stared at the wet spot with great interest. His eyes narrowed when he looked up at Jordan, who stood half a head taller than he. "Why do you want the cart?"

"We need transport."

"Do you, now? That is a fine beast you have with you."

"One horse is not enough."

The man stared at Isabella with a leering grin. "I would not mind holding such a lovely lady close while we rock together on a single horse."

Isabella wondered if a snap of her whip would startle the man enough to rid him of that horrendous expression that made her feel as dirty as his clothes. That would only draw more attention to her, and she did not want that.

As calmly as if the man had not spoken, Jordan said, "I am interested in purchasing your wagon."

The man started to reply, but paused and stared at the weapons Jordan wore. Something flickered through his eyes, gone too swiftly for her to guess what it had been. Leaning against the wall, he cursed as a stone rocked beneath him. "My wagon cannot be bought for talk. Do you have coin?"

"First tell me what you want for it and a horse to pull it."

Isabella's gaze settled on the long knife stuck in the brown-haired man's belt. Bloodstains darkened the nicked edge. She hoped it had been used only to kill the rare chicken found on the farm or to steal a rabbit from the priory's lands. Her fingers tightened on her whip.

"Fair price," the man replied. "Fortypence."

With an icy chuckle, Jordan motioned with his head toward Isabella. She moved away from the wall as he did, but she kept her hand on her whip.

The man called, "Twentypence."

Jordan shouted back, "If I keep walking, will you become more reasonable?"

The farmer scraped his tongue along his full lips, then said, "Tenpence."

Jordan smiled, but when he turned to face the man, his face was once more somber. She struggled not to laugh, realizing he was enjoying the chance to bargain with the knave.

Jordan counted the agreed amount into the man's hand, careful not to reveal if he had more. "Thank you—"

"Zane." He grinned a nearly toothless smile. In a smooth motion, he made the coins disappear amidst his rags. "The wagon and the horse are yours. If anon you decide to sell them back to me, I shall give you a fair price."

Jordan waved toward the swaybacked white horse beyond the cracked fence. "Hitch up the beast, Zane, before it drops dead. As much as I have paid you for it, I would like to get some use out of it."

"Hitch it yourself. It is your wagon." He pulled a long piece of grass from the clump by the wall and began using the end to clean his few remaining teeth.

Handing the reins of his mount to her, Jordan pushed past the filthy man and whistled to the other horse. It raised its head in dull curiosity and lumbered toward him. Isabella wondered if the ancient beast could pull the wagon to La Tour du Courtenay. If Jordan had any doubts, she saw no sign as he hitched the white horse to the cart. The wheels wobbled while he led the horse toward her.

Beside the wall, Zane cackled a laugh.

Jordan ignored him as he took the reins of his gray horse and lashed them to one of the broken boards on the cart. When he lifted her into the cart, she discovered it was as filthy as its previous owner. She sat because her gown was already caked with mud.

When Jordan drove the wagon onto the road, she clutched the side. They bounced into puddles. Looking back, she saw Zane had vanished. No doubt, he planned to spend his windfall. She guessed by the morrow's end, the tenpence would be in the possession of some malter or innkeeper.

It took almost as much time to drive back to the grave as to walk. When Jordan turned the horse to enter the field, it was reluctant to go more than a few steps when fresh grass was beneath its nose.

"This is ridiculous," Isabella said when the gray horse passed them and drew even with the white horse.

"It is. You could give a snap of that whip."

"I would not use it on such a feeble animal. It appears half starved."

He snorted. "I am beginning to think you carry it just to gain attention. You never use it for any common purpose."

"I did not say I never do. I use the whip when it is appropriate, but not with this poor horse."

"Such gentle-heartedness can get you in trouble."

She folded her arms in front of her and gave him the stern frown that worked so well with the sisters when they intruded on her work. "My decision has nothing to do with gentle-heartedness, Jordan. It has to do with not frightening the poor horse out of its few remaining years." She raised her chin. "A carefully considered decision based on reason instead of impatience."

"I stand corrected." Jumping out, he motioned for her to remain where she was. "And as the horse seems unwilling to pause in its dining, I will get Ryce and bring him here."

She nodded, biting back her offer to help. In the short time she had spent with Jordan, she had seen that arguing about anything to do with his friend was futile. She wanted to apologize for being curt, but he walked away before she could speak. She sat in the cart until he returned with the blanket-covered body. Helping him settle it in the cart, she edged aside so he could climb in.

Instead, he leaned forward until his eyes were again even with hers. How easy it would be to fall into their depths and discover if fire or ice waited there! And how dangerous. She was not here to explore those enigmatic eyes. She needed to find the missing pages before war swept through England again. Yet she could not think of anything other than his strong arms on either side of her and how his lips parted as he moved even closer.

Was he going to kiss her? Was he going to kiss her when his friend's *corpse* lay beside her? She realized she did not care about what was wrapped in the blanket. She only cared about how his mouth would feel against hers.

"Thank you," he said quietly.

"What?" She had not expected him to say that. She had not expected him to say anything.

"Thank you helping me fulfill my vow to Ryce." His eyes darkened even more as his voice became taut. "I promise you that I will be as unswerving in helping you accomplish what you have pledged to the queen."

"Thank you." She did not know how else to reply. Why wasn't she pleased and smiling when he promised her exactly what she hoped he would?

Sister Isabella is the most logical one in the Abbey. She had heard the abbess say that many times, and each time pride had filled Isabella. Sister Dominique was lauded as the most skilled with a staff and blade, and Sister Rosanna and her twin, Sister Blanche, were more gifted with unarmed combat than anyone else in the Abbey.

But . . . Sister Isabella is the most logical one in the Abbey.

It was time she remembered that.

Clearing her throat, Isabella turned to pick up the reins. Her mind worked better when she was not immersed in his beguiling gaze.

"I will hold you to that vow," she said.

"Is that all you will hold me to?"

Foolishly, she looked back at him. His face remained somber, but she had heard faint amusement. Before she could find herself caught again by the mysteries in his eyes, she slapped the reins just hard enough to make the horse take a couple of steps forward. The motion forced Jordan to stand before he fell onto his nose.

"It seems to me," she said, "that you have enough obligations."

She waited for his sharp response, but he only asked, "Can you drive?"

"I think so." She could not remember ever riding in a cart

before, but how difficult could it be to control the old horse once they persuaded him to leave the field?

"Good." He unlashed his horse from the wagon. Swinging easily into the saddle, he said, "Follow me."

Isabella had little confidence that the white horse could keep pace with Jordan's fine steed, but the wagon bounced along the rough road at a pace slightly better than a walk. Even so, it would be past dark before they could reach Kenwick Castle. Traveling once the sun was gone would be foolhardy. She wondered if Jordan had given any thought to where they would spend the night. Her blanket was wrapped around his friend's body, and the spring nights were chilly. The idea of lying on the cold ground without a blanket was not something she looked forward to.

Shouts intruded into her thoughts. Looking back, she saw a half dozen men racing after them at top speed. Bent low over their mounts, they clearly were chasing something. At a shouted order to halt, she realized it was the cart.

She slapped the reins on the horse's back, determined not to let the men, who must be thieves, catch them. The wagon moved only a bit faster. She called to the horse to hurry. The shouts were closer.

When Jordan drew his horse in front of hers, she yanked on the reins before the white horse could plod into him.

"Are you insane?" she gasped.

"Perhaps, but we cannot outrun them. I would rather lose my purse than my cargo."

Before she could answer, the men surrounded the cart. They carried bare knives that glistened malevolently in the faint sunshine. A blond man, the only one who wore a sword, regarded them with a satisfied smile before motioning for them to alight.

Although she was sure Jordan would demand an explanation, he nodded. She eyed the well-armed men as she let Jordan help her down from the wagon. Slipping her hand under her cloak, she did nothing else. There were seven men, and in spite of the abbess's assurances that her nephew was a tested warrior, she doubted she and Jordan could fight off all seven.

The blond man dismounted and swaggered toward them. His tunic was stained with what might have been the ale whose scent wafted around him. Patting the white horse on the haunches, he smiled triumphantly. "You were a fool to think you could break the law in this shire."

"The law? Are you the sheriff?" Jordan asked.

"I am the bailiff." The man's chest puffed out with pride.

"Why did you stop us?" Jordan's voice was chill.

The bailiff ignored the question. "What are your names?"

"I am Jordan le Courtenay. This is Isabella de Montfort."

She was surprised he did not use his title or hers, then realized he was concerned that the men would hold them for ransom. A bailiff kidnapping people within his own shire?

"She is not your wife?"

"No."

The blond man motioned for her to step aside. "Our business is with the thief, not with the woman."

Unable to stop herself, she blurted, "Thief? Jordan? That is absurd!"

"Absurd?" His blond eyebrow cocked as he gestured to his men. He turned to her as if there were nothing unusual about Jordan being ordered to put his hands behind him so the men could bind him. "The wagon you were riding in is stolen."

"It is not stolen. Jordan bought it."

"From Widow Eglantine?"

She shook her head, trying to see past him when she heard Jordan curse. "He bought it from a man. We saw no woman."

The bailiff smiled. "The wagon and horse belong to Widow Eglantine. She came in from her fields to find them gone. This man has them. That shows me that he stole them."

"Jordan *bought* the wagon. Find the man who sold it to him, and you will learn the truth."

"Isabella," Jordan said with a serenity she wished she could copy, "it will be all right. Do not argue with him."

Shock riveted her. Why was he surrendering willingly to a false charge? Didn't he realize that thieves were hanged? Horror threatened to strangle her as she wondered if he had no wish to live now that his best friend was dead. No, she could not believe that. The abbess would not have sent her to find Jordan if there was any chance he was ready to give up his life, and, just as important, he was riven with that awe-inspiring rage he kept so tightly restrained.

"What do you have in the back of the wagon?" asked the bailiff, freeing her from her uneasy thoughts.

Isabella glanced at Jordan. He motioned with his head toward the wagon. She knew he was worried about the fate of his friend's corpse. He was a warrior! Why was he not fighting for what was so important to him?

If he was going to do nothing . . . She stepped forward. A large knife rose to block her way. In astonishment, she looked at the blond man, but he was focused on Jordan.

"I asked you a question," the bailiff said. "I would like an answer."

Jordan said calmly, "You wanted to know, Bailiff . . ."

"Gamell," he answered as grudgingly as if he were the one being interrogated. "What is in the back of the wagon?"

"A corpse," Jordan replied with a serenity that amazed her. "My friend whom we are taking to where he can have a decent burial. If you will let us go, we will continue with that task."

Several men crossed themselves and took a step away from the wagon, but Gamell reached for the blanket covering the body.

"Touch that shroud, and you will rue it." Jordan's voice was not raised, but a shiver skidded down Isabella's spine. She could not doubt he meant his warning even though his hands were bound behind him.

Gamell snatched his hand back; then his face turned a furious red. He snapped an order, and his men shoved Jordan to his knees on the road. One held a knife to Jordan's throat.

"Speak the truth, thief. Otherwise—"

Isabella did not hesitate. She leaped toward the blond man. He moved back, shocked. She drove her foot into his knee, knocking him to the ground. He shrieked in pain as he curled up on the road. At the same time, she brought her fist down on his wrist, sending the sword flying. His men stared, giving her the moment of hesitation she needed. Uncoiling her whip, she lashed it out. The tip struck the hand of the man holding the knife to Jordan's throat.

The man dropped the blade with a cry. When she motioned the man away, he glanced toward the bailiff, then edged aside. Another man reached for his knife, and, ignoring the pain in her shoulder, she snapped the whip again and again as she slowly turned to make sure none of the men was trying to sneak closer. She was startled when sparks exploded as the end struck a stone on the road. She was curious why, but now was not the time for discovering the answer.

Jordan stood, staying close to the wagon. When he arched a single ebony brow, she was overwhelmed with the unreasonable need to giggle. She *had* told him that she was willing to use the whip when necessary.

Stepping back until she stood beside him, she let her whip slither through the dirt. The men watched it like kittens fascinated by a piece of thread. She took advantage of their distraction to reach behind Jordan and draw the knife they had found in the grave.

"Hands," she hissed.

He glanced at her, then shifted his hands toward the wagon. She leaned against him, hoping Gamell's men thought she was abruptly frightened, and walked her fingers down his arm as she sought the ropes. She tried to ignore the strong sinews beneath his sleeve and how her fingers trembled. Of course she was trembling! That witless Gamell wanted to arrest Jordan.

"Careful," Jordan murmured.

"I am being careful not to cut you," she said in a whisper so low only he would be able to hear it. She found the rope around Jordan's hands.

"That was not what I meant," Jordan said as quietly.

She was shocked by the laughter in his words. What could he find humorous about their situation? She tried to shift the knife to cut into the ropes, but the wagon bounced behind her. As Gamell shouted a curse and struck the wagon with his fist again, the dagger tumbled out of her hand.

"Are you scared of a *woman*?" Gamell snarled at his men as he gripped the wagon while he stood on one foot. His other leg dangled at a nearly impossible angle, and she guessed it was broken.

She snapped the whip toward a man who was edging closer. He jumped back with a fearful yelp that drowned her soft gasp as her shoulder burned with agony.

No one came nearer. She swept the road beneath the wagon with her foot. Where was the knife?

"Maybe they are realizing," she said to hide her attempts to find the knife, "that you need to search for the real thief. This wagon was sold to us by a man named Zane."

The men shared uneasy glances, and she knew the name meant something to them.

"Find him," she continued, "and you will capture the true thief."

"He has a dark beard long enough to drop halfway down his tunic and is dressed in tatters," Jordan added and, for the first time, she heard pain in his voice. When he winced and shifted his arm, she saw a thin line of blood seeped down his right side. What had happened to him? "And he has tenpence I gave him. He should not be difficult to find."

Gamell hopped toward them. "*You* have the stolen wagon."

"Bought fairly from the man who took it," Jordan argued. "We had no reason to believe it was stolen. How can you fault us when the crime is not ours?"

Isabella added, "You need to listen to Lord le Courtenay."

She heard Jordan mutter something, but ignored it. If the bailiff and his men refused to be swayed by facts, maybe they would be intimidated by Jordan's title.

"A lord is he now?" Gamell guffawed. He frowned at his men, and they laughed with far less enthusiasm.

She tried to catch the men's eyes. If she could persuade just one to listen to the truth, he might convince his fellows. They all looked away. She could not tell if they were ashamed or scared.

"Yes, I am Lord le Courtenay," Jordan said coolly. He winced as he squared his shoulders, then groaned.

Isabella whirled to examine the blood on his tunic. Shouts came from every direction. Her arm was grasped. She broke the hold as she had been taught at the Abbey, but her other arm was seized. She was jerked almost off her feet. Her hand burned when her whip was yanked out of it. As she reached for it, a hand slapped her hard across the face. She reeled into the grass beside the road and fell to sit on the hard ground.

Through the ringing in her ears, she heard Jordan shouting her name. She tried to answer. The words were in her mind. They could not reach her lips.

"Murder, too," she heard Gamell crow.

"No." The word echoed through her head. Had she said it aloud?

There was a rattle and the sounds of hoofs on the road. Dust swarmed over her. She struggled to stand, but dropped back into the grass. Something was thrown at her. She did not have the strength to react. It struck her in the head. A flash of pain. Nothing more.

Chapter 5

Isabella limped across the road to where her whip had flown out of her hand when she was struck. With great caution, she bent to pick it up. Her head whirled like a leaf in a maelstrom. Whether Gamell and his cronies had intended to knock her senseless or a stone had popped from beneath the cart's wheels, she could not guess.

One thing was clear. She had made a mess of everything. The abbess had trusted her to seek out Jordan le Courtenay and gain his assistance. Now she was delayed on her journey to Lincoln, and the earl was accused of theft and—if her memory was to be trusted—murder. The bailiff was soft-witted, for anyone with a bit of sense would see that Sir Ryce had been dead for months. She wondered if there was anyone with any sense left in the shire.

Coiling the whip, she looked along the road to where the end had struck a stone and sent sparks flying. Which one? Some glittered, and she guessed they were quartz or flint. Others were as dull as her spirits.

She lashed the whip to her belt and looked for her sack. It must be in the wagon with the corpse. She shuddered. Once she found Jordan and cleared his name, she would clean her bag. She was not squeamish, but did not want the bag that had touched what was left of the dead man against her.

Isabella took a deep breath and let it out quickly when she saw something lying on the road. At the best speed she

could manage, she lurched toward it. Cautiously, she bent to
pick up the dagger that had been in Sir Ryce's grave. Gamell
and his men must not have noticed it as they hurried away
with Jordan.

Sticking the knife next to her own on her belt, she knew
she had to keep Jordan from enduring Gamell's idea of justice. She looked at the walls of Kenwick Priory and turned
in that direction. The prior would know who could help her.

She chided herself as she crossed the open field. If she
had spent more time studying with Nariko, she might have
been able to keep the bailiff from taking Jordan and the cart.
What good were bits of stone and herbs when facing an ad-
versary? She should have paid more attention to all the lessons. With the flat of a sword, she could have slapped
Gamell's men aside, or a quarterstaff could have knocked
them senseless long enough for Jordan to get the cart away.

How had the bailiff found them so quickly after they purchased the wagon from Zane? Someone must have informed
him that she and Jordan were using it. But how and why?
Even if someone had happened along the road while Sir
Ryce was removed from his grave, how could that person
have alerted the bailiff in time for Gamell and his men to
stop them such a short distance along the road?

There was an answer, and, as with any other puzzle she
faced, she must find it. Her hands fisted at her sides. How
disappointed the abbess was going to be if she failed!

Forcing her unsteady legs to the quickest pace possible
without falling on her face, Isabella was relieved to reach the
priory's gatehouse. It was a simple structure with a double
door set beneath a room where the brother in charge of the
gate probably slept.

The doors were open, so she walked through and into the
small courtyard where outsiders would be welcome. Home-
sickness surged over her, and she wondered why she had
ever been excited about leaving St. Jude's Abbey. Within the
Abbey, the madness of the world was kept away. She longed
for the moment when she could complete her duties and return home.

After bidding Jordan farewell . . .

She frowned when a twinge, as painful as the ones that still rippled through her shoulder, slashed her. She had met the man only a few hours ago, and he was an endless surprise. In one way, he was much like the abbess: He was stubbornly determined to do what he believed was right. But it was a masculine determination that followed a logic she found difficult to understand.

Why he had acted as he had when the bailiff halted them? He was an earl, and she had expected that he would remind the bailiff that Gamell should show him respect. Instead, Jordan had gone with them without much protest.

Once he realized you were out of danger.

The thought bursting into her head amazed her. Why hadn't she realized before that might have been why he was so compliant?

A monk in dark robes rushed to greet her, saving her from having to answer the unanswerable question.

"Can I help you?" he asked.

"I am Lady Isabella de Montfort. I wish to speak to the prior."

"Now?"

"Yes. Please tell the prior that I am sorry to disturb his daily prayers, but I must speak with him without delay."

The monk's eyes grew wide, but he bowed his head and asked her to wait in the courtyard. She was tempted to tell him that she respected and understood a community's need for isolation. Her promise to say nothing of St. Jude's Abbey kept her silent.

A bench was set against the gray stone wall, but she did not sit. She suspected she might not be able to stand again. Her legs wobbled even when she locked her knees in place. Kneading her hands, she tried to be patient as the minutes passed without the brother returning. Her head ached more with every breath.

If she had just been better trained, she might have—

"Milady, you wished to see me?" asked a deep voice from her right.

Isabella whirled to face the man, then wished she had not. Her headache exploded within her skull, and everything around her began to fade into darkness once more. No! She would not allow herself such weakness. She had made enough mistakes already. She had to remain strong to get help to save Jordan.

As her eyes focused, she saw the prior was more than a head shorter than she was. He wore a cassock as simple as the other brother's, but it was white. Only the thick gold crucifix suggested he was someone of importance. He might once have worn a tonsure, but time had stolen most of his hair. When he held out his hand to her, it shook with palsy.

"Thank you for seeing me," she said.

"Brother Valens said it was urgent."

"It is. I need your advice on where to turn for help for Lord le Courtenay."

The prior sighed. "The earl is devastated by the barbaric death of his friend. If you have come to plead for the knight to be laid to rest within these walls, milady—"

"Lord le Courtenay has been accused of theft and murder."

Groping for the bench, the prior sat heavily. "I am shocked. He seemed a good man, unlike the titled men who have done the devil's work."

"He *is* a good man." Knowing she must not withhold any fact that could gain the prior's help, she added, "His aunt is the abbess at St. Jude's Abbey."

"That is good. She will be able to pray for his soul, which has been tainted by his crimes."

She dropped to her knees beside the prior. "Please heed me. The earl has not done the crimes of which he is accused. The victim of the so-called murder is the man who was buried by the wood, and Lord le Courtenay bought the wagon and horse from a man he believed to be their rightful owner. A man named Zane."

"Oh, dear God." The prior clutched his crucifix as if he faced Satan.

"What is it?"

"Zane is a thief and a liar, and I doubt there is a commandment he has not broken."

"Come with me and tell Gamell that. The bailiff will heed you."

"Milady, I cannot leave the priory." He lowered his eyes, clearly wanting to avoid hers. "My duties are here."

"If you can save Lord le Courtenay . . ."

"I am sorry, milady. My duties are here."

"Then tell me how to find the man Zane."

"No, milady. You must stay out of the marsh. It eats folks alive."

"Eat?" She stared at him, astonished a prior would say such a thing. "You know that is impossible."

"They go in. They never come out again."

"Give me directions to find Zane, so I may save Lord le Courtenay." She reached to take his hands, then faltered as the ivory-handled knife cut into her side. She shifted it along her belt before looking back at the prior, who still wore his horrified expression.

"Milady, where did you get that dagger?"

"It was in the grave of Lord le Courtenay's friend."

The prior crossed himself. "You must get rid of it, milady."

"Why?" She hoped his answer would not confuse her further.

"It belongs to the Brotherhood."

"Here in the priory?"

"No, milady." His voice quivered. "It is not *a* brotherhood as we have here in Kenwick Priory. It is *the* Brotherhood."

"I don't understand."

"You do not need to understand. You need to rid yourself of that dagger posthaste."

She started to draw it, pausing when he choked as if someone had their fingers about his throat.

"Not here," he managed to whisper. "Take that cursed thing away from my priory."

"Prior, my only concern right now is to save Lord le Courtenay."

"You need to worry about yourself, milady, while you carry—"

"First I must save Lord le Courtenay."

"So be it." He heaved himself to his feet and scurried through a gate, which closed behind him. A bolt slid into place, locking it. Why was the prior of Kenwick Priory so frightened by a knife made by a brotherhood?

Isabella tried to imagine the abbess being intimidated and could not. Putting her hand on the bench's seat, she shoved herself up. Her legs were steadier beneath her. She turned and paused when she saw a young man standing behind her.

He was lanky with hands that seemed too big for his growing frame. His dark hair fell forward over his brown eyes, and the hint of an uneven beard edged his jaw. He wore mail that did not reach either his elbows or knees. At his side, he carried a sword. She could not help but wonder how well he was able to wield it.

She said nothing, waiting for him to break the silence. If Gamell had sent one of his men to find her, she would not surrender. She did not recall any of the bailiff's men having mail, but she slid her hand over the haft of her knife.

"You spoke of saving Lord le Courtenay," the young man said. "Why is he in need of saving?"

She doubted Gamell's men would be coy, so she answered honestly, "He has been accused of theft."

"Theft? The earl?" He shook his head vehemently. "Impossible. He has too much honor."

"You speak as if you know him well."

He bowed toward her. "I am Emery, the earl's squire."

"We are well met, Squire Emery, because I need your help in proving that Lord le Courtenay is innocent."

"Tell me what I need to do to help." He bowed his head again. "I am willing to offer my life to save Lord le Courtenay."

"I hope it does not come to that." Looking at the locked gate, she recalled the prior's words about the marsh. *They go in. They never come out again.* But she had no other idea of what to do. The thief named Zane knew the truth. Putting her hand on the knife, she quelled her shiver and motioned for the lad to follow her. "First we need to go into the marsh and—"

"Do not go to the marsh," interrupted a voice from behind her.

Isabella saw a man who wore a monk's simple robes. "I must find Zane and take him to Kenwick Castle to save—"

"The earl is not at the castle. He is at the Drake and Gander Inn at the crossroads just north of here," replied the monk.

"How do you know that?" Emery asked, his hand slipping to his sword's hilt.

Putting her hand over the squire's to halt him from drawing his sword against a monk, she said, "Let him answer. How do you know that, Brother . . . ?"

"Maurice, milady. I know because the inn is where justice is dealt out by the sheriff and where hangings are held." He shuddered so hard his cassock rippled. "There was a hanging held less than a fortnight ago when a man was accused of stealing his neighbor's sheep."

"Thank you, Brother Maurice. We will go to the inn to keep the earl from hanging for a crime he did not commit." She ignored the young man's grumble. Their quarrel was not with the monk.

"I hope you can save him." The brother locked his hands behind him. "He seems to be a good man. Not like the other who came to stand beside that grave."

"Other?" asked Emery. "Who else sought Sir Ryce's grave?"

The monk shrugged. "I did not speak with him myself, but one of the other brothers did and was not pleased with the man's haughtiness." He lowered his voice and added, "He even swore on sacred ground."

"Was he a member of the Brotherhood?" she asked.

"Brotherhood?" The monk regarded her with bafflement. "I told you, milady, that he came from beyond these walls."

Realizing Brother Maurice did not know what she was referring to, Isabella thanked him for the information he had shared and motioned for Emery to follow her out of the priory. She was unsure how much time it would take to convene a court and sentence Jordan to death.

Jordan shifted on the hard bench. The chains connected to the manacle on his right wrist jangled, and he swore as pain scored his side where he had been cut by the bailiff's man. He could not imagine how he would have been able to mishandle the situation more. Not only had he failed to protect Isabella, but he had let those dolts take Ryce's corpse. They refused to tell him what they had done with it, other than to say he would learn when the sheriff on the morrow sentenced him to death.

And there was nothing he could do but sit in a cramped space no bigger than a cupboard and watch the stars appear beyond the window to pock the night sky. If he could free his wrist, he would find a way to sneak out of the room in what he guessed was an inn. He could smell spilled ale and burned food. At the thought, his stomach grumbled, reminding him that he had not eaten anything but a slice of bread since sunrise.

He paid that discomfort no more attention than he did the pain in his side. Running his finger over the manacle again, he snarled another curse. He could not free himself without the key, and the bailiff had made a great show of latching the ring on to his own belt before shouting to his men to bind his broken leg.

Leaning his head against the wooden wall, Jordan thought of the vow he had made not to draw his sword again in war—either a real battle or in a tournament. He had not guessed he would be tempted to break that vow so quickly. When he had seen Gamell strike Isabella, a single thought had gripped him. He wanted to see Gamell's blood.

The heavy odor of charred food made him sneeze. The smoke was getting thicker. He tried not to think about food. Instead, he focused his thoughts on Isabella. He should be grateful Gamell had left her by the road. She probably was safe behind the priory's walls now. Once he cleared his name, he would go to Kenwick Priory and offer anew to help her fulfill her obligation to the queen. Not that she needed his assistance, for she had knocked Gamell from his feet with a single, disabling blow. It had been an amazing sight, but a woman who dared to challenge a man with allies could soon find herself wishing she had begged for their mercy instead.

"Such a woman needs protection from her own illusions," he said to himself and the stars who were his only witness as he vowed, "I shall safeguard her on her journey for the queen."

He sneezed again as the smoke tickled his nose. Was the innkeeper scorching a whole side of beef? It was Lent, so nobody should be cooking meat.

Shouts erupted from beyond his door. He heard benches crash and a door slam.

"Fire!" shouted someone.

Jordan jumped to his feet. The chain caught, tugging him back. He stretched and pounded on the door. By God's blood, he was not going to meet his end chained like a beast to a wall in a burning inn.

"Gamell! Let me out!"

No one came.

The smoke thickened. He choked on every breath. His eyes burned as if twin fires had been set behind them.

Turning, he put his foot against the wall where the faint shadow of flickering flames danced. Maybe he could pull out the iron ring holding his chain. He began to cough, and his foot slid down the boards as he fought to breathe.

The window!

He had to get air.

He tried to move, but collapsed to his knees. Tears coursed down his face. He struggled to raise his head, because the smoke was worse where it was pouring beneath the door.

He could not move.

He could not breathe.

He could not . . .

Something cracked behind him. Strong hands clasped his arms. Mail cut into his sliced side as he was lifted to his feet. He groaned, even though the pain showed he was still alive.

"Get out of here!"

He could not identify the man's voice or the person whose reply was muffled. Was he losing consciousness again?

No! He would not surrender to death. He had two vows to complete.

"I—I—I cannot—I cannot go," he managed to choke out. "Wall. Hooked to wall."

"Sword . . ." The one word was clear among the other muted sounds.

By God's blood, he was not going to let them kill him. He forced his fingers to close into a fist and raised it toward the closer person. No, there was only one person with him in the room. Where had the other one gone? No matter. He was going to make this one pay for trying to kill him. He did not know which of Gamell's men it was. The man's face was covered with a cloth. Jordan tried to take aim so his fist would hit some part of the man's face. It was not easy when his eyes blurred with the tears falling down his cheeks.

"Jordan! Don't!"

He recognized *that* lilting voice.

Isabella!

He lowered his fist when she drew the cloth aside. Pulling in a breath, he struggled to ask before he choked on the smoke within it, "What are you doing here? Get out! The inn is on fire. You could—"

She muttered something as she pressed the material to her face. She coughed as she held a piece of undyed wool out to him. Lowering her own cloth, she ordered, "Put it over your mouth and nose and breathe shallowly. We need to get out of here while we can still see."

As he obeyed, he did not bother to tell her that he already was having trouble seeing. The cloth and whatever crunched within it as he shaped it to fit over his mouth and nose did help sift out the smothering smoke. It allowed him to say, "I cannot go. I am hooked to the wall."

"I know. I will get you loose."

She raised a sword. Before he could caution her that the sword would not cut through the iron links, she drove the tip into the wall. The wood tore around the bolt holding the chain to the wall. He tugged as she rammed the sword into the wall again and again.

"I am free!" he shouted as he pulled the chain to him and wrapped it around his arm like a cloak. Keeping the cloth and whatever was within it close to his face, because it was holding the smoke at bay, he took the sword as she began to cough. His fingers recognized the familiar crest on its hilt. "Emery?"

"I sent him to get the wagon. We saw it behind the stable."

"Ryce?"

"I don't know. We did not look inside because we wanted to get to you. We will know when we get to the wagon. Come with me. We need to get out of here."

Hearing her cough more, he groped through the smoke until he found her arm. He grasped it and steered her toward the door. He bumped into the wall. She grabbed his arm with her other hand. With a shove, she pushed him through the doorway.

She had pushed too hard, Isabella realized, when she heard Jordan hit the wall on the other side of the narrow passage. He groaned as he had been doing when Emery forced the door open. There was no time to apologize, because she could not guess how long it would take before Gamell and his men realized the inn was not on fire—that they had been fooled by smoke devices she had set—and came to make sure their prisoner had not escaped. She swallowed her rage at how they had abandoned Jordan to die, reminding herself that if they had not she would not have been able to free him.

"This way," she whispered, but doubted he could hear her past the thick wool. Smoke was finding its way through the charcoal she had rubbed into the fibers, and she doubted the wool would protect them much longer. Her eyes burned as if the inn were truly aflame.

Her toes found the steps at the end of the short passage, and she stumbled out of the inn and toward the stables behind it. The containers of smoke were set at the front of the inn. She hoped nobody would notice that there was no fire beneath the smoke until she and Emery could help Jordan into the wagon and make their escape.

When the smoke thinned, she tossed aside the piece of wool and reached up to lower Jordan's away from his face. "It will be easier to breathe now without that," she said.

"Charcoal," he said, amazed as he ran his finger through the rough fragments embedded into the fabric.

"I discovered that it helps sift out smoke." She tossed his on the ground.

"Isabella, we need to help fight the fire. If anyone else is still inside—"

"There is no fire."

"No fire?" He coughed hard, putting his hand to his side where he had been cut. "The smoke . . ." He coughed more.

"There is no real fire."

"I saw . . ."

Again she answered what she guessed he was trying to say. "We set out a few torches to make it look like a fire, but there is no real fire. Only smoke. I told you that inside, but you must not have heard me."

"How can there be so much smoke without fire?"

"I will explain once we are away from here. Emery is waiting behind the stables. Can you walk that far?"

"I think so." His voice was weak.

She paused beneath a broad-branched tree. "Let me help you."

Stepping forward, he said, "Gladly."

She started to put her arm around his waist, but he shifted to put his hands on either side of her face. He tilted it back slightly. Her heart thudded as fiercely as his fists had on the door before they could get it open. She stiffened, knowing she should not . . .

Then his lips found hers, and all thought vanished into sweet pleasure. His kiss was gentle but contained the heat of a welcome hearth in midwinter. She leaned into it, wanting to experience every bit while she could. As his fingers raked through her hair, pressing her mouth even more tightly to his, she curved her arms up around his back. He drew back enough to run his tongue along her lips, and her breath escaped in an eager sigh. His tongue delved into her mouth as if he wanted to find the source of that sound. Quivering, she savored his zealous exploration. She did not hesitate when it withdrew, and she slid her own tongue along the slippery warmth within his mouth.

With a laugh, he whispered, "You are a bold one."

"Me? I am only following your lead." She twisted a strand of his hair around her finger.

"Will you continue to do so?" He cupped her chin and kept her from stepping back. "Will you do as I ask and stop risking yourself when you have a duty to perform?"

Isabella jerked her chin out of his hand. When she rocked on her feet, she refused to hold on to him to steady herself. She grasped a tree until her knees locked in place. By St. Jude! He was chiding her after she had rescued him from the noose, after she had let him kiss her, after she had—

Shouts came from the direction of the inn.

Jordan motioned for her to follow him toward the black bulk of the stables. As she ran by his side, he asked, "How have you done all this?"

"It is a reaction when elements are mixed." She edged around the side of the stable. Her foot sank into something soft, and she grimaced. "I used some sulfur and some iron oxide and some—"

Emery appeared out of the smoke. "We have to go *now*. The bailiff has discovered you are missing, milord. I overheard him calling for a search party to find you and hang you right away."

"We need to get the wagon first," Jordan replied.

"Milord—"

Isabella did not wait to hear Jordan tell his squire that

they would not leave without Sir Ryce's body. Freeing her arm with a quick snap, she paid no attention to Jordan's gasp of surprise. She sped toward where the wagon was waiting.

She gasped when she saw a silhouette leaning over the wagon, his back to her. She could not tell who it was, but her only allies were running to catch up with her.

With a shout, she ran forward. She reached for her whip, but halted. If she swung it back, she might strike one of the men behind her. She drew the knife that had been in the grave with Ryce. She put it to the man's back.

"Move away from the wagon," she ordered. "We will not let you steal it."

Her name was shouted from behind her. She ignored it as the man whirled and swung his arm. She ducked beneath it, then reached up to grab it. With a sharp motion, she leaned forward. The man was flipped onto the ground. He landed hard, but rolled to stand.

She did not give him the chance. Squatting over him, she put the knife to his throat. "Who are you?" she demanded as she heard footsteps slowing as they came toward her.

The man beneath her did not answer. Instead, from behind her, she heard Jordan say, "Lady Isabella de Montfort, allow me to introduce you to my friend Bouchard, Lord Weirton of Kenwick Castle."

Chapter 6

Isabella had never been so embarrassed—not even the day when she had come into the refectory smelling of some elements she had been mixing, and the odor of rotting eggs had made half the sisters ill. What was wrong with her? She never did anything without thinking through all the consequences.

Scrambling to stand, she looked down at her boots instead of the prone man. "Forgive me, milord. I thought— When I saw you—"

Jordan reached past her and, holding out his hand that still wore the manacle, brought the man to his feet. Isabella stepped aside and squared her shoulders. She could not give in to the temptation to fade in to the smoke. She had promised the abbess that she would seek Jordan's help to fulfill the Abbey's pledge to the queen. Nothing—not even her inexcusable behavior—could release her from that vow.

Taking a deep breath, she raised her eyes. The two men were grasping each other's arm in a warrior's greeting. Lord Weirton was even taller than Jordan, but appeared as thin as the reins draped over the wagon. Only his lips were thick, seeming out of place on his lean face. In the light of the brands, the baron's hair matched his scarlet tunic.

Brands!

She whirled to see Gamell and his men in an arc by the stable. None spoke. They stared, uncertainty on their faces, at the man she had knocked off his feet. Dismay sank

through her like mercury on a cold day. Was Lord Weirton
the sheriff who had been sent to sit in judgment in the court?
King Henry had appointed barons to serve as sheriffs. Even
if Lord Weirton was not the sheriff, whoever held that post
would have sent for the baron upon Jordan's request. In the
midst of the ambush on the wagon, she had forgotten that.

"Isabella," Jordan hissed.

She looked at him, and he gave the slightest nod toward
the baron. Hoping her cheeks were not as crimson as Lord
Weirton's hair, for she had humiliated herself anew by turning her back on him, she forced herself to face the baron.

The baron openly appraised her, his gaze sweeping over
her before lingering on the knife she held in her right hand.
She braced herself for his fury, but a smile eased across his
lips as he reached out to take her hand and bow over it. He
acted as if he had not noticed the dagger, but she knew he
had.

"Ah, le Courtenay," he said with a chuckle. "I can see
why you were delayed in returning to Kenwick Castle, although I must say my sister Odette will be dismayed."

"Lady Isabella did not delay me." He scowled at Gamell,
who was trying to ease back into the pack of men. "Yon
bailiff did."

"Gamell?" called Lord Weirton without turning or releasing Isabella's hand.

Gamell crept forward. He was leaning heavily on a thick
branch. Someone had wrapped a bandage around his leg, but
Isabella knew it would not heal correctly unless straight
sticks were held tightly on either side of it.

Jordan stepped forward to put himself between her and
the bailiff. She thought Lord Weirton would not release her
hand, but he did as she shifted so they were not all clumped
together.

"Milord," Gamell said, putting his fingers to his forelock
and giving an awkward bow.

"Why are you standing about when fire burns the inn?"
Lord Weirton demanded.

"We searched but could find no signs of a fire, save for a

few torches driven into the ground. There is only smoke. It is very confusing."

"You are easily confused." He waved his hand toward the men. "Send them to put out the fire. You stay here to explain this debacle to me while your men douse the fire. Send them. Now!"

Gamell hesitated, then motioned for his men to disperse. They vanished into the smoke still pouring out of the inn. The bailiff's trembling lips suggested he would gladly have gone with his men.

"Why did you delay Lord le Courtenay from his journey?" The baron spoke with the stern impatience of a parent who had already chastised a slow-witted child for the same offense. "You are sworn to *protect* those traveling through our shire, not to harass them."

"He stole—" Gamell gulped so loudly that Isabella could hear it even though he stood more than a sword's length away. "We were told he had stolen the wagon from a widow."

"Stole?" Lord Weirton's eyebrows reached almost to the hair drooping across his forehead, which glittered with sweat.

Isabella watched the baron while Jordan explained—yet again—how he had purchased the wagon from a man who he had believed owned it. Lord Weirton's gaze kept flicking toward the bailiff. She could not tell if Jordan noticed, but Gamell did. Each glance made him shrink more into himself.

"But he has a dead body in the back of the wagon!" Gamell interrupted in a last-ditch attempt to salvage his pride.

With the same serene tone he had used before, Jordan said, "I am moving Ryce de Dolan to a proper grave."

Lord Weirton nodded, but looked at Isabella. He appraised her as if he had never taken note of her before. His hand rose to rub the underside of his chin when his gaze once again lingered on the knife she held.

Her fingers curled more tightly around its carved haft.

Jordan had called the baron his friend, but she wondered if she would ever describe Lord Weirton the same way.

"And she is helping you in this endeavor?" the baron asked.

"Yes." Jordan added nothing more.

"I see." He focused his gaze once more on Gamell. "And so should my bailiff. Le Courtenay, why don't you return with Lady . . . ?"

"Lady Isabella de Montfort," she said quietly.

Jordan frowned. Why was he distressed that she had to remind the baron what her name was?

If Lord Weirton noticed Jordan's expression, he ignored it while he went on. ". . . your lady to Kenwick Castle? Odette will see to your comfort. I would like to discuss this matter further with my bailiff once his men have put out the fire making this throat-searing smoke."

"I told you, milord, that there is no fire," Gamell said.

"Where there is smoke, there is fire." His voice hardened. "And be silent until you are asked a question." His friendlier tone returned. "If you take the road to the right, you will reach Kenwick Castle by dawn."

"We are going to La Tour du Courtenay," Jordan said as he put his hand on the wagon. The chain struck it with a sharp *clang*.

Gamell did not wait for Lord Weirton to speak. He fished a key out from somewhere beneath his tunic, almost toppling to the ground when the branch wavered beneath him. When the baron held out his hand, the bailiff reeled forward to give the key to him.

Lord Weirton muttered something and gestured for the bailiff to step aside. Gamell stared at Isabella for a long moment before obeying.

She let her breath slip past her taut lips when the bailiff moved away. She refused to lower her eyes before his venomous glare, and she let no hint of dismay show on her face. If the bailiff thought he could not daunt her, he might stop trying.

When the manacle was unlocked and taken off, Jordan

rubbed his wrist. He tossed the chain toward Emery, who did not catch it because the lad was staring at Lord Weirton, his eyes wide and his mouth agape.

"Give it to Lord Weirton, so no other person is treated thusly," Jordan said.

Emery shut his mouth, nodded, picked up the manacle, and held it out to the baron.

Looking at Lord Weirton, Jordan continued. "We have need for the cart, but I understand the true owner needs it to work in the fields." He reached under his tunic and pulled out a small pouch. "There is enough in here to allow the widow to buy herself a pair of wagons and decent beasts to pull them." He threw it to the baron. "Will you arrange for the coins to reach her without falling into someone's hands?"

"Gladly." The baron chuckled, but with little amusement. "It seems an appropriate task for Gamell to undertake once we have finished our discussion."

"Good. Isabella?" Jordan held out his hand to her.

She hesitated. "Your side—"

"Isabella, do not dawdle." He used the same impatient tone Lord Weirton had when speaking with the bailiff.

"I am not dawdling! If you do not have at least the good sense God gave to a goose to know that you need some attention—"

He seized her wrist and tugged her toward him. She raised her arm, determined to break her hold on him, when he said quietly, "We need to leave *now*."

Not sure what put tension in his voice, she faltered. Her thoughts fled to the moment when he had pulled her into his arms. She had never guessed a man's kiss could weaken her as utterly as Samson was undone by having his hair cut. All concerns about completing her task had disappeared as if they had never existed.

Now, as Emery came around the wagon again, a brand in his hand, she looked into Jordan's eyes. Shadows swept across the left side of his face, but his right was brightly lit. She could see the lines of pain etched around his mouth. His lips were taut, and his eyes drilled into her like a nail into soft wood. When his grip softened and his fingers teased the sensitive skin on the underside her wrist, her legs seemed as unsteady as the bailiff's. She wanted to put her arms around Jordan's shoulders to hold herself up and against him.

"Now," he said in little more than a whisper.

"Yes." Her fingers tingled with the yearning to trace his lips and savor the pulse of his breath with each word he spoke.

"Now."

"Yes!" Her craving for his kiss overwhelmed everything else, and her hand rose toward his nape to draw his mouth to hers.

He put his other arm around her waist. "We need to—"

"Yes." She understood all about needs when she could not imagine anything she needed more than his kiss.

"—leave *now*." He gave her a not-too-gentle shove toward the back of the wagon.

Isabella blinked as she realized she had been alone in her fantasy. Strong emotions had burned in Jordan's eyes, but not the same ones absorbing her, allowing her to think only of how his touch had thrilled her.

"Lady Isabella," said Lord Weirton as he held out his hand, "allow me to assist you into the wagon."

She stared at his hand, not wanting to put her own on it. But she must not insult a man Jordan knew and clearly respected.

As she started to put her hand on his, Lord Weirton gave a slight shudder. "There is no reason for you to ride in the wagon with a corpse. I can offer you another horse if you come to Kenwick Castle."

"Weirton," Jordan answered before she could think of an answer, "Lady Isabella and I appreciate you clearing up this matter with Gamell, but we must continue on to La Tour."

"Of course, although, as I said, my sister will be greatly distressed, le Courtenay." He glanced at the wagon. "I trust you will welcome us to attend the memorial service."

"If you wish."

"Odette will wish, so expect us at La Tour within a day or two. It may take some time to deal with the matter here," the baron said, and his eyes narrowed before he walked toward the bailiff.

Isabella had not expected to have sympathy for Gamell. It shocked her after the man had threatened to hang Jordan and left him to die in the "fire." Yet, as she watched Gamell cringe like an oft-beat dog, she pitied him.

"Emery," Jordan said, giving her an excuse to look away from what she did not want to watch, "help Lady Isabella onto your horse. A lady should not be driving a bier. I hope you will take that task."

His squire faltered, then said, "I would be glad to do so, milord."

Isabella considered for a fleeting second offering to drive the wagon, but she was exhausted and had no interest in the constant need to urge the horse to keep moving. When Emery cupped his hands to give her a toss-up onto his black horse, she thanked him and swiveled in the saddle to watch Jordan heave himself heavily onto the back of his horse. Again she wanted to suggest they wait until she could tend to his side. She said nothing. The abbess had described him as honorable; Isabella would have chosen another word.

Stubborn.

The wide stream was so shallow that Isabella could have walked across without dampening more than the top of her boots. Even so, she could see in the midmorning light sifting through the trees that someone had gone to the trouble of erecting a bridge wide enough for a single horse to cross. The bridge was supported on both sides every two to three feet by thick, flat stones leaning against each other. It was a complicated structure to build across an easily fordable stream.

"Someone must have grown tired of wet shoes," Emery said as he drew the wagon even with where Jordan had halted his horse at the top of the gently sloping bank. "I think it would have been far simpler to take them off and carry them to the opposite shore."

"Keep the horse going. If you let it stop, you may never get going again," Jordan said with a wave. When the wagon edged down the bank, he added, "We should reach La Tour by sunset. That way, we can have everything ready for the memorial service by the time Weirton and Lady Odette arrive. We—" He cursed as he wobbled in the saddle.

Isabella jumped down off the squire's horse. Putting up her hands, she steadied Jordan before he could topple to the ground. Emery started to turn the wagon back toward them.

Jordan opened his mouth, but Isabella cut him off by saying, "You heard Lord le Courtenay, Emery. Keep going. We will catch up with you within the hour."

"Isabella," Jordan began, "I can—"

"I am sure you can, but I doubt *I* can endure watching you weave in the saddle like a dancer trying to cross a rope."

Emery chuckled and slapped the reins, ordering the horse to enter the stream. His smile vanished when the horse refused to move. With a string of curses that Isabella had never heard, he jumped out of the wagon, grabbed the horse by the bridle, and led it into the water.

Isabella smiled. "It seems the poor beast is not as affronted with the idea of getting its hoofs wet as long as someone else gets wet, too. Now for you, Jordan . . ." She realized abruptly that her hand was stroking his leg in tempo with the horse's slow splashing through the stream. Yanking her fingers away, she pointed to the near end of the bridge. "Sit there, and let me tend to your wound. We don't need to be burying you next to your friend."

"Do you ever mince words?"

"I did not think you so sensitive to the truth." She walked to the stone that had one end hidden in the riverbank. It was large enough to stretch over the water lapping against the shore. She used the time to regain her composure. She was exhausted, which explained why her emotions were unsteady. She was certain that once she slept, she would be able to control them.

Sitting, she watched as Jordan swung down slowly from his saddle. His steps were even and calculated. He had shown some weakness, and she guessed he was determined not to reveal more. What he could not know was that she had seen many of her sisters at the Abbey attempting the same trick, and she had become wise to it. Suffering in silence was appropriate when confronting a foe, whether real or during lessons overseen by Nariko, but once the battle was over being stoic was dangerous.

"Sit here," she said, patting the stone beside her.

"You are making too much of a simple wound." A scowl hardened his face. "I have endured much worse."

"So I can see."

That had been the wrong response. His eyes sparked with fury as lines dug into his forehead almost as deeply as the scar.

"Stop acting as if I am insulting you." Fatigue honed her tongue. She was tired not only from no sleep, but from having to watch every word she spoke. "What *more* must I do to prove to you that I am your ally in your task as I hope you are my ally in mine?"

"Isabella—"

"Be quiet, and sit so I may tend to your wound." She freed her frustration. "The next time you are injured, you can stamp about and scowl, but I need you hale to help me. I will not have you suffering from evil humors because you are too accursedly obstinate to listen to good sense." She pointed to the stone beside her. "Sit and be silent."

Isabella was astounded—pleasantly so—when Jordan obeyed. Sitting next to her, he turned sideways when she motioned. She noticed, as he did so, the gray arcs beneath his eyes that matched the smoke stains on his clothes.

"How long has it been since you last slept?" she asked in a gentler tone.

"A full night's sleep?"

"Yes."

"A year or two."

She frowned. "I was asking seriously."

"And I was answering seriously. When one travels with the king or one of his sons, sleep is very scarce. All the Plantagenets live hard and drink hard and wench hard. It is expected that the men serving them do the same."

"I see."

"What do you see?" he asked, shocking her, for he sounded like his aunt.

"I see why you have slept too little." Bending to look at the dried blood on the right side of his tunic allowed her to avoid his eyes. Everything would be simpler if he were not so *male*.

A manly musk surrounded him like an invisible aura. His muscles rippled with such an enticing wave. Even though her sisters trained daily, there remained a softness about them that had been banished from his body that was as unyielding as the mail he must have worn in battle.

"Where is your hauberk?" she asked as he drew his tunic over his head, wincing.

"I did not think I needed my mail tunic when visiting my friend's grave, especially when I believed that grave was in a priory." He tossed his tunic on the stone before bending down to get a handful of water and splash it on the wound. As the water dripped down his bronzed skin, he glanced at her and gave her a lopsided grin. "I shall not make *that* mistake again."

Her stomach did a leap as her heart thudded unevenly. She had not imagined how charming such an expression could be on his face. It stole the sternest lines and eased the searingly hot anger in his eyes, giving her a glimpse of a man who enjoyed a good jest and the company of favored friends.

She wanted to learn more about that man, but when he raised his shirt to reveal where he had been cut along his right ribs, she gasped in spite of herself. She had seen more severe wounds, and she had seen lacerations that had been infected with evil humors before the person had sought healing help, but she was surprised Jordan had been cut so viciously. He had hidden the pain well.

"That bad?" he asked, a hint of humor in his question.

"You are still alive, aren't you?" She copied his light tone. He did not want sympathy, so she must be careful not to give him any.

"You are the healer, so you should be telling me rather than asking."

"You talk too much. I asked you to be quiet so I can concentrate."

He chuckled, then winced again.

Taking a pouch off her belt, she opened it and drew out two items. She unrolled a length of thread from the ball she always carried. Cutting the thread with her knife, she put the ball aside. She peeled away linen from the other item. It protected a small glass container. Opening the top with care so she did not spill the liquid inside, she drew out a precious brass needle and shook it.

"Is that wine I smell?" Jordan asked.

"Yes."

"To ease the pain of your ministrations?"

She held up the vial where she kept her needle. It was partly full of rich red liquid. "If you think there is enough within to help, you are welcome to drink it."

"Why do you carry so little?"

"It is to protect my needle from evil humors." She dipped the thread into the glass and drew it out slowly. "As well as what I will use to close the cut on your side."

"How does wine keep away evil humors?"

"I don't know, but I learned that it was so. I have never had a patient suffer from putrid flesh." She threaded the needle. "I am sorry I do not have more wine to ease your pain."

"Do what you have to do." He raised his head and gazed at her steadily as a smile tipped his lips. "But do it quickly. I have no interest in shaming myself by squealing like a child with a scraped elbow."

Isabella examined the wound again. It was the length of her longest finger, and it sliced across his ribs, so she knew each breath he took was painful. Yet, he seemed to be drawing in air easily and releasing it. Her own lungs refused to fill while her gaze swept over his firm abdomen where layers of muscles were outlined as clearly as his ribs. Her finger quivered as she imagined running it along those tight muscles. Would they grow harder beneath her touch?

"Are you all right?" His word brushed against her ear, heated and tempting.

She shivered, wondering how something so deliciously warm could raise gooseflesh along her. Wishing he would say something more so the sweet fire could sweep over her anew, she knew she must answer.

"*I* am fine."

"I see."

His clipped answer told her that her voice had been too whetted. She focused on her work, pushing the needle through his torn skin. He flinched slightly at each stitch. When she put her hand on his left side to tilt him slightly so she could draw the skin closed, she felt another length of puckered skin on his other ribs. She wondered if all who served the king and his sons were so battered.

"You seem to have learned much during your time at my aunt's abbey," he said as she paused to rethread the needle.

"Without the concerns of the rest of the world, it is simpler to concentrate on one's studies." She hoped she could continue to give him these half answers.

"Did you learn to make the smoke devices at the Abbey, too?"

She was glad she did not have to meet his eyes as she prepared to take another stitch. "Why would you think I learned to do that at the Abbey?"

"If you didn't, then where did you learn to do it?"

Instead of answering, she drew another section of the torn skin together and drove the needle through it. He gave a muffled grunt, but did not recoil.

"I know my aunt, and she would not be content to spend all her time studying religious works. She believes women are capable of much more."

"Yes, she does."

"Which leads me to believe that any abbey she oversees

would be filled with like-thinking women capable of much more."

"She would accept nothing less. That is why I am grateful that I have had the opportunity to study at the infirmary there." She did not add that she was also grateful she could speak the truth without disclosing the true reason St. Jude's Abbey was unique. She tied off the thread and broke it. "That was the last one."

"Good." He reached for his shirt on the stone behind him.

"Wait. Let me get some salve to put over the stitches."

"I appreciate all you have done. To ask for more—"

"Would save me work later. If an evil humor attaches itself to the torn skin, it could fester. That would require far more of my time and medicines."

Isabella was pleased when he did not question her further. Putting the needle and the remaining thread on another stone, she untied the largest pouch on her belt. She drew out another glass container wrapped in lamb's wool. Opening it, she put her finger in the light brown ointment.

"I am sorry if this hurts, but it speeds healing."

"What is in it?" he asked.

"Unsalted butter, the plants speedwell and bugle, and honey. It is a simple remedy, but works well." She dabbed thick cream along the stitches and skin around the wound. "I created it to soften the udders of cows, but it seems to work just as well on bruised and broken skin. I can put some on your wrist, too."

He grasped her arm. "Enough, Isabella. A man can endure only so much."

"I am sorry if I hurt you."

"Hurt me?" He laughed. "You have spent too much time around women."

"I don't understand."

He tilted her hand up and pressed his mouth to her palm. Sensation exploded through her. His thick hair fell forward to brush her arm, a hundred individual caresses, each a delight.

"Sweet," he whispered.

"I told you that there is honey in the salve."

"I am speaking of the flavor of *you*."

She closed her eyes and let the pleasure surround her as he kissed her palm again. When his tongue traced a line up her wrist, she wanted all the joy he could give her. Every bit of it, all she could imagine and all that was beyond even her fantasies.

A moan slipped from her lips when he drew back her long sleeve to place gentle nibbles along the inside of her elbow. She leaned toward him, breathing in the very male-ness of him with each uneven gasp. So much naked male flesh awaited her exploration. She slid her hand over the center of his broad chest. At her touch, his heart's beat accelerated like a runaway horse.

She thought she heard him whisper her name as his arm slipped behind her and pulled her close to him. Whatever he said vanished into a groan when her sleeve struck his lacerated skin.

Isabella pushed away. "You should know better than to attempt such things when you are wounded."

"Me?" He laughed, but she heard pain beneath it. "*You* should know better. You are the healer."

"I do know better. I was not thinking clearly. That is . . ." She looked away before she could say something else stupid. "Do not exert yourself until the skin has had a chance to grow together."

"And then?"

"Then we need to find what the queen seeks and take it to her."

Jordan chuckled again as he tucked one finger beneath her chin and brought her eyes back to meet his. "I suspect, while you were in training, you ruled over the infirmary with a steady hand."

Her hand was far from steady when he touched her. Trembling fingers threatened to send her supplies tumbling into the water. At that thought, she turned to pick up the needle. She dipped it in the water to wash away any blood, then slipped it into the glass carrier. As she wrapped it, she said, "I will tend to it if we light a fire tonight."

"Tend to it? How?"

"Holding it into the fire burns away any humors that were in your blood. While those humors do not make you sicken, if they were to enter someone else's wound, they could be deadly." She picked up her pouches. Tying them to her belt, she stood and put one foot on a support stone. Every inch of her longed to be close to him, so she needed to keep space between them. "I learned much of this from reading materials written in Italy almost a hundred years ago by a female physician named Trotula. She wrote about the illnesses and conditions of women, but I have found her basic information works as well for men as for women."

"So you have vast experience with men?"

"Why are you twisting my words?" She frowned. "Your aunt told me you are a man of honor, but I see nothing honorable in denouncing me after I answered your many questions and tended your wound."

She walked away. Let him bring the horses across the stream. She was suffused with the irrational desire to strangle him. The thought shocked her. She was a healer, and she had vowed never to do intentional harm to anyone she was treating. But she had made that pledge before she met Jordan le Courtenay.

A broad hand caught her arm, and she was spun to face Jordan. Her foot slid to fall between two stones. She fought for her balance, and he steadied her. As soon as she was sure she would not tumble into the water, she peeled his fingers off her arm.

His face was as hard and expressionless as the stone beneath her feet. When one hand settled on his sword, she regarded him with as chilly a scowl as his. Even so, heat was building between them. Not only from anger. There was more. It was as if—having pressed his mouth to her—he had released some fiery storm that swirled in wild abandon, drawing its power from both of them.

"Don't wander off on your own," he ordered.

"I would not have walked away if I were not furious at your crude speech."

"Crude?" He seemed honestly surprised.

"I do not need vast experience with men," she said, "to know that a lady should not be treated rudely."

"You are an accursedly difficult woman to apologize to."

"Apologize? You want to apologize? Why didn't you say so?"

"Because you will not give me the opportunity."

She arched a single brow. "You have the opportunity now."

"Then let me say that I am sorry you misunderstood my question, Isabella. I did not mean to accuse you of anything. Rather, I was curious how many men you have had the chance to treat within the walls of St. Jude's Abbey."

"There are men working for the Abbey. Their work is often difficult, and they can be injured. I have helped with their healing." She lowered her chin from where it jutted at him. "I believe we are both too tired to have a battle of words, Jordan. We are only half armed with our wits."

"On that, I can concur wholeheartedly. You should have stayed at the priory last night and rested."

"Even then, I was not thinking clearly, for I should have known that Lord Weirton would be sent for. Sheriffs do not try murder in their courts." A giggle slipped past her lips, and she clamped her hand over them.

"What is amusing?"

"It is not really amusing. I should have compassion for Gamell, but I cannot help being glad the baron chastised him."

Jordan smiled. "The bailiff has suffered already from your amazing defense of the wagon. Once my side is healed, I would like to learn that kick you used."

"I would be glad to teach you."

"How did you learn that?"

"When one has four brothers . . ." She let her voice trail off, hoping he would misconstrue her words.

"I understand." He motioned for her to go to the horses.

"And I want you to understand, Isabella, that if we encounter such trouble again, you must let me handle it while you remain behind sturdy walls like Kenwick Priory's."

"I cannot make such a promise, even if I could have stayed within the priory."

"Are you saying you were not welcome within the walls of Kenwick Priory?"

"Yes."

"Why?" Jordan jumped off the bridge and held up his arms.

She ignored them as she leaped down beside him. He should not risk his stitches. Just as important, she should not risk losing herself in his thrilling embrace.

Drawing the dagger that had been in Ryce's grave, she placed it on his palm. "Because of this."

"The prior refused to help because of a knife?"

"Because it belongs to the Brotherhood."

He scowled. "If you are suggesting that Ryce stole from the priory, you are mistaken."

"I am not suggesting that. I made the same error assuming it belonged to someone within Kenwick Priory's brotherhood of monks. It belongs to—as the prior put it with this exact emphasis—*the* Brotherhood."

"Who or what is that?"

"I had hoped you would know." She tapped the crest engraved in the haft. "I assume this identifies the members of the Brotherhood."

Tilting it, he said, "The crest depicts a knight riding with a squire leading the horse. The carving is done by a skilled artist, but otherwise, the dagger is quite commonplace."

"Maybe in appearance, but the prior was frightened by what it represents."

"Frightened? Are you sure?"

"Quite sure. The poor man was so terrified that he could hardly speak. Just the way he spoke the name of the Brotherhood sent chills through me." She shivered as she looked past him to the trees edging the stream and the shadows stretching out under them.

"But what would scare a prior other than concern for his immortal soul?"

"I don't know, but whatever it is must be connected with that knife and the Brotherhood. If that something could endanger our quest, we must avoid it."

"Avoiding the Brotherhood sounds like an excellent plan."

"I agree, but how can we avoid what we don't recognize?"

"They have no interest in us."

"They had an interest in your friend, who may have been a member of the group. That could be why the knife was in his grave."

He ran his finger along the haft. "Or it was dropped there by one of those who slew him."

"By mistake, or as a warning to anyone who opened the grave?"

"I don't know." His mouth grew straight. "But I mean to find out."

A strange feeling whirled through her as he spoke the words like a sacred vow. It was a feeling she had seldom experienced.

It was fear.

Chapter 7

Slowing his horse in the shadowed center of the bailey of La Tour du Courtenay, Jordan looked at his familiar home through drizzle. Sheep and cattle wandered in the bailey, and the castle's residents continued with the tasks that never were completely finished, not even at the hour when the sun brushed the western horizon.

What did Isabella think of the round keep set on the hill at one side of the bailey where the wall sat atop a steep bank dropping into the river? Two years ago, only a month after Jordan's youngest sister wed, his father had died and La Tour became his responsibility. Those two years had brought a few changes—a new well, stone atop the stable roof instead of thatch, a door on the kitchen. All other alterations had been set aside when he was called to serve young Prince Richard. Several parapets on the keep were still missing. He had planned to replace the wooden and earthen walls with stone, but there had not been time to arrange for the work to start.

He laughed mirthlessly. In spite of its old-fashioned defenses, the castle had survived the wars of the Plantagenets better than he had.

"Do you wish help alighting, milord?" Emery asked in little more than a whisper.

Jordan looked at the lad by the wagon. Emery was always eager to serve him and thought of Jordan's needs first. He had once served another lord, but that man had been killed in a foray. Jordan could not remember which one. It had been after his own squire died of a horrendous wasting disease. Emery had been looking for another man to serve, so Jordan had accepted his offer of service. It was a decision he had never regretted.

"I can manage, Emery. The wound is healing well." He patted his side as he swung his leg over the horse. When his squire looked away, he put his hand more gently to his side where the stitches strained with every motion. He glanced at Isabella.

She was looking around with curiosity. Smoke stains still clung to her clothes beneath her cloak, and her left cheek was smudged, emphasizing its curve. Or was that the bruise the bailiff had inflicted on her? He swallowed his fury at the thought, glad that Weirton would see that Gamell learned some manners. Isabella's hair was wild around her face, but she sat straight on the horse. All signs of exhaustion had vanished when they approached La Tour, and he recognized the pose of a warrior ready to face any foe without giving quarter, even if the only enemy was the warrior's fatigue.

"If you are sure you are set, milord . . ." Emery tugged on the horse hooked to the wagon, turning it toward the small chapel built against the bailey's palisade.

Jordan guessed the lad had his doubts. It had been all right for his squire to fret over him before, but Jordan did not want Isabella guessing how sapped he had been by the head wound he suffered in Aquitaine. It rightly should have left him dead.

His fingers gripped the front of his saddle as he eased himself to the ground. Pain no longer shot up his right leg, and he could walk now without limping. Such agony had haunted him after he had the good fortune not to die in Aquitaine.

"Welcome home!"

Jordan smiled as a bent man rushed to him. The thick cape flapping in his wake made him look like a monstrous bat, but there was nothing evil about the old man who had served as the steward at La Tour for as long as Jordan could remember. "Lew, I should have known you would be the first to welcome me home."

Dropping to his knees awkwardly, the old man reached for Jordan's hands to press them to his nearly bald head. He choked as he stared up at the scar near Jordan's right temple.

"I have been told I was lucky, Lew." He motioned for the steward to come to his feet. "And maybe I am, for I was not buried in an anonymous grave along with my comrades."

"'Twas God's will that brought you home alive."

He did not want to disagree that he had seen only hell during the forays that did not spare even holy houses. "I could use something to wash the dust of the road from my mouth." He turned again to gesture at Isabella who sat with unexpected patience on her horse. "As would my guest."

"Have you brought a wife?" asked Lew with the candor he had earned from his long service to the le Courtenay family. "You chose a very lovely one, milord."

"Lady Isabella is not my wife."

"Your betrothed?" Hope clung to the steward's voice. The only surviving son of his parents, Jordan had, in Lew's opinion, an obligation first to sire a thriving heir for La Tour.

Jordan shoved that conversation back into the depths of his memory. "I met her yesterday not far from Kenwick Priory, Lew. I would not want her to be embarrassed by an overly enthusiastic and very mistaken comment."

"You can trust me, milord."

"That I can." He clapped the old man gently on the shoulder, even though he suspected nothing less than a fierce ocean storm could knock Lew from his feet.

Going to where Isabella still sat on her horse, Jordan said, "Welcome to La Tour du Courtenay."

"It is magnificent!" Her words came out in a gasp as he put his hands on her waist, then shifted them a bit higher as her many pouches blocked him from getting a good grip.

"I am pleased you think so." He was amazed the banal words were true. He was pleased by her appreciation of the castle . . . and by how her slender form fit perfectly in his hands.

As she leaned forward to put her hands on his shoulders so he could help her dismount, their eyes were almost even, as they had been when they stood together in the smoke outside the inn. The powerful emotions within hers were the same as when he could not resist kissing her. Spellbound by the anticipation of exploring each of those strong passions, he drew her down with care. She slid off the horse and against him. The slow, steady caress with those beguiling curves would make a monk rethink his vows. She was a splendid woman, and the tightening along him told him what he already knew.

He wanted her.

He wanted her in the privacy of his bed where her hair would spread like a river of gold across his pillow while she reached her arms up to curve around his shoulders. He would slake his hunger for her lips and then taste her breasts and the firm, flat line of her abdomen before feasting on her most private pleasures. Just the touch of his tongue against her would make her writhe with need as she opened herself and welcomed him deep within her.

A groan broke his enchantment when one of her pouches grazed the wound she had stitched closed. Releasing her, he frowned when she hit the ground with a thud.

"Are you always so gallant?" she demanded. "You jarred every tooth in my head."

Knowing he should apologize, he did not. He was tired of apologizing, especially because she was right so often. He still owed her an apology for not checking more closely that Zane was the true owner of the cart. But how could he explain? To tell her of his thoughts of her gazing up at him with her incredible eyes while he moved with her, firing them both to ecstasy . . . No, he could not speak of that.

"Isabella, I am tired and thirsty and starving. You must be, too. We can stand here and argue, or you can go into the hall and find something to ease your thirst and some bread to fill your stomach."

"Me?" Her vexation vanished. "What about you?"

"I have duties to complete before I can rest."

She looked at the wagon Emery was drawing to a stop in front of the small church with a cross on its roof. Sorrow darkened her expressive eyes. "If you want—"

"I *want* to eat my fill and drink until my brain is flooded and sleep until I cannot sleep a second longer." It was his turn to be annoyed, or maybe he had been annoyed since he had met her. He could not be certain, and he did not want to waste time counting the ways she had irked him. "But I need to tend to my duties. If you really want to help, go inside so that I might complete them."

"I would rather go with you."

"Why?"

"So when you topple onto your face, I can stand over you and remind you that I—as your healer—am telling you that your friend would forgive you for eating before you prepare his memorial service."

"Because you sewed me up does not make you obligated to watch over me." *You cannot begin to imagine the true wounds festering within me.* If he said those words aloud, she would pester him with questions until he regretted ever speaking them.

"Very well. If you will not be sensible, let me help you."

"Isabella—"

"We can argue here until the stars come out, or we can tend to arrangements for Sir Ryce."

Did she have any idea how irritating—and desirable— she was when she stood in front of him, her lips parted as she prepared her next retort? Those lips had been so sweet beneath his.

God's blood, he needed to stop thinking of such things. It would take several days to reach Lincoln and probably several more to locate the queen's pages and at least a sevenday to escort Isabella back to St. Jude's Abbey to continue her studies at the infirmary. At the very least, they would be together for a fortnight. If he let his body dictate to his mind, it would take far longer because he would want to find every possible moment to linger with her in some hidden corner where he could explore her beguiling body. A man with even a bit of sense—and he considered himself one in spite of allowing a foe to slice into his skull in Aquitaine—would do whatever was necessary to hurry each leg of the trip so their time together was as limited as possible.

He motioned for her to follow him. Walking to where Lew was watching, he did nothing to ease his steward's curiosity about what they had been discussing.

Lew matched his steps and held a tankard out to him. The steward must have had it ready in the keep. Taking it, Jordan drank deeply. The hops grown along these rolling hills were unlike any others, and he savored each sip.

He nodded to familiar faces, but nobody approached him. Did they think they would be blighted by whatever had caused his scars? If they had any idea of the scars within . . .

He put aside his hateful thoughts while Lew babbled about the alterations planned for the castle. He tried to listen, remembering those eternally long months when he believed he would never see La Tour again.

When Jordan handed him the empty tankard, Lew said, "You look pale, milord."

"We have traveled far." He glanced over his shoulder. Isabella had not caught up with them. She was exhausted, but refused to rest until her patient did. He was pleased to see that someone had brought her a tankard also and that she was drinking from it as she followed.

"If you are hungry, I can have food brought."

"Lew, I do not need you mewling like an overwrought nursemaid. I already have someone else doing that."

"The lady is worried about you, milord."

Jordan did not answer as Isabella cried, "Look at that!"

His hand was on his sword's hilt as he spun. When he saw her looking up at the sky, he cursed under his breath. What was she doing *now*? Lew glanced at him, startled, but he pretended not to see the steward's frown. Isabella was his guest at La Tour, and it behooved him to treat her as he would any guest. That was difficult when he could not imagine any other woman who acted as she did. Or any other woman he wanted to hold in his bed.

Shaking that image from his head, he raised his eyes when she pointed toward the sky. Colors arced across it, brilliant in the center and fading near the ground.

"It is just a rainbow," he said.

"Just? Isn't it amazing?" In the air, she traced the arch. "Haven't you ever wondered what creates such a splendid sight?"

"Not really."

She looked at him with disbelief. "You are an intelligent man, Jordan. How can you not be curious about the world around us?"

Lew chuckled under his breath.

Not wanting to deal with both of them at the same time, Jordan said, "Lew, Lord Weirton and his sister, Lady Odette, will be arriving on the morrow, so have preparations made for their arrival."

"As you wish, milord." He could not hide his grin. "And I will make certain myself that all is as you would wish for you and Lady Isabella."

"That is very kind of you," Isabella said before Jordan could answer.

Lew bowed his head, but gave Jordan a conspiratorial grin before he walked toward the bridge to the gate opening onto the keep.

Jordan walked around the now empty wagon and reached for the round ring on the church's door. It matched the heavy iron hinges that squeaked as he opened the door.

A cloud of incense and the odor of guttering candles swarmed out, inviting him to enjoy the knowledge that he had done as he pledged. The chapel was no wider than the gatehouse. Two small windows were set into the thick walls. The altar was constructed of unsmoothed stones that had been taken—it was said—from a stone circle farther along the river. A cloth that his mother had embroidered was draped over the top, and a simple pair of gold candlesticks were atop it.

"What a lovely church," Isabella said from behind him. "It invites prayer and solitude."

"Solitude, yes."

"Do you want me to leave?" she asked, and for the first time he heard her fatigue.

God's blood! She had helped him to do as he had vowed to Ryce. She had tended him with a healer's kindness and fought by his side with a warrior's skills. More than a warrior's skills, because she had knocked the bailiff from his feet with a well-placed kick unlike any he had seen before. And he *was* grateful, but she was a constant reminder of the turmoil among the Plantagenets—father and sons and mother—that he wanted no part of again.

"No." He walked toward the altar before Isabella could ask more questions. Staring up at the rafters, where birds chirped in the last light washing in from the windows, he saw a motion near the altar.

The shrouded remains of his friend were set on a table by the altar, and a short, fleshy man walked around them, waving a censer. Clouds of musky incense surrounded him.

"Myrrh," Isabella whispered when she came to stand beside him.

"I know."

She slipped her hand into his. "It is the saddest of fragrances."

He closed his fingers over hers, then, giving in to temptation, raised her hand to his lips and kissed it gently. Even in the faint light, he could see tears welling up in her eyes.

"Why are you grieving?" he asked. "You never met Ryce."

"I am sad because I know how difficult it is for you to bid him farewell."

Jordan was saved from answering when the priest put down the censer and walked toward them. In his white cassock, he resembled a duck, waddling on each step.

"Father Eloi," he said, "this is Lady Isabella de Montfort."

"Milady," Father Eloi said with a slight tilt of his head. "You are a good friend, milord, to do your friend such honor and have him buried here with your parents and grandparents and their parents."

"I want him to lie in consecrated earth." Jordan explained what he had discovered at Kenwick Priory.

Father Eloi frowned. "The monks were wrong, milord. Sir Ryce was a good man, and he deserves a good rest."

"I am glad we agree."

"Foolish prior," grumbled the priest. "He worries so much about the state of his soul that he forgets he already has been declared dead."

"What?"

Isabella said, "A monk is declared dead to the outside world when he enters a holy house. It is a sign that he gives up all claim to worldly goods."

Jordan forced his shoulders to ease from their rigid stance. He was letting every word unsettle him. Not that he did not have a good excuse, but he should be willing—even eager—to endure all he had and more.

"Thank you for reminding me," he said with the best smile he could force.

It must have looked like a grimace, because her brows lowered. "Are you feeling unwell?"

"I am well, thank you." He raised his voice as he added to the priest, "I would like the service tomorrow after the sun reaches its apex." He looked around the otherwise empty chapel. "If someone wishes to say prayers for Ryce's soul, there will be time."

"As you wish, milord."

"I will return after I have arranged for food for Lady Isabella."

Father Eloi gave him a sad smile. "You should eat as well, milord. Sir Ryce would want you to remember the many times you enjoyed a hearty repast together."

Jordan's throat tightened with grief. If he had asked more questions that last night when Ryce was enjoying La Tour's hospitality, he might have been able to persuade his friend to ride with him the next morning to serve Prince Richard. His mouth tightened. Why would he have wished such a fate on his friend? Ryce could have died as futilely in Aquitaine as he had at the tournament. Ryce, at least, had been fighting for a prize he wanted. For what had Jordan almost lost his life?

Motioning for Isabella to precede him out of the church, he did not offer his arm. Only a fool would invite her to stand so close that her ethereal fragrance washed over him. And he had vowed, when he discovered he would survive, that no one would ever label Jordan le Courtenay a fool again.

Chapter 8

W hen Isabella entered the dusky bedchamber on the top floor of the circular keep of La Tour du Courtenay, she was pleased someone had unpacked her sack and taken it away to be cleaned. Her other gown was hanging from a hook, and a laundered shift waited across the foot of the bed. It was not hers, and she guessed from the scent of mint and cloves rising from the linen that it had come from a storage chest.

She walked to the bed, taking care not to jostle the chair beside a table. The room's sole window was wider than she had expected. The rushlight on the table gave off enough light to let her see most of the room. Above her the ceiling was lost in shadow.

The bed was wondrously carved with ivy and flowers and grapes, and from the wooden canopy hung dark green curtains that had been embroidered with the same fruits and flowers. Rushes crackled beneath her feet, and the aromas of dried lavender and rosemary drifted around her.

She smiled. The scents brought memories of her stillroom. Would she have time to visit the stillroom here? Her smile faded. She recalled that she and Jordan must leave as soon as Sir Ryce was interred. Already two days had been lost, and they must not delay any longer getting to Lincoln Cathedral.

Rain splattered on the window, and she turned to close the shutters. She paused as she stared out into the night. In the light from the hall below, the wooden curtain wall shone damply, and voices, faint and indistinguishable, came from the bailey. Closer, she heard footfalls and muted conversations on the keep's outer wall where Jordan's watchmen marked the passing of the night's hours.

She sat at the table and rested her chin on her palm. She was too exhausted to move, but her mind was whirling like dust raised in the wake of a racing horse. How was she going to fall asleep when she could not stop thinking about Jordan? He was an enigma. He showed a clear distaste for battle; yet his castle was well guarded, proof that he understood the need for caution. When a fool like Gamell believed he had the authority to imprison a man falsely, it revealed the distrust and decay in the chain of loyalty from tenant to king.

If she could develop the formula for the exploding powder known in the distant east, maybe she could convince the king and his sons that it was too dangerous to continue their fighting. She was amazed that she had not thought of the experiment all day. Most days, the lack of an answer plagued her like an itch in the center of her back.

Instead she had thought about Jordan. When he touched her, when he kissed her, she sensed there was so much more to him than a man who restrained his emotions so completely.

"Keep your mind on your task," she said to herself as she stared at where water was seeping beneath the window's shutters.

Rising, Isabella undid the belt around her waist. She carefully set the pouches on the table and looped the whip over the back of the chair. The dagger with the odd crest was still stuck in her belt, replacing her knife she had lost somewhere. Pulling the blade out of her belt, she carried it to the bed and lifted aside the pillow. Even though the idea of sleeping with something that had been in a grave made her stomach cramp, she smoothed the pillow over it.

Loosening the laces on the front of her gown, she pushed it over her shoulders. The fabric reeked of smoke and sweat, and she sneezed as she stepped out of it. Tossing the gown on the floor, she wished she had time to clean it. Not that it mattered, for the journey to Lincoln would leave it filthy again.

She undid her boots and left them on the carved chest at the foot of the bed. The pattern of a hart trying to flee the hunters caught her eye, but she concentrated on taking off her socks and dropping them by her boots. The right sock had a hole in the heel. Once she was clean and ready for bed, she would sew it closed.

Seeing a bucket of water near the unlit hearth on the other side of the bed, she took off her shift that was gritty with smoke. No hair shirt could have been more uncomfortable, and the soot had left reddened spots on her right breast and left hip. Lastly, she lifted the ribbon holding the key over her head, placing it with care on the bed.

She knelt and put her hands in the bucket. Cupping them, she drew out cool water to rinse her face. A cloth and some strong soap were next to the bucket, so she wet the cloth and washed. She sighed with delight at being free of the dirt.

Running her fingers through her hair, she undid what was left of her braids. More soot tumbled around her, so she ducked her head in the bucket before lathering her hair. She rinsed her hair in the same water and hoped no remnants of the smoke would cling to it. Squeezing the long strands over the bucket, she doubted she had ever appreciated being clean as much as she did now. She tossed back her head and let her hair fall down her back, as water puddled behind her.

"What is *this* doing here?"

At Jordan's voice, her head snapped up. She wrapped her arms around herself, but they offered little cover. Edging toward the bed, she grasped the curtain and pulled it around her.

She stood, keeping the curtain between her and his eyes. In spite of herself, she gasped when she saw he was wearing only his breeches that clung to his muscular thighs. Droplets of water edged along the firmly drawn lines of his chest as he threw her gown over the chair where she had left her whip.

Only then did he look in her direction. His words slurred as he said, "If you are here to chide me about getting my stitches wet, you can rest assured that I did my best to protect them." He raised his right arm over his head and chuckled. "Come and check for yourself if you do not believe me."

"You are drunk!"

"I would have thought you, as my healer, would want me to ease the pain left by an hour of sitting with my friend's corpse."

Isabella did not dare to let her outrage lessen. She could feel sorry for his loss, but that did not change the fact that he had walked into her bedchamber, half dressed and intoxicated.

"What are you doing here?" She pulled the bed curtain closer to her, but halted when she heard threads hooking it to the top of the bed snap.

"I could ask you the same."

"You could, but why don't you answer my question first?"

He sat on the chair. Leaning forward so he could lock his fingers together between his knees, he said, "As you wish. I am here because this is where I sleep when I am at La Tour."

"This is *your* room?"

"Yes."

"But I was brought here." She pointed to the shift on the bed. "That was waiting, and it cannot be yours."

"Not likely. I don't sleep in a woman's shift." His eyebrows arched rakishly. "Don't you want to know what I wear when I sleep?"

"No."

He shrugged. "I thought you were more curious, Isabella."

"Not about what you wear to bed."

"You need to stretch your imagination in new directions." When she did not answer, he looked at the shift. "That appears to be the perfect size for you." His forehead furrowed in deep thought. "Although we are nearly the same height, you are decidedly narrower across the shoulders and waist than I am." He eyed her up and down. "Or so I assume, for it is impossible to tell when you are wrapped in that heavy curtain."

"If this is someone's idea of a jest . . ." She sputtered on her dismay, unable to continue.

"Do not look for trouble where there are only misguided intentions."

"Whose?"

He chuckled. "Do not fire daggers at me with your eyes, Isabella. If I wished to lure you here, I would not arrange for a serving woman to bring you. Lew must have misunderstood me when I spoke to him about making sure you were at home in La Tour." He picked up the shift and tossed it to her. "My apologies, Isabella."

She caught the garment but wondered how she could pull it on without loosening her grip on the curtain. As if she had asked the question aloud, he turned his back.

"You could leave," she said.

"I could watch."

Deciding the best answer was none, she hastily pulled the shift over her head and smoothed it into place while making sure he did not look at her. She lifted the cover off the bed and wrapped it over her shoulders. The heavy blanket trailed behind her as she stepped out from behind the bed curtain, but did not reach low enough to cover her ankles. She shrugged it to adjust it better, and it tumbled to the floor.

"Do you need some help?" he asked without turning.

"I am fine."

"An undisputable fact, but do you need help?"

Heat scored Isabella's face, and she hoped she was not crimson with embarrassment. By St. Jude! She was one of the Abbey's ladies. She should not be bothered by an uncooperative blanket.

Picking it up, she settled it around her again, this time making sure it covered her. "All right," she said.

He faced her, and his gaze slid along her from where her

drenched hair fell over the blanket to where her toes showed
beneath it. "Do not be offended when I say I preferred you
the other way."

"You have had too much to drink."

"And you talk too much." He folded his arms over his
chest, a motion she feared would strain his stitches.

"That may be true, but you are drunk on too much wine
and too little sleep."

"You are always the healer, aren't you?"

"How can I stop being what I am? Can you stop being a
lord in the king's service?"

"I do not have that luxury." His voice hardened. "You
should gather your things and leave, Isabella."

"And go where?"

"God's blood, you are the most confoundedly logical
woman I have ever met! Stay here, if you wish."

"But this is your room."

"Use it or not, as you wish." He strode toward the door.
"I shall find somewhere else to sleep tonight."

She did not know what to say but "Thank you. I am sure
you have been looking forward to returning to the comfort
of your own bed."

Pausing by the door, he looked at her. "Are you asking me
to stay, Isabella?"

"What gave you that idea?"

"You keep talking even after I said I was going to leave."
He walked to her, each word in rhythm with his steps. "You
talk about the comfort of my bed and how much I have been
looking forward to it."

Ignoring every instinct that told her to keep at least an
arm's distance between them, she did not move. "Jordan,
you are too exhausted to think clearly. I have some dried
poppyheads. If I crush them and put them in some wine for
you to drink, you will sleep well."

"And if I have no interest in sleeping?" He slipped his
fingers beneath her wet hair, letting them curve around her
nape.

"Jordan . . ." No other words came to her lips as he

brushed his across them. Quivers slithered down her spine all the way to her toes, which curled into the rushes on the floor.

He lifted his mouth away and regarded her in silence. He took a step back. She put out her hands to halt him. When her fingers touched the flesh stretched taut across his chest, she slid them up toward his shoulders and closed the distance between them again. With a moan, he pulled her to him and captured her lips.

There was nothing gentle about his kiss. It tasted of wine, and she was intoxicated by his tongue demanding entrance into her mouth. She did not deny him—or herself—the pleasure. When his lips glided away from hers, he left a trail of teasing nibbles along her chin before stroking her ear.

She heard a soft "Oh!" and only belatedly realized it had come from her lips as he traced each whorl of her ear. Heat soared where they were pressed close. She raised her arms to wrap them around his shoulders. The blanket fell back to the floor, and only the thin linen separated his naked skin from hers that yearned to be even closer to him.

When his hand moved up from her waist to cup her breast, she was swept by the fires his touch kindled. His thumb toyed with the tip as he deepened his kiss until she was gasping against his mouth. He gave a low, husky chuckle before he put his arm behind her knees and swept her up against his chest.

Her foot struck the chair, and she heard something fall to the floor with a thump. *My whip*, whispered a small voice within her mind, but she could think only of how wonderful his skin tasted as her lips explored the hard line of his freshly shaven jaw.

"I never knew," she whispered, "anything could feel so amazing."

She reached up to comb her fingers through his hair and tilt his mouth back over hers. He gave her a kiss that was too fleeting. She was about to protest, then, as she savored the motion of his body against hers, discovered he was carrying her across the room. He leaned her back on the bed, spreading her hair across the pillow. He bent to bury his face in the curve of her neck where her pulse exploded like thunder.

When she reached up to draw him to her, he caught her hands and folded them between his own. He shook his head, regret stealing the passion from his eyes.

"No?" She stared at him in disbelief.

"*You* are too tired to be thinking clearly," he said, brushing more hair away from her face. "But I am not as drunk as you have denounced me for being, for I can hear that."

"Hear?" She was baffled.

"You said you had never felt these sensations before." His hand curved down toward her breast before he jerked it away, clasping it behind him. "Your words reminded me that you are not a woman who is willing to trade herself for a bauble. Even more important, I must not repay you for helping me fulfill my vow to Ryce by taking your maidenhead tonight." Picking up the blanket, he settled it over her even though she was pushing herself up to sit. His hands on her shoulders leaned her back into the pillows again. "Sleep well, Isabella."

"Jordan—"

He put his finger on her lips, then bent to kiss her lightly. Blowing out the lamp on the table, he vanished into the darkness.

She sat up and was about to call his name. She clamped her lips closed. What would she do if he came back? She had been so enthralled by his lips and fingertips that she had not thought beyond the rapture. Now she was no longer lost in pleasure, and the facts were simple. She belonged to St. Jude's Abbey, the only place where she could hope to continue her studies and find the answers to her experiments. Jordan's life was here at La Tour, and once she completed her task for the queen, they both would return to where they belonged.

Dropping back into the pillow, she stared at the top of the bed that was lost to the darkness.

Your words reminded me that you are not a woman who is willing to trade herself for a bauble. Even more important,

I must not repay you for helping me fulfill my vow to Ryce by taking your maidenhead tonight.

Jordan was right. She talked too much.

Isabella woke and did not move. Her thoughts, caught in the cobwebs of sleep, struggled to understand what her body already knew. Rain splattered once again on the shutters, but that familiar sound had not pulled her out of sleep. Then she realized the window was not on the side of the room where it should be. She loved her room on the eastern corner of the cloister where she woke to the earliest rays of the sun.

This window faced north, and the bed had a softness she never had known at the Abbey.

Rushes crackled so softly she would not have noted the sound if she had been in her own bed. Someone was in her room. Not her room. Jordan's bedchamber.

Reaching beneath her pillow, she slowly drew out the knife she had placed there earlier. She kept it beneath the blanket as she blinked away the last vestiges of sleep.

Then she saw a shadow move.

It was a man. He was standing by the table and opening some of her pouches. Was he insane? If he mixed some of the elements together, there could be an uncontrolled explosion like the one in the barn at St. Jude's Abbey!

"Don't touch that!" she shouted, jumping off the bed and holding out the knife.

He whirled, hitting her arm. The knife flew out of her fingers and disappeared into the darkness. With a laugh, he slashed at her with his own.

"Where is it?" he demanded, his voice a guttural rasp.

"Where is what?" She leaped back as he swung the knife again.

"You know what I want."

"I have no idea."

"Liar!"

She jumped aside again and hit the chest at the foot of the bed. She toppled to the floor. Getting up quickly, she screamed when he drove the knife toward her. She did not hesitate. She drove the flat of her foot up under his chin. It knocked him to the floor. He crashed hard and slid on the rushes. His shoulder hit the wall. He groaned once, then was still.

Light swept into the room, and Isabella whirled to see Jordan in the doorway. Behind him were several people, both male and female, trying to peer past him to discover why she had screamed. One of them—it might have been Lew, but she could not see past Jordan to tell—held a brand.

Jordan crossed the room in a few quick steps. Looking from her to the man lying in the corner, he grasped her shoulders. "Isabella, are you all right?"

"Yes," she said. Or, to be more honest, she tried to say the word, but it came out sounding like a snake's hiss, unsteady and undulating.

"What happened?"

"I woke to find him sneaking in here." She clasped her arms in front of her to halt the trembling as she thought of how easily he could have killed her while she slept. If she did not hold her arms tightly to her, she knew she would wrap them around Jordan, and she was not sure how he would react in front of his retainers. Telling herself to focus on what had happened, she added, "I thought he was a thief, but I don't know what he wants."

Over his shoulder, Jordan asked, "Lew, do you recognize him?"

"No." The old man inched into the room followed by the serving woman who had brought Isabella to the chamber earlier. Neither of them met her eyes.

Isabella wanted to tell them she had more on her mind than a misunderstanding. Turning away, she went to find the knife that had been knocked from her hand. She put it on the table and opened the medicinal pouch on her belt. One packet would be all she needed. She closed the pouch and put it on the table.

Going to where Jordan was squatting next to the man, trying to shake him awake, she motioned for him to move aside.

He did not stand. "Isabella, he attacked you once. If you expect me to watch while—"

"He has been senseless for several minutes. He will be groggy when he wakes, and I doubt he could attack anything with the headache he is going to be suffering." She pointed to the spot on his chin, which was already swelling. "He may not be able to answer any of your questions until that eases."

"He will not answer anything while he is unconscious."

"If you will step aside, I can remedy that." She crushed the small packet she had taken out of the pouch and held it beneath he man's nose.

He choked.

"What are you doing?" Jordan asked.

"A strong odor wakes even a senseless person." She wafted the packet beneath the man's nose again, and his eyes popped open. Tossing the herbs on the floor, she asked, "How are you feeling?"

He mumbled something, but closed his eyes.

Looking over her shoulder when she heard coughing, she smiled when she watched Lew go to the window and throw aside the shutters. "I warned you that it was very pungent."

"What is in it?" Jordan asked.

"*Hammoniacus sal.* Your aunt calls it smelly salts."

"She is correct about that." He stood and, crossing the room, tossed the packet out the window.

"I—" She choked as an arm encircled her neck, pulling her back against a wet body.

Jordan drew his knife as the man forced her to her feet. She heard gasps of horror from near the door, but she was being too tightly held to look anywhere except straight ahead.

The man's arm closed around her throat as he ordered, "Give me the knife, milord."

Jordan tossed his knife at the man's feet. "Let her go."

"Not that knife!"

"It is the only one I have."

"Play the fool, milord, and your lady will die." He compressed her throat.

The room was eclipsed by blackness, and her head

seemed to be floating away on some gentle zephyr. Then she was jerked back to reality as she heard Jordan talking to the man, whose voice was growing increasingly desperate. She fought to focus her eyes, but a hand was in front of them. The man's hand. She must have lost consciousness, and he had pushed her head back against him.

She blinked. There was something imprinted on the man's wrist. A design. She fought to see more clearly. A horse and a man. No, there were two men, and one was leading the horse.

The same design as the crest on the dagger.

"Then she will die!" the man behind her screeched. His hand shifted away from her face, and she saw him raise his knife.

The serving woman screamed again and must have grabbed Lew's arm, because the light from the brand rocked up and down the walls.

That distraction was all Isabella needed. Ramming her elbow back into the man's stomach, she clawed at the arm around her neck. He groaned, and his arm loosened slightly. She whirled to face him. The flat of her palm struck his chin in the same spot her foot had. He reeled back, groaning and spitting blood.

He swung wildly, but she ducked beneath his arm. She grabbed it and pushed back his sleeve.

"What is this?" she asked.

All color vanished from his face. He shoved her backward. She careened into Jordan. Her legs entangled with his, and they both fell to the floor.

The man grabbed the knife from the table, knocking her medicinal supplies onto the floor. He cheered with triumph.

Isabella jumped to her feet. Both Jordan and Lew shouted as she ran toward the man, who spun to face her with the knife. She edged away a step and moved in an arc just beyond his reach. He picked up a container and flung it at her. She ducked, and it hit the bed, scattering pungent herbs everywhere.

He turned to run, and she grasped the whip from the chair. It snapped loudly as it struck the man on the right arm.

He cried out in pain. The knife hit the floor and bounced into the darkness.

Horror stole the last bits of color from the man's face. Pulling a flask off his sword belt, he opened it and downed it in one gulp. He shouted, *"Semper minax, nunquam summissus!"* He ran toward the door, wheeled when he saw the others there, and climbed up on the window ledge. He threw open the shutters and leaned out.

"No!" she cried, but the man was gone.

The serving woman screamed again and fell to the floor with a thud.

Isabella ran to the window and looked out. Even in the faint light, she could see the dark form on the side of the hill.

Jordan shouted orders to Lew to send guards out to capture the man.

"It is too late," she whispered as she gripped the edge of the window. *"Semper minax, nunquam summissus.* Always defiant, never humble. Just like on the knife's crest."

Defiance had gained the man nothing but death. If he had been alive and able, he would have been fleeing now. Even if he still breathed, his body must be so broken that he could not possibly survive beyond the dawn. On the morrow, there would be two bodies committed to the churchyard. She wondered if anyone would mourn the man who had chosen death over being captured.

Tears rose up from some place deep within her, a place where grief had torn open her soul and left a barely healed scar. A grief of having everything and everyone she had loved in one moment ripped away, her father, her mother, her home. A resurrection of a loss so consuming, it flooded out, unstoppable and uncontrollable. She thought of how someone would be waiting for that man to return, and he never would. That someone would never know why.

When Jordan's arms turned her away from the window and against him, she put her face on his shoulder and wept for the dead man, for the ones who loved him, and for the pain she still could not forget.

Chapter 9

Jordan knew he would have awakened with a headache . . . if he had been able to sleep. As he climbed the uneven steps down to the gatehouse connecting the keep to the lower ward, too many thoughts banged against his skull, each one demanding his attention. He had tried to silence them with a bottle of wine and then another and still another. Nothing had smothered the condemnations his own conscience fired at him like a row of skilled archers.

Isabella was a guest of La Tour, and he had been barely able to control himself. That she had been in his room, separated from him only by sheer fabric, was no excuse for acting as if she were a camp follower. She was the queen's servant, due the respect he would give to the king's men.

And she fought with the skill of any of the king's men. Over and over in his mind, all through the long hours of the night when he tried to wash that image away, he could see her besting the thief not once, but twice while Jordan watched.

Jordan le Courtenay—an earl vowed to serve his king, dying for him if necessary—had let a woman—*his* guest—fight off an intruder by herself. What a laughingstock he would be if anyone learned of the struggle in his bedchamber! No one would because Lew would hold his tongue and make sure the serving woman did, too. As for Isabella, he suspected she saw nothing out of the ordinary with her role as a heroine.

He cursed under his breath. She was a heroine, rescuing herself and who knows how many other people if the intruder had sought other prey. Why had the beast wanted the knife that had been in Ryce's grave? If the Brotherhood wanted the knife returned, they needed only ask.

As "good morning" was called, he replied automatically to the people in the lower ward. He realized he was walking toward the church and turned away from the small stone building. More guilt stabbed him. He should have sat awake all night with Ryce's corpse and prayed for his friend's soul. Even knowing that Ryce would have thought him a fool to ignore the company of a pretty woman did not lessen his feeling of having failed his friend.

The lower ward was crowded. Not far from the church, several children were chasing chickens. It must be a game, because no meat—not even fowl—could be eaten during the Lenten season. Their shrieks of excitement should have been a welcome back to the life he had left behind in La Tour, but they reminded him, as he continued in the opposite direction, of how he could not feel at ease even in his home.

As he was looking away, Jordan's eyes were caught by a flash of gold. Isabella was squatting on the ground with her back to him. Before he could walk in another direction, she looked up. Her face was dirty, hiding her bruised cheek. With her hair pulled back in a loose cascade at her neck, she seemed surrounded in gold.

"Good morning!" he called, trying to sound cheerful.

"I did not expect to see you before the memorial service." She slowly came to her feet. Her trip-worn gown was damp along the hem, but the bodice still bore the dirt and smoke stains from freeing him at the inn. She had risked her life for him so many times already. His gaze rose to the bruise on her cheek, and the red heat of his fury blurred her face. He forced it down. If there was vengeance, it was Isabella's to demand, not his.

That thought should please him because he had vowed not to let someone else's abused honor propel him headlong into battle again. It did not. He had made that promise to himself when he survived Prince Richard's honorless foray. Then he had been fired up with bloodlust. Now . . . The passion when Isabella regarded him with genuine sympathy was even more powerful than the yearning to serve his liege lord and gain commendation for his bravery.

He tore his gaze from hers. He did not want to let her compassion touch him, because then he would have to feel other things. Other things like the sorrow that gnawed at him and bone-deep regret.

He noticed, for the first time, that she had spread out the contents of the pouches she wore on her belt. "I see you are busy. I will leave you to your work." He saw her face harden. He wished he had not spoken, but it was too late. He walked away.

"Jordan." She said no more; yet it was enough for him to face her.

"Yes?"

"Thank you."

He scowled, pain lashing across his forehead. "Thank you for what?"

"For not being angry with me for what happened with the thief."

"Angry with you?" he asked, astonished by her comment. "You halted an intruder. Why should I be angry with you?"

"I was told before I left to meet you that men prefer to do the fighting. I have failed to allow you to do what you would have wished to do."

"If you think I wished to fight a thief who managed to sneak into my bedchamber, then you are wrong."

"I know you did not want to fight him any more than I did."

He had not guessed he was so transparent. "Why do you think that?"

"You agreed swiftly to help me when I said we might prevent another war between the king and his sons." She smiled and set her fingers on his arm.

The double assault on his senses hardened every muscle along him as his pulse thudded through his skull, sweeping aside the ache he had been suffering and replacing it with another. This ache arose from deep within him because he longed to be deep within her. Good sense had kept him from joining her in his bed last night, but he was beginning to think that good sense was highly overrated. He wanted to feel her golden hair flowing over him as she surrounded him with her warmth.

"So I appreciate what you did last night," she said in the same soft, bewitching voice. "I know how difficult it was for you."

Was she still speaking of him having to see that cur holding a knife to her throat, or was she now talking about how he had walked away when he wanted to spend the night with her?

"It is over," he said.

"It is." She looked past him toward the window in his chamber far above them. "I don't understand anything about men." She put her hands to her lips as her eyes grew wide.

Knowing that she had said something she had not intended, he gave her a wry grin. "That makes us quite even."

"You don't understand anything about women?"

He was astounded when he chuckled. "I doubt any man from Adam onward has ever understood anything about women. That is not, however, what I meant. What I meant is that I fail to understand my fellow man."

"You will have to explain further." A smile eased the tension on her face. "I understand nothing about men other than how to heal their wounds."

Heal mine, he wanted to shout. His body tightened with the anticipation of her touch, which could help him forget, for as long as he held her, what haunted him.

Edging away, so he did not give in to the temptation to pull her into his arms and continue what good sense had halted last night, he said, "I speak of men who do not appreciate the value of what they have and aspire to obtain what others possess."

"You are speaking of the king and his sons."

"Among others."

"I don't like to talk about wars and battles and fighting among families."

"I understand. As the only sister among four battling brothers, you probably have been torn between each as they try to get you to side against the others."

She stared at him in astonishment. She began to speak, then closed her mouth.

"What is it?" he asked.

"Nothing important."

She was lying. He was as certain of that as he was that he wanted to hold her close. Why would she be false about such a question when she had spoken the truth about other, far more sensitive topics? A half dozen answers rushed through his mind as he recalled the tales of her barbaric brothers. It was no wonder that she had gone to St. Jude's Abbey to study healing. Not only had that allowed her to escape the feud, but she was gaining knowledge that she might need to save the life of one of her brothers.

She knelt and gathered up the small pouches. As she put them within the sack she had been wearing when they met, she asked, "Do you think your opinion about the king and his sons is why your aunt suggested I obtain your help?"

"My aunt and I have not spoken since my father's funeral two years ago."

"Yet she asked me to find you, and she must have had her reasons. Your aunt sees with very clear eyes."

"Are you suggesting my aunt is a mystic?"

"No, just very insightful." She sat on her heels and raised her eyes toward his. "You are alike, Jordan. She considers the facts deeply and is not swayed by the opinions of others, even if her opinion is unpopular."

"You are right. In that, my aunt and I are alike."

"No wonder she thinks so highly of you." She picked up the bag and stood. "I hope you have her clear eyes, too. Did you see the thief's left arm?"

"I watched Emery and some of the lads take the body away, if that is what you mean. I can assure you that he is dead."

"No, that is not what I meant. He had a symbol scorched into his skin. It was hidden beneath his shirt until his sleeve fell back."

"You were barely conscious, Isabella. If you mistook a mark from birth as something else—"

"I did not mistake anything. He had a symbol burned into his skin." Slinging the sack over her shoulder, she grabbed his left arm and pushed back his sleeve. Tapping the underside of his wrist, she said, "Right here, and it was identical to the symbol on the knife found in Ryce's grave."

"The Brotherhood's symbol."

She nodded.

"That tells us nothing we did not already know," he said, drawing his arm out of her hand. He doubted he could endure her touch—even a chaste one—much longer without showing her exactly how little she understood men. Again he silenced the alluring images of her naked flesh pressed to him.

"One thing you may not know, Jordan, is that the man did not die just from his fall. He died from poison." She drew a cracked flask out of her sack. "It has a residual flowery scent. I would guess it is a poison made of lily of the valley."

"But why drink poison before jumping out the window?"

"He wanted to be sure he died."

"That is insane. No rational person would do such a thing."

"You are right. No rational person would." She shivered so hard he could see it. "What *is* the Brotherhood?"

"I don't know, but if the Brotherhood wants the accursed knife back, I will gladly give it to them."

"But—"

"There are no 'buts,' Isabella. No knife is worth anyone's life, not even a thief's. If he wanted it so bad, let him be buried with it."

She recoiled from his gruff tone, and he wanted to apologize. How could he tell her that if he did not let rage come between them, he would not be able to control his craving for her?

He strode away. Climbing the hill to the gate, he stormed through it. Nobody spoke to him as he went up to the wall that encircled the keep. At the top, he stopped when he reached the point where he could see the farthest across the lands of La Tour du Courtenay.

The gentle rolling hills flattened out into the plains that ran to the horizon and the sea beyond. Copses broke the expanse. Some fields had been plowed, but others still waited. The scattered cottages looked as if a child had tossed them among the fields.

This and only this should be his concern. That was what he had pledged when he had made his bargain with God to spare his life in Aquitaine. Now he was wondering if he had, instead, been negotiating with the devil, who was offering him a taste of the hell awaiting him.

At the sound of light footfalls, Jordan looked up from the list of accounts Lew had given him to review. Was Isabella seeking him out? He could not silence the burst of hope at the thought of seeing her smile, of caressing her hand, of listening to the music of her laugh.

A serving woman paused in the doorway to his office next to his private chamber, and hope faded once more. She curtsied and said, "Milord, the lord and lady are here."

He was puzzled for a moment, then realized the serving woman must be speaking of Weirton and his sister. "I will welcome them in the great hall."

She curtsied and left.

Jordan stood and rubbed his eyes while he fought a huge yawn. He was grateful that Weirton had kept his promise to come to La Tour to attend the memorial service. He was even more thankful that Weirton's sister was with him. Certainly the lady would want to spend time with Isabella, talking about whatever interested ladies. That would allow him to keep space between him and Isabella. He hated the idea, but maybe then he would be able to get some sleep and not let his need for her blind him.

When he came down the curving stairs to the great hall, he saw the servants gathered and talking lowly. They scattered when he came near, and he knew they were gossiping about Weirton and his sister. He had joined in many such conversations as a child. Now the obligations of the castle's lord were his.

The great hall rose to wooden rafters that crisscrossed the ceiling. Arched doorways led to other chambers. Stacks of wood waited by each hearth that was half the height of the doorways. Fires gave off smoke and the scent of oak. On one wall, mounted heads from past hunts had been a source of pride for his father. Tables were set at the far end in front of a raised table used only for formal occasions. Three circular lamps, each with a half dozen candles, hung from the ceiling, but they were not lit. Sunshine poured through small windows set near the ceiling at each end and through the pair on either side of the hall.

As Jordan walked across the hall, rushes crackled under his feet. An unpleasant odor rose. After he greeted his guests, he would have fresh rushes spread on the floor.

Weirton strode toward him, grasping Jordan's arm. "It is good to see you back at La Tour, le Courtenay."

"It is good to be here."

"You will not be so foolish again."

"Foolish?" Jordan knew he should not take offense at Weirton's words, but he did.

"Following that young fool Richard in his endless quest for war."

Jordan nodded. He could not disagree with the truth, but he did not want to talk about the past. "I trust your journey was uneventful."

"No travel with Odette is uneventful."

"Why is that?" He hoped the lady was not demanding and arrogant.

"See for yourself." He raised his voice. "Odette, do come and greet our host, Jordan le Courtenay."

A woman stepped out into the light, and Jordan stared. He could not halt himself.

Stunning.

There was no other word to describe her. Such fragile features and fiery red curls would keep a man from thinking of anything but her. He doubted the top of her head would reach his shoulder, and as she untied her cloak to hand it to a servant, he could not keep from staring at her slender hands that were so tiny he suspected he could hold both on his palm. Her breasts were surprisingly lush above her slender waist.

"My sister, Lady Odette," Weirton said with a smile that suggested he was responsible for her beauty. He took the twig cage she was carrying and set it on the floor.

"Milady." Jordan bowed his head, sure that fatigue was stupefying him, making him see impossible flawlessness.

"We appreciate your welcome, Lord le Courtenay." Her voice was soft, suggesting the very sight of him had taken her breath away.

He almost laughed at that idea. He was hardly at his best, and he guessed she was accustomed to men trying hard to impress her in the hope of obtaining one of her smiles.

"Come," he said, motioning toward a nearby table, "and wash dust out of your throats."

"You are very kind, milord." She put her hand up, and he placed his beneath it. Edging closer, she smiled at him as if she had been waiting all her life for this moment.

That thought was unsettling. Before he could answer, he heard Weirton draw in a quick breath. He followed Weirton's gaze toward where Isabella was entering the hall with her sack tossed casually over her back and her whip slapping her thigh with each step.

"Lady Isabella," crowed Weirton, "how good to see you again."

Isabella halted in midstep and faced them. Her eyes widened, but she was smiling as she came toward them.

Jordan could not help comparing the two women. Lady Odette was small and fragile. Isabella was his height and had proven she was capable of defending herself and anyone else. While Lady Odette's russet hair swirled around her like a sunset cloud, Isabella's golden curls were windblown and tangled. Lady Odette was perfection, but his gaze kept returning to Isabella as Weirton introduced her to his sister.

"Lady Isabella de Montfort, this is Lady Odette Weirton."

"I am pleased to meet you, Lady Odette," she said before looking at Weirton. "It is very kind of you, milord, to come here to be with Jor—with Lord le Courtenay on this day."

Isabella chided herself for using Jordan's name casually. She had seen, from the corner of her eye, Lady Odette's shock. Shifting her bag off her shoulder, she set it on a bench. Half of her herbs had been ruined during the debacle near Kenwick Priory.

"I knew Ryce de Dolan well, too," Bouchard Weirton said as he took her hand and bowed over it. He squeezed it. "You will be pleased to know, milady, that Gamell has been duly punished for his attack on the two of you."

Drawing her hand away because she was unsure what he meant by compressing her fingers, she said, "I am not pleased to know that, milord."

"You are not?" He glanced at Jordan, clearly hoping that Jordan would explain what she meant.

She resisted reminding the baron that she was quite capable of explaining herself. "I never wish to hear of another's suffering."

"You have a tender heart, milady."

"It is the way of a healer."

Lady Odette interjected, "You are very tall for a woman. Are all the women in your family such giants?"

"I have only brothers."

"Are they giants, too?"

"Yes," she said, even though she had no idea. She was unsure why the lady was trying to goad her, but she would not be baited into saying something that would reflect poorly on St. Jude's Abbey. Nobody at La Tour knew she was from the Abbey, but that did not matter. *She* knew.

"I cannot believe the outrageous stories I have heard about you, Lady Isabella. Chasing a man so relentlessly that he ended up falling out of a window." Her bright green eyes widened as she gave a small shiver. "Do not take what I am about to say the wrong way, but I am so very glad you were the one attacked, rather than me. I would have had no choice but to wait for Lord le Courtenay to come to my rescue." She smiled at him.

Isabella frowned. How had the lady heard of that? She was vexed that Jordan would make light of the horrible events.

When he motioned for Lord Weirton and the lady to choose a tankard from the table, he said quietly, "I suspect Lew was eager to talk about what happened. He has known Weirton for many years, so he probably saw no reason not to brag about your skills. After all, they are no surprise to Weirton. He saw what you and Emery accomplished at the inn."

She let the stiffness sift out of her shoulders. He was right, and she was overreacting. Taking the tankard Jordan handed to her, she swallowed her gasp when her fingers brushed his. He shifted his hand so that his fingers covered hers for the briefest moment. It was enough to send shivers of longing all the way to her toes. As she saw the hunger in his gaze, she fought her other hand that wanted to stroke his face as she brought his lips to hers.

A shriek tore Isabella out of the fantasy as Jordan yanked his hand away and reached for his sword. She grabbed the handle of her whip, but halted when she realized the scream had come from a serving woman who was staring at a cage made of twigs.

"What is *that*?" cried the serving woman, backing fearfully from the table where the cage had been set.

"Stop it!" ordered Lady Odette. "You will scare him."

"Scare who?" Isabella asked.

"Peppy."

Lord Weirton motioned as if he were the host. "Le Courtenay, there are some things about which I wish to speak with you privately. Shall we leave the ladies to their discussion while we have ours?"

"Most certainly." Jordan bowed his head toward them. "Ladies, if you will excuse me . . ."

Lady Odette gave a soft sigh as Jordan walked away with her brother. "An amazing man."

Isabella wanted to agree, but was disconcerted by the

lady's expression. It reminded her of one of the sisters at St. Jude's Abbey when she was about to begin a contest of skills—determined to win and unwilling to accept defeat, no matter the cost. What Lady Odette expected to win was obvious. She wanted Jordan, and she did not intend to let him slip away. Lord Weirton must share her interest, because he had brought her to La Tour.

Did Jordan have an interest in the lady? He had been holding her hand when Isabella entered the hall; yet, there could be no mistaking the desire she had seen in his eyes. Or had she? Had there been only a reflection of her longing?

"Are you ready to come out, dearest?" Lady Odette was holding an acorn in one hand as she reached for the door to the cage with the other.

"What do you have in there?" asked Isabella.

"My pet squirrel."

"A squirrel?" Her nose wrinkled.

"It is my dear Peppy." The lady opened the cage.

Isabella watched in amazement as a gray squirrel scurried up the lady's arm. It accepted a nut from her and sat on her shoulder to chew, its small eyes focused with obvious suspicion on Isabella.

"You have a squirrel for a pet?" she asked.

Lady Odette patted the squirrel's head, something the creature must not have liked because it snapped at her. "All ladies are carrying such sweet creatures. I assumed you would know that."

"I have been deep in my studies, and I am afraid that I have not had time to discover what is of interest to others."

Lady Odette gave her a broad smile. "Then you must allow me to teach you everything, Lady Isabella."

"That is not really necessary." She tried to imagine her sisters' reaction if she returned to St. Jude's Abbey with some sort of vermin draped over her shoulder.

"Oh, but it is. Bouchard told me that, because of that stupid bailiff, we are indebted to Lord le Courtenay and you. If I can make amends for what you endured by sharing such tidbits of information, then it will provide a small repayment."

Isabella was about to demur, then remembered that, once she and Jordan found the pages, they must place that precious packet in Queen Eleanor's hand. To make a mistake in the queen's court would not only embarrass herself, it would bring shame to the Abbey. If Lady Odette's instruction could help, Isabella must be an eager student.

"That is very kind of you, milady," Isabella said.

Lady Odette lifted the squirrel off her shoulder and cradled it in her arms as if it were her child. It made a furious clicking sound at her, but she ignored it. "Then let us begin with how you address Lord le Courtenay with such familiarity. I heard your error, and you are fortunate that only Bouchard and I heard it."

"But Jordan asked—"

"You need to listen, milady, not argue."

Isabella said nothing as Lady Odette explained all the reasons a woman should not use a man's given name. As she tried to follow the convoluted rules, which made little sense to her, she wondered if she had agreed to the lessons too quickly. She may not have traded her soul to the devil in exchange for the information, but she knew she was going to have a devil of a time following them.

No matter.

She had skipped out on too many lessons at the Abbey. If she were as skilled as many of her sisters there, she could have saved that man from death and discovered the truth of why he wanted the knife. She suspected she would need everything the lady could teach her while she searched for the queen's pages and returned them to Queen Eleanor. She must think of that instead of how, once their task was completed, she would be saying farewell to Jordan.

Lord le Courtenay, she reminded herself. She suspected learning to address him again with such formality would be the toughest lesson of all.

Chapter 10

Father Eloi wafted incense around the stone coffin that held Ryce's bones. When the priest went to repeat the blessing over the shrouded form on the floor in front of the coffin, Jordan's fingers tightened until he was sure his cracking knuckles would be heard throughout the church.

The nameless cur did not deserve to share a rite with Ryce de Dolan. His friend had been an honest man, dedicated to a chivalric ideal. The shrouded man had been a thief and would have murdered Isabella if she had not proven herself his better.

A bird sang in the rafters.

He saw bits of sunlight spilling through the thatch above the rafters. Like the rest of the castle, the church was in need of repairs. He wished he could stay and tend to them, but he had promised Isabella to journey with her to Lincoln.

Lowering his head, he glanced to his right where she stood gazing at the floor. Her lips moved to match the words Father Eloi spoke. She wore her dirty gown. None of them had had a chance to change, because the priest had insisted—once he heard Weirton and his sister had arrived—that the ceremony be held without delay. Even in the muddy and torn gown, she demanded his attention. No, demand was the wrong word. She never asked to be admired. That was another way in which she differed from other women.

He knew the danger of letting his gaze linger too long on her. God's blood, he had been ready to bed her, acting with as little honor as the nameless thief. She had risked her life to save his, and he had treated her as if she were a pleasure woman.

Pleasure woman. He had not guessed, until he first kissed her, that so much passion was within her. He should have, because, since his return from Aquitaine, he had hidden his own feelings from everyone.

Hearing a deeper voice repeat the prayers, he looked to his left where Weirton and Lady Odette stood. Even wearing dirt from the journey to La Tour could not detract from Lady Odette's ethereal beauty.

Weirton had let him know that his sister had been eager to meet him. Only a reminder that they were at La Tour to bury Ryce had halted Weirton from a blatant suggestion that Jordan should consider marrying Lady Odette. Once the service was over, Weirton was sure to bring up the subject again.

As the priest finished his prayers and turned to offer a blessing, Jordan looked at his friend's coffin. Next, he knew, the mourners would go with the coffin to the churchyard where it would be buried. More prayers, and then the service would be over. Another life wasted in the absurd pursuit of prestige and a woman's favor.

He would not be so stupid. It was the vow he had made the day he heard of Ryce's death, and he intended to keep it. He would fulfill his pledge to Isabella and return to La Tour. He would concentrate on doing the repairs the castle needed before he burdened himself with a wife. When he chose one, he would do so with great care. He would not throw his life away to win a woman who went to share another man's bed without shedding a tear over his grave.

Another vow. A smile played at his lips. He needed to stop making promises.

"Are you all right?" asked Isabella in a wispy whisper.

"Yes."

"I am pleased to hear that."

The chill that had encased him for months thawed a bit at her gentle kindness. He had no time to reply as he joined the others following the coffin into the churchyard. He saw her slip her arm through Lady Odette's and steer her and Weirton along so quickly they had no chance to speak to him. He was grateful that she knew he needed to be alone.

Father Eloi's words were few by the grave. When the priest stepped away from its edge, he clasped Jordan's arm wordlessly before returning to the church and his other duties.

In the silence left in the priest's wake, Isabella said, "Lady Odette, I am certain you would appreciate a chance to rest after your long trip from Kenwick Castle. Lord Weirton, I know you wanted another tankard of Lord le Courtenay's ale."

"You have many ways of healing those around you," Weirton said. "You clearly learned your lessons well at St. Jude's Abbey."

Isabella's face grew ashen, and Jordan knew she was stunned that the baron had discovered where she had been studying. He was not. Weirton was a clever man, who liked to know everything about those around him. Why was she so shaken? Within minutes of their first meeting, she had mentioned to Jordan that she studied at his aunt's abbey.

A smile quickly settled on her lips, and he wondered if he had been mistaken. Standing by a grave was enough to make anyone pale.

"There are many types of healing," she replied. "Each person is different."

"As I said, milady, you have learned your lessons well." Weirton and his sister turned to leave the churchyard.

Isabella started to follow, then paused. Her hand slipped into Jordan's, and she gave it a gentle squeeze before she turned to leave.

"Isabella?" Jordan called lowly.

She looked back.

"Thank you," he said.

"You are welcome." She gave him a sad smile before she walked away.

He stood where he was and watched while she went toward the gate to the upper keep. Even when she was out of sight, he continued to stare across the lower ward and wondered why he had failed to see the truth. He had made so many vows, and keeping some meant breaking others. He had promised to keep out of the deadly games played by the Plantagenets, but had agreed to help Isabella serve the queen. He had vowed never to let another person be as important to him as his parents and Ryce had been, because he did not want to suffer such a loss again. But, in such a short time, Isabella had become a part of his thoughts.

"What should I do, Ryce?" he asked, even though he knew the answer his friend would give him.

Women! They are the bane and the boon of manhood.

He wondered if he had ever truly understood his friend's words before now.

It was only a small explosion, but enough to knock Isabella off her feet. A cloud of smoke rose in the twilight to block out the evening star, and shrieks came from every direction. Rolling over on the damp ground, she pushed herself to her feet. The experiment should have worked, but the explosion had been uncontrollable. She still had not found the correct elements to add together to make the compound Nariko had seen in the distant East. She was beginning to think it might be easier to find the philosopher's stone and turn lead to gold.

The acid she had made from mixing sulfur and water in an open container had detonated when she added iron to it. She had not even had time to stir in charcoal fragments. As she stamped out the small fires burning in the fresh grass, she sighed. How many more attempts must she make before she found the correct mixture?

And she should have known better than to use the acidic mixture without taking care. If she had been thinking clearly, she would not have been so reckless. But, even as she prepared the experiment, the image of Jordan's face during the funeral invaded her mind. She wanted to offer him some comfort, but knew of no herb or healing stone that could ease such grief.

"Lady Isabella?"

At the call of her name, she turned to see Lew rushing toward her as fast as his bandy legs could move.

"What happened?" the steward asked, puffing.

"An accident." She did not want to explain, especially when her experiment had been an absolute disaster.

"Are you hurt?"

She looked at her scraped hands, then hid them in her dirty gown. "I am fine."

"I am pleased to hear that." He sat on a stump that someone had left by a stack of wood. "Pardon an old man's lack of manners. It has been a long day. Spring cannot come soon enough for these old bones."

"We all are exhausted." She tried to smile but failed. Bending, she gathered the glass containers that had not shattered. She set them aside and picked up the shards of the bowl that had held the mixture.

"Maybe it will be quieter now that Lord le Courtenay has brought his friend to rest here. He can take the time he needs to heal."

She wrapped the glass containers in lamb's wool and put them into her bag. "If he takes care, his side will heal where I stitched it closed."

"I do not mean those wounds. I speak of other ones."

"I have seen his scars."

The old man rubbed his hands together as if seeking to warm them. "Lord le Courtenay has never flinched when there was a call to serve, but each time he has gone away, he has returned changed. He laughs less and keeps more to himself."

"What warriors see and hear and do requires them to harden their hearts so they can honor their sword-sworn oaths without hesitation."

"Maybe you are right, but there is a more important reason for him to remain in La Tour. He has a duty to perform here. Without an heir, La Tour will have no future. For an heir, he needs a wife, and how can he woo a wife if he is always away?" Lew brightened slightly. "But that problem appears to be taken care of."

"Why do you say that?" She had not seen anyone peeking into her room when Jordan thrilled her with his splendid kisses. Jordan's appearance in the doorway at the same time as his servant would have shown Lew that she had been alone with the thief.

"Isn't it obvious?" Lew chuckled. "Lady Odette. There could be no other reason for Lord Weirton to bring her to La Tour." He clambered to his feet. "I should not be keeping you here talking, milady, when I was looking for you to let you know that the evening meal is ready."

Isabella was relieved for the excuse to take her leave before the steward saw her reaction. He confirmed what she had been thinking, but having Lew say aloud that the baron and his sister had an ulterior motive for their visit to La Tour made the situation too real. Did Jordan suspect? He was an insightful man, so he could not be unaware of Lord Weirton's plans. Maybe the impending visit was the reason Jordan had pulled himself out of her arms last night.

Lord Weirton! How had he learned that she had studied at St. Jude's Abbey? As she had by Ryce's grave, she warned herself not to give in to panic. A casual remark made by Jordan—or by herself, even though she did not recall making any such comment—could have revealed the truth. Lord Weirton would surely assume that she was a lay student at the Abbey. As long as the baron knew nothing more, no damage had been done.

Hurrying through the gatehouse and up the steps to the keep, she could not escape her thoughts that went this way and that like a leaf bouncing amidst rocks in a stream. She must find a way to regain her poise before she joined the others for the evening meal.

She peeked into the great hall. A few servants were loitering there, but no one sat at the raised table that had been covered by a cloth embroidered with gold and silver threads in an ornate pattern. If she went through the hall, she could reach Jordan's chamber and change quickly.

The servants stared in astonishment when she entered the hall, and she guessed she looked even worse than she had imagined. Glad there was no polished surface to show her reflection, she rushed across the hall.

Whispers abruptly filled the hall like a swarm of maddened bees. All the servants looked to the right. Isabella did, too. Framed by an arched doorway were Jordan and Lord Weirton and his sister, whose fragile, angelic looks contrasted with her wild red curls. Isabella spared the baron and Lady Odette a single glance before her gaze fixed on Jordan as she slowly stopped in the middle of the hall.

His tunic was a lighter shade of red than the lady's hair, and its sleeves were trimmed with the silver and gold design on the tablecloth. The hilt of his sword glistened where it hung from his leather belt that emphasized his battle-hardened body. Boots encased his lower legs, revealing a strength she knew was no illusion. She had never seen him look so much like an earl.

Isabella took a step toward the door, then stopped short. She watched as Lady Odette stood on tiptoe to say something to Jordan before slipping her small hand into the crook of his arm. The lady leaned toward him in an obvious invitation for him to bend to give his reply.

Something bit into Isabella's stomach. It bit so hard she almost looked down to see what was there. She did not need to, because she recognized the hideous, hateful feeling of being inadequate. Even if she had been wearing the best gown the Abbey could provide, she could not compete with the glory of the clothes worn by Jordan and the Weirtons.

She squared her shoulders as she put her fingers on the handle of her whip, reminding herself that she was the queen's representative at La Tour. It did not matter what she wore. It only mattered that she did as she had promised.

And she should have been prepared. The abbess had warned her about the peculiar dance between men and women when they were—or at least one was—interested in marriage. Being told about it and witnessing it herself were very different. She had not imagined that a woman could be so focused on the pursuit of a man.

Walking across the room, she smiled. "Good evening, milords, Lady Odette."

"What happened to you?" Lord Weirton asked, his eyes narrowing. "You look as if you have been dragged through a sty."

She gave him a cool smile. "Luckily I do not smell that way."

Lady Odette put her hand delicately to her nose. "There is a peculiar odor."

"It will dissipate." She glanced at Jordan. Why was he saying nothing? Was he horrified that she had appeared in his hall looking as she did? Worse, was he disgusted?

Lord Weirton took her hand and bowed over it as he had earlier. "Lady Isabella, allow me to say you are always a surprise."

"Thank you." She was not sure how else to answer.

"It is a shame that your charming gown is ruined," Lady Odette murmured. "Or maybe it is just as well, for now you can be rid of it. That quaint style is no longer fashionable."

Isabella did not let her smile waver. Either Lady Odette chose her words poorly, or she was determined to make any other woman appear lacking in comparison with her perfect beauty. Isabella was unsure which, but she was not going to allow the lady to goad her into anger.

"How fortunate," she replied, "that I still have the opportunity to wear such a charming gown."

Lord Weirton chuckled. "Fortunate for all of us."

"If you will excuse me, I will leave you while I clean up."

"You will return, won't you?" The baron offered his arm. "May I escort you through the hall, Lady Isabella?"

"Thank you," she said, wondering why Jordan was silent.

As she placed her hand on Lord Weirton's arm, he led her away from his sister and Jordan. Isabella had no doubts that leaving the two of them alone had been the baron's plan.

"In spite of the dirt on your face, you look well after your ordeals," Lord Weirton said.

"An illusion," she answered, resisting the urge to look at Lady Odette and Jordan. "It has been the most challenging week of my life."

"And the most unusual, I daresay."

"Why?"

He laughed easily. "Do you often rescue wrongly accused men in such a dramatic way or protect a castle from an intruder?"

"No." She smiled and warned herself again not to presume the worst from an ordinary comment. "In fact, my life before now has been quiet."

"Something I never thought I would hear a de Montfort say."

"You speak of my brothers, not of me. We are different in many ways."

Lord Weirton paused by the door by the stairs leading up toward the private chambers. "I see that, milady. My sister has made several comments in my hearing that would have—if she had spoken them to your brothers—brought on a blood feud that would have embroiled our families for generations."

"As I said, I am different from them."

"Le Courtenay tells me that you are planning on leaving La Tour for Lincoln."

"Yes," she replied, glad that she was prepared for such a question. "I have heard there is a skilled healer in the community at Lincoln Cathedral. It is said he has devised a way to combat the wasting sickness that steals too many lives. I hope to learn from him."

"So you might share the new information with your teacher at St. Jude's Abbey?"

"I learned there, so it seems reasonable that I would share new techniques with her."

"That is very kind of you, milady. You offer your service with both skill and a sense of obligation worthy of a lord's daughter."

"Thank you." She hoped her smile did not appear as

strained as it felt. "Lord le Courtenay has kindly offered to escort me as a favor to his aunt."

"That *is* very generous of him," the baron said. "The road between here and Lincoln can be treacherous. It is wise for the four of us to travel together with our retainers."

"Four?"

"My sister will not be interested in remaining at La Tour du Courtenay, once you—once we leave. I promised her"—he smiled in Lady Odette's direction—"a chance to enjoy company other than mine. As well, a larger group would give any thieves second thoughts."

And offer your sister more time to persuade Jordan to make her his wife. Isabella did not speak the words. It was unworthy to think such things. She should be relieved there would be more people traveling the lonesome roads with them.

"I hope you need not have any more weeks as disturbing as this one," Lord Weirton continued. "Is it true that the intruder was after a knife found in Ryce de Dolan's grave?"

She shrugged as she walked under the arch. "What he wanted is something we can never know, because he died before he revealed the truth."

"It does not matter now because the knife is where it belongs, buried with de Dolan."

"It is . . ." She hesitated when she heard a giggle from the far side of the hall.

Lady Odette had her hand on Jordan's arm. She was laughing brightly, slanting toward him so her voluptuous breasts brushed his sleeve. He looked over her head toward where Isabella stood in the doorway.

The length of the hall vanished as his gaze locked with Isabella's. The lady's lyrical laugh diminished into the rush of her own heartbeat when she saw emotion tightening his face. An answering need welled up as if he had pulled her into his arms. That was where she wanted to be. She was tired of half-truths and pretensions.

If Lord Weirton spoke again before returning to where his sister clung to Jordan, she did not hear him. She watched as

Lady Odette strolled across the room by Jordan's side. The lady's mouth was moving, so Isabella assumed she was speaking to Jordan. Even when he nodded to the lady, he did not break the connection with Isabella until they reached the steps to the raised table.

Isabella released a slow, unsteady breath when he looked away. Had she breathed in all that time? Or had it been only seconds that had been stretched taut with the tension linking them?

She could not compete with Lady Odette, who had a courtly polish not taught at St. Jude's Abbey. A smile tipped Isabella's lips, for she knew that the lady could not vie with her in a knowledge of herbs and the elements.

Each person has talents uniquely her own, and it is silly and quite useless to compare one's skills with anyone else. She had heard the abbess say that when a newcomer to the Abbey wondered if she would ever be able to accomplish all expected of a sister.

She needed to remember that as never before.

Chapter 11

Closing the last packet, Isabella set her sack on the table in the otherwise deserted stillroom. She had found a haven in the cramped space close to the kitchen while the others supped. She had spent the past hour replenishing her medical supplies. Doing so had given her an excuse not to return to the great hall to watch Lady Odette give Jordan coy "come to me *now*" smiles.

Picking up the sack, she put the pouches in the section where she kept herbs separate from the elements for her experiments. She had dill for stomachaches; rosemary to prevent nausea as well as keep evil spirits at bay; dried newts and beetles for toothaches; fennel for fevers; and mandragora for headaches and to bring on sleep.

"And hart's tongue," she whispered as she put the final pouch into the bag. "To prevent unchaste thoughts." She had never used it for that purpose before. At St. Jude's Abbey, she had prescribed it to halt hiccups. She was tempted to try some to get Jordan out of her mind.

She settled the sack over her shoulder, drew on her cloak, and went out into the night. She stared at the hall where lights still blazed. Jordan would want to know why she had not joined him and his other guests for the evening meal. She would have to find a way to be honest without revealing the confused state of her emotions.

Walking toward the gate that led to the stairs and the lower ward, she paused as she emerged on the other side of the wall. There was a narrow lip on the hill. She guessed it was necessary to prevent the stone walls from sliding down into the gatehouse, but it seemed to offer an advantage to an attacking force. Ladders and narrow siege towers could be set against the walls.

She looked down the hillside and realized any invaders would have to carry heavy ladders or sections of a siege engine up the steep sides. If the grass was wet, it would be like trying to climb a glass mountain. Four or five feet of flat area outside the wall presented no danger.

Isabella leaned back against the uneven stones. Above her, she could hear the voices of the guards walking the parapets. One mentioned Lady Odette, and another chuckled. She forced herself not to listen further.

Fog was rising from the freshly plowed fields, leaving the keep an island set upon a cloud with the stars and the moon shining brightly overhead. She walked along the shelf between the wall and the sheer drop into the dry moat, putting some distance between her and the chatting guards. The grass was damp with dew, so she took extra care where she put her feet. The wind was chill, reluctant to relinquish its wintry power. She drew her cloak closer as she paused to stare at the stars.

They were moving in the same dance she had seen every night since she had begun watching them from the roof of the refectory at St. Jude's Abbey. So many nights, she had struggled to stay awake as she plotted their course across the sky. She had discovered the motion altered with the seasons, but the pattern remained identical year after year.

"Do you hear music we cannot?" she asked softly. "Is the moon playing a wondrous tune? Do you—"

"Always talk to the stars?"

She looked to her right, startled. "Jordan, what are you doing out here?"

"I could ask you the same." His words sounded a bit slurred as if he had again drunk too much wine.

"I like to watch the stars."

"And talk to them?" He remained in the shadows, so she could barely see him.

"I was talking to myself." She was about to add more, but gasped as a falling star streaked across the sky, brilliant for a moment, then gone. She pointed toward the sky. "There."

"What? I saw a flash."

"It was a star falling to its death. Each star has only so much light. If it expends it all in a single flash, it goes dark."

"How do you know that?"

"You just saw that for yourself. One of the most important tools in discovering the answers to the heavens is simply to open one's eyes and observe."

"And what of questions on earth?" He came closer, emerging from the shadows to lean on the thick, stone wall. His face in the moonlight was so emotionless it could have graced his friend's death mask.

"I don't know. I guess it would depend on the question."

"I guess it would." He stared out where the moonlight frosted the top of the fog below them.

Lew's voice echoed in her head, *Lord le Courtenay has never flinched when there was a call to serve, but each time he has gone away, he has returned changed. He laughs less and keeps more to himself.* She knew, as his steward did, that Jordan's outward wounds were minor compared to the pain searing his soul. Reaching out a single finger, she traced the scarred line near Jordan's right temple.

He caught her wrist and lowered her hand away. "You have avoided touching that before."

"I did not realize that."

"I did."

She found it difficult to swallow, but whispered, "I am sorry."

"You have nothing to be sorry for."

"Nor do you have anything to be ashamed about. Sometimes accidents happen. And—"

"And sometimes," he interjected, "things happen on purpose."

"Or *for* a purpose."

"What possible purpose could be gained by such a wound?"

"I don't know. What happened?"

His finger stroked the sensitive skin beneath her wrist. "Nothing extraordinary. Prince Richard was determined to punish some of his vassals who spoke out against him. We rode upon a castle in Aquitaine, as we had before. A blow sliced through my helmet and knocked me senseless. I was left for dead while the other knights enacted the prince's vengeance. By the time I regained my senses, the rampage was over and most of the residents of the castle were dead or wished they were. The only honor of that day belonged to those who died before the looting and rape began."

She drew her hand out of his grip as his mouth straightened. "You cannot assume the blame for others' actions."

"I was one of them."

"But you were unconscious."

"During that battle."

She could not keep from recoiling. "You have participated in looting and rape before?"

"I never stepped in to stop it, so that makes me as guilty as anyone else riding beneath the prince's banner."

"Trying to halt battle-intoxicated warriors could be suicidal."

"Is my life worth more than the lives of those murdered?"

"I cannot answer that," she said, stepping closer again. Lew had been right. The wounds hidden within Jordan had not healed. They remained raw and festering. "But I do know that the abbess said you are a man of honor."

"And you believe her?"

Isabella was astonished at his fury. So seldom did he reveal his true emotions that she was doubly shocked each time he did.

"I do not question the abbess's opinions," she said, knowing that apologizing might whet his rage further.

"So, if she had not told you that, you would not believe me when I give you my word that I shall help you."

"Why are you asking me such an absurd question?"

"Because you seem to believe there is something honorable about fighting to the death because that is what you have promised to do." His mouth worked; then he snarled, "Or seek death in a tournament."

"Seeking death? I thought tournaments were sport."

He folded his arms over his chest and stared up at the sky as the breeze rippled through his cloak. "You apparently know nothing about tournaments."

"I know only that they are popular among young men who use them to keep their warrior skills honed."

He looked at her. "So you have never witnessed one?"

"No."

"It is chaos just as in a true battle. Men on horses charge at each other, and the fighting ensues."

"But they fight with dulled swords and unsharpened knives, don't they?"

"No, for how can they prove their abilities when no blood is shed?"

She put her hand on her stomach, which was threatening to spew everything in it. "That is barbarous!"

"More than you can guess. When a tournament's battle cannot be contained within the field set aside for it, the fighting can spill over into a village or among the barns of a farm. Those who live in those buildings are not safe."

"You are jesting! No knight would kill an innocent person simply to prove he was a great warrior. Not in a *game*!"

He took a strand of her hair and twisted it around his finger, tilting her toward him. The scent of wine drifted from him. "My dear Isabella, sweet innocent Isabella, you have no idea what a man will do to prove his prowess on the battlefield or beyond it."

"But to slay people who have committed no crime other than being in the way—"

"Often that is crime enough."

She stared at him, seeking any sign that he was spinning her a tale and waiting to see how much she would swallow before he could not restrain his laughter any longer. She found none. He was serious.

"That is barbarous!" she whispered as she had before.

"Now you can understand *why* I am willing to help you."

"But will succeeding truly put an end to the dying? Yes, it may halt a war between the king and his sons, but while there is peace, more tournaments will be held."

"One problem at a time, my dear Isabella."

She unwound her hair from his finger. "You should not address me so."

"Would you prefer me to address you as Lady Isabella?"

"It would be more appropriate."

"More appropriate?" He laughed, but there was little amusement in it. "If you wish to speak of what is appropriate, wouldn't it be most appropriate to address you as *Sister* Isabella?"

She stepped away from him. "How did you know? How long have you known the truth?"

"I did not know with any certainty until now, for you told me you are not a nun."

"I am not a nun, but I am called a sister within the Abbey." Isabella closed her eyes and sighed. She had done exactly as the abbess had asked her not to do. Opening her eyes, she asked, "What did I do that betrayed the truth?"

"You hid the truth well. Weirton planted the suspicions in my head when he spoke of how no one had heard anything about a de Montfort daughter since your father's death and how your mother had been cloistered shortly after Lord de Montfort died."

"You must not tell anyone what I have told you."

"There will be no need. Who would believe a cloistered sister can do the things you do?" He lifted her whip and ran his fingers along its braided handle. "Are you unique at St. Jude's Abbey, or has my aunt been overseeing an unusual religious house?"

"You are asking questions I should not answer."

"Who constrains you? My aunt?" His dark brows rose. "Or is it the queen?"

"I told you. I should not answer those questions. Please do not ask me more."

"I am not the only one asking them." He looked at the sky. "You missed an interesting meal. Weirton has many questions about you and how you came to be at Kenwick Priory when you were bound for Lincoln."

"What did you tell him?"

"That women seldom reveal the whole truth until it benefits them. Fools that men are, we let ourselves become enmeshed in the pursuit of you in the hope we will learn the truth. Too often, that leads us into a quagmire we should have avoided, for you err in believing we feel more than lust for you."

His words sliced into her, each one as sharp as a honed blade. "You seemed quite aware of what you were doing when you kissed me in your bedchamber. You can deny the truth all you wish, but you felt something for me other than lust. If it had been only lust, you would not have stopped."

"That is where you are wrong, Isabella! I don't feel anything for you or anyone else."

She grasped his arm and pinched hard.

"Ouch!" He shook off her hand.

"So you do have feelings."

Rubbing his left arm, he snarled, "How much more of your nonsense am I going to have to endure?"

"As much as I must endure when you say you did not feel something when you kissed me!"

"If I did feel something other than lust, it was a mistake."

"It is very generous of you to admit that *now*, but I do not believe it."

"No?"

His mouth slanted across hers as he jerked her to him. A desperation burned through his lips with an icy fire. Pushing her back against the wall, he slid his hands down to her waist and then up to cup her breasts. She should shove him aside, tell him curtly that she wanted more than lust, but she moaned into his mouth in the moment before his tongue surged into hers. Clutching on to his sleeves, she stroked his tongue with her own.

The taste of him told her how ravenous she was for more.

His skin was rough beneath her lips as she sampled his cheeks and his neck that was sharp with a day's growth of whiskers.

His breath seared into her hair as she drew his earlobe into her mouth and nibbled gently on it. She heard herself panting when his thumbs teased the tips of her breasts through her gown. When he undid the ribbons holding her bodice closed, his hand slipped beneath it to sear her skin. The key struck his hand, but his eager fingers pushed it aside. His other hand grasped her skirt, raising it as he pressed even nearer. She was imprisoned between the unyielding stones and his equally hard body.

She murmured a wordless protest when he drew his hand away from her breast. He silenced her with another deep kiss. He grasped the other side of her skirt, lifting it until the night's chill touched her bare skin above her stockings.

Bunching her dress between them, he ran his hands down her naked thighs. His thumbs slid along the inner length, slowly drawing her legs apart. She writhed against him, no longer able to control her own body. The mastery of his touch urged her to cede every bit of herself to the rapture he offered.

When his hands glided up her legs, he slipped his fingers over her hips to cradle her bottom. He lifted her against him. Her legs wrapped around him as her dress dropped between them. The fabric could not hide his hardness pressed against her. That he was kissing her with such craving to prove he offered her no more than lust did not matter. She wanted this pleasure with him.

"Lord le Courtenay!"

The shout ricocheted off the wall. When Jordan's title was bellowed again, Isabella recognized Emery's voice.

She ran her mouth along Jordan's neck and whispered as her lips came close to his ear, "Tell him to go away."

"No." He set her on her feet and started to smooth her skirt around her. She heard his breath catch as he pulled his hands back and stared at them as if he could not believe they had betrayed him into touching her again. "I have to answer him."

"Jordan—"

"Don't say anything." The desperation she had sensed in his kiss filled his voice as he put out his hands to keep her from coming closer. "Don't do anything to make me want you more." Picking up the bag that had slid off her shoulder—when?—he held it out to her.

She took the bag without speaking.

"I am sorry," he said before he walked toward where his squire was rushing along the narrow ledge of earth.

"Because you started or because you stopped?"

He paused long enough to say, "Both."

Jordan paced the floor of his private chamber. When he climbed the stairs from the great hall after dealing with Weirton who had sent Emery to find him, he had not been surprised to discover it was empty and that Isabella had requested to use another room.

God's blood! If Emery had not interrupted them when he did, Jordan had few doubts that he would be in his bed now with Isabella. *Sister* Isabella! Whether she had taken a nun's vows or not, she belonged to his aunt's abbey.

That thought rocked him to the very depths of his being.

"Milord?" asked Lew from the doorway.

Jordan was baffled that the steward did not come into the room; then he realized Lew was concerned about intruding. Laughter clawed at his throat. He had guaranteed that Isabella would treat him with the cool distrust she showed Weirton. Would he ever forget the pain on her face as he thrust her away from him?

"Come in, Lew," he called. Motioning to the table where a bottle of wine was open, but untouched, he added, "Help yourself if you wish to quench your thirst."

With a smile, Lew poured himself a generous serving. "Some for you, milord?"

"I have had more than enough."

The old man glanced toward a chair.

"Sit," Jordan said.

Lew did, his smile broadening. He took a sip before saying, "Lord Weirton and his sister are now in chambers more to their liking."

"Good." He had been amazed that Emery would rush out of the keep, shouting his name, when the problem was that Lady Odette preferred a chamber without a window. She did not want to let her squirrel escape. Such a matter could have been handled by the steward or even the squire. If Emery had not interrupted . . . He shook that thought out of his head.

"You will not rid yourself of her that way, milord," Lew said and tilted back the glass. "No woman has ever been banished from a man's mind simply because he wants her to go."

"I hope you are wrong."

"I am right about this, milord, for I have many more years of being plagued by such thoughts than a young man like you. She is an unforgettable woman."

"You are right." He went to the window and folded his arms on the deep sill as he had dozens of times in the past. With a curse, he pushed away. It had been from this window that the intruder had leaped to his death.

"So you are not going to forget her."

He began pacing again. "Once more, you are right."

"Why not then do what is best for both your state of mind and La Tour and marry her?"

Jordan paused in midstep, then looked at Lew. "That is one of the most outrageous statements you have ever made. Should I concern myself with my state of mind or yours?"

Lew drank deeply and wiped his mouth with the back of his hand. "La Tour needs an heir, and with the rumors of trouble between Prince Richard and his father, you may be drawn into battle once more. You must think of La Tour, milord, and make sure there is a legitimate heir before you leave. When we believed you had been killed . . ." The old man shuddered so hard Jordan could hear his remaining teeth click together.

"I was not killed, and I am not leaving again."

"You are leaving with the dawn."

"To go to Lincoln, not to go into battle."

Lew came to his feet and put the glass on the table. "The road to Lincoln has dangers of its own. If you survive the journey there and back, what will you do when the call to serve comes next time?"

"I have considered ignoring it."

"Don't jest about such things, milord!" Horror raised the old man's voice higher with each word. "If you fail to do your duty, La Tour could be forfeit, and all its tenants turned out."

"Lower your voice before you wake half the household." Jordan went back to his pacing. "I will decide what I will do if the call comes. With luck, it will not." *With luck and the completion of Isabella's task for the queen,* he added silently.

"But you must be ready to go, and how can you leave without having sired an heir?"

"Lew, you sound like an old hen. I am not your only chick, and you do not need to fret over me."

Stepping in front of Jordan, the steward crossed his arms over his chest. "I am not the one fretting. Milord, look at yourself. You cannot get the lady out of your mind because she is not in your bed. Why not wed her and get her with child? That would take care of all the problems."

"You make it sound simple, Lew."

"It is. Father Eloi will marry you within the hour, and she can be yours tonight." He lowered his voice to a conspiratorial whisper, "Remember the old saying, 'Marry in April when you can, joy for maiden and for man.'"

"What about, 'Marry in Lent, you will live to repent'?"

Lew's shoulders sagged. "Ah, there is that to consider. Easter is coming soon. If you remain here, you can enjoy courting the lady. It is possible she will be seeded with your child by the time you stand in front of the priest. No one will note if the baby comes a few days early."

"No, we are leaving at dawn as planned."

The old man seemed to shrink into himself.

Jordan sighed and went to the table. Pouring more wine into the glass, he brought it to Lew. "You need not worry, Lew. I am well aware of my obligations, but it is not as simple as you would deem it to be. The lady has obligations of her own."

"To marry, and she has chosen you. Lady Odette—"

"Lady Odette?" he repeated in astonishment. "Are you talking about Weirton's sister?"

"Aren't you?" Lew's rheumy eyes widened. "No, you are not. You thought we were discussing Lady Isabella, didn't you? *She* is the lady who is keeping you awake? She dresses like an urchin and experiments with fire and . . ." He crossed himself. "She has bewitched you!"

"God's blood, Lew! Enough! She has not worked any magic on me. I promised I would take her to Lincoln as a favor to my aunt." He walked in the opposite direction, chiding himself. He must be careful what he said about his aunt. If he—with too much wine drowning his brain—could see the truth, others might as well. "It does not matter. I am not marrying either of them tonight." He held up his hand as he heard Lew draw in a breath to retort. "Or any time in the foreseeable future. Don't nag me, Lew. I am well aware of my duty as I have been since the day it became obvious that I was going to be my father's only surviving son."

Lew gave a deep sigh. "As you wish, milord."

"Take the bottle with you."

"Thank you, milord."

He listened to Lew's slow footsteps. As the steward reached the door, Jordan said, "I thank you for your loyalty to La Tour."

"It is my home, too."

"I understand." Walking to the steward man, he put his hand lightly on the other man's shoulder. "I will consider your words."

"About Lady Odette?" Hope rushed into Lew's eyes.

"About everything you have said."

Lew raised the bottle in a silent salute before leaving.

Jordan remained by the open door. He needed only to go

out into the passage and take a half dozen steps to the left, and he would reach Isabella's room. Her hair would be a golden rippling sheen across her pillow, and her body would be warm enough to thaw the ice deep inside him. He groaned.

Maybe he should give Weirton the answer to the question the baron had posed less than an hour ago. He could marry Lady Odette and do his duty to La Tour. The lady was willing, and it was an easy solution.

He would not make another pledge until he had accomplished what he had already vowed. He must help Isabella find the casket of pages for Queen Eleanor. After that, she could return to her studies at St. Jude's Abbey as Sister Isabella, and he could marry another woman who would give the castle an heir.

It was, he decided as he shut the door, a perfect plan, logical and in everyone's best interests. So why did he feel as if someone had driven a fist into his gut?

Chapter 12

Shifting her sack from one shoulder to the other, Isabella waited outside the stable in the predawn chill. She wondered what was delaying Jordan and the Weirtons. She kept glancing up the steep hill, hoping Lord Weirton and his sister would appear before Jordan did. For the past hour, as she struggled futilely to get a few last minutes of sleep before the journey, she had imagined what she could say to Jordan. It was ironic that words had been so comfortable between them when they were strangers and now were troublesome. She hoped she was not right when she wondered if that was the way he wanted it, because he had admitted he had no feelings for her.

"Other than lust," she whispered.

"Milady?" asked a boy who was leading a horse out of the low stable. "What did you say?"

"Nothing of import." She walked around the black gelding. She shook her head. "I will need something with more stamina for the ride to Lincoln."

"Milady, this horse was a favorite of Lord le Courtenay's mother." His mouth became a stubborn line. "A lady should ride a gentle beast."

"We are going to be traveling with few breaks, so I need a horse able to tolerate the journey. How about that one?" She pointed to the white horse in a stall near the door.

"The stallion? He is not a lady's mount."

"I can handle him. Saddle him for me."

The boy hesitated, his eyes flicking from side to side. She knew he sought someone to help him persuade her to take the quieter horse. Reluctantly, he nodded and, leaving the gelding in obvious hope that Isabella would change her mind, went to saddle the stallion.

She patted the black gelding on the back. "You deserve an easier time than this journey."

The horse swiveled its head to look at her, and Isabella smiled. When the gelding whinnied softly, she dared to believe that the horse had understood and was thanking her for selecting another mount.

A hand grasped Isabella's shoulder. She reached up and seized it, but froze when she heard the stable boy gasp out Lord Weirton's name. Halting the motion that would have sent the baron to the ground, she released her tight grip on his arm. As she faced him, he was rubbing his arm.

"Forgive me," she said.

"I should not have sneaked up on you." Lord Weirton continued to knead his arm. "I recall what you did when we first met. It seems you are a dangerous woman."

"A woman needs to be prepared for the perils along the roads." It was an insipid reply, but the best she could do. How many more mistakes was she going to make before she found the brass casket with the pages? Nariko had warned the sisters to think before reacting because the skills she taught could cause injury. Isabella had paid too little attention to that admonition as she had with so many of the lessons.

"Very wise of you, milady. It seems you have learned much more than a healer's skills."

She did not reveal her dismay. Had Jordan broken his promise and shared with the baron what she had admitted about St. Jude's Abby last night? No, Jordan kept his word. She must not let the baron unsettle her into betraying herself.

"There are many lessons to learn in life." She was proud of the innocuous answer.

His gaze slithered up and down her. He frowned, and his

voice hardened. "Are you wearing the knife that was in de Dolan's grave?"

"Yes." She touched the sheathed knife on her belt. "I need to return it to Lord le Courtenay."

"I thought you said it was buried with de Dolan."

"I did not get a chance to answer, if you will recall."

Lord Weirton's smile returned. "You are right. I hope we will have a chance for uninterrupted conversations on the way to Lincoln. I must say that you look well rested. Odette found very little sleep last night."

"Because she was anxious about going to Lincoln?"

"Among other matters."

Isabella looked away and stroked the black's face. Was the baron trying to make her feel worse with a secretive smile?

"Once we are on our way," she said, "Lady Odette will see there is nothing to be uneasy about. She will be well protected."

"She is aware of that, but . . ." He sighed. "Forgive me. I should not speak of how le Courtenay has changed. He is not the same man he once was."

She stared, openmouthed, at the baron. She had not imagined he would turn the conversation in such a direction.

"You seem shocked, milady."

"I am," she admitted.

"At the changes in le Courtenay? I had thought you two did not know each other before he left on his most recent foray to Aquitaine."

"We did not."

"So you cannot know how eager he was to serve whenever King Henry or one of the princes called his lieges forth to protect his kingdom. Now he seems reluctant to engage in any battle." He took the reins of a dark brown horse, handed to him by a different stable boy. "Even to save a fair lady."

"If you speak of the incident with your bailiff, I can assure you that he saw little peril in the situation. I was the one in error."

"I do not speak of that, but of what happened the night you arrived at La Tour."

She scanned the baron's face and saw nothing but honest curiosity. "He did all he could to protect my life, but he could not halt the intruder from taking his own. If one of us had not reacted swiftly, we both could have died."

"So you reacted."

"As I said, it happened quickly. If I had not been able to unarm the man, Jordan would . . ." She realized the baron was looking past her.

Looking over her shoulder, she saw Jordan and Lady Odette. The lady held her pet's cage in one hand and had her other tucked into the crook of Jordan's arm. She was smiling triumphantly. Jordan's face was taut.

"Do not let me interrupt your tale," he said. "It is not often that a lady is the hero of her own story."

"There is nothing more to add." She regarded him as coolly as he did her. "The situation came to a regrettable end."

Lady Odette waved her hand in front of her face and gasped, "If something like that ever happened to me, I would have to depend on a brave man to come to my rescue."

"You might think differently," Isabella retorted when she saw Lord Weirton nod his head at his sister's words, "if you knew that no one else could save you. Any motion made by Lord le Courtenay would have meant my death. I knew that as he did. That is why I had to save myself."

"If there was no one else to save me, then I would die."

"Without a single attempt to save yourself?"

"What could I do that a brave man could not?" She ran her fingers along Jordan's arm. "I would gladly die with his handsome face as my last sight."

Laughter burst out of Isabella at the lady's ridiculous comment.

Lady Odette recoiled. Her lips pursed as she looked at Jordan, who regarded her with as little expression as he had shown Isabella. The urge to laugh struck Isabella again. Did Lady Odette expect him to chide Isabella for speaking the truth?

With a sniff, Lady Odette started to whirl away. Her skirt bounced behind her, showing the fury Isabella guessed was on her face. She halted when the stable boy came around the side of the stable leading the white stallion.

"I cannot ride that beast!" the lady gasped.

"He is for Lady Isabella." The boy glanced at Isabella, then added, "The black is for you, milady."

Isabella bit her tongue to silence her groan of dismay when Lady Odette gushed her thanks. She should have realized that the lady would not be willing—or able—to ride a beast with any spirit. Wondering how many days traveling at such a slow pace would add to their journey, she stroked the stallion and checked the saddle to make sure it was set for her.

"Let me help you, milady," Jordan said behind her.

Isabella watched him assist Lady Odette into the saddle on the black gelding. The lady giggled and chattered like her pet squirrel. After Lord Weirton mounted and settled himself comfortably in the saddle, his sister handed him the cage, which he attached to the board at the back of his saddle.

Jordan came toward Isabella and asked, "Do you need help?" His mouth twisted. "I know the answer is no, because you prefer to do things on your own."

"The answer is no because you should not be straining the stitches in your side by tossing me into the saddle."

"I think I proved my stitches can survive lifting you."

Fire scored her cheeks as his answer resurrected the heat of their feverish kisses. Was he undisturbed by what had happened, or was he concealing the truth again? One thing she knew was true. She would be a fool to allow him to put his broad hands on her waist as he lifted her into the saddle. Last night had been all the proof she needed that she could not control herself when he touched her.

"Thank you, but I will be fine," she said.

"As you wish." He went to his gray horse and swung into the saddle with ease.

Isabella lashed her bag onto the back of the horse before she climbed into the saddle. She calmed the stallion that

shifted beneath her. Ahead of her among the half dozen retainers traveling with them, she heard Lady Odette and her
brother asking Jordan about what he planned to do to rebuild
the castle. The lady's comments made it clear that she
planned to be spending the future at La Tour.

Pausing only long enough to be certain her herbal sack
was secure, Isabella set her horse to follow the others'
through the gate from the lower ward.

She was the only one who looked back in farewell.

Isabella sat on a stone and opened the packet of food that
Emery had handed her when they stopped shortly after the
sun reached its zenith. The squire had said nothing as he returned to serve the others. He lingered close to Lord Weirton as if he were the baron's squire instead of Jordan's.
Whenever Lord Weirton spoke, Emery would nod with enthusiasm.

She took out dried bread and pungent cheese, trying not
to think that Emery regretted his decision to serve Jordan. It
was understandable that the lad wanted to serve a knight
who would not hesitate to go into combat where Emery
would have the opportunity to perfect his skills.

Sitting as close as possible to Jordan, Lady Odette kept
up a lively patter about how excited she was to be on this sojourn with Lord le Courtenay and her brother. Isabella noticed how the lady's delicate fingers touched Jordan at every
opportunity.

Isabella took the packet and rose. The servants, four men
and a woman, glanced at her, but neither Jordan nor the
Weirtons seemed to take notice. She walked through the
trees to sit on a hummock beside a brook. The splash of the
water over the stones drowned out the voices behind her. It
also, she discovered belatedly, hid the sound of footfalls.

"You should not be so far from the others," Jordan said as
he squatted beside her. "If I had intended to do you evil—"

"If?"

"There was no evil in anything we have done."

"Lust is one of the seven deadly sins."

"Sins are not evil, just mistakes."

Her laugh was so sharp it hurt her throat. "At last, something we can agree upon."

"One other thing we can agree on is that you insulted Lady Odette when you laughed."

"If she sent you here to tell me that I need to apologize, she need not."

"You don't intend to apologize?"

"Of course I do." She took a bite of the cheese. "I must find the way to do so. I shall have plenty of time, for we have not traveled a league since we left La Tour. I can see that we will not reach Lincoln before Holy Week."

"You sound resigned to that fact."

"Railing would gain me nothing. Lady Odette's horse cannot journey far each day, so we will be going slower than I had hoped."

He shifted to sit on a boulder behind him. "A completely logical view of the situation."

"You make logic sound bad."

"It is, because it blinds you to the majority of the people in the world who are ruled by longings and fears. I understand those strong passions. I understand them all too well, as you have seen."

She put the cheese onto the bread on her lap. "I did not expect you to say that."

"What did you expect me to say?"

"That you wished you could be logical and ignore everything you think or feel."

He smiled coolly, but his eyes were heated with emotion. "You are an accursedly insightful woman, so you must see that I owe you an apology, too."

"You already apologized." She stood, not wanting to rehash that acrimonious moment by the wall. She had spent too long during the night going over and over each moment. "We should get under way if we hope to cross the Trent by sunset tomorrow."

"Yes." He came to his feet and motioned for her to precede him to where the Weirtons waited with the horses.

She took a pair of steps, then halted. He put his hands on her shoulders to stop himself from bumping into her. When her heartbeat leaped and pounded like thunder through her head, she tried to silence it.

"Listen," she whispered, hoping he could hear the soft sound now lost beneath her reaction to his touch.

"For what?" he asked as quietly, and she knew, as his warm breath glided along her nape, teasing the hairs that refused to remain in her braid, that she had made another mistake.

"I thought I heard something."

"I hear nothing but the stream and us." He lifted his hands off her shoulders and moved to where he could face her. "What is it, Isabella? Your voice is trembling."

"You are right." She kept her words even as she pushed past him. "It was nothing."

His words had been a vicious blow. He had been honest when he said he felt only lust for her. Why couldn't she believe that instead of hoping he was thrilled all the way to the heart when he touched her?

To the heart? She was as silly as Lady Odette. If Jordan le Courtenay had true affection for any woman, she had seen no sign.

Isabella said nothing as she went, with Jordan following, to where Lord Weirton was assisting his sister onto her horse. The baron made some jest about Isabella reconnoitering to keep them safe, but only Lady Odette laughed.

Again Jordan offered Isabella help; again she declined. Taking the stallion's reins from Emery, she mounted. Lord Weirton gave the signal to start, but she paused as the faint sound she had heard by the stream touched her ears again.

"What is wrong?" Jordan asked as he brought his horse next to hers. He put his hand on her reins. Even though there was a handsbreadth between his fingers and hers, the motion seemed too intimate. She readjusted her hands and saw his frown.

She sighed. She had not meant to insult him also.

"I heard . . ." She shrugged. "It is nothing. We need to go."

She thought he would ask more questions, but he sent his horse after the others. Glancing around, she was about to give the order to follow when shrieks echoed through the small wood.

A dozen men rushed out from under the trees. They held knives and shafts. They swung both at the riders. Lady Odette screamed in terror.

"Go!" Isabella shouted to her horse as she loosened her herbal sack from the saddle and flung it over her shoulder. She hoped she would not need it. Holding the reins with one hand, she reached for her whip with the other. She whirled it over her head and snapped it out in front of her.

A man screeched in pain. She could not see which one because her horse reared back, frightened by the whip. She struggled to control him. It whinnied in terror. Two men were striking it with the long sticks. With a curse she never imagined she would use, she swung the whip. The men scurried back from the lash and the flailing hoofs of the horse as it stood on its rear legs again in fear.

Lady Odette's cries for help rose above the cacophony.

"Go!" Isabella called again.

This time, the horse obeyed. She steered it directly at where the lady was surrounded by men who were tearing her gown as they tried to pull her off her horse.

Isabella did not hesitate. Jumping off her horse, she cracked the whip toward the men attacking the lady. They scattered as the others had. She ran forward and slapped her hand hard on the gelding's haunch. The horse raced away with Lady Odette clinging to it. She saw Lord Weirton hurry in pursuit.

The others . . .

She whirled as she heard another woman cry out in fear. The serving woman! Isabella ran toward where she was being yanked from her horse.

Her foot caught on something, and she fell to the ground. Her whip bounced into the low mat of last summer's grass by the side of the road. Pain arched across the top of her foot along with the gush of heated blood. She looked down to see that the top of her left boot was sliced as well as the skin underneath. . . . A sword was lying in the dirt.

She grabbed it and jumped to her feet. Her left leg almost collapsed beneath her, but she locked her knee in place as she put as little weight as possible on that foot. The sword felt odd in her hand. A small projection from the hilt interfered with her grip.

Before she could decide which battle to join, Jordan grabbed her arm and tugged her toward the side of the road. She tried to stumble after him, but dropped to one knee.

"Are you hurt?" he shouted.

She got up and raised the sword. "Behind me, Jordan!"

"What?"

"Protect my back, and I will protect yours!"

He said something, but she did not hear it as her sword struck another. She had to concentrate on each move. When she returned to the Abbey, she would study much more intensely with Nariko.

The man holding the sword was more inept than she was, and she used one of the few tricks she had mastered to send his sword flying into the brush along the side of the road. As he ran to get it, another man swung his blade at her. She tried to keep him away while she kept her back pressed to Jordan's, but she had to step aside to avoid the knife that was almost as long as a sword. Every attempt she made to move toward Jordan was stymied when the man jabbed at her. Blood poured out of the cut on her foot. She slipped and fell to one knee. Fabric tore, and more pain rushed outward from her knee.

Suddenly the man twisted the knife, and her sword sailed out of her hand, stinging as the projection on the hilt scraped across it. The man advanced on her, licking his lips.

"Isabella!" Jordan shouted.

She tossed her bag on the ground and ripped the top open. Her fingers found the packet she needed. Yanking it open, she upended it into her hand. She held up her hands and blew. A black cloud rose, striking the man.

He sneezed violently again and again. Rubbing his eyes, he roared like a beast in pain. His comrades stared in disbelief. She raised her hands again, and they fled.

Jordan and Emery slashed at the men, who, shouting warnings to each other, vanished into the wood as quickly as they had appeared. Emery called to give chase.

"Let them go," Jordan said as he lowered his sword. "We cannot leave the others unprotected."

"They are not unprotected." The lad wiped a hand across his bloody cheek and winced. "Lady Isabella can guard them." His voice fell to a whisper. "How did she scare them away?"

"I don't know, but I am going to find out. Gather the others and see how they fare." Jordan put his sword in its scabbard as he went back to where Isabella sat on the road. Her torn skirt was spread around her, making her look like a flower battered by the storm.

She raised her head and met his eyes. "Are they gone?"

"Yes."

"Was anyone badly hurt?" Her face was paler than he had ever seen it.

"Emery is checking on them."

"He will have to run quite a distance to find Lady Odette and the baron."

His mouth tightened at her unspoken accusation. "Weirton had to make sure his sister reached safety."

"I understand." She shifted and winced. "But we could have used his sword in the battle."

"We did quite well without him, thanks to you." He picked up the sword that had been knocked from her hand. When he snarled an oath, she asked what was wrong. He answered, "This."

She took the sword and ran her finger along the small round crest on the hilt of the sword. It was the familiar symbol of the two men: one leading a horse, the other astride.

"Were *they* members of the Brotherhood?" she asked.

"Was I wrong to assume the Brotherhood was made up only of knights and lords?"

"There are those who ride and those who walk on these crests. That may symbolize two levels of members within the Brotherhood. Whose sword this was we will probably never know." He closed her fingers over the hilt. "It is yours, Isabella, won fairly in battle."

"Hardly fairly. I tripped over it in the road when I went to assist Lady Odette." She handed it back to him. "I have very few skills with a sword."

Emery interjected from behind Jordan, "But you have other skills. What did you do to that man, milady? Was it magic?"

"Magic?" She laughed, putting her hand over her heart.

Jordan could not keep his gaze from watching the quick rise and fall of Isabella's breasts as her musical laughter seeped into him. With her hair half in its braid and half falling around her shoulders, she was magnificent. His palms itched to sweep along her splendid curves as he drew her mouth to his and sampled the joy in her laugh.

Emery leaned toward him. "Is she mad with fear?"

"Not likely." He saw his squire recoil at his terse tone, but he could not apologize.

"They thought *I* am a magician?" Isabella asked as her laughter eased.

The squire nodded so vehemently his chin almost hit his chest. "I saw them making the signs against magic as we gave chase." He grinned. "Maybe they thought we were the devil's minions come to steal them off to burn for all eternity. What did you do, milady?"

Picking up a leather packet that had been hidden in the folds of her skirt, she tapped it. She raised her hand to show the black specks on her palm. "Pepper. I blew pepper into his face. It burns the eyes and tickles the nose. There is nothing magical about that."

"Other than your wisdom to know how to baffle them with such ease." Emery chuckled. "Well done, milady."

"Emery," Jordan said as he stood. "You have your duties."

His squire stopped laughing and went to collect the weapons left behind when they were attacked.

Isabella remained seated on the ground. "Why did you scold him? He was enjoying the silliness."

"There is nothing silly about an accusation of practicing magic."

"There is when one is using common herbs."

He grasped her shoulders and leaned toward her. "God's blood, Isabella! If they are so gullible to believe that a puff of pepper is magic, how do you think you will ever convince them of the truth? Fools cling to their stupid ideas, even when presented with the truth. It is far more comforting for them than to admit they were mistaken."

"Are you speaking of the attackers or of someone else?"

"I have already offered to apologize again, Isabella. Must you hear me offer to do so every hour on the hour?"

"Maybe."

He stared; then his lips twitched. She arched a single eyebrow at him, and he laughed. He could not recall the last time he had felt such genuine amusement welling up in him. Seeing amazement in her eyes, he took her hand.

When he brought her to stand, she stumbled with a moan. His good humor sieved away as he noticed, for the first time, the bloodstains on her gown. He knelt as he tilted her against him. Around a spot covering her knee, there was a rip. The blood there was already drying, so he lifted the hem of her skirt to examine the deep stain there. He swore vehemently when he saw the blood oozing through a slit in the top of her boot.

"In my bag, there is a packet marked with two red circles," she said, her voice weakening on each word. "It contains leaves from leeks. If you mix it with some honey and a bit of flour, it will ease the bleeding."

Jordan kept his arm around her as she slid down to sit on the road. As her head lolled against his shoulder, he called to Emery and Lady Odette's serving woman—what was her name?—Dedia. He repeated Isabella's instructions to them, and they rushed to find flour and honey among the food supplies.

With care, he searched in the sack, surprised by how many different items it held. He found a small packet with two red circles embroidered into the leather.

"Keep your eyes open," he ordered when her heavy lids lowered.

"I am trying."

"I know you are." He ran his thumb along her chin. How many times had it jutted at him as she spoke some retort? He did not care as he reveled in the soft warmth of her skin.

"Stop that!" she hissed. Her eyes popped open, and she glowered.

Just as he had hoped. She had every right to be furious with him, for he had not treated her with the respect he should offer a lady, especially one from his aunt's abbey.

When Emery and Dedia returned with the flour and honey, they followed Isabella's instructions to pound it together with leek leaves. They spread it on the wounds on her foot and on her knee. She bit her lower lip, but did not make a sound other than to thank them when they had wrapped clean fabric around her foot.

Jordan draped her arm around his shoulder and helped her with care to her feet. He sneezed. He ducked out from beneath her arm and, taking her hands, turned them palm up. When he brushed his fingers across them, black specks flew in every direction.

"You are a peril to everyone around you, even your allies," he said with a smile.

She hobbled to pick up her whip. "Is that what we are? Allies?"

"I would like to think so, because we are bound together in a common task."

"Then it is ridiculous for us to snarl at each other and look for hidden meanings in simple comments." She coiled the whip and hooked it to her belt before taking the bag he handed to her.

"That is true." He whistled for his horse. As it trotted toward him with the white stallion right behind it, he asked, "Are you suggesting we declare a truce?"

"We are two reasonable people who need to work together. We should be able find a way to dampen our baser desires."

"That may be simpler to say than to do." He put his arm under her knees and lifted her. He heard her breath skip a beat when she slanted across his chest, cradled in his arms.

Her voice was unsteady when she said, "You are a strong-willed man, and I am a strong-willed woman. We have both overcome challenges before. Why can't we do the same now?"

"Another simple question." He drew in a deep breath, then let it sift out past his taut lips as her hair tickled his cheek and the soft pressure of her breasts threatened to send his head spinning right off his neck. "We need to trust and depend on each other while we complete our work. A truce is the only way to achieve that."

"Then that is what we must do." She grasped the saddle on the stallion and slid up into it with his help. Looking at him with her amazing eyes the color of a stormy sky, she said, "I will do my best to make sure our truce stays in place. Will you?"

"I will." Another vow! God's blood, he hated taking more vows, especially one he wondered, even as he spoke it, if he would be able to keep.

Chapter 13

Isabella woke with aches along every inch of her. From her throbbing foot to her shoulder that still protested snapping her whip, she was in miserable shape. She promised herself that, if she did not feel better by nightfall, she would boil some linseed in milk and apply it to every spot where she hurt.

Lady Odette's twittering voice did not help. The lady acted as if she had suffered the most and barely acknowledged Isabella's injuries. Lord Weirton had offered his congratulations and his sympathy, but never mentioned that he had ridden much farther from the attack than was necessary to keep his sister safe. Instead he focused on the sword she had found on the road.

"It is clear why we are still alive," the baron announced with a wide grin as he ran his thumb over the crest on the sword. "We had guardian angels watching over us."

"If so, I did not see the Brotherhood coming to assist us," she replied, vexed that he was not giving credit to those who had held off the ambush.

"But they left this sword so we might know we were not alone."

No facts would change the baron's mind. Jordan must have known that already, because he said nothing while they broke their fast with bread and honey and fresh water from a nearby brook. He cleaned his sword with a heavy cloth and then did the same with the sword with the crest on it. At Lord Weirton's request, he returned it to the baron who was eager to have it hooked to his saddle, ready if they were attacked again.

The sun was barely over the horizon when Isabella limped to where the stallion was saddled and waiting.

Emery rushed to her. Last night, before they went to sleep rolled in blankets on the cold, damp ground, Jordan had exacted a promise from his squire that no more damage was done to her.

"Allow me, milady." He bowed as he locked his fingers together.

"Thank you." She put her hands on the horse's back and raised her left foot onto his linked hands. Before he could lift her into the saddle, she drew back to look at the sunlight glinting off something among the trees. "What is there?"

"Where?"

She drew her knife. If at all possible, she wanted to avoid using her whip until the pain had lessened in her shoulder. "Come with me, Emery."

"Where?"

"I saw something sparkling in the sunshine. It don't think it reflected off steel, but I want to be sure."

He faltered as he glanced across the clearing to where Jordan was speaking with Lord Weirton. "Let me call Lord le Courtenay."

"No!"

"No?"

"I don't want to frighten Lady Odette." She inched toward the trees, motioning with the knife for him to follow. "Follow me." She did not wait to see if he would obey, because she knew he would.

Isabella had limped only a few paces when she smiled and put the dagger into its sheath. "It is a stone cross put up by the ancients." She looked at the monument that was so tall that she would have had to stand on tiptoe to touch the top. "I would appreciate you not mentioning to anyone how I let the glitter of quartz in the stone unnerve me."

"If you do not mention to anyone that I tried to keep you

from confronting a stone cross." The lad walked around the weathered cross and examined it from every side.

She laughed. "That sounds like a fair bargain." Running her hand along the rough granite, she marveled at how it had been raised among the trees. Maybe the trees had not been there when the cross was set in place.

She bent to pick some leaves off a plant growing over the base of the cross. Alehoof, she knew by the heart shape of the nascent leaves. It would not be ready for harvesting for another month.

Emery cleared his throat. "I heard you and milord talking about the Brotherhood." He stood with his hands clasped behind him and his feet planted far apart.

"And Lord Weirton?"

He nodded.

"Do you know something of them?" she asked.

He glanced in both directions, then lowered his voice. "Enough to know that it is not wise to speak of them openly. Lord Weirton was cautious and did not speak of them by name."

"They do not wish their name known?"

"They do not seek glory as the Knights Templar or the Knights Hospitaller do."

She pushed herself to her feet. "Then the Brotherhood is a knightly order?"

"Yes, they are brother knights who seek to serve England rather than to travel to Outremer to fight in a Crusade."

"How is it that you know so much about the Brotherhood when Lord le Courtenay knows so little?"

"Squires talk to each other."

"And some of the squires you have spoken with serve knights who belong to the Brotherhood?"

His face became a sickish gray. "I—I should not say. The members of the Brotherhood are supposed to be known only to each other."

"That," said Jordan as he stepped from behind the stone cross, "does not make it easy to become a member, if one is so inclined."

Emery gulped. "If you wish to join the Brotherhood, milord—"

"You will be the first to know." Putting one hand on the cross, he asked, "What else do you know about the Brotherhood, Emery?"

"The Brotherhood was established to protect England when King Henry is on the Continent. They are sworn to do whatever is necessary to serve the king."

"Even theft and ambushing innocent travelers?"

"But they would not have attacked us! They would have protected us."

"Protecting Isabella did not seem that man's intent when he held a knife to her throat."

Isabella paid no attention to Emery's sputtering answer. From his description, the Brotherhood sounded like a counterpart to St. Jude's Abbey. When the queen had been imprisoned after fomenting rebellion with her sons, there had been anxiety that the Abbey would be disbanded, for the women within its walls vowed to offer up their lives for the queen. *Do whatever is necessary to serve.* The Brotherhood's pledge could have belonged to the ladies of St. Jude's Abbey.

When Jordan led the way back to where the rest of their group waited, she was pleased that his steps were slow enough for her to keep pace. He had not asked how she fared this morning. He knew, because he bore the marks of even worse wounds.

She faltered at a vicious curse and a pained whinny, then pushed past Emery who had stopped in front of her. In disbelief, she watched as Lord Weirton raised a thick branch and struck his horse.

Rage stripped the pain from her, and she ran across the clearing. "Stop that!"

He ignored her. "You worthless beast!" He lifted the stick again.

She grabbed it. Yanking it away, he whirled to confront her with the stick raised. She grabbed his right arm, turned to push her hip into his side, and flipped him over her back.

He struck the ground hard. The stick bounced across the ground to halt at the feet of his shocked sister.

"Milord," Isabella said, walking away to pick up the branch, "do not treat your steed with such ill will again." She broke the stick over her knee and tossed it into the trees. "If you do, I swear I shall see you suffer as fiercely."

She ignored the stares from the servants as she went to the poor horse. It calmed as she stroked its back gently and then scratched its nose.

"I must ask you to pledge," she continued into the silence, "that you will not strike your horse or any other beast so savagely again. I know it is discussed whether such creatures have feelings like our own, but they are as sensitive to pain as we are."

Lord Weirton stood slowly and brushed dirt from his tunic. He looked from her to Jordan, who, once again, wore no expression. "If she again takes me from my feet like that, I will forget she is a woman and drive my sword through her."

She continued soothing the horse, but stepped away when the baron motioned for her to do so. She met his gaze as she kept her face as stolid as Jordan's. Lord Weirton lowered his eyes first, then swung up onto the horse. He shouted for someone to help Lady Odette into the saddle.

Isabella remained where she was as the Weirtons and their retainers rode out of the clearing. Even when she heard Jordan walking toward her, she did not move.

"Weirton does not easily suffer being made to look like a fool," Jordan said.

"I did not make him look like a fool. I made him look like the savage he is for treating his faithful horse with such cruelty."

"He is a well-respected baron with many friends among the king's advisors. He has never, not even during the insurrection that ended with the queen's imprisonment, wavered in his support of the king. Other barons might have seen the opportunity to obtain more power, but Weirton was steadfast in his support for King Henry."

She nodded and let her shoulders loosen from their stiff line. "You are right. I must apologize for knocking him from his feet."

"He will not believe you are sincere."

"Because I will not be sincerely sorry that I halted him from beating his horse, but I will express my regret for how I reacted." She faced him. "I will do so because he is your friend."

"Thank you, Isabella." His lips eased into a smile.

It took every ounce of her self-control not to press her mouth to that smile. With the early morning sunshine flowing down through his dark hair and emphasizing the low mat of whiskers along his stern jaw, he was so utterly desirable that she wondered how she could resist surrendering to the passion that filled his eyes each time he looked at her.

"You are welcome." Did he have any idea the simple words meant far more? She yearned to tell him that he was welcome to kiss her with blistering passion that seared her.

Stop it! She had arranged the truce between them, the truce that made them allies, nothing more. And he had agreed. She could not break it when it was less than a day old.

As she walked toward where the white stallion waited, Jordan caught her arm. He jerked his hand back. She wondered if her heart would ever beat again, for it had halted the moment his hand touched her. She should say something. He stared at her, saying nothing. She wished he would speak or move to break this enchantment. She could not. She would be happy to spend the rest of her days and nights gazing into his eyes.

"When we stop for the night," he said, his voice once more without emotion, "I would appreciate you showing me how you knocked him off his feet."

"As I told Lord Weirton, it is a simple trick."

"So it should not take you long to teach it to me."

She thought of pulling him close as she had Lord Weirton, and a heated flush surged through her. Even as she nodded, she knew she should find some way to avoid the lesson.

It would be difficult when she could not wait to touch him again.

The stream ran wild between its banks. Still high from spring rains, the water flowed over boulders that would be difficult in any season. It was too wide for the horses to cross with a single leap, and trees crowded the far bank, offering little space for them to land even if anyone was rash enough to try.

Jordan drew his horse in and shook his head. "There will be no crossing here."

"There is a ford to the south," Weirton said.

"But going south takes us in the wrong direction," Isabella argued. "Lincoln is north."

"I am well aware of that, milady," Weirton said in the clipped tone he had used with her all day.

"If we take care, we can lead the horses through there." Her finger outlined a path between the boulders.

"It is possible." Jordan let his admiration slip into his voice. Isabella's clear thinking and logic no longer took him by surprise.

"Of course it is. Why don't we cross here?"

"Don't be stupid, milady. The horses might slip and throw us." When Lord Weirton turned his back on her, she bristled.

Jordan put his hand on her arm before she gave voice to the fury in her eyes. She was always rational. Why was she being irrational now?

Her fingers covered his, and the familiar unsated yearning riveted him. He leaned toward her, but halted when she lifted his hand off her arm. She did not look at him, and he knew he should be thankful. If he saw the need in her eyes as he had at dawn, he doubted he would be able to keep from pulling her to him.

Sliding off her horse, Isabella lifted her whip off her belt. Letting it fall to the ground, she shook it to get tangles out of the braided leather.

"What are you doing?" he asked.

"Crossing the river." She raised the whip with one swift motion. It rippled through the air, the end wrapping around a branch. She gave it a tug. Before he could do more than gasp, she swung across the river, landing on the opposite bank. She did not loosen the whip, but sent it flying back across the river.

Jordan caught it and smiled. Was there no end to the surprises Isabella had for them?

"Why don't you try it, Lady Odette?" Isabella called.

"Me?" Lady Odette gave a shudder. "You cannot expect me to do that. No true lady would do such a thing."

He hoped Isabella could not hear the lady's offensive words. And they were offensive. Isabella might not have every ladylike gesture that Lady Odette had perfected, but she was far more intriguing. She was curious about the world and deeply committed to the queen. And her movements fired a flame that only making love to her would extinguish until he wanted her anew.

From the other bank, Isabella called, "You should rethink that, Lady Odette. It is fun."

The lady blushed.

"Let us get you across the river," her brother said, putting his arm around her shoulders, "in a manner appropriate for you."

Jordan looked from Isabella's shocked expression to the Weirtons. When Emery came to stand next to him, he handed the whip's handle to the lad. Emery sailed across with a shriek of delight and sent the whip back to Jordan.

The sounds of the Weirtons' horses grew faint. It would take them more than two hours to reach the ford and return to where Isabella stood. The many vows he had sworn made him curse. He had no choice, for one pledge—to be sure his friend's sister went unharmed during their journey—took precedence over all others, even one he had made to the queen's lady.

Gathering the reins for the white stallion and his squire's horse, he mounted his. "Emery," he shouted over the pounding water, "keep Lady Isabella safe until we reach you."

Isabella's eyes widened. "Aren't you crossing here?"

"I am vowed to protect Lady Odette." He tossed the whip to her.

Anger and hurt glistened in her expressive eyes. "And to help me do as I promised."

"I shall do that, for we will continue to Lincoln as soon as we have caught up with you. It should be by midafternoon."

He did not give her a chance to answer. Slapping his hand on his horse's flank, he led the other two horses with him after the Weirtons. He knew the trip was going to take far longer and be much more complicated than he had ever envisioned.

Chapter 14

The forest remained cool and damp in the spring twilight. After traveling through open fields, Jordan hoped they could traverse the forest's length without incident. There were rumors of outlaws among the trees and glades. He was confident that he and Weirton—and Isabella—would protect Lady Odette. Even Emery was competent with a sword, as long as he did not get too excited and swing it wildly, presenting more danger to himself than any foe.

Still, Jordan was pleased when the lamps hanging on an inn appeared out of the thickening gloom. He had suggested halting more than an hour ago, but Weirton had insisted they continue to this inn. The baron seemed indifferent to his sister's fatigue, and Jordan did not want to embarrass Lady Odette by insisting they halt.

The yard in front of the inn was bare. Many had stopped here before them. That surprised Jordan, because the inn was not on the main road to Lincoln. They had turned off that road when Weirton announced they should stay at the thatched inn. The name on the inn had almost been wiped away by years of wind and rain and sunshine.

He dismounted and stretched. He watched Isabella steer her horse around him. She had said little after he had reached where she and Emery waited with unexpected patience by the stream. Weirton had worn an arrogant smile, but that had disappeared when she refused to be baited by his pointed comments.

He held up his hands to help her alight.

She shook her head, and her hair glistened like true gold in the last of the day's light. "See to Lady Odette. She is too tired to get down on her own."

"You want me to help her instead of you?"

Her fingers tightened on the reins, but her voice was serene as she said, "Your honor demands it, Jordan."

He tried to think of something to say, but anything that came into his mind would have sounded petty. She was doing as she had promised: treating him like a valued ally. *He* was the one vacillating, wanting to toss that agreement aside.

Going to where Lady Odette was tapping her fingers on her saddle, he tried to imagine Isabella waiting for someone to help her. He pushed that thought aside when Lady Odette's smile returned, bright and inviting.

"How kind of you, milord," she cooed as he lifted her from the saddle and set her on her feet. "Bouchard was correct when he described you as a chivalric gentleman." Her smile suggested that she was the match for such a man.

He did not want to disillusion her, so he offered his arm and led her toward the front door where the innkeeper—a portly man whose red nose suggested he enjoyed sampling his own ales—was greeting Isabella. The innkeeper's smile was as broad as his belly while he ogled her. She seemed indifferent to his admiration.

Lady Odette was not. "Look at that cur! If he leers at me like that, I swear I shall have his eyes cut out."

Jordan smothered his laugh as he wondered what the lady would do if the innkeeper paid her no attention. That would offend her even more.

He did not discover how Lady Odette would react to his amusement, because when the innkeeper looked past Isabella, the man hastily threw the door open widely and stepped aside to let them enter.

Jordan's head brushed the lowest of the rafters in the uneven ceiling. The odors of charred food and stale drink filled the narrow space. He noticed several half-filled tankards on a table in the center of the room.

"Do you have other guests?" he asked as the innkeeper followed them inside.

"Not overnight guests, milord."

He was taken aback by how the man addressed him, then realized Isabella must have told the innkeeper their names. "Where are the drinkers who left their ale unfinished?"

The innkeeper glanced from him to Weirton, then focused on his feet. " 'Tis not for me to say, milord. Those who mind their own business and no one else's live longest in the forest."

"That is always a good way to live one's life," the baron replied. "We need rooms for the night."

"I have three only."

"Odette, you and Lady Isabella—"

"Will stay together." Lady Odette's expression suggested that arguing would be risky. "She can protect me from whatever might come creeping into our room."

The innkeeper began to protest that he did not allow vermin into his inn, but the lady ignored him and fixed her gaze on her brother as she tapped her toe with impatience.

"That sounds like an excellent plan," Isabella said with a smile. "If you will show us to our room, Walter . . ."

Jordan watched as the innkeeper hurried up the stairs. Isabella could take care of Lady Odette, but the sudden emptying of the inn at their arrival disturbed him. Weirton's acceptance of the lack of an answer had kept Jordan from asking more questions.

Two doors faced each other across a hallway so narrow he was surprised the innkeeper could pass through it. A third door was set farther along the passage. When the innkeeper opened one door, he edged aside to let them enter.

It was not as bad as Jordan had expected. The fresh smell of a recently restuffed mattress on the bed platform was complemented by broom marks on the hearth. The room with its one small window and heavy rafters had been recently cleaned.

"No." Weirton gave the chamber a quick glance. "This will not do for you, Odette. I hope the other rooms will be more comfortable than this one." His nose wrinkled as he looked at the bed platform and then at the innkeeper. "And my sister has no interest in sleeping in filth."

"I will sleep here," Jordan said, annoyed with Weirton.

"No need for you to suffer here." Weirton motioned toward the door. "You can have the back room if you wish."

"Nonsense. This will do for me." He unhooked his cloak and tossed it atop the mattress.

"As you wish." The baron gestured for his sister to come with him.

Isabella remained by the hearth as the others went out of the room. She ran her fingers along the stones and asked, "May I remain a moment longer?"

"Tired ears?"

She smiled as the sound of the lady's voice, outlining the changes the innkeeper must make in order for the room across the hall to meet her most basic standards, came into the room.

"Lady Odette knows exactly what she wants," he said.

"And from whom she wants it." She sat on the edge of the hearth and regarded him with a broadening smile. "You need to be cautious, Jordan."

"I know." He rested his elbow on the mantel over her head. "I appreciate the warning."

"You are my ally, and I don't want to see you waylaid by a lovely woman's wiles before we complete our task."

"Can't you show a bit of jealousy?"

"I cannot imagine being like her any more than she can imagine being like me." Isabella laughed and looked up at Jordan when he did not join in.

He was watching her with undisguised hunger. He glanced quickly away, but she knew he was having as much trouble as she was at forgetting what they had shared.

She ran her fingers along the stones of the hearth. She must guard every minute against reaching out to him. Even a chance touch could tear down the wall between them.

Seeking another topic, she said, "Walter the innkeeper is frightened."

"As he well should be." His breath sifted past his clenched teeth. "The peace is fragile, and, if civil war breaks out again, it will be people like our host who are caught up in the fighting."

"Maybe the Brotherhood will prevent that."

"Don't make decisions based on what Emery told you. He is a boy who gossips with other boys and kitchen maids. If the Brotherhood is truly concerned about England's future, why do they hide? The Templars and the Hospitallers do their work openly." His smile returned. "I would prefer to depend on you completing your task, Isabella. Queen Eleanor comprehends the dangers of more battles between father and sons. She was wise to found St. Jude's Abbey."

"Shh!" She put her finger to her lips. "Take care what you say."

"I will watch what I say, but you risk giving away the truth each time you do something amazing like crossing the stream or flipping Weirton off his feet."

Isabella stood. "You said you wished to learn the way I knocked Lord Weirton from his feet."

"Yes."

She was glad he let her change the subject again. "This is as good a time as any."

"In the rain?"

"It is raining?"

He took her arm and steered her toward the small window. Reaching past her, he threw the shutters open. Water splattered her gown.

"I am sorry," he said.

She smiled. "Nonsense. It will help wash away the filth from the road, so I do not look like a wretched hag when we reach Lincoln."

"I doubt that would be possible, Isabella."

Realizing that his hand was still on her arm as his breath caressed her ear, she inched away. She pretended not to have heard his compliment. "If you do not mind getting muddy, I will be glad to show you what I did to knock Lord Weirton off his feet."

"And how you aimed that kick at Gamell, too. You disabled him with a single motion." He glanced out the window. "It seems as if the storm is already ending."

"Spring showers come and go rapidly." Trivial comments prevented her from speaking her true thoughts.

Jordan must have felt the same because he kept up the silly chatter as they went down the stairs and, after collecting one of the tankards from the table, outside. The night air was chillier than when they had gone in.

"Here?" He opened a gate to a small grassy area.

"It will do." She emptied the tankard before setting it on top of the rail fence. Looping the strap of her sack over the gate, she faced Jordan.

"What do *I* need to do?"

Isabella smiled as he asked the question she had when she studied with Nariko, who supervised all the lessons, whether she was the main instructor or not. Tall and slender, Nariko always wore her shimmering black hair in a single braid. Her robes were an unblemished white, even when she had been practicing for hours.

During Isabella's most recent lesson with Nariko, she had spent more time chatting than practicing. Nariko had known she was avoiding using a bow.

"You may need to shoot some mistletoe out of a high tree," Nariko had said with mock seriousness. "Think how useful it will be then."

Isabella chuckled. "Nariko, you always try to see the positive side of every problem."

"And you the negative."

"I hope not!"

Nariko's smile crinkled her eyes that were the same shape as the tapered point of an arrow. "Don't you realize the rest of the Abbey's sisters are in awe of you?"

"It is *you* the sisters revere."

"Maybe so, but they admire what you have learned and what you help them learn. What I teach may help them in a fight, but what you teach is a way to survive—and heal if they are hurt—when they are far from the Abbey."

"When? It has been at least a dozen years since Avisa, Elspeth, and Mallory were called away."

"They served the queen as we all must. We should be honored by the sacrifices we must make, even leaving our beloved home." She looked to the east and sighed.

Isabella remembered her shock when she wondered if Nariko might be lonely. Nariko's esteemed father, her only connection with her homeland at the edge of the world, had died years before. Zuki, her daughter, was as much a part of England as Nariko's husband.

Isabella had not asked. Some things were not spoken of among the sisters, especially what their lives had been before they came to St. Jude's Abbey.

"Isabella?"

Jordan's voice shattered her thoughts. She blinked and focused her eyes on him. Now her life was not within the Abbey. Now she served the queen. Until she completed her task, she would not be able to return to the cocoon of her home in the Abbey.

If she returned . . .

"Bend your knees," she ordered, hoping she could lose herself in the lesson and forget the uncomfortable thought.

"Like this?"

She shook her head as she went to stand beside him. "You need to keep your knees deeply bent, so you can go either up or down."

"Like this?" he asked again.

"Deeper." Bending, she put a hand behind each knee. "Lower yourself until you are touching my hands."

He did as she asked.

"Remember that feeling," she said as she stepped back. "Now I want you to try this."

She dropped into the position she had asked him to take. Thrusting herself upward, she raised her left leg and swung it. The side of her foot struck the tankard, sending it to clatter beyond the fence. She landed as lightly as she could, but agony shot across her left foot. She ignored it. Part of learning to defend herself had been lessons in not letting pain distract her.

"You expect me to do that?" He shook his head with a rueful smile. "It would take me a thousand attempts before I could knock it off."

"I think it took me that many to learn." Clasping her hands behind her, she said, "But that is the motion I used when I struck the bailiff in the knee. I did not aim my foot as high."

"No wonder you left Gamell hobbling."

"Using such tactics in addition to other weapons can give an advantage to any warrior."

"Even a lady warrior?"

"Especially a lady warrior." She savored the camaraderie between them. She wished this could be enough, but she would not lie to herself. She longed for him to teach her the wonders shared by a man and a woman.

He glanced down at her foot. "You should be careful."

"I always am."

"Yes, you are, but you need to be extra careful." He pulled off his tunic to reveal he wore mail over a padded shirt. He went down to one knee to lift the mail over his head and let it fall to the ground with a rustle of the links. Standing, he drew his tunic back over his padded shirt. "We still have several days of riding to reach Lincoln. You need to be healthy when we get there."

"I will be. It is my first duty—and yours—to serve the king and queen."

He hefted the heavy mail and draped it over the fence, which creaked with the weight he had worn without any sign of strain. "You do not need to tell me what I know well. I have never failed to fulfill my obligations to the king. If I am called again, I will not shirk in my duties."

"But you have said you hope the call will never go out again for war."

"Don't you?"

"Yes."

He wiggled his fingers and faced her. "Now teach me how you flipped Weirton so he looked like a beetle on its back."

Isabella warned Jordan to be cautious about his stitches, but she otherwise gave him no quarter as she showed him the steps to pitch someone onto the ground. He tried to copy her moves and asked dozens of questions. Again and again, he tried to toss her to ground. Each time, she halted him and left him on his back. He rolled to his feet and showed he was ready to try again until she had downed him for at least the tenth time.

That time, he stayed on the ground.

Isabella knelt and stroked his hair that was damp with their exertions. "I think you have done enough for your first lesson."

"I did not knock you off your feet once." He turned onto his back. "Do you realize how ignoble it is for a war-tested warrior to fail against a woman?"

"As ignoble as it would be for me to be defeated by you."

He chuckled. "Fair enough. I can see now why you were chosen for your task."

She gazed at the first stars breaking through the twilight. "It seemed so straightforward when the abbess asked me to retrieve what the queen sought."

"My aunt made the request of you rather than the queen?" He sat and faced her.

"The king keeps the queen under close scrutiny. She uses intermediaries to make her wishes known."

"So you have never met the queen?"

"No."

"You have a treat ahead of you, Isabella."

"You have met the queen?"

He nodded. "I was a child, but I remember how anxious my parents were about every detail when the queen spent a night at La Tour. I saw her from a distance. She was the most incredible woman I had ever seen." He winked. "Until I met you."

"Jordan, save your compliments for Lady Odette. There

is no other woman in the world more formidable and dazzling than the queen." She put her hand over her stomach as
it growled. "It is past time for our evening meal." Standing,
she held her hand out to him. When he took it, he winced.
"Sore?"

"You sent me to the ground one time too many, I fear."

"Do you think you will have trouble sleeping?"

He stretched his arm and grimaced as he stood. "It feels
as if each of your stitches has come loose."

"Let me check."

He blocked her fingers from reaching for his tunic. "No,
Isabella, that would not be wise."

She started to retort that she knew how to look for damage without hurting him further. She closed her mouth. He
was warning her about the danger of touching him. Even a
virtuous, well-meaning brush of her fingertips against his
skin could ignite an inferno.

She reached into her sack and pulled out a packet with a
blue cross embroidered onto it. "Use only a small amount of
the powder in a glass of wine." She set the packet on his
palm. "Do not use more than what you can pinch between
your fingers, for it can create strange images. It will ease
aches and allow you to sleep."

"There is another way I could ease my aches." He put his
hands on either side of her face and brought her to him. "I
would rather have you prescribe me a bit of you."

"You know that is impossible," she whispered, even as
her body was begging her to surrender to the rapture promised by his eyes.

"Not exactly impossible. All you need to do is say yes."

"And then what?"

He brushed his lips against hers. "You know the answer
to that, Isabella."

She did. Drawing out of his arms, she pulled the straps of
the sack over her shoulder and went through the gate. Every
part of her—save the most logical part of her mind—
yearned for her to go to him. She was running by the time
she reached the inn door. Hurrying up the stairs, she went

into the room she would share with Lady Odette and closed
the door.

She leaned against the door and sank to the floor. How
many more times could she resist his eager kisses? She
knew the answer. As many as she must.

Sleeping was impossible. Isabella was hungry because she
had not gone down for the evening meal, but it was not her
grumbling stomach that kept her awake. Her mind kept drift-
ing to how Jordan's eyes had been ablaze with craving.
When he had held her outside the keep at La Tour, there had
been no thought of what was right and what was wrong.
There had been only the need. The need for his kisses, the
need for his touch, the need for whatever they could share, a
need whetted by the awareness that her most incredible fantasies would be eclipsed by the true rapture of his embrace.

"Stop it," she ordered under her breath.

Jamming the thin pillow under her head, she tried to get
comfortable on the floor. Lady Odette had claimed the bed,
setting her squirrel's cage on one side and curling up on the
other. Rather than argue, Isabella had considered herself
lucky to get a blanket to use on the floor.

But sleep was impossible. At the Abbey, when she could
not sleep, she had gone to her barn and worked on some experiment. She had known then that she would not be disturbed.

She stood and glanced toward the bed where Lady Odette
was snoring softly. She dressed quickly, trying not to groan
when she put her sore foot into her torn boot. Groping for
her sack, she found it in the feeble moonlight and slipped
out.

Isabella glanced at the door across the hallway, but hurried down the stairs and out of the inn. Lingering might
mean Jordan opening the door. Could she tell him no again?

The night was cool and damp as she lifted down one of
the lanterns beside the door. She could not guess how the
elements might react under these conditions. She had taken
care to keep her barn clean and dry. Some elements erupted

when water was added. No efforts had allowed her to control those detonations. She wanted to find the combination that let her decide when the explosion took place and how powerful it would be.

Odors from the byre drew her in that direction. It was less likely that someone would wander by.

Her knees were wet as soon as she knelt. She set her bag on a unused stone trough. There was barely enough light for her to find the packets she needed.

She dug a small crater. With care, she stirred together equal amounts of sulfur and charcoal. She stiffened, hoping the mixture would not explode before she could determine if she had the right formula. Picking up a twig, she opened the lantern and lit one end of it.

She leaned away as she held the twig out to the elements. It sparked. Only for a moment, and with a sharp *snap* that startled her. She put her hands up toward her face to halt herself from crying out in triumph, but paused. As if she had been stung by a bee, her fingers burned.

Lifting the lantern, she looked down at where a puff of smoke was rising. Small white crystals glistened in the light. She looked from it to her fingers. The burn and the glitter could mean only one thing. There must be saltpeter in the ground, maybe left by chickens.

Could saltpeter be the ingredient she had been missing? Who would have guessed that such a lowly product created in dung heaps and latrines would provide the answer to the puzzle?

Her joy tempered. She had no idea how much saltpeter had been in the ground. The explosion had been too small to be effective as anything other than a curiosity. She still had a lot of work ahead of her, but she had made an amazing leap forward.

She would try again on the morrow when the sun was out. Jordan would want to make an early start, but she suspected Lady Odette would insist on lingering over breakfast. That would give Isabella a chance to try for more and bigger detonations.

Jumping to her feet, she spun about. She had done it! She would learn more and be able to show, upon her return to the Abbey, her sisters and the abbess all she had discovered.

But she needed to share this excitement with someone *now*!

Jordan!

He was the only one who would appreciate how exciting that one small spark was for her. Gathering up the sack and the lantern, she rushed to the inn. She set the lantern on its hook before going up the stairs.

Her excitement dimmed when she faced Jordan's closed door. Should she knock? She raised her hand, then lowered it. What was she thinking? She would be a fool to go into his room when she wanted to celebrate, because she could not imagine a better way to celebrate than in his arms.

She reached for the latch on the door to the room she shared with Lady Odette. She paused again. Lady Odette would be horrified that Isabella had been working near an old dung heap.

Jordan had expressed interest in what she had learned at his aunt's abbey. She had taken a chance on trying the experiment. She needed to take a chance that she could curb her longings so she could share the wondrous news before she burst with joy.

With a smile, she knocked on his door. Some things were worth the risk.

Or so she hoped.

Chapter 15

The leather hinges on the door squeaked, and Jordan heard the cat jump off the bed. Light footsteps sped it out of the room. Disgusting! He was traveling with two exquisitely beautiful women, and the only one sharing his bed was a cat.

As if his thoughts had gained life, he heard, "Jordan, may I come in?"

Isabella!

"Come in," he answered, his voice rough from sleep. He lifted his head from the pillow . . . or he tried to. It felt as if his mail shirt rested on his skull. His eyes did not focus. Could the herbs Isbella gave him still be making him dizzy as they had after he swallowed them?

In the light from the hearth, he saw Isabella's captivating silhouette. She tiptoed toward the bed, as soundlessly as the cat. Then she gasped and pointed at the far side of the bed.

"What is it?" He tried again to raise his head. Again something pinned him to the bed. He turned slightly and stared in disbelief at the redhead lying beside him. Lady Odette's arm was curved over his waist, and her head tucked against his shoulder. She nestled closer, her voluptuous body reforming along him.

Isabella walked toward the door, indignation in each sway of her hips. He had to halt her before she assumed . . . What did she need to assume? The truth was right before her eyes and his.

Shoving Lady Odette off him as gently as possible, he swung his legs out of bed. The floor seemed to rock beneath him, and he wondered if he would be able to walk. He needed to hurry. With every step Isabella walked away, the chances of him halting her grew less.

Somehow he reached the door before she did. He put out his arm to keep her from leaving.

"You can rot in hell!" she snarled.

"Isabella, you must listen to me."

"What is there to listen to? She is in your bed!"

"A surprise to me." He yawned.

"What?"

"She must have slipped in after I went to sleep."

"You expect me to believe that story?"

He shrugged and yawned again. "Whether you choose to believe it or not, I vow it is the truth. My side was hurting after your lesson, so I used some of those sleeping herbs you gave me."

"Some?" Her anger eased. "I told you to be careful and use only a small amount."

"I put only what I could pinch between my fingers in wine. That is what you said, right?"

"Yes."

"I drank a few sips. After that, I hardly remember lying down, but I would have remembered if someone else had already been in the bed."

"Would you?"

He chuckled. "Maybe. Maybe not. I know I would have remembered if *you* had been there."

"Enough, Jordan." She walked around the bed to where Lady Odette was lying on her back with her hand stretched out across where he had been sleeping. In a low whisper, she asked, "Why are you standing there? Help me."

"What are you doing?"

She lifted Lady Odette's limp arm over her shoulder and brought the lady up to a sitting position. "Help me unless you want her brother insisting you marry her after bedding her."

"I said I did not—"

"I may believe you, but will Lord Weirton?"

Jordan stumbled on his answer, astounded that she had accepted his word once he pledged that he spoke the truth. She had known him such a short time; yet she showed so much faith in him. Only one other person had ever shown him such trust: Ryce de Dolan. Only one other person had he trusted as much as he had Ryce: Isabella de Montfort. Not because she was from St. Jude's Abbey, but because whenever she made a promise, nothing—not even common sense—would deter her from doing as she had promised.

And he had to do the same.

Going to the bed, he motioned for Isabella to step aside. Lady Odette collapsed like a wilting flower into the bed. He lifted her and cradled her against his chest. She seemed as fragile as that dying leaf. He looked down at her perfect features and wondered why he felt no desire for her. She was the kind of woman he had favored—eager and willing—unlike Isabella, who never did quite as he expected. If Weirton's sister had discovered Isabella in his bed, there would have been screeching and fury. Much as there would have been if Weirton had chanced upon his sister in Jordan's bed and insisted on marriage to preserve her reputation. Had that been the lady's plan? Had she purposely slipped into his bed in hopes of forcing him to make her his wife?

As if he had asked the question aloud, Isabella said, "You must not delay returning her to her own bed. If Lord Weirton peeks in here . . ." She did not need to finish saying what they both knew. "Do you need help?"

"I am steady enough to carry her."

"It is good that she is tiny."

He started to nod, then halted when his head felt too light. He must keep his head—and his wits—about him. The floor seemed to rise and fall like a ship on a maddened sea, but he put one foot in front of the other and edged toward the door.

Isabella slipped past him, and the scent from her hair weakened his knees further. She smelled of freshness and the night and a magic she denied possessing. He had never known that her enchantment could have an aroma, but it did—mystical and beguiling.

Then she was gone. She had opened the door and slipped

out into the hallway as noiselessly as she entered. He walked as swiftly as he could to the door. He stepped through the doorway just in time to see her lift the latch on the door across the hallway. She swung it open just long enough to let him into the room.

It was dark. When Isabella whispered close to his ear to wait where he was while she lit a candle, a heated tremble rushed from his head down his spine. Every muscle grew taut as he longed to throw Lady Odette onto the bed and bring Isabella back to his own, where he would let her spin her spell around him while he taught her the special magic of their bodies merging into one.

He swallowed his groan as he heard her furtive motions. His fantasies were a torment, and he had guaranteed that they would remain unsated when he agreed to be her ally and nothing more.

"Close your eyes," he heard her say.

He did and opened them slowly when the glow from a rushlight burned through his lids. With care, he went to the bed that was narrower than where he had been sleeping. He placed Lady Odette in the middle of it.

The lady murmured something that sounded suspiciously like his name, clutched the pillow, and buried her face in it. She was glorious with her red curls draped over her, barely concealing the curves that had been pressed into his chest. Her lips were parted with the gentle breaths of sleep that moved her firm breasts. She would make some man a demanding and delightful wife, but not Jordan le Courtenay.

"One problem solved," he said as he turned from the bed.

Isabella was no longer in the room. Where had she gone, and how had she slipped away without him noticing? His mind must be working even more slowly than he had guessed. He had to find her. He had to know why she had come into his room in the first place.

He walked out of the room, closing the door behind him. His door was ajar. Hope lightened his feet as he pushed it open farther. He was not surprised to see Isabella sitting cross-legged by the hearth. She looked up as he shut the door.

"Come and sit with me," she said, patting the stones.

He wanted to tell her that they would be much more comfortable on the bed, but knew she had selected the warm stones by the hearth to keep herself away from his bed.

As soon as he was sitting beside her, she asked, "Did Lady Odette awake?"

"No. Did she take some of your sleeping potion, too?"

"I did not give her any, but she may have sampled your wine to fortify herself for when she seduced you."

He smiled. "So you think she needed to *fortify* herself?"

"You are a very daunting man." She ran a single fingertip along his cheek. "And she wants to be your wife. I am sure she feared losing her opportunity to force you to marry her."

He took her finger and brought it to his lips. Hearing her sharp intake of breath, he released her hand. Was he witless? Neither of them needed to *fortify* themselves to seduce each other.

"I owe you my gratitude," he said, even as other words burned on his tongue, words asking her to be his.

"You would have done the same for me."

"You are an amazing woman, Isabella de Montfort."

"You are my ally in serving the queen." Her mouth tipped in a tired smile. "And you are the nephew of the abbess of St. Jude's Abbey."

"Such a relationship is no guarantee of being trustworthy."

"Are you trying to persuade me to call you a liar?"

He chuckled. "I am trying to express how much I appreciate your confidence in me."

"Why wouldn't I have confidence in you?"

Draping his arm over her shoulder, he said, "The fact you ask is an example of what makes you astounding." He yawned.

"You need to go to bed. That potion is a strong one."

"I will once I know why you came in here."

"I noticed something odd when I was in here earlier."

"Odd?"

"Here." She pointed to a stone on the edge of the hearth. "It is not as warm as the others."

"Stones heat at different temperatures."

"I know that, but this stone is identical to the others around it. Even so, it is not as warm as the ones next to it. That suggests there is something unusual about it."

He squatted beside her. "How can it be the same and different at the same time?"

"I don't know." She grasped his hand and pressed it against a stone. "Feel how warm this is?"

"Yes, it is warm." His voice became a husky whisper. "And so am I."

"The fire—"

"Is not as warm as your fingers." He lifted her hand from the stone and draped her fingers over his. "Your fingers are not soft like Lady Odette's, but their touch can heat a man's fantasies and more."

"Don't, Jordan." She drew her hand away. "Don't say things like that when you know where it could lead."

"I know exactly where it could lead."

She raised her eyes to meet his. "To lust."

"Yes."

"But that is not enough for me."

He stood. With a curse, he slammed one fist on the hearthstones. "I thought you were not like the rest of them, Isabella."

"Not like who?"

"The women who always want something in return for the pleasure they offer."

She came to her feet. "Any pleasure I offered you was given freely and with no obligations. I am not Lady Odette. I am Isabella de Montfort of St. Jude's Abbey."

His fury refocused on himself. She was being honest, as she had been from the moment they had met. She had even revealed the truth about having been a sister cloistered at St. Jude's Abbey when he asked. And he should be as honest himself. Why was he not claiming her soft lips as he loosened her honey gold hair to drift along him? Because he had made her a promise, and he would keep it. No matter how difficult it was.

"You are right, Isabella."

"I am?" Her bluish-gray eyes widened again.

"Don't act surprised. You have proven yourself to be right more often than you are wrong." He knelt beside her. "Show me what you discovered."

"Are you sure?"

"I am, Isabella." He could not keep his voice from caressing her name as he wished he was stroking her soft skin.

"Then let us start over. Do you feel how warm it is?" She put her fingers on the stone, then shifted them aside when he touched it.

"Yes."

"Now this one." She pointed to the next stone. "Can you feel the difference?"

"Yes." He was amazed how much cooler the second stone was. Running his fingers along the other nearby stones, he found that all but the one she had pointed to were the same temperature. "Do you know why?"

"There is only one logical answer. There must be something blocking the heat."

"That is logical."

She gave him a smile that threatened to harden him to stone, for it was saucy and seductive. She drew a large packet out of her sack that he had not noticed was lying on the hearth. She opened the pouch to reveal a collection of tools. Smiling, she withdrew a metal rod about the length of her longest finger. She handed it to him.

He drove the chisel between the stones as he wished he could plunge himself into her. Pieces of mortar scattered everywhere, falling in a fine dust around them, but she paid it no mind.

With a laugh, she said, "Don't destroy the whole hearth."

"I will do my best." He clenched his jaw as he pushed hard against the bar, wishing she would keep talking. That kept his thoughts from where they should not be going.

Accursed truce!

The stone popped out and slammed on the bed, making a deep gouge in the wood. The innkeeper would not be pleased. Jordan hoped an extra coin or two would ease the innkeeper's ire.

If there only was a way to ease his craving for Isabella . . .

She stretched out on her stomach and peered into the space where the stone had been. Strands of her unruly hair flowed across his boot, teasing him to finger it.

"Do you see anything?" he asked.

"Maybe." She reached into the space and withdrew a pouch much like the ones she wore. Sitting, she undid the strings at the top and tilted it over her hand. A single small item fell out.

"What is it?" he asked.

"It looks like a pilgrim's token. It is . . . Oh, sweet heavens, it has *Semper minax, nunquam summissus* stamped on it."

"The Brotherhood! What is it doing in there?"

"It may be no more than an accident. It was set on the hearth and slipped between the stones. On the other hand, it may mean something to the Brotherhood's members. They may have left it here as a greeting or a warning to their fellows. Without knowing more about the Brotherhood, we cannot know for certain."

He took the token and turned it over. As he had expected, the reverse showed the now-familiar symbol of the two men—one mounted and one leading the horse.

"First the knife in Ryce's grave, then the sword, and now this token hidden beneath stones. There must be some connection." He rubbed his forehead. "Why can't I see it?"

Isabella smiled. "The sleeping potion is very potent. It can keep you from thinking clearly."

"But I need to think clearly."

"You need to sleep."

He ran his fingers slowly up her back. "It seems such a waste of time."

"I have never found sleep a waste of time, for it refreshes the mind and the body." She laughed, and he wondered if any sound had ever been as glorious. Was she talking, or was she singing? Either way, every movement of her lips sent music swirling through him.

"There are other ways to refresh the mind and body," he said.

"If you are suggesting . . ." An appealing flush rose up her face.

"Say the word, and we can renegotiate our truce to include all you wish."

"And what you wish?" She ran her fingers along his cheek and across his lips.

"It is the same thing we both want." He brought her to her feet and led her around the end of the bed. "We want each other."

Reaching behind her, he lifted her braids to fall down in front of her. He undid them by combing his fingers gently down them. When his fingertips grazed her breasts, she quivered and whispered his name.

He could no longer wait for her to agree. With a groan, he drew her down into the bed and beneath him. He framed her face with his hands and murmured, "Say the word."

"Jordan, we should not—"

"Yes, we should." He ran his tongue along her neck and smiled when she trembled. "Say the word."

He pressed her more deeply into the bed as he ran his fingers up her sides. Shimmering, piercing sensations rippled through him as she clung to him, and he was overpowered by her reaction to his touch. Her fingers tightened on his back as his fingertip roamed a sinuous path along her breast. When he bent to sample the gentle curve visible at the top of her dress, she moaned with the consuming need.

"Yes. Yes, Jordan."

He had never heard more beautiful words. He captured her lips, not giving her the chance to retract them. As he pinned her soft body to the bed, her fingers inched up his back, holding herself to him. He knew then that she ached to be a part of him as he was part of her. She gasped against his mouth. The longing threatened to overwhelm him, when her tongue delved past his lips to inflame him with its fiery touch. When he tasted the flavors of her mouth, he knew no other woman had been so worth the chase and that she would excite him as no other woman had. He wanted to share ecstasy with her.

He loosened the ribbons along her gown, peeling back the bodice to reveal her linen shift. When his finger brushed the tip of her breast, it strained against the fabric. He freed it so he slid his finger up its sumptuous slope. She writhed beneath him, and he watched her face as the craving became the desperate desire he had suffered from the moment he saw her dazzling eyes.

"Tell me this is what you want, sweet one," he murmured as he rolled onto his back to let her breasts spill out of her gown as her hair fell in a golden storm around them.

"*You* are what I want." Her breathless voice was nearly muted by the pounding of his heart as her hand moved down his chest.

A tempest raged through him with every heated breath as she guided his mouth to hers. She did not halt her eager exploration when she reached his waist, but continued lower until he grasped her wrist to halt her.

If she touched him now, he would explode. He wanted to savor her more before he surrendered to ultimate rapture. It took him only moments to draw her gown and shift down and toss them to the floor. He thumbed her quivering breasts before running his tongue through the warm valley between them.

She trembled and whispered, "Now. Please."

"Not yet." He sat and rid himself of his clothes. Slowly, he drew her back over him, relishing each inch of her on him.

She gave a soft mewing sound in the moment before her mouth moved along his neck. Her lips left heated tingles on his skin. Her legs moved against his as she trailed kisses along his chest and down across his abdomen. Her fingers, bolder than he had ever imagined, reached down to cup him between the legs. Now he was the one squirming with uncontrollable need.

"I want this to be within me," she whispered as she lightly ran one finger up and down him. "Now. Please."

He gazed up into her eyes that were twin storms of passion. Her touch, each gentle stroke, matched his pulse. He could wait no longer.

With a groan, he pulled her beneath him and rose above her. Even in the madness of his hunger for satiation with her, he remembered to be careful as he moved into her. A soft cry burst from her, but he silenced it when his mouth claimed hers anew. It took every bit of his willpower to restrain himself as he waited for her to become accustomed to him within her.

Slowly he taught her the rhythm of lovers. Her hands curved up his back before gliding down to press him farther into her. Her eagerness shredded the last of his control. Her gasps as she was consumed by ecstasy were the last thing he heard before he gave himself completely to the joy. It was everything he had fantasized and more.

Isabella brushed her hair into a braid and twisted it around her head. She pinned it in place and picked up her sack. Behind her, she heard Lady Odette complaining about the incompetence of her maid.

It was easy to ignore the lady as she savored her happiness. What an incredible night it had been! And she had not had a chance to share the tidings of her discovery with Jordan yet. Would he be excited, too? She knew Nariko would be that Isabella had managed, even if by accident, to make the material that could be exploded in a controlled manner. The martial arts instructor had urged her again and again not to give up. Now, after so many false steps, Isabella had shown she was worthy of being counted among the sisters in St. Jude's Abbey.

"Are you already ready?" asked Lady Odette when Isabella settled the sack on her shoulder and went to the door.

"We planned to make an early start today."

"I have not yet had anything to eat." She patted her pet on the head. "And Peppy cannot travel without having his meal."

The squirrel made a chittering reply that Lady Odette took for an agreement.

"I will see you downstairs then." Isabella was glad for

any excuse to leave the room. She had not wanted to return last night, but if Lady Odette had awakened to find Isabella gone, there would have been endless questions to answer. She did not feel like answering them. She just wanted to be happy.

A light rain was falling when Isabella came out into the yard after stopping long enough to get a piece of bread lathered with honey from the innkeeper. Not even a torrent could have diminished her joy. Seeing Jordan checking his horse's saddle, she rushed to him.

"Good morning," she called.

He turned and leaned one arm on his saddle. "It is a very good morning now that you are here, Isabella." His smile was so beguiling that she was tempted to toss aside what she wanted to tell him and slip into his arms.

"You look as if you are feeling better."

"Much better."

"So am I."

His smile broadened. "I am very pleased to hear that."

"I wanted to tell you this last night—"

"But you got diverted."

She regarded him with bafflement, then, instead of asking questions, said, "I wanted to tell you that I did it, Jordan! I was able to complete the experiment that I have been working on for years."

"Experiment? What experiment?"

She quickly explained, although she omitted Nariko's name and how she had come to have such knowledge. She did not want to chance someone overhearing, so it was better that she suggested the information had been brought back from Outremer by some returning knight.

"Like Greek fire?"

She regarded him, puzzled. "Greek fire? What is that?"

"I thought you considered yourself a student of the elements and how they work together."

"I am." She laughed. "That is why when I don't know something, I ask."

"As you have been asking Lady Odette for information on how a lady acts?"

Waving aside his question, she asked, "What is Greek fire?"

He knelt and picked up a stick. The odor of sulfur rose from it, but he paid it no attention as he drew the simple figure of a man in the loose dirt. "I saw a picture of this once." He added a cylinder about the length of the man's arm. "The ancient people used a tube that held liquid and spouted fire. It was so powerful it could engulf a ship within seconds."

When she squatted beside him, she balanced her chin on her palm. "I wonder how they created it."

"The knowledge is lost. Is that what you are trying to make?"

"No. What I am trying to make is a mixture that when blended properly will explode when lit."

"And you studied this at my aunt's abbey?" he asked.

"Yes."

"As well as healing herbs."

"Yes."

"And the way you fight with such amazing moves." He brushed her cheek with a crooked finger. "You are a sensational woman, Isabella."

She took his hand and folded it between her own. "Jordan, what is truly wondrous is how the explosion was one I could control. I have worked for so many years to achieve this."

Lifting her hands to his lips, he kissed one, then the other. "I am very proud of you, Isabella. It is not often one gets to have a dream come true. Now both of us did last night."

"Both of us?" She wanted to ask what he meant but saw Walter, the innkeeper, coming out of the inn. She released Jordan's hand. "I think we have said enough for now. It would be better not to speak of what happened."

"You may be correct." He gave her a roguish grin. "But I cannot stop thinking about it."

"About what?"

"About last night."

"What are you talking about?" It was not like him to speak in riddles.

His smile straightened into a frown, leaving a deep crease in his forehead. "Isabella, why are you being coy? You said you were as eager as I was. Are you going to deny that now?"

"I cannot deny anything when I have no idea what you are talking about."

"How you shared my bed last night after we found— what we found in the hearth."

"Shared your bed? You think I—You believe we . . ." She began to laugh.

"Isabella." His voice was a rough growl. "This is not funny. After we discussed what we found, you joined me in my bed. When I woke, you were gone. Why are you acting as if I am lying?"

She put her hands up to his cheeks so his eyes could not avoid hers. "Jordan, I am not accusing you of lying. I am sure you believe what happened was real. What you need to remember is the herbs I gave you to help you sleep can make you see things that are not real."

"So it was only a dream?"

"Maybe not exactly a dream, but something similar. I warned you that some of the herbs create strange visions that can seem very real."

"You did not find me in your bed last night?"

"My bed? Lady Odette was sharing my bed. No one else." She frowned. "And you were sleeping very soundly in your bed when I checked on you in the middle of the night."

"What about the pilgrim's token? Are you telling me that we did not find it?"

"Yes, I am telling you that everything you believe happened after you took the herbs was a dream caused by the herbs."

Shock widened his eyes, even as his mouth grew taut.

His gaze roved over her, and she wondered what he sought. As if she had asked the question aloud, he said, "I should have known it could not be real when you were so open with your passions, not hiding behind duty and obligation. You were eager and brazen, touching me as a man wants to be touched. When you leaned over me, and your naked breasts pressed to me and begged me to make love to you, I should have known it was nothing but a delusion."

He walked away toward the fenced area where she had taught him two of the moves she had learned from Nariko. He fisted his hands and slammed them onto the gate. Tension billowed from every inch of his taut body. Not only tension, but grief, too.

Isabella was surprised when tears welled up in her eyes as she hastily looked away. She was shocked by his words . . . and her reaction to them. Her fingers had tingled when he spoke of her touching him. When he had described her bare skin against his, she had been unable to breathe.

Now he stood with his shoulders sagging as if the walls of La Tour stood upon them. She had known Jordan just days, but in that time, she had seen him unhappy too often. His cheerful smile had been such a treat, and now it was gone. How she longed to bring him the joy she had known when her experiment finally succeeded! When she heard him curse, she knew there was one way she could bring him that release from sorrow. She could make his fantasy come true.

Looking at her, he said, "It was wonderful to hold you like that, Isabella, even if it were no more than the herbs creating images in my head."

"We should not talk about this any longer."

"Why not?"

"Because it was not real."

"What is real? Denying what we truly feel?"

"We must."

"I am no monk, Isabella, vowing to forsake pleasure in every form."

Hurt by his brutal tone, she lashed back, "No, you are a man who is afraid to feel anything but lust and grief and guilt. If that is all you can feel, Jordan, then you are right to deny it. I feel joy and hope and excitement and love, and I will feel each of them as fully and as greedily as I wish."

She did not give him a chance to reply. Nothing he said could bridge the chasm that had opened between them, swallowing her happiness.

Chapter 16

The city of Lincoln was awe-inspiring. Isabella was unsure which direction to look in first. Shops and wooden homes with thatched roofs crowded the streets amidst the shops. The shambles, where the butchers worked, was hidden away from the main route through the city. Churches, their square towers rising above their roofs, marked each neighborhood.

But Isabella's gaze was drawn up to the double towers that marked the west front of the grand cathedral. Set on the hill, the cathedral and Lincoln Castle stood above the city. The castle's great tower completed the imposing look, seeming to brush the clouds.

She wanted to admire it longer, but had to watch where she steered her horse through the busy streets. The market was set at the bottom of the hill by the city wall. Odors from the fish market and the poultry market assaulted her as Lord Weirton motioned for them to follow him up a steep street toward the castle and cathedral.

Isabella's heart beat with such excitement she feared it would leap right through her skin. "We are here," she breathed. "At last, we are here."

"Did you doubt I would do as I promised?" Jordan asked beside her.

"No," she replied hastily, trying to hide her astonishment that he was talking to her. In the past four days, he had said less than a half dozen words to her. Even when she had removed his stitches yesterday, he had spoken only a terse "Thank you." She had acted as if she did not care, but his coolness annoyed her as much as her failure to re-create the controlled explosion. After all, her only crime had been to suggest he try the medicine made of crushed poppyheads. She was not responsible for his dream that he had sworn was real.

When he arched a single eyebrow, a wisp of a smile played along his lips. She doubted she had ever seen a more welcome sight. While they had spoken only when necessary, she had discovered how much she missed his rare laughs and offhand comments.

"All right," she said. "I may have had doubts, but that is only human."

Before he could reply, Lady Odette moaned piteously as she had for the past hour. As they climbed the hill, she clung to her saddle and groaned with every step the horse took. The lady refused to explain when her brother asked what was bothering her.

Isabella did not need to ask. She recognized the signs suffered by some women during their monthly flow. The lady was pale, and she held her hand low over her abdomen.

Edging her horse closer to Lady Odette's, she took the reins that were hanging loosely from the lady's hands. If the gelding was frightened by a cart or the shouts of peddlers, the lady could be injured.

Quietly, Isabella said, "I am carrying parsley, milady. I will prepare some to ease your pain as soon as I can."

The lady's only answer was another groan.

"We are almost there," Lord Weirton called back. "The house with the green door."

"We are almost there," Isabella repeated when the lady hunched over the saddle.

A hand settled on her arm, and sweet embers of desire burst forth once more. She looked to her right to see Jordan's concern. Giving him another quick smile, she motioned for him to catch up with Lord Weirton. Three horses took up the whole breadth of the street, and it was narrowing as it climbed toward the cathedral.

He nodded and rode ahead of her and Lady Odette. When Lord Weirton turned to his left, Jordan looked back to make sure she had seen. Again she motioned for him to keep going.

A narrow gate connected the house with the green door and the house next door. One house on the hill above was constructed of stone, but the rest were of weatherworn wood. That wear, she knew, was a good sign that fire had not destroyed the street in many years.

The yard behind the house was cramped. A small byre beyond the circular well would have barely enough space for their horses. She wondered where they would store their saddles and harnesses as well as food for the horses. That would have to be someone else's concern. She had to tend to Lady Odette and then go to the cathedral to find the brass casket with the pages.

Lord Weirton dismounted. "You are welcome to stay at this house for as long as you remain in Lincoln."

Jordan swung down easily in spite of their long hours of riding. "I did not know that you had a house so far from Kenwick Castle."

"It belongs to a good friend of mine. Conrad d'Alpin."

"*Brother* Conrad?" asked Emery as he jumped out of the saddle.

"Brother?" asked Jordan. "As in the Brotherhood?"

The squire shifted nervously from one foot to the other as he stared at the ground. "I should not have repeated what I heard whispered among other squires, milord. Forgive me."

Lord Weirton's laugh broke the tension. "The lad is tired, so foolishness is falling out of his mouth."

"Is d'Alpin involved with the Brotherhood?" Jordan asked.

"Why are you asking me? I don't listen to rumors spread by squires." The baron spread out his hands. "D'Alpin is a good man who allows us to use his house. To repeat gossip belittles that kindness."

Isabella saw Emery slink away, leading her horse and his. The poor lad must wish he had not opened his mouth. How much did the squire truly know about the Brotherhood? When she saw Jordan watching his squire, she guessed he was as curious as she was.

A door at the back of the house opened, and a man peered out. He was short and thin and wore a brown tunic that brushed the top of his worn shoes. His hair fell into his eyes, giving him the appearance that he had just been roused from a nap. Introducing himself as Aldus, a servant in Lord d'Alpin's house, he held the door for them to enter.

Lord Weirton assisted his sister down a trio of steps into a sparsely furnished room where a single serving woman waited. Pegs would hold their cloaks and a bench was set against one wall. The hearth was so tall that Isabella could have walked under the mantel without bending. It was unlit and the stones had been swept clean.

Asking them to wait while he alerted the other servants, Aldus hurried through another door.

Lord Weirton did not wait for the door to close before he grumbled, "A decent welcome would have been a comfortable place to sit and something to drink."

"Oh, Bouchard, you do not understand true discomfort," his sister said with a whimper.

As the baron tried to offer her sympathy, Lady Odette slipped her cloak off, confident that someone would catch it before it fell on the floor. The serving maid rushed forward to grab it, then let out a squeal as Peppy ran down Lady Odette's arm and jumped onto the cloak.

Isabella put a steadying hand on the young woman's shoulder and gave her a commiserating smile. The serving woman took a shuddering breath before squaring her shoulders. She set the cloak and the squirrel on the bench.

"Peppy, my sweet," Lady Odette cooed as she held out her hand. The squirrel jumped into it and scurried up to her shoulder, where it sat and chattered at the maid. "Do not touch my Peppy unless I ask you to."

"I will not." The serving woman curtsied and, gathering

up the cloak, rushed out of the room before the lady could scold her further. She exchanged an uneasy glance with Aldus, who was coming back into the room.

The serving man wore a practiced smile. "Lord Weirton, I have arranged for food for your companions."

"Food?" cried Lady Odette. "If you bring food in here, I will be sick."

When Aldus gasped, Isabella said, "Lady Odette is feeling poorly."

"Poorly? If she brings bad humors, we—"

"You, Aldus, have nothing to fear from her condition."

The serving man's expression of horror would have been amusing under other circumstances, and Isabella was tempted to remind him that the women who worked in the kitchen endured a monthly bleeding, too, but she did not want to unsettle the kind man further.

"It would be for the best of everyone," Jordan said with quiet authority, "if the lady be given privacy."

She was unsure if it was Jordan's seconding of her request or if Aldus wanted to arrange to be as far as possible from a bleeding woman, but the serving man hastily led them out of the entry room.

With the help of Lady Odette's maid, Isabella put the lady to bed in a windowless room on the ground floor. Isabella was not surprised when Lord Weirton suggested that his sister choose another. A strange odor of damp clung to the reed mats on the floor. Lady Odette would not heed him, insisting she could go no farther, and he relented. The chamber was barely big enough for the three of them in addition to the bed and a simple chest set beneath a lamp hanging from a brad on the white stone wall.

At Isabella's request, water was brought in a small cup. She put five drops of oil from parsley seeds into the cup and offered it to Lady Odette. "Drink it, milady. It will ease your cramping."

Lady Odette took it and sniffed. "It is odious."

"It is a small amount. Drink it, and you will be able to rest."

With a scowl, the lady complied, and soon fell asleep.

Isabella went out into the passage where Lord Weirton was sitting on a chair set beneath one of a trio of windows that offered a view of the steep street. The green door was open to let in fresh air.

He came to his feet as she stopped into the passage leading to a set of stairs to the upper floor. "How does she fare?"

"She will be fine by the morrow. For today, she needs to rest."

"That is good news. We have been fortunate to have your skill, milady."

"I am glad to be able to help."

"If all women thought that way, our king's life would have been easier. His wife could have done better to serve him rather than her favorite son."

"It is not for us to judge the queen."

"I would expect you to defend her, milady, for she is said to be much like you—educated and opinionated." With a quiet laugh, he added, "Do not take that as an insult."

"I consider it a compliment to be compared to the queen."

"I thought you might." He smiled, and she returned it. Maybe she had misjudged the baron, who had seemed to think first of himself. She realized she had not been mistaken when he added, "I wish Odette a wonderful future." His eyes flicked toward where Jordan was standing by a window that overlooked the street, and his smile became predatory.

Isabella should not care about the baron's plans to marry his sister to Jordan. She should gladly wish the Weirtons on him. She should crow from the rooftops that they deserved each other. But she knew it was not true. Jordan was a man of honor, as he had shown by staying away from her so they were not tempted by passion.

"Lord Weirton," she said quietly, "I think your sister would appreciate seeing you when she woke."

"You expect me to wait in there while—"

"I know your sister would not be the only one who would appreciate your solicitude toward her." She glanced toward Jordan.

The baron pushed past her to go into the room, shutting the door behind him.

"Do you always manipulate people with such ease?" asked Jordan as he came to stand beside her.

"No. That is why I will be forthright and ask you if you will come with me on the morrow to meet whoever is handling the bishop's duties at the cathedral."

"Why do you ask? I agreed to help you."

"I was unsure if you had changed your mind." The words she had been holding in burst out.

"I do not renege on a vow, Isabella." Hurt dimmed his eyes. "I thought you knew that."

"I do know that." With a sigh, she said, "Forgive me. All this talk of the Brotherhood has unsettled me."

"That is no surprise after the attack on you at La Tour."

Setting her sack on the floor, she opened it and drew out the sheathed knife. She held it out to him. "You should have this. It is not mine. It belonged to your friend."

"You fought to keep the man from taking it. I think Ryce would want you to have it to honor your courage." He took the knife and slipped it into the sack. "And it would please me, too, because Ryce would not be lying in holy ground now if you had not saved my life."

"Lord Weirton would have kept you from hanging."

"Possibly, but you freed me from Gamell's prison. Ryce always appreciated a grand gesture, so it is only fitting that you keep the knife." Handing her the sack, he added, "It is not like you to be frightened."

"I am not frightened. Just curious about the Brotherhood."

"I saw that when we found the token."

"Token? What token?"

Shaking his head, he said, "Forget I said that. Another part of the dream I had at the inn." He did not give her a chance to reply before he asked, "If you are not disturbed by Emery's comments, what is bothering you?"

"I am anxious that I shall fail the queen. How can I go back to St. Jude's Abbey and admit failure?"

He did not reply for a long moment, then asked, "So you intend to return there?"

"It is my home, Jordan, just as La Tour is yours. You must know how I miss it, because you missed La Tour when you had to be away."

"I never thought of it that way. You seem so unsuited for a cloistered life that I just assumed you were happy to be out in the world." He took a step closer. "And I guess I was foolish enough to think you might have other reasons to remain beyond your abbey's walls."

"Jordan, what you dreamed . . ." Heat slapped her cheeks, and she knew she was blushing again. She wished he had never told her about his fantasy. The images played through her head when she tried to sleep.

"I know. I will not speak of it again."

"Good." She walked toward the stairs at the end of the hallway.

From behind her, she heard, "But I will never forget it."

Neither will I.

Where was Jordan? He had promised to meet her at midmorning to climb to the cathedral. Isabella tried not to fume as she paced by the green door. Passersby stared at her, but she paid them no mind. She felt oddly vulnerable without her whip and her sack of herbs and elements. She could not imagine wearing such things in a cathedral.

Or her filthy gown. She had taken her other gown out last night, but the heavy skirt was wrinkled. Even so, the simple tawny gown with its light blue bodice ribbons and its fanciful embroidery was the finest she had ever worn. The sleeves dropped almost to her knees and were edged with thick ruffles. Beneath it, she wore her torn boots, but her hair was wrapped neatly around her head under a silk veil, and she knew she looked her best.

The bells tolled from the top of the street. She had waited an hour for Jordan because the bells had been ringing when she finished checking on Lady Odette, who whined anew before swallowing another dose of the parsley oil.

Gathering up her skirt, she strode up the hill. It was so steep that she had to slow down as she passed the lone house built of stone. An odd arch hung over the entrance door with strange carvings on either end. Two other arches curved over windows on either side of the upper floor. The one in the center was simple and unadorned.

She wondered how anyone could build a house on such a sheer slope, but buildings edged both sides of the narrow, curving street. Trees clung to small patches of earth, as determined to remain there as the residents. By the time she neared the top, she doubted if two horses abreast could have maneuvered between the buildings.

The hill continued to climb, but more gradually, when she reached the plateau where the two great buildings faced each other from against opposite walls of the city. Looking at the castle, she saw one tower stood at the very edge of the hill. It was topped by a wooden structure with windows that offered views in every direction. Such an observation tower would offer first warning and enable the castle's steward to post soldiers on the stone curtain wall that must have been raised recently because the stones had not weathered like the ones at La Tour.

She turned her back on the castle. In front of her beyond the buildings at the crest of the steepest part of the hill was the massive cathedral with its twin towers. She was amazed by its sculptured front where rows of arches marched above the doorways and windows. Among them, carved figures dipicted stories from the Bible that could be understood by everyone. Smaller doors opened into the cathedral aisles. A spire sat atop each end of the facade and the towers blocked out the sky on either side of the tallest door. Birds fluttered around the eaves and in and out of the towers where bells marked the hours. Voices wafted through the open doors.

Glancing down the street, she hoped she would see Jordan. They had traveled so far and experienced so much together. She wanted him with her when she made the final steps on the journey to bring the queen what she needed to save England from another war.

He was nowhere in sight.

Isabella sighed. She had not guessed the end of her quest would have lost its thrill when he was not with her to share it.

She could not wait any longer. She had agreed to find the pages and return them to the queen with all possible speed. Delaying to help Jordan had been necessary, but loitering on the street in the spring sunshine was not. She strode purposefully to the closest open door.

Song greeted Isabella as she entered the grand cathedral. Excitement returned to pump through her when she gazed up at the row of windows marching along the nave. The soaring columns holding the arched ceiling were far above her head.

She admired how sunlight poured through the windows set high in the walls on either side of the nave. Ahead of her at the far end of the long nave was the transept where the choir was set beneath the single tower. Carved wood and stone vied for her attention. She wished she had a dozen eyes so she could see everything at once.

"Welcome," said a man as he hurried past her, his footsteps hushed on the stone floor. Before she could answer, he vanished into a chapel to one side of the entrance.

Wanting to explore every inch of the cathedral, she did not have the luxury of time. She must find the small brass casket. She walked around the simply carved stone font that seemed out of place amidst the grandeur. As she reached the other side of the heavy, stone basin, she saw a man sitting on the floor. He was carving an intricate pattern on what she guessed would be a massive cover for the font.

Looking up, he gave her a tired grin.

"That is lovely," she said in a whisper. Even so, the sound seemed to gain strength as it reached toward the ceiling.

"I hope the new bishop will be pleased with it." He ran his hand over what she realized was a lamb. The outline was rough, but the flower it held in its mouth looked alive.

"Has a new bishop been named?" She was unsure how she hoped he would answer. A new bishop might be able to provide her with the location of the pages, or a new bishop might hinder her in such a search. Whoever was named would have the king as well as the archbishop to thank for his promotion to the prestigious post.

"No new bishop yet," the stone carver said, putting his chisel with care against the outline of the lamb. "He will come when the good Lord deems it the right time."

Isabella smiled at his gentle reminder of patience. If she had had more, Jordan would be beside her to share this final part of their journey. She had been wrong to deny him that.

She turned to go out the door she had entered. She paused when she saw Jordan standing on the other side of the font. Like her, he had changed from his traveling clothes, and he looked as impressive as he had in the great hall at La Tour. Heat surged up through her before slipping back down her legs to curl her toes within her boots.

She slowly closed the distance between them, not caring what they had promised each other, not caring that they stood in the cathedral. His gaze burned into her as her hands lifted toward him, needing to rediscover his burly muscles and his gentle touch.

He took one and bowed over it, kissing it with no more passion than if they were strangers. Dismay swept away her anticipation of his touch. When he released her hand quickly, she started to protest. He gave the slightest shake of his head and looked past her.

"Good morning, Father," he said.

Isabella tensed, but made sure she was smiling as she faced the priest. "Good morning, Father."

"Good morning. I am Father Joseph. May I help you?"

Her smile became more genuine. First they needed to find the brass casket, and then she and Jordan could find a way to celebrate.

"I need to speak," she replied, "with whoever has assumed the bishop's duties until another bishop is appointed."

"The canons share the duties along with the dean."

"May I speak with the dean?"

"He is not here, but I saw Canon Anthony in one of the chapels. Shall I take you to him?"

"Yes, thank you."

"Please follow me."

Jordan took her hand and placed it on his arm as they walked along the cathedral's magnificent length. Columns led to arches that opened into galleries. No chairs broke the length of the cathedral, even in front of the pulpit that was made of the same polished wood as the choir pews. The screen was decorated with symbols and plants.

"Why didn't you wait for me?" Jordan asked so low that the priest, walking several feet in front of them, would not hear.

"I did wait. For an hour by the bells in the tower here."

"I was delayed for a good reason."

"Tell me about it when you can." She squeezed his arm. "I will be more patient next time."

"You? Patient?"

"Prepare to be amazed."

"I always am with you, Isabella." His laugh enthralled her and brought a curious glance from the priest.

As she stroked his arm, she hoped that they would find a way to bridge the chasm between them. She was not sure how, but she dared to believe it was possible.

Chapter 17

"Canon Anthony is in here," Father Joseph said as he paused in front of a small chapel to one side of the grand nave.

"Thank you," Isabella said.

He tilted his head toward them and continued toward the front of the church.

A man was on his knees before the statues of several saints. He wore a tonsure and robes as simple as the those of the monks at Kenwick Priory. When he stood, the light from the candles near the altar rail glittered off the gold chain holding a wooden cross on his chest.

"You are seeking me?" asked the man.

"Canon Anthony, we hope you can help us," Jordan said. "I am Jordan le Courtenay, and this is Lady Isabella de Montfort. We are seeking an item given to the bishop for safekeeping."

"The bishop is no longer here."

"We understand that, but we hope you can help us."

"What sort of item did you give to the bishop?"

"A casket—"

"A brass casket," Isabella interjected.

Jordan glanced at her, then said, "A *brass* casket containing some pages. It is not large."

The canon rubbed his chin. "It is possible it is still here. Does it belong to you?"

"My aunt, an abbess at a small abbey south of here, sent us to find it."

"An abbess, did you say?" Canon Anthony smiled. "You are doing a wonderful deed to collect it for your cloistered aunt."

Isabella smiled, too, pleased that Jordan had not revealed that they were there on behalf of the queen. The cathedral and the city were closely connected with King Henry. The church leaders might not be willing to help the queen.

"Do you know how long ago it was delivered to the bishop?" the canon asked. "I have been in my post since I was appointed by the king's natural son, Geoffrey, during his tenure as bishop of Lincoln." He paused, and she guessed he wanted them to make a comment.

Isabella had no idea what to say, for the king's illegitimate son had resigned from the church during an argument with his father, one of the many that he and his brothers had with King Henry. Deciding on the banal, she said, "So you have been in your position for at least two years."

"Eight, milady, for Bishop Geoffrey was long the bishop of Lincoln."

"Then you are well familiar with the cathedral and where the bishop might have stored such a casket."

"Of course." He stepped past them. "Let me show you the cathedral while I send a brother to search. There is not much left behind because the bishop took anything of importance to Rouen." Calling to a passing monk, he gave quick instructions to find what they sought.

The monk hurried away to do as he was bid.

Hope exploded through Isabella again. Could it be this simple? Just ask and the casket would be brought to them? She swallowed a chuckle. Would the canon be aghast if she danced about and sang with joy when the monk brought her the casket? She put her fingers over the key she wore beneath her gown. She imagined going to the queen and presenting her with the brass casket. Jordan would be by her side, handsome and worthy of being a liege of the king. Once he saw that with the delivery of the casket to the queen a war had been averted, could he set aside the pain from past battles?

"Milady, you can see why we are proud of our choir," the canon said, intruding into her reverie. "Several master wood-carvers worked on it."

"It is beautiful." She looked at the wooden benches facing each other across the stone floor. Columns were painted with bright colors, and light shone through windows above, warming the space. It seemed somehow intimate in the vast cathedral.

Jordan pointed to the hinged seats. Several were tilted back to show more carving. "Which master carver hid his work *under* the choir's seats?"

"Those are misericords," the canon said. "They are, fortunately, infrequently seen in England, although I understand many churches are filled with them on the Continent."

"What are misericords?"

Isabella knelt to look at the raised bench. "Misericords are follies. The carver's idea of a biblical scene or a jest." She put her hand on a seat. "As one must stand for a long time during some Masses, these half seats were created for older brothers and priests to lean on." She lifted another to reveal an angel gazing down at a child in her arms. "Most of the time the misericords are hidden, but when the seats are open for services, the carvings are visible."

"Is that a pig?" Jordan squatted down and chuckled. "It is playing a pipe."

Again Canon Anthony sighed. "The carvers took too many liberties. Bishop Alexander, who was bishop when the cathedral burned fifty years ago, had many tasks to complete in the wake of the fire. He could not supervise all the workmen, and that is the result."

A monk rushed up to the canon. Isabella realized he was the man sent to find the casket. When she saw his hands were empty, she drew in a shaky breath.

"I searched through the items the bishop left in his office," the monk said. "I found no brass casket there."

"Are there any other places it might be?" asked Isabella, her voice trembling. She could not fail the queen. She could not fail St. Jude's Abbey!

"Do not despair, milady," the canon said. "We will continue to search throughout the cathedral and the chapter house. The bishop's palace is not much more than a ruin, but we will look there also."

"How long do you think it will take?"

"Is there a reason for you to recover this casket so quickly?"

"Yes." She tried to devise some story that was not a lie. She could not tell him that the abbess had insisted Isabella take the casket to the queen before the month's end, which was barely a fortnight away. Inspiration came as she said, "Lord le Courtenay's aunt asked for us to return it to her by the end of April. She must have a good reason for making such a request."

"We will endeavor to find the casket before then." He gave them a beatific smile. "Have faith, milady." Looking at Jordan, he asked, "Where can we send word when we find the casket?"

"To Lord d'Alpin's house on Ermine Street."

"Lord d'Alpin?" The canon's face paled. "I did not realize— That is, we will do all we can to find the casket with all possible haste." Without adding more, he herded the monk away.

Jordan frowned. "I had no idea d'Alpin's name would inspire such a reaction from a churchman."

Walking toward the doors, Isabella did not reply. She needed to gather her shredded hope and have faith as the canon had urged.

"I am sorry," Jordan said as they emerged into the sunshine. "If they have not found the casket within a day or two, we can take over the search."

"Why would we have any better chance of finding it than they would? They know the cathedral and its precincts."

"But we want to find it more."

"That is true." She paused as they reached steep Ermine Street. "Why were you delayed, Jordan? If you want to find the casket as much as I do . . ."

"I was talking to Emery."

"About the Brotherhood?"

He offered his arm when her boot slid on a cobble. She put her hand on it, and he covered her fingers with his. "He evaded my questions and said too frequently that he did not have an answer. The lad knows more than he is revealing."

"If the previous lord he served was a member of the Brotherhood, he may have overheard much. He would not want to betray the memory of that lord by divulging it now."

"Logical as always, I see."

" 'Tis not logic, but compassion. He had a shattered expression when he spoke of Lord d'Alpin and the Brotherhood. He wants to serve you well, Jordan, but he is still bound by his promise of service to the lord who died."

"We have all made too many vows."

She did not answer as they half walked, half skidded down the street. When they reached the house with the green door, he held it open for her to go inside.

"I assume you want to check Lady—"

She silenced him by putting her finger to his lips before crooking her finger for him to come with her. He did as she walked past the door where Lady Odette's voice could be heard ordering her serving woman to do something. She climbed the stairs and, opening another door, stepped into the room she had been given for her use.

Jordan remained in the hallway. "If you wish to speak of our plans to search, we should do so elsewhere."

"Let Canon Anthony and the monks look today and tomorrow. I don't want to think about that." She cupped his chin and kissed him lightly on the right cheek. "I want to think of us."

"The us who made a truce we would be no more than allies?"

"Why did you ever accept such a silly offer?" She brushed his left cheek with her lips.

"I thought it was what you wanted."

"So did I. It was a very rational decision based on the facts." Gently she drew his face toward her as she stepped back into the sun-washed bedchamber. "But there is nothing rational about desire, is there?"

"Nothing at all." He smiled as he closed the door, then reached behind him to lower the bar into place.

She trailed her fingers up his cheeks. "I have been miserable, Jordan, when we pretended to ignore each other. I *missed* you, and I want to be with you without any promises. You are right."

"About what?"

"We have spoken too many vows." She whispered against his ear, "Show me what you dreamed."

He caught her face in his strong hands and brought her gaze to meet his. "If you will show me what you have dreamed."

"What makes you think that I have dreamed about you, Lord le Courtenay?" she asked with feigned haughtiness.

"Your eyes tell me, for desire glows from them."

"Make my dreams come true."

"We will make *our* dreams come true."

She gasped at the sudden intensity in his voice, but the sound vanished as his mouth claimed hers. He pulled her to him as he steered her toward the bed. When they reached it, he leaned back, drawing her down over him as his tongue pursued every bit of pleasure awaiting in her mouth.

But even that did not seem enough because his lips tasted every inch of her face, leaving a fiery trail along her cheeks, forehead, eyelids. She guided his mouth to hers again. When she touched him, her longing intensified into madness to know all of him.

His fingers sought the ribbons holding her bodice in place, but he did not undo them. She stared down into his eyes as he drew his lips away from hers. Knowing that he was offering her a final chance to change her mind, she was astonished. He had spoken of feeling only lust, but was it possible this tender, enticing man longed for more? She dared not speak the word *love* or admit how her heart was empty without him in it.

"You are an incredible woman who never has turned

away from any battle. I cannot be the hero you deserve," he said as he edged away and sat with his back to her. "You deserve a man who would be willing to die for you."

"Why would I want that?" She ran her fingers up his back. "I want a man who is willing to live for me."

He gave her a puzzled frown. "I don't understand."

"I know." She sat and stroked his face. "You are determined to shut yourself off from life because you want to avoid any sort of confrontation."

"With you, that is impossible."

"That is because I want to experience every bit of life, the joys as well as the griefs, the excitements as well as the frustrations. You should want the same." Rising to her knees, she put her cheek against his shoulder. "Don't be afraid."

"Afraid?"

She smiled at his astonishment. "There is nothing about you that is horrible, not what you have experienced, not what you do not want to experience again. Nothing you have vowed—even when you have questioned your sword-sworn oath—is wrong because you made that pledge with your heart. How can anything decided by the heart be wrong?"

"That is not logical."

"Which is why we have hearts—to tell us anything is possible if we want it enough." She sifted her fingers through his hair to urge his mouth back to hers. "And I want you."

He whispered her name in a choked voice before his mouth pounced on hers. In his deep, probing kiss as he pushed her into the mattress, she tasted his need for healing, a need that no herbs in her sack could cure.

She arched her neck to give him freer access as his lips sought along her jaw. When he loosened the ribbons on her bodice and pushed it aside, his heated breath scorched her.

"What is this?" he asked as he lifted the key from the hollow between her breasts.

"Can't you guess?"

"The key to the secrets in your heart?" He gave her a rakish grin that incited the quiver deep within her.

"I don't think I will have many secrets from you after today." She lifted the ribbon over her head and set it on the thick windowsill. "For now, I am not the queen's lady."

"No, you are mine."

Her gasp at his intense tone became a moan when his tongue traced the curve of her breast above her shift. He drew her gown lower, then hooked a finger in the strap of her shift and pulled it down to fall over her gown. Rolling onto his back, he pulled her over him and drew the tip of one breast into his mouth. A craving, as hot and potent as a flame, shot through her, settling in the void between her legs, hot and moist.

As he shoved her gown even lower, he asked, "Where is your whip?"

"I did not . . ." she whispered, struggling to form each word when her mind was drowning in pleasure. "I did not think I should wear it to the cathedral."

"There is something very beguiling—and very naughty—about a lady who wears a whip and is willing to use it."

She smiled as she traced a line along his chest until she reached his belt. "If you want me to get it . . ."

"No, because then you might fight your way free of me."

"That is something you need not worry about." With a grin, she added, "I could use it to make you do as I wish."

With a quick motion, he brought her back under him as he pushed her gown and shift down over her legs. He laced his fingers through her hair and reclaimed her mouth.

She was overwhelmed by the feelings assaulting her. His eager lips, his hot tongue, the rough fabric of his tunic, the pressure of him above her, the need for him to be within her, each an individual torment.

"I do not need any whip to force you to be my prisoner," he growled in her ear. He pushed one knee between her legs as he drew her hands down to her sides. Pressing them against the bed, he etched her skin from chin to belly button with his tongue's hot, silken trail.

Sensation, powerful and unstoppable, rose through her

when he continued his exploration lower. She quivered when he placed gentle nibbles in the inner curve of her hip. A cry erupted through her gasps as he pushed her legs apart enough for his tongue to penetrate her with liquid fire. Her fingers curled into his palms as she tried to free herself from his captivity.

His laugh brushed her like a thousand intimate caresses. "You are my prisoner, and you will do as I wish for as long as I wish."

"Let me go!"

"No, for I want to sample ecstasy with you again and again and again until you are as docile as a spring zephyr."

Her answer vanished into another gasp as he drove his tongue into her, exciting her in ways she could never have imagined but now would always crave. She writhed beneath his skillful siege on her senses. Each touch left a fluid spark in its wake. His breath, though heated, brushed a cool breeze across her. He teased and delved and caressed, pausing each time just before she could reach joy's zenith, sending her higher and higher with each new assault of delight until she was begging him for release. She thought she heard his pleased laugh in the moment before she lost herself in rapture.

Some time later—she could not be certain how long— she opened her eyes to see his smile close by. She tilted up her mouth to welcome his kiss that was redolent with the flavor of her satiation and his ravenous hunger for her. She watched, loathe to move, as he stood and tore off his clothes with an eagerness that pierced her with a renewed craving. His body, although scarred from battle, was lean and muscular. He slanted toward her, and she stared at the hard shaft that would soon be part of her. She ran a curious finger along it, and he gave a throaty moan before he pulled her tangled gown over her feet. He tossed it aside, then drew off her ragged boots and threw them atop her other clothes. He pressed her back into her bed. As she reached to put her arms around his shoulders, he held her hands to the bed again.

"Let me go," she whispered, unable to gather the strength to speak more loudly.

"You are *my* captive, so stop telling me what to do. Just tell me what you like."

"Tell you?" The fire deep within her fled up to her face. "I—I don't know if—that is, I don't know how . . ."

"Don't be afraid," he whispered.

"Afraid?" she asked as he had.

"What did you tell me? That there is nothing about me that is horrible? Maybe so, but I can tell you that there is much about you that is wondrous." He lifted her hands and slid them up her, the rough texture of his fingers between hers like coarse ashes along her skin. "I want you to understand how wondrous your body is, how much pleasure it gives me." He ran her palms up over her breasts, pausing so his fingers could toy with her nipples. "Here you are so lush that I seek every chance I can to feel your softness on me." He drew her hands down toward her hips. "Here you are so strong when you plant your feet and prepare to face a foe." Slipping her hands along her legs, he murmured, "And here you will pull me close when I am part of you."

"But I don't want to touch me." Her soft moan contradicted her words as he ran his fingers between hers along her thighs. "I want to touch you."

"As you wish." He steered her fingers up to his shoulders and then across his chest. "How is that?"

"Wonderful."

"And how is this?" He let her hands brush the hard muscles layered across his abdomen.

"Splendid." She closed her eyes as she savored each ripple beneath his skin.

When he did not ask another question, she opened her eyes. His gaze seared down into her as he pressed her hand against the silken shaft that pulsated at her touch. He closed her fingers around it, sliding his hand to her wrist. His finger inched up and down her hand, but she did not need his guidance as she stroked him until he was gasping against her hair.

He pulled her hand away as he tugged her beneath him again. She gasped when he pressed her hands to the bed, but before she could speak, he captured her lips. Then he was inside her. His fingers tightened around hers as her body enclosed his. He moved slowly, so slowly the rapture threatened to consume her. She wanted more. She had to have more. But he pressed her to the bed, giving only what he wished, holding back his pleasure and hers, increasing her anticipation of ecstasy. It was too much, and she lost herself in the explosion once . . . then again . . . then a third time. Each time, as she shivered through the fall back into reality, he was above her, pinning her hands to the bed, his gaze focused on her face as he gauged each peak of pleasure she found.

She whispered his name, and he closed his eyes in the moment before his mouth retook hers. His slow strokes deepened and quickened. She matched his motion as passion escalated between them. When he shuddered against her, she surrendered once more to a bliss made sweeter because this time he shared it with her.

Isabella opened her eyes as she heard rain striking the windowsill. The droplets glittered on the key and ribbon hanging over its edge. She closed her eyes and snuggled closer to Jordan. She did not want her obligations to intrude yet. She wanted to linger here with him for . . . forever. Had he guessed, when he asked about the secrets of her heart, that the greatest one was that she loved him? She had tried to hide that even from herself, but, lying in his arms, she could not pretend not to understand why she had been so wretched when they tried to keep a distance between them. She slipped her arm across his bare chest.

He smiled at her. "I am a fool, Isabella."

"It is about time you admitted that." She laughed, elated at his light, teasing tone that she had heard so seldom.

"Don't you want to know why I am a fool?" He kissed the top of her head lying on his shoulder.

"Tell me."

"I was a fool to think my fantasies—inspired by your

sleeping potion—could be as wonderful as it would be to hold you like this. Truly hold you."

"Then hold me."

"Gladly."

The sound of the storm beyond the window vanished as she was drawn once more into the tempest she wanted to share with him for as long as she could. For two days, they did not have to worry about finding the casket. She would gladly use that time to discover ever more ecstasy with him.

Chapter 18

"Imay be able to help," Isabella said when she stood by Lady Odette's bed the next afternoon.

Lady Odette refused to get up, even when Isabella assured her that exercise would ease her cramps. In the corner of the room, her maid's face bore a bright red mark where Lady Odette must have struck her. The squirrel chattered crazily in its cage, but Isabella ignored it.

Lady Odette wrinkled her nose. "No more of those odious herbs. I fear I would vomit anything I tried to swallow." With a groan, she put her hand against her forehead. "I may anyhow."

Isabella paid no attention to the lady's lamentations. Instead, she opened the pouch she had brought with her and knelt by the bed. Her fingers knew each stone by touch, and she easily pulled out the red jade that was smooth on only one side.

"What are you doing?" asked Lady Odette.

"I can explain, or I can help you." She placed the stone on Lady Odette's abdomen. When the lady tried to see, Isabella warned her to remain where she was.

"What are you doing now?" Lady Odette asked when Isabella opened her pouch again.

"You have complained of a headache, too." She drew out a jagged crystal. The points were faded to white, but the center remained a vibrant purple. "This can help."

The lady regarded her with dismay. "It is sharp. It will cut me."

"If you would prefer to set its place yourself, take it."

"I am not a healer." Lady Odette scowled, then winced.

Isabella put the stone in the center of the lady's forehead. "Close your eyes and think of what gives you pleasure."

"Like Lord le Courtenay?"

"If he gives you pleasure." She was relieved that the lady's eyes were closed.

"Maybe if he *would* give me pleasure, I would not suffer from my monthly curse." She opened one eye. "Do you have anything in that pouch to make him mad with desire for me?"

"I am a healer, not a conjurer."

Isabella was uncertain if Lady Odette heard her or not because the lady did not reply. Gathering up her pouch, she motioned for the serving woman to come with her. She closed the door once they were in the passage outside the lady's room.

"Is there something I should do for milady?" the maid asked past her swollen lips.

She unhooked a second pouch from her belt and poured some leaves into her hand. "Take them."

"Parsley? To make more oil for my lady?"

She wondered why the serving woman was loyal to a lady who abused her. "No, put these leaves on your face to take away the bruising."

"Thank you, milady. You are very kind."

The bed chamber's door opened and slammed against the wall.

"What are you doing?" demanded Lady Odette. She reeled back to sit on the bed as if the act of standing had been too much for her. "I am in here suffering from the most hideous pain, and you two are loitering outside my door."

Isabella ducked as the lady threw the stones at her. They clattered to the floor past her, and she heard one shatter. The amethyst had not been easy to obtain, and now it was broken into useless shards.

"Maybe," Isabella said, freeing the rage that had built in her since the lady first spoke condescendingly to her at La

Tour, "if you showed more kindness, as a lady should, to those around her, you might find others more concerned about you."

"What do you know about being a true lady?" With a sneer, Lady Odette eyed her up and down. "You denied your birth by going to an abbey to study healing. A lady does not do that." She reached out and flicked the whip hanging from Isabella's hip. "You look like a herder."

"I have never pretended to be anything but what I am."

"A whore who has tried to lure Jordan le Courtenay into her bed." Again her nose wrinkled. "He has better taste than you!"

Isabella laughed. She could not halt herself.

Lady Odette stamped her foot, then stormed past her up the stairs, vowing to inform her brother. Isabella was about to tell the lady that she would have to wait because Jordan and Lord Weirton had left the house earlier that afternoon, but faltered.

What could cause a strange empty echo in a stone floor?

She went into the bedroom, trying to find the exact spot where Lady Odette had driven her heel against the floor. She pounded her feet several times. All she heard was a dull thud. Moving farther from the wall, she tried again.

There!

Peeling back the reed mats, she saw a break between the stones where the grout had been chiseled away. It outlined a square no more than two feet in each direction. It looked as if the stone was meant to be moved.

But how?

She ran her fingers along the stone and realized there was a circular indentation where the grout had been chiseled away. It was not much wider than her thumb, but round. She dug into the small circle, hoping for a latch that would allow her to move the stone. The shallow opening had small metal brads reaching out into it. Something must fit in there, held in place by the brads.

Grabbing her sack, she reached in for the pouch containing her healing stones. She frowned when she realized it had

opened, scattering the contents through her bag. Raking
everything out of the bag, she took care none of the elements
spilled. The stones clattered to the floor.

She tried them all in quick succession. Some were the
wrong size. Some were the wrong shape. Most were both.
Sighing with defeat, she put the stones into the pouch. She
started putting the pouches into her sack, then froze when
she saw the knife from Ryce de Dolan's grave.

Not daring to breathe at her own audacity, she looked at
the crest on the haft. The crest belonged to the Brotherhood.
The owner of the house was rumored to be a member of the
Brotherhood. Was it possible . . . ?

She placed the knife over the spot. The crest on the haft
fit perfectly in the hole. Giving it a gentle turn to the right,
she pushed on the stone. Nothing happened, so she twisted
the knife to the left.

She watched in astonishment as the stone lowered into
the darkness with the faint squeak of leather hinges. Two
stones on either side folded back as well.

Rising, she took down the lamp on the wall. She held it
above the hole. Very slowly, she edged the lantern down into
the darkness.

The light cascaded along a ladder toward what appeared
to be a floor more than a tall man's height below her. Why
would there be an opening from the chamber to the house's
cellar? She moved the lantern and saw the stone walls beneath her disappeared into the distance in both directions. It
was a corridor cut out of the earth, a tunnel that passed under
this house and continued beyond it.

She lifted the knife out of the indentation and stared at it.
The crest had been the key to move the stone. That belonged
to the Brotherhood. The secret tunnel must as well. Had
gaining entrance to the tunnel been the reason the man who
attacked her at La Tour wanted the knife?

Drawing her feet under her, she opened her sack again
and removed the pouch of the healing stones. She put them
into another pouch on her belt and slipped the knife into its
sheath before hooking it next to her whip. She could not

guess whom she might meet in the secret space. Even if she met no one, she might need the crest to open another door.

She set the lamp on the floor beside the opening and swung her feet onto the ladder. Slowly she descended, pausing to pick up the lamp. Amazed, she saw a handle on the underside of the stone. It must be the way to open and close the door from beneath the floor. Her stomach cramped at the thought of becoming trapped.

She wished Jordan was with her. She would look around a short distance—no more than one hundred steps along the tunnel—and then return to wait for him before investigating farther.

She hooked the lamp onto a rung and balanced with care as she drew the stones out of her pouch, one at a time. She gripped the handle on the stone and raised it into place, jamming the healing stones into the edges so it could not close completely. If luck were on her side, nobody would notice anything unusual other than that the reed mats had been pushed aside.

Taking a deep breath, she moved down through the narrow circle of light. She tried not to think what the darkness might conceal.

The lower rungs were slippery. She grasped the ladder, and the light from the lamp fluttered wildly. Her frantic breath was so loud that she was surprised it did not echo along the tunnel.

When her foot touched solid earth, she whispered a grateful prayer. She leaned her head against the ladder and tried to stop panting as if she had raced up Ermine Street twice.

Isabella raised the lamp to look around. The top of the space was damp with water that also gathered in puddles on the uneven floor. She was surprised to discover the space was not much wider than her outstretched arms. If there was a cellar beneath Lord d'Alpin's house, it did not connect to the tunnel.

Going to one wall, she held the lamp close to the stone. It glittered with many different kinds of mineral, and she wondered if the walls were made of limestone. Whatever the rock was, it could support both the castle and the cathedral, so she need not worry about it collapsing around her.

The tunnel stank of rot and dampness as she walked along it, counting her steps. From overhead, she could hear footsteps, but she could not guess if she had passed from beneath Lord d'Alpin's house to another. The tunnel's floor slanted upward, but not as steeply as Ermine Street. She could not tell if it ran parallel to the street or off at an angle.

As she held up her lamp, she gasped. A wall to her left was illuminated. She had not imagined such colors were beneath the earth. Rich shades of red and even blues and grays rippled down long icicles of stone. Water dripped from the ends into pools on either side of her. The pools were not deep. She could not see where the water flowed away because her small circle of light did not reach that far. She had not noticed when the tunnel widened. It was now twice the breadth of her extended arms.

She quelled the yearning to examine the pools more closely. She had not climbed down into the tunnel to look at water.

At that thought, she lowered the lamp. She hoped nobody had seen its light. Or *nothing* had. There could be beasts in the tunnel and the caves that might open off it.

Another thought she silenced. She must be careful not to wander so far that she could not find her way back to the ladder leading up to Lord d'Alpin's house. She needed to continue straight ahead.

Running her fingers along the wall, she noticed a change in texture as the walls became closer again. Had the wider section with the pools been natural while the tunnels carved out by men? How could they have been created without anyone knowing? She warned herself not to assume that the Brotherhood had built these tunnels. They might be only the latest tenants beneath Lincoln. The Romans had arrived over a millennium ago.

Isabella paused as her fingertips warned her that the wall was veering outward again. She had gone almost a hundred footsteps. Far enough. She was not sure how much longer she would be able to go undetected.

It was difficult to turn back, because she wanted to keep exploring. She hurried along the tunnel, counting her steps again. How long would she have to wait until she could speak to Jordan alone and arrange for Lady Odette to be out of her room so they could sneak into the tunnel again? Perhaps during the evening meal they could devise some excuse to slip away without arousing suspicion.

She laughed, the sound contorting as it bounced off the walls. Lady Odette would do everything she could to keep Isabella and Jordan from leaving the table at the same time.

The light from her lamp reflected off the pools of water, startling her. She laughed again, this time uneasily. The tunnels fueled the imagination, so she must be careful not to let hers create danger where there was none.

She reached one hundred steps from where she had turned around, but did not see the ladder. Either she had miscounted, or she had taken a different length of pace coming back. Holding the lamp higher, she scanned the tunnel ahead of her.

Her wrist was seized. A hand clamped over her mouth before she could draw in a breath.

She had been discovered!

Chapter 19

Isabella reached to grab the arm near her face. If she could knock her captor senseless, maybe she could escape without him identifying her. Or had he already seen her?

"Isabella, don't."

"Jordan?" she whispered against the hand.

She was whirled so fast to face him that she had to clutch on to his arm to keep herself from spinning away. He grasped her hand to keep the lamp from hitting the wall; then he pulled her to him. His mouth on hers made her want to forget where they were and what might be hidden in the tunnel. Running her fingers up his chest, she curved her arm around his shoulder and teased his tongue to chase hers into her mouth. She was shaking when he raised his mouth, overpowered anew by the yearning he aroused.

"What are you doing *here*?" Jordan asked as he took the lamp from her, holding it up so they could see each other. His face was a complex pattern of shadows.

"Exploring."

"This is no place for you to poke your curious nose. These tunnels could collapse without warning."

She stepped away and rapped her knuckles gently against the wall. "I doubt there is another tunnel in England as solidly built as this one."

"It is not only the construction that concerns me."

"I know. It is who uses these tunnels."

He set the lamp on a small rock protruding from the wall.

"How can you be sensible and do something so risky at the same time?"

"Because there are secrets here, and there may be answers as well. How did you get down here?"

"Probably the same way you did. I was told you were tending Lady Odette, so I went to her room. I found nobody there, then saw the mats had been shoved back, revealing a stone not flush with the floor. Hold out your hand." He dropped several small stones onto her palm. "I assume these are yours."

She knew the stones by touch. "These are my healing stones. I put them in the trapdoor to make sure I could get back up through it. What if you cannot open it again?"

"Going back that way is out of the question. Before I shut the trapdoor, I tried to make sure the mats were covering it again. I don't want anyone to know we have discovered this tunnel. Weirton was upset when his sister insisted on using that room. I suspect we now know the real reason why."

"I agree. I cannot trust him. Do you?"

He shook his head, making new shapes in the shadows on his face. "If he is not involved with the Brotherhood, he wants to be. He praises them every chance he can."

She drew Sir Ryce's knife and pointed to the crest. "This served as the key to open the trapdoor."

"Very clever."

"Isn't it? A member of the Brotherhood can carry this, and no one ever will know that it grants entrance to places like this."

"Yes, the Brotherhood is clever," He ran his finger along her cheek. "But I meant you. You are very clever to see that the crest fit into the stone."

She laughed. "I was so curious what was beneath the stone that I was ready to try anything to open it." Looking both to her right and left, she asked, "Which way do you want to go?"

"There is a wall not far beyond the ladder, so we need to go in the direction you were exploring."

"I did not see a way out, but I went only about one hundred steps along the tunnel."

Lifting the lamp from the wall, he said, "There must be other ways in and out of the tunnels. People would be noticed coming and going from d'Alpin's house, and there would be whispers."

"Which Emery would have heard."

"The lad has showed a propensity for learning all the rumors, whether they are true or not." He gave a wry chuckle.

"You have changed." She traced the strong lines of his face with her fingertip, delighting in the upturn of his lips as she touched them. "Laughter is much easier for you now."

"I have more to laugh about now."

"Me?"

His finger under her chin brought her lips to his. "Yes, you." His kiss was a swift promise of more pleasure after they left the tunnel. "Let's go."

Isabella did not resheathe the knife as she followed Jordan. She wanted to remain in the circle of light, but her mind kept wandering to how easily she could raise her fingers and stroke his strong back.

When they passed the pools with the incredible colors on the walls, he did not slow. She had been certain that he would be curious about what had been hidden beneath their feet. What hadn't he told her? Had he learned more about the Brotherhood? Or was there another reason he was rushing? She did not ask. If he had a reason to hurry, it would be a valid one.

Her fingers tightened on the knife as they passed the spot where she had turned around. When a glow appeared in front of them, she whispered, "Maybe we should look for another way."

He put his finger to her lips. "Do not speak so loudly."

"I am whispering!" She drew his hand away. "I know that there may be other ears listening to what we say."

"I know you do."

"Then why did you halt me?"

"I enjoy any excuse to touch you."

She was astounded when he winked at her. He was enjoying himself. He *was* as curious as she was to discover what the Brotherhood was concealing.

"We need to see who is ahead of us," he said.

He blew out the lamp, leaving them in thick twilight. She heard steel slide against wood and knew he had drawn his sword. Sliding Ryce's dagger into its sheath, she loosened her whip. She trusted her skills with it more.

The light did not move as they inched forward. She strained her ears, but heard only her rapid heartbeat. Again the walls fell back to widen the space between them. She motioned for him to remain by the left-hand wall while she edged along the other side. By the left wall, he would be better able to swing his sword. Her whip would go in whichever direction she snapped it.

Jordan gestured for her to halt while he inched to where he could peer past the wall. She bit her lip as sweat threatened to loosen her grip on the whip.

"No one," he whispered as he lowered his sword and motioned for her to follow him.

The space was lit by a pair of brands. A single pool was at the right rim of the light. The floor did not slant. They could not have reached the top of the hill yet.

"Look at this!" she whispered, not knowing how far her voice would carry along the tunnel.

She pointed to carvings in the stone. She could not tell if the lines, which looked as if a great beast had randomly clawed the wall, were symbols or words or just something made by the water oozing down the walls. "What do you think these represent?"

"I don't know." He drew in his breath sharply as he plucked one of the brands from between the rocks and held it to the floor several feet ahead of her. "Did you see *this*?"

She gasped. Cut into the floor was a larger version of the knife's crest. Now she could see that the man on the horse wore mail, as did the horse. The smaller man, who led the horse, did not.

He bent and traced a line that went from the man in front

of the horse to the one riding it. "What is this? A quarter-staff?"

"Or a rein?"

Disgust twisted his mouth. "That suggests too many terrible things."

"Like the Brotherhood wishes to put the rest of the world under its control, holding the leash on everyone?"

"Yes." He stood. "You need to get out of here immediately."

"Why?"

He grimaced again. "I assume it would be worthless to say—as I tried before—that a woman's place is not in a dank tunnel where she is tempting death."

"You assume correctly."

"And if I were to suggest that, you would tell me that if I am leery of what lurks here, *I* should take my leave."

"That is also a good assumption."

He held out his hand. "I should have said that we both should leave here right away."

"Just a minute."

"Isabella . . ."

She paid no attention to his impatience as she bent to peer at the symbol. "Hold the brand a bit to the right so I can make out the words carved beneath it."

"It probably says you would be a fool to linger." He grasped her arm. "Just as Ryce was when he got involved with the Brotherhood. I will not lose you to them, too."

"Do you think he was a member?" she asked as she went with him to where the walls slanted toward each other again.

"No."

"You sound so sure."

"If you had known Ryce, you would be certain, too. He lived his life with as few obligations as possible."

"Save to you."

He nodded. "Now you understand why *I* had to arrange for his burial."

"I have understood that all along." She ducked as the tunnel's ceiling dropped lower. "But it is curious how the knife got into his grave and why someone wanted it enough to kill himself when he failed to obtain it."

"There are too many unanswered questions about the Brotherhood." He looked back at her. "The most important question now is how we get out of here."

When the tunnel ended in a narrow staircase, Isabella saw the steps marched up in uniform order. She wondered how long ago they had been cut into the earth.

Jordan relit the lamp as he put his foot on the first step. "Stay close, Isabella."

"Finally! An order I am happy to follow." She tried to laugh, but the sound fell flat, deflated by the unease boiling within her. It had strengthened as they had passed the carving in the floor. Had the carving been a warning to turn back?

"There are not many steps."

She nodded, but he could not have seen because he was already climbing the stairs. Hurrying to follow, she was assaulted by odors flowing down to her: the reek of water that had sat for too long, murky and isolated.

Stronger than the smell was a miasma that could not be seen or felt or tasted or smelled.

Evil.

Torment.

Pain.

With a gasp, she pushed past Jordan and put her hand out, blocking his way.

"What is it?" he whispered.

"I—I—I don't know." She lowered her arm to her side. Every instinct warned they needed to take care, for something more horrible than anything they had already seen waited at the top of the stairs.

"Did you see something?"

"No," she had to admit.

"Hear some—"

"Nothing!" She started to face him, then halted. Turning her back on whatever was above would be stupid. It might leap from the shadows and swallow her in a single gulp.

"Isabella, what is it? You look as pale as a corpse."

Knowing how foolish she sounded, she said, "There is something awful up there. Not a beast or a person, but something that lingers there, waiting for its chance to consume the unwary."

"That sounds like an old tale to scare naughty children."

"I have never felt like this. It is like having some invisible creature crawling along my flesh, leaving a trail of slime that burns with fear."

He stepped up beside her and put his arm around her shoulders. She leaned against him, glad for his strong arms.

"We can go in together," he said. "I doubt there is much that can withstand us both."

She was tempted to say that whatever waited within the cavern had a power that could overwhelm them so quickly that they would be dead before their next heartbeat. She remained silent. She had to hope whatever it was would flee the light.

The cavern was twice the size of the cave below. The roof was far above her head near the doorway, but lowered toward the far wall. The rough walls were striated with color that came alive in the light. The floor was smooth, as if a river used to run through the cavern.

"Better?" asked Jordan.

She smiled ruefully. "I appreciate you not telling me how silly I was."

"Don't be so sure that there is nothing here because you cannot see it." He swept his torch back and forth to send light flowing in the very back of the cavern. The squeak of rats was followed by the skitter of small feet.

"I was not talking about rats."

"Neither was I. The way to hell is below the ground."

"Hell?" She shivered. "I hope Satan is not responsible for anything here."

They went into another tunnel. Like the cavern, the walls were rough. Sharp points of stone were as numerous as briars in a thicket. They jabbed her as she tried to weave a path through them. The tunnel led steeply uphill, and she wondered how close they were to the surface. She slowed when she saw something against the wall. A ladder!

"Jordan?"

"I see it. Wait while I go up." He shoved the brand into her hand and went up the ladder.

It had more rungs than the one from Lady Odette's chamber. When he reached the top, she stepped back to give him light to search for a handle to open it. If he could not find one, they would have to continue on.

He came down the ladder. He put his finger to his lips when she started to speak.

Motioning for her to follow him along the tunnel, he leaned toward her and whispered, "I heard voices from people above us."

"Could you hear what they were saying?"

"From what I could discern, they were discussing what they planned to serve for the master of the house's dinner."

"They? Women or men?"

"Women, I think, but the stone muffled their words and distorted their voices, so I cannot be sure."

She sat and set the lamp by her feet. "Do you think they know there is a tunnel beneath them?"

"They will know if we pop up through the trapdoor."

A slight smile eased her taut lips before she said, "So we have to keep going."

Stroking her face gently, he said, "Or we can go back."

"We have not reached the end yet. We can decide what to do when we get there."

He smiled as she stood. Taking the brand, he turned to continue up the tunnel. She glanced at the ladder and sighed. She should have guessed it would not be simple.

The tunnel twisted like a snake. To avoid the cellars of those who did not belong to the Brotherhood or because the rock was too difficult to cut through? Maybe it was for another reason altogether.

Her lamp flickered. "Jordan, it is going out!"

He glanced over his shoulder and held the brand higher. He suddenly yelped. He tossed his brand toward her. His sword clattered on the floor. Waving his arms wildly, he tried to throw his weight on his rear foot. He wobbled forward . . . and down into a hole.

Dropping the lamp, she grasped his arm and sat. She tried to pull him toward her, but she slid on the smooth floor. Jamming one foot against the wall, she kept herself from being dragged forward. He grabbed her arm with his other hand. She winced as her shoulder flared with pain. She gritted her teeth as she shoved her other foot against the wall and tried to edge backward.

She could not move.

She had to try something else. She drew her feet up under her and rose to a squat. Pain shot down her legs as she used her body as a lever to pull him away from the hole. Slowly, so slowly she would have sworn that time had stopped, she was able to move away from the hole.

Stones clattered into what sounded like a bottomless abyss as he pushed against the edge of the pit. Every muscle protested while she kept making slow, painful steps. Then he released her arm. She fell and called his name.

"Hush, Isabella," he said as he crawled to where she was lying. "I am alive, thanks to you."

She threw her arms around him and pulled him down to her for a kiss that she hoped would say all she could not. He slipped an arm under her, cradling her close.

The light fluttered again and dimmed. She sat and stared at the lamp. She should have brought more than one. Picking up the brand, which still burned, she held it out so she could look into the hole. There must have been a bottom, but she could not see it.

Jordan pushed himself up to stand and cursed when his knees wobbled. If Isabella had not been so quick, he would be dead now. Reeling toward her, he picked up his sword and shoved it into its scabbard. "Thank you, Isabella. I owe you my life . . . again."

He was not surprised when she pretended not to hear him. She was not comfortable with gratitude for something she believed anyone would have done. He had to wonder about what life was like at St. Jude's Abbey to persuade her to think as she did.

"What sort of people," she asked, "build a tunnel and fail to fill in a hole in the floor?"

"People who want to make sure nobody enters without the key to traversing the tunnel from one end to the other."

"What is the Brotherhood trying to hide?"

"That is a question too dangerous to ask."

"Not too dangerous to ask, but maybe too dangerous to answer." She uncoiled her whip and snapped it across the hole in the floor.

"What are you doing?"

"Hoping to find something to snag, so we can get across."

"In the dark?"

She handed him the brand. "Hold it up to give me as much light as you can."

He did and watched as she sent the whip flying at a large chunk of stone. She struck it several times, but each time, the whip uncoiled from around the stone when she gave it a tug. Long after he would have given up, deciding it was hopeless, she wrapped the end of the whip around the stone again, and this time when she pulled on it, the whip remained in place.

When she took a step back to gain momentum to swing across the hole, he halted her.

"Me first," he said.

"But, Jordan—"

He silenced her protest with a kiss that made his knees weak again. She felt the same, he knew, because her fingers gripped the front of his tunic. Gazing into her eyes, he whispered, "I am going first, Isabella. If something happens, go back up to d'Alpin's house."

"Don't talk like that."

"Promise me you will."

"I will not make that promise." She gripped his arm. "I will—"

"You must fulfill your obligation to the queen. You cannot do that if you die here."

Her shoulders dropped, and she nodded. Lifting her hand off his arm, she held out the whip's handle.

He took it and gave her the brand. Turning to look across the pit, he hoped there was not another hidden trap on the far side. He launched himself into the air. He landed with a thud that echoed in both directions along the tunnel. He sent the whip skimming over the hole back to her.

When she caught it, he held up his hand. "Toss the brand across, Isabella."

The fire on the brand whooshed as it flew to his side. He picked it up and held it high again. He watched, not daring to breathe, as she swung toward him. She was almost to him when he heard a *crack*. Small pebbles rained down.

He jumped forward, dropping the brand again, as he grabbed the long drapes of fabric falling from her sleeves. Threads snapped, but he did not release her as he threw himself backward. She tumbled to the ground beside him. With a cry, she snapped the whip sharply just before the rock it had been wrapped around crashed to the floor between them and the hole.

"Are you all right?" he asked.

"I will need to get more parsley leaves to ease all our bruises." She wound the whip and hooked it to her belt again. Rubbing her elbow gently, she stood.

He got to his feet, too, and grimaced as he grabbed the sputtering brand. It would not last much longer. Taking Isabella's hand, he continued along the tunnel. He watched every step because he doubted the pit was the only trap the Brotherhood had set.

When the tunnel opened into yet another chamber, he was not surprised to see the Brotherhood's emblem cut into the floor. He heard Isabella draw in a sharp breath at the same instant he saw a flash of light.

"We have to look for another tunnel," she whispered so lowly he could hardly hear her.

"How can you be so certain there is one?"

She gave him a scowl that reminded him of Lew's when he made some comment unworthy of an earl. "Whoever built these tunnels must have ways to get out if one section collapses."

Taking her hand, he ran with her toward a darker spot on the wall. A tunnel? He cursed silently. It was a pool. Looking over his shoulder, he doused the brand in it. He stepped into the frigid water, taking care not to splash. She did the same. Hunkering down, he shifted her between him and the wall. In the darkness, he hoped nobody would notice them. His tunic was dark, as was his hair. With her golden strands hidden behind him, there should be nothing to catch the light.

Footfalls resonated through the cavern. He tried to gauge how close they were. Concentrating on them was grueling when her rapid, shallow breaths caressed him.

Two men. He could tell by their different voices. As they came closer, he heard them laughing together like good friends. The empty space deformed their words so he could not understand one.

"Who are they?" Isabella whispered.

"I don't know."

"Can you look?"

"No."

As the men came nearer, he held his breath. How long would it take them to pass by? If they went down the tunnel, they would see the trap had been triggered. Maybe they would believe the intruder had been lost in the pit.

The voices vanished into the distance. He risked a glance over his shoulder and saw light glowing out of a tunnel he had not noticed. It was on the opposite side of the cavern from the one he and Isabella had used.

He waited until the light was almost gone, then stepped out of the pool. His feet moved awkwardly, frozen by the icy water. Helping Isabella out, he knew her soaked skirt must be a weight against her legs.

"We have to go into the tunnel they came out of," he said as he hurried her across the cavern while they still could see.

"In the dark?"

"Let's hope we find another torch." He glanced back. The light was growing dimmer.

"If they discover that we have found the tunnel, the Brotherhood will not be willing to let us wander about with that knowledge."

"Only if they are certain we are the ones who breached their secret maze."

"If we confront them across bare blades, they will be." She took his hand as they entered the tunnel. "Put your hand against the other wall, and we will follow it as long as we can."

"As long as there are no other traps. God's blood, we were so close. One of those men might know why the knife was in Ryce's grave."

"I know."

He heard her sorrow, and he wanted to apologize. How had he shifted his grief onto her shoulders along with the obligation of discovering why Ryce had died? He had agreed to help her, but not for such a price.

"How have you come to know me so well," he asked, "when I have told you so little?"

"There are many ways of telling. When I began my studies, I discovered if one observed with all the senses, it was possible to learn amazing things."

"Once we are out of this accursed tunnel, I shall have to let you tell me all you have learned about me. It should be . . ."

Was that light ahead of them? He blinked several times, but the light remained. It was no illusion.

"Do you see it?" she asked.

"Yes. It is—Isabella!"

He knocked her to the floor. Something struck the wall to her left. Splinters of stone exploded, and she moaned. In the dim light, he saw blood blossom on her left hand.

"Isabella?"

"I am all right. Just a small cut." She edged over onto her side and looked at him. "How are you?"

"Unharmed this time." He came to his feet and ran his hand along a stone that hung on a thick chain.

"Look at the wall. We are not the first to pass this way and trigger the death trap."

He peered at the limestone. The variegated strands of color were not simply elements. Some, rusty and scattered, could be dried blood. Bile filled his mouth, and he looked away.

"We have to go," she said urgently. "If someone heard . . ."

Taking her right hand, he hurried her forward. He hoped they were not walking into another trap, but going back was impossible.

Beneath his feet, the floor changed from raw stone to pieces cut and mortared together. No one was in a large round room when they entered. Overhead, the rock had been engraved with the Brotherhood's crest.

"Chains," Isabella said with a groan. She wrapped her arms around herself. "Chains and axes and knives."

Jordan looked around the room and saw more blood-stains. "For torture."

"You did not need to confirm what I was thinking." She tried to smile, but her lips quivered. "Who are these people?"

Going to a table where a huge book was open, he scanned the pages. "God's blood!"

"What is it?"

"Look at this." He ran his finger along the letters that were written in red. He hoped it was red *ink*. "They are vowed to keep England safe, and to that end, they hope to keep Richard from becoming king. They believe he will ruin England by constant war. They pledge to see John become the next king."

"But the only way that can happen is if Richard is dead."

He pushed away from the table. "Murder does not seem to bother them." He put his arm around her shoulders. "If I don't make it out, go to the cathedral. Even the Brotherhood has to respect sanctuary."

"I am not so sure of that." She lifted her whip off her hip again.

He drew his sword as he led her toward a doorway. Stairs led up, and he did not hesitate. The curved steps revealed they were in a tower. He heard Isabella gasp when they entered a room with arrow slits, but he had already guessed they were in the castle.

Ahead of them was a ladder leading up to ground level. They would have to climb it and find a way to slip out of the tower undetected. Someone high-ranking in the castle must have arranged for the tunnels to be connected to this tower. If he and Isabella were discovered here, they would be slaughtered after being tortured.

He paused at the bottom of the ladder. When she laughed softly, he could not keep from staring at her.

"I am not mad," she said through her chuckles.

"But what can you find amusing about our situation?"

"You."

"Me?" How many more ways could this woman astonish him?

"You cannot decide whether to go first up the ladder, in case there is someone at the top, or if you should let me lead the way because you are uncertain if we have been followed." Her humor vanished as she put her hands on his arms. "Whatever happens, we shall face it together."

He drew his arms from beneath her palms and, sweeping his arm around her waist, drew her against him. "Let me go first, Isabella. You will have warning if someone is coming through the tunnel."

Climbing up the ladder quickly, he stood at the top as she hurried after him. He went to the door of the small circular room and looked out.

"There are several people nearby and more in the ward," he said.

"Follow my lead."

Before he could ask her what she meant, she coiled her whip, hooking it to her belt as she eased out the door and knelt. Had she lost her mind in the dark tunnels?

As he stepped out of the tower, ready to defend her, she stood and shoved a handful of greenery at him. He caught it before it could fall to the ground.

When she walked away toward a spot farther along the

wall, she called, "Hurry! I need more alehoof if I am to help cure the stomachaches along Ermine Street. Evil humors are spreading from one house to the next very fast."

A man, carrying a bare sword, rushed toward them. "What are you doing?"

"Stay back! I am trying to stop half the city from becoming ill," she shouted. Raising her hands as if supplicating heaven to heed her, she continued in the same loud voice, "You need to get inside and close your shutters. Evil humors are abroad and hunting for victims." She waved the guard away. "Evil humors have attacked me, too. If I touch you, they will swarm over you."

The man turned gray, and he backpedaled for several steps before turning and running. He shouted Isabella's instructions to his comrades. They glanced at Isabella digging frantically into the weeds; then they fled, too. She gathered a few more handfuls before she stood.

Jordan was able to hold back his laughter until they went through the gate and onto Ermine Street. "Did you learn to lie like that at my aunt's abbey, too?"

"The abbess prefers we tell the truth." She tossed the weeds onto the street where the first strong rain would send them down toward the market. Pausing, she glanced at the towers of the cathedral, and her smile faded away. "I truthfully hope the canon has sent a message that he has found the brass casket."

Her words struck him like a blow, and his exhilaration at discovering the truth about the Brotherhood drained away. If the casket was not recovered, the Brotherhood might be saved the trouble of killing Richard. The prince could die in another insurrection, an insurrection leaving England in ruins and easy prey for the Brotherhood.

Chapter 20

Isabella stood in the middle of the cathedral's nave and wondered what the abbess would think of her plan. She knew Jordan would not like it, but what choice did she have? Earlier, even before the sun had risen on Palm Sunday morning, one of the brothers had delivered a message from the canon. He had seemed not quite sure if she could read it, even when she said she could, so he had read it aloud.

> *Dear Lady Isabella,*
>
> *It is with great regret that I must inform you that, despite every effort, we have been unable to locate the brass casket you described.*

It was signed with Canon Anthony's name.

"The casket has to be here," Isabella said as she looked at Jordan. He had explained his bruises—and hers—to the Weirtons as the result of trying to keep a thief from stealing Isabella's healing stones. "The canon said the bishop kept important items either in his house or here in the cathedral."

"He may not have known the casket was important."

She gave him a wry grin. "If the queen gave something to you to keep safe, wouldn't you consider it important?"

"Yes, and I have tried." He traced her lips with his thumb.

She slanted toward him, then reminded herself why they were in the nave. "Jordan, can you keep people away?" She unlooped her whip and looked at an arch connected to the outer wall. "If I get up there, I will have a view of the whole cathedral."

"Up there? Have you lost your mind?"

"It is possible, but it is also possible that it may be the most enlightened idea since the beginning of time."

His hand screened his eyes from the light coming through the windows set above the arch. "No, it seems more likely that you have lost your mind."

"I must try, Jordan. You cannot be protective of me because we are . . ." She glanced around the cathedral and lowered her voice further. "Because we are lovers."

"You are asking the impossible."

"Something I learned from your aunt." She moved closer to the arch. "Anyone?"

"No . . . Wait!" He motioned for her to hide the whip.

Wrapping it around her waist, she concealed the handle within the heavy folds of her gown seconds before a monk appeared out of the shadows. She bid the brother a good day, locking her hands over the leather braid around her. Neither she nor Jordan spoke as the brother walked out a door.

"Anyone else?" she asked.

He grabbed her and kissed her deeply.

"Stop," she pleaded. "I must concentrate on what I have to do. If I think about being in your arms, I may fall."

"I will catch you."

She stepped away and looked at the top of the arch. "Trying to catch someone plummeting from that height would be dangerous."

"I know I cannot talk you out of this, so be careful, Isabella."

Pulling off the whip, she sent its end up toward the arch. The leather wrapped around a carved head. She gave it a tug and smiled. It was much easier when she could see. As she had practiced over and over at the Abbey, she climbed the whip.

She swung her leg over the arch. Grasping the petals of a flower carved into its side, she clambered onto the narrow stone ledge. A flick of her wrist loosened the whip. She pulled it up and out of sight from the floor.

Scanning the cathedral below, she watched people come and go on their private errands. Everything looked just as it should.

There had to be something she was missing. There had to be! But what was it? She did not want to climb down and admit to Jordan that she had failed. Worse, she could not imagine telling the queen that she had failed.

"Lord le Courtenay, I did not expect to see you here at this hour of the morning." Canon Anthony's voice boomed. "I was so sorry we could not find what Lady Isabella sought. Such disappointing tidings on Palm Sunday."

She pressed against the top of the arch. Canon Anthony must not suspect why Jordan was loitering by the wall.

"She understands that you have done your best," Jordan replied. "I thought I would come and express my gratitude that the worst of winter has left us."

"And with it Holy Week. If you will excuse me, I need to check on preparations for the next Mass."

Isabella shifted to watch the canon stride toward the choir. He looked small in front of the carved screen and the beautiful benches with their misericords. The wooden creatures on the screen seemed to be watching him, too.

She gripped the stone arch as she stared, unwilling to believe what her eyes were showing her. All the heads on the screen were looking toward the floor of the choir. It could not be a coincidence. They must have been carved that way for a reason. Were they guarding a secret cache, a cache known only to the bishop?

Wrapping the whip around the arch again, she slid down it so quickly she scorched her hands. Flapping her fingers to cool them, she said, "I think I know where the casket is."

Jordan grinned. "Where?"

"Come with me." She grabbed his hand, not caring that hers hurt. She forced her feet to a stroll, even though she wanted to run the length of the nave. Kneeling in the choir, she lifted a choir bench to reveal its misericords. Carved flowers were set on either side of a man wrestling a bull. Both looked toward the floor.

"It is a misericord," he said impatiently. "You explained what they were before."

She lifted the wooden seats on either side. One showed the angel and the baby. The other was decorated with a lion holding its own tail in its mouth. "See?"

"See what?"

"See what they have in common with all the carvings on the screen!"

"They all—" His low whistle of astonishment echoed oddly through the cathedral's high ceilings. "They are looking toward the floor."

"Or what is beneath it." She dropped to her knees and ran her fingers across the stones. "Maybe Lord d'Alpin's house is not the only one with something hidden beneath its floor." Drawing her dagger, she dug its tip between two stones.

He put his hand on hers. "Isabella, you don't know which stones might cover the hiding place, if there is one. You cannot pull them all up."

"The canon might notice."

"He might when the choir tripped during the next service." He squatted next to her and ran his hands along the stones.

"What are you doing?"

"In my dream after I drank your potion, you showed me how stones can have a different temperature based on what is behind them." He smiled as his hand paused over two closely set stones. "These are cooler than the rest. There may be a space beneath them."

"I told you that in your dream?"

He cupped her chin. "Everything else in my dream has come to pass. Why not this?"

"Why not?" She handed him Ryce's knife. "Use this for a good purpose now."

"Ryce would have liked that." He jammed the knife into the narrow crack between the two stones, but withdrew it when chanting came from around them. "It is the beginning of a service."

She grimaced. "'Tis another sign of our ongoing misfortune that we had this epiphany on Palm Sunday."

"We can come back tomorrow when the cathedral will be less crowded." Standing, he put the knife in his belt. "It will be waiting for us, Isabella."

"I hope you are right."

Jordan sat on a chair in the main room of Lord d'Alpin's house. On the only other chair, Lady Odette waited for him to reply to her latest question. He wished he knew what she had asked. His mind was not on her or the topic of a gathering once Lent was past.

Where was Isabella? She had not said where she was going. Since their sojourn beneath the hill in the strange tunnels, he had kept close to her. She would not have returned to the cathedral because they needed to work as a team: one to dig out the casket, the other to keep watch so they were not seen.

"Milord . . ." Lady Odette gave him a scintillating smile. "Jordan, if I may."

"I am honored to have you use my given name, milady." He would have agreed to almost anything to put a polite end to their conversation.

"May I ask of you a great boon?"

He looked at Lady Odette. "Of course, milady."

"Tell me about yourself."

He cursed silently. If he was witless enough to let her trap him, he deserved having to sit with her instead of discovering where Isabella was. He opened his mouth to answer.

The house shook. Sound like the loudest thunderclap slammed into his ears. Lady Odette's mouth was wide open, and he assumed she was screaming, but he could not hear her cries as the house shuddered again. A flash of fire erupted beyond one of the windows.

Eruption! Isabella!

Running, Jordan shoved aside servants paralyzed with fear. He tore open the back door. The odor of sulfur struck him as he saw a small circle of fire. The horses were rearing with fright in the stable, and several more servants were cringing against the building.

In the middle of it all stood Isabella with a glorious smile.

He raced to her and pulled her back from the flames. Kicking dirt in the direction of the fire, he was not surprised when she pulled herself away.

"Stay back!" he shouted when she ran *toward* the blazing pile of whatever it was.

She paid no attention to his warning. He started to give chase, then, through the thickening smoke, saw her pick up a bucket and pour water over the fire. It hissed, then surrendered in a light gray billow of smoke.

"I did it!" she cried as she flung her arms around him. "I did it *again*!"

"Your controlled explosion?"

"Yes!"

He swung her around. As he set her on her feet, he framed her face with his hands and leaned forward to kiss her. He halted when he heard the door slam behind him.

"What is happening out here?" Lady Odette stormed into the yard, her nose wrinkling. "It stinks."

"There was an accident," Jordan replied. "Fortunately no one was hurt, but everyone was scared."

"What kind of accident causes such noise?" She put her hand to her head. "My ears are ringing as if the cathedral's bells were in them."

Isabella went to her. "Come. We will get some fresh bread and grind it fine. Once we heat it and put it against your ears, the ringing will ease."

"You reek, too!" Lady Odette snarled.

"As you will, if you linger here, milady. Let us get you inside and tend to your ears before the ringing becomes permanent." She steered the lady into the house. She paused in the doorway and smiled at him. He did not think he had ever seen her so happy, except when she was in his arms in her bed. He hoped they would find the casket on the morrow, because he wanted to see her that happy again.

*   *   *

*   *   *

Isabella yawned as she opened the door to her bedchamber. The room was dark because she had spent hours by Lady Odette's bedside, soothing her. As she entered, she saw Jordan sitting on the windowsill. He crossed the room and drew her into his arms.

"How is Lady Odette?" he asked.

"According to me or to her?" She laughed. "She is fine."

"And you?"

"I did it, Jordan! I proved the experiment worked by repeating it. I needed to have equal amounts of charcoal and sulfur and almost twice as much saltpeter. It works. It really works."

"Now you can teach the formula to others."

She sat on the bed and drew off her shoes. "I am not sure that is wise. It can create very powerful explosions."

"My aunt will help you decide what to do."

"Yes." She was glad the room was dark so he did not see her expression as he sat beside her and kissed her neck. She loved him. Did he love her? If he did, why did he keep acting as if she were going back to St. Jude's Abbey while he returned to La Tour?

As he drew her down into the bed, she wished she could push that thought aside as easily as he did her clothes. She wanted to celebrate tonight and again tomorrow when they found the queen's small casket beneath the choir floor.

"Isabella?" he asked, puzzled. "What is bothering you?"

Knowing she had been too distant while lost in her sad thoughts, she smiled. "I still have so much to learn about being with you."

"Then let me give you another lesson." His raffish smile enthralled her as he whispered, "Or two."

"Or maybe I can teach you something." She let his teasing lure her out of her doldrums.

"You?"

"I have a few experiments I would like to try with you."

"Didn't you tell me that no experiment is valid until you recreate it at least once more?"

"Yes."

"Or maybe more?"

"Yes."

"Then let us get started on your experiment, sweet one."

With a laugh, she straddled his chest, sliding down his firm torso until she could lean forward to press her mouth to his. He moaned as she shifted to run her tongue along his ear. Against the inside of her thighs, his sides pulsed with his rapid breaths. His heart thudded beneath her breasts as his sweaty sheen heated her skin.

She wanted him and she wanted to enjoy being with him. She would savor every minute . . . while they could be together. As she spiraled with him into ecstasy, she could not help wondering how long it would be until she had to tell him farewell.

Chapter 21

The bells in the cathedral towers welcomed the morning,
mixing in with shouts from peddlers and cries of fishwives.
Wagons rattled along the street, bouncing on the cobbles, as
the horses strained to climb Ermine Street.

Isabella stepped onto the street, jumping aside as a small
keg that had escaped from a dray rolled past. She listened to
the day's sounds. Something was not right.

When her hair was drawn to one side, warm lips brushed
her nape. She stretched her arms behind her and pressed
back to Jordan's firm chest. *That* was not what was wrong.

"Where is your smile this morning, sweet one?" he
asked. "You have achieved what you had begun to think was
impossible. You— Good morning, Weirton."

Isabella stiffened at the baron's name, but as he greeted
them jauntily, she knew he was not what was wrong either.
Maybe the odd feeling she had had in the cavern still haunted
her. There had turned out to be no reason for her alarm then,
so why was she giving the same feeling any credence now?

"Where are you off to on such a glorious morn?" asked
Lord Weirton.

"The cathedral." She saw no reason to lie because, if the
baron truly wanted to know where they were bound, he
could watch where they went. "And you?"

"Down the hill and back up," he replied with a smile. "I
am meeting some friends." He looked at Jordan. "As I have
told you, my friends are eager to meet you, le Courtenay.

Why not come with me while Lady Isabella enjoys her prayers?"

Jordan was torn. She could tell by how he hesitated. He was tempted to go with Lord Weirton, hoping to learn more about the Brotherhood and Ryce's connection to them. She was about to tell him to go when he said, "Some other time, Weirton. I promised Isabella that I would go with her this morning."

"And a promise to a lady should never be broken, even when my friends are growing impatient." He laughed and slapped Jordan on the shoulder, but she saw the banked irritation in his eyes when he glanced at her.

"He is determined for you to meet his friends," Isabella said as soon as Lord Weirton was out of earshot.

"I would rather not."

"But—"

"Let's find what we came to Lincoln to get, and we can leave the Weirtons behind."

She smiled as he offered his hand. "That is the best idea I have heard today."

"It is early." He gave an earthy laugh. "I plan to have an even better idea for you later."

"I look forward to it."

He arched his brows. "So do I."

As they climbed the hill toward the cathedral, Isabella wished Jordan would keep jesting. The heavy feeling of something wrong slowed her steps.

"Did you notice," he asked, "there are no birds singing?"

Her eyes widened as she paused. He was right. The usual sounds of people moving through the city were not woven through by birdsong. "At this hour, there should be birds everywhere."

"You study nature, Isabella. Do you know why the birds would abruptly disappear?"

"I have no idea." She looked over the lower section of the city spread along the river below them. The streets were busy with people going about their business as they would any Monday. With Easter on Sunday, everyone wanted to be prepared for the festivities that accompanied the religious celebration.

"Look at that!" Jordan pointed to a leashed dog by a house. The dog whined, and its tail was between its rear legs.

Going to it, she tried to soothe it. The dog howled and shivered. Was it being hurt by the leash? She untied the rope, and it fled down the hill.

"That is bizarre," he said.

"Yes." Slowly she stood. "Before you ask, I have no idea why it acted like that."

"You could have been bitten."

She put her arms around his shoulders. "I leave that to you."

With a grin, he tweaked her nose. "Such salacious words from the daughter of a nun."

She stepped away and held out her hand. "As soon as we find what we seek and take it to the queen, I want us to discover if my mother is still alive and where she is." When he did not take her hand, she asked, "What is wrong?"

"I did not realize you expected me to help you with that quest as well."

She slowly lowered her arm to her side. "Oh." She did not know what else to say. It was true that Jordan had never spoken of a time after they delivered the pages to the queen, but she had foolishly assumed that he wanted her to remain in his life. Tears burned in her eyes. Did he wish to return to his life that was filled with no emotion—no joy, no grief, no excitement, no anger? A life where nothing was asked of him, so he had to give nothing?

Walking up the steep street, she knew he would follow to help her locate the cache where the letters were hidden. Such a vow he would never break.

Isabella entered the cathedral. Before she could step through the inner doors into the nave, Jordan stepped in front of her. He took her hands and drew her to one side of the nave.

As people came in and out of the church, he said, "You did not give me a chance to say anything."

"Your face said it all. You intend to do no more than you pledged—help me find the casket and take it to Queen Eleanor to prevent another insurrection." She lifted her fingers out of his grip. "And you are right. You never promised me anything else."

"You know it is more than that. I have been away from La Tour for too long. I need to supervise the updating of its walls and defenses. If war comes to La Tour, the castle needs to be ready."

"Is that all you can think of? War?"

"Isn't that why we are in Lincoln? To halt a war?"

She could not argue with that, and she did not want to argue about anything else. He was being reasonable, just as she usually was, but when her heart was involved, logic seemed worthless.

"I do understand, Jordan. I—" She gasped as a rumble exploded around them.

He frowned. "Are you experimenting with more of that sulfur and saltpeter powder?"

"No!"

"If someone else has ignited it . . ."

She shouted over the rumble and the sound of people yelling in fear. "I did not leave any of it out."

She grabbed his arm as the sound grew louder. It was as if every beast in the city were growling. Overhead, the circle of candles rocked as if the cathedral had set sail. The noise deepened as the floor moved beneath her feet. Had the gates of hell opened to spew forth disaster?

She looked up as the chains on the lamp creaked a warning. Tugging on Jordan's arm, she ran toward the west entrance. Something was wrong with the building. It was shaking like someone suffering with a fever.

As she stepped into the entry, he caught her by the shoulders and twisted her to face him. His mouth moved, but she could not hear what he was saying. She looked past him and saw one of the bolts holding the circle of candles to the vaulted ceiling break. The brass ring swung out, striking the wall. Glass burst out of a window and fell in a dangerous shower.

"We have to get out!" She could not be sure he heard her scream, so she seized his arm and pulled again. "Now, Jordan!"

She reached for the door between the two great towers. Suddenly the floor moved beneath them again, this time more violently. She was thrown away from Jordan. Fighting the floor that moved like a slithering snake, she leaped forward to clasp on to his arm again. She heard stones groan as they struggled to remain in place.

"We need to get out!" she cried, trying to stand.

He pulled her to him and pushed her to the floor. When she shouted again, he shook his head. The door had burst open. Giant chunks of rock were raining down onto the yard. A monk ran to escape the stone, disappearing in the thickening cloud of dust.

She uttered a desperate prayer when she looked behind them as Jordan motioned for her to go with him into the cathedral. The giant brass circle dropped to the floor along with a section of the roof. Chairs and several people were crushed beneath the cascade of stone.

Rising as far as her knees, because the floor was too unsteady for her to stand, she caught flailing hands, pulling fleeing priests, monks, and worshipers into the small haven. A shower of dirt and cobwebs fell from overhead. Within the nave, the floor rippled as if the stone had transformed into sea waves.

The arches supporting the roof crumbled. More stone crashed to the floor or struck the wall. Glass burst from windows. The font fell over and rolled toward a woman who was fighting to escape the nave.

Isabella yanked her whip off her belt. Sweeping it out, she aimed toward the woman. The woman tried to catch it. Isabella pulled it back and snapped it again, this time wrapping it around the woman's arm. With a tug, Isabella gave her the unspoken message to use the whip as a guide through the suffocating dust.

The woman stumbled forward, and Jordan rushed out to help her the last few steps. Isabella reeled in her whip, leading them to safety. When the woman dropped to the floor and wept hysterically, Isabella drew back the whip to send it again into the maelstrom of stone and glass and splinters.

"No!" she shouted, but the sound did not reach her own ears when the rest of the roof fell. The floor shattered beneath the giant pieces of stone. Dust struck her with dozens of tiny blows.

Flinging out her whip again, she could not see where it went into dirt and pebbles erupting in every direction. She gave it a slight tug, hoping someone could see it and follow it.

"Isabella! Where are you?"

She gasped when she realized she could hear Jordan's shout. The floor beneath her knees was once again motionless. Above her head, the bells clanged in the tower. The motion of the earth had rung them.

Throwing herself into his arms, she cried, "Are you hurt?"

"No. You?"

"No."

"What happened?"

She drew back enough so she could stroke his dust-covered face. "It is called an earthquake."

"It felt like the wrath of God."

She was about to agree, then heard a scream. She ran to where she could see a woman pointing to hands reaching from the rubble. Her stomach lurched with horror, and she started to turn away; then she saw the fingers move. She knelt to try to see under the slab of stone. Was it possible someone was alive under it?

Gripping one hand, she called, "Squeeze my fingers if you can."

The hand tightened around hers until she wanted to cry

out in both excitement and pain. A mumble eased out from
beneath the stone. "Don't leave me."

"I am going to pull you out. If you can push free, do!"

She heard no answer as more rock came down atop the
rubble. Smoke erupted up in a dozen places. Fires must be
burning beneath the stones. Anyone who was imprisoned
beneath the debris could burn to death before they were rescued. A moan escaped from her own lips when the fingers
compressed hers even more, but a deeper pain came from
her heart.

"Isabella, are you sure you are not hurt?" Jordan knelt beside her.

"I am all right."

"We need to get out of here. The rest of the walls may
come down at any minute."

She motioned with her head toward the hands. "There is
someone under the slab. I need help to get him out."

He put his hands between hers and tugged.

"Not too hard," she said through clenched teeth. "Whoever is under there may be hurt, and there must be others still
alive beneath the fallen roof. We have to find them and get
them out while we can."

"You are the healer. You tell us what to do."

Us? She glanced over her shoulder to more people behind
them. Everyone was coated with the gray dust that crunched
between her teeth with each word she spoke.

"Draw him out with care," she said, releasing the hands.
She stood. "Look and listen for survivors. Don't move any
stones without checking that no others are leaning on them.
There must be more people alive in the cathedral. We have
to find them. If you see the cloister's healer, let him know I
am here to help."

The people scattered to explore the edges of the destruction. Other voices came from every direction, and her orders
were repeated to anyone who came near.

Bending, she watched as Jordan slowly pulled on the
hands. She heard soft groans as a man appeared from beneath the broken stone. The man was covered with the

crushed stone, so she could not guess how old he was. His
right arm hung limply, dragging across the floor. Jordan
found two broken pieces of wood, and, tearing a piece from
the man's own tunic, they set and immobilized his arm.

"Milady?" asked a trembling voice behind her.

She looked up to see an elderly monk. The side of his
face was scraped, and his few remaining wisps of hair were
thick with dust. "Yes?"

"I am Brother James, the healer."

"Is your stillroom still standing?"

"Yes."

"Thank heavens," she breathed as she came to her feet.

"What do you need, milady?"

She recited the ingredients she always had at hand at St.
Jude's Abbey. "Broom flowers, water fleur-de-lys, red nettle
roots, hemlock, primrose, eryngo leaves, plantain leaves,
anise, cumin, fennel, carui, and unsalted butter."

"I understand. That is a pain ointment that works for
many injuries."

She smiled. "We will need splints for broken bones, and
clean thread and needles to sew wounds. While you boil all
the herbs and mix them with the butter, please also break up
some poppyheads and stir them into wine. That will bring
sleep to those who are in pain and who suffer from shock."

Pausing only long enough to tell Jordan she was going
with the monk to set up care for the injured, she nodded
when he said he was joining a search party. She wanted to
tell him to be careful, but knew he would do whatever he
must to save lives.

Isabella needed all the skills she had learned at St. Jude's
Abbey as the morning became afternoon. Smoke hung in the
air, and she knew the cathedral was not the only building
burning. She had taken one glance at the city below and seen
the plumes of black rising. Was anyone alive to douse the
flames? If not, the whole city within the walls could burn.

Brother James helped as she outlined where to put the pa-
tients and how to decide which ones needed to be seen first
and which ones could not be helped. She heard the mumble

of last rites coming from every direction across the yard at the west front. People came from the broken buildings along the hill, those who could not walk carried by those still able.

When the earth shuddered again, screeches and cries of terror came from every direction. More huge chunks of rock collapsed into the ruined cathedral. Where was Jordan? She could not see through the new clouds of dirt and dust. If he died . . . Tears rose in her eyes at the thought.

She did not have time to worry. Again and again, she was called to check on one of the injured. Monks went from one person to the next, offering the herb mixture she had created. She watched as one person after another allowed the ointment to be lathered on wounds, swallowed the poppy potion and drifted off into sleep, a brief respite before facing what lay ahead.

It was growing dark when Brother James told her—quite sternly because she had ignored his previous suggestions—to rest. He shoved a cup of wine into her hand. "Do not come back to work until you have finished it."

"If I drink it quickly on an empty stomach, I will be ill."

"Precisely." He gave her a tired smile. "Sip it, milady, and I will send someone to find bread for you to eat."

Thanking him, she went to sit on the low wall between the cathedral and the bishop's house. The latter had completely given way, and nothing remained but a pile of stone.

She set the cup on the wall beside her and leaned her elbows on her knees. Resting her forehead against her palms, she let the turbulent shivers rush through her. She could no longer halt them after a day of watching people suffer and die.

Someone sat beside her. Not just someone. Jordan. She knew that with a sense that had no name.

Raising her head, she looked at him. A scrape along his face had lengthened his scar. Dirt and dust gave his hair the gray of a man many years his senior. His tunic was ripped across one shoulder, and as he put his arm around her, she realized his other sleeve was completely torn away.

"How are you?" she asked as she handed him the glass of wine.

He took a deep drink, swirled it around his mouth, then spat it onto the ground. "For a man who had a cathedral fall down around him, I have to say I am doing well."

"I have been so fearful for your safety."

He tilted the cup to her lips and waited until she had taken a sip. He drank more, swallowing it this time. "You have had cause to be. The whole center of the cathedral's roof gave way as well as the central tower."

"You rescued many people."

"And saw more dead." He sighed. "If this had happened yesterday when the cathedral was full on Palm Sunday, there would be even more who were killed."

"I thought about that, too." She placed the cup on the wall and rubbed her hands together.

Taking them, he massaged them gently. "And how are you, Isabella?"

"Tired, but alive, and for that I am grateful."

"Many people can say the same because of you."

"Not everyone we rescued will survive."

"But they did not die alone under broken stone."

She caressed his cheek, being careful not to touch where blood had dried into a jagged riverbed. "Thanks to you."

"There were about a half dozen of us crawling over what remains of the cathedral."

"How long do you think the fires will burn?"

He frowned. "Don't tell me that you are still planning to look for the casket in those ruins."

"What other choice do I have? I made a vow to recover the casket and bring it to the queen."

"How do you expect to find anything in that?" He gestured toward the smoking rubble.

"I don't know." She stared at the ruined cathedral. "I honestly don't know."

Chapter 22

Jordan hated weakness, especially his own. As he sat on the side of the bed where Isabella still slept, he put his hand to his head and held his breath while he waited for everything to stop spinning. It had been almost a fortnight since the earthquake and the devastation at the cathedral and nearly a week since he had been caught in a collapse of stone while trying to retrieve Canon Anthony's body. How much longer was he going to suffer from a weak head?

The city of Lincoln was trying to make order out of chaos, but it was difficult because many houses had been destroyed, especially along Ermine Street. If the monks had not given him and Isabella a room overlooking the cloister, they would have been sleeping in the open as others did. Emery had another room across the corridor, and the lad had been very helpful in looking first for survivors, and then for corpses.

Jordan had heard that the Weirtons had sought a haven in the castle, which had not suffered any major damage. He had seen Weirton once in the past two weeks. He had not been able to satisfy his curiosity if the tunnels and caverns beneath the hill had survived. He suspected not all had because several houses had been swallowed by the earth, and he guessed they had been situated over the labyrinth built by the Brotherhood. His suggestion that Weirton and his sister come to help tend the injured had been met with incredulous disdain. He could not keep from thinking of the Brother-

hood's symbol with the man held by a rein. The Brotherhood did not deign to help those lower in class; they used
them.

Jordan pushed himself to his feet, taking care not to move
the mattress hard enough to wake Isabella. She had worked
for long hours every day and most nights since the earthquake. He rocked to one side as if the warm breeze coming
through the window were a storm wind. He tried to com-
pensate, but bumped into the wall on the other side.

"Jordan?" Isabella sat up, the blanket held to her breasts.

"I am fine," he said.

"You do not look fine." Pulling her shift over her head,
she slipped out of bed.

"You do." He tried to give her a lascivious smile, but it
must have looked more like a grimace.

Isabella's arm around him gave him a way to steady himself. He was astonished to discover she was steering him
with slow, even steps past the table by the window. He
squared his shoulders, not wanting to strike the table that the
brother who usually slept in the chamber used as a desk.

"No," he muttered when he saw she was guiding him
back to bed. "There is still work to do."

"There will be work to do for months to come. You need
to rest until you are stronger."

"I promised that I would continue to look for the brass
casket."

She sat with him on the bed. Leaning her head on his
shoulder, she said, "The month will be over in three days.
The queen will have left England, and it may be too late."

"That does not sound like you, Isabella."

"I am trying to be logical."

"Logic says the casket is in the cathedral. If we can get to
where the choir was, we can find it."

"Beneath tons of stone?"

A knock came at the door. As Isabella slipped her gown
over her head, lashing it at her waist and reaching for her
belt with her pouches and whip, Jordan pushed himself to
his feet and went to the door. He smiled when he saw Emery

with a tray containing bread and slices of beef, which tasted better after abstinence from meat during Lent.

"Come in." Jordan held the door as the lad set the tray on the table. "What news do you hear?"

"Nothing good," his squire answered. "In the shaking last night, more houses fell down on the other side of the river. How long does the shaking continue, milady?"

Isabella shrugged. "I wish I knew. The ancient Greek scientists wrote that the quaking of the earth is caused by great winds, but we have not had such winds here."

"Maybe because they are caught underneath us and are trying to escape."

"Like steam from a pot? That is a very interesting idea." She smiled. "Emery, if you decide a knightly life is not what you want, you would make a good student."

Seeing his panicked expression as a guffaw burst from Jordan, Isabella decided not to tease the lad more. She was thrilled to hear Jordan laugh, because he had been as somber as a statue in the cathedral. Laughter was a good sign that the balance was returning to an injured body; evil humors could not endure amidst happiness.

She selected a piece of bread and two slices of beef. She held them out to Jordan just as another knock came at the door. Motioning to Emery to help himself, she went to the door and opened it. With a smile, she greeted the brother standing in the corridor.

"Milady, there are many requests for your medicines," he said. "We need to prepare more."

"Can Brother James read?" she asked.

"Yes."

"Wait here."

Isabella went to the table. Opening the ink jar, she quickly wrote the formula for the medicine and held it out. The breeze snatched it from her fingers, and Emery stretched to grab it.

The mark on his wrist was visible even from across the room. She did not need to be closer to recognize the emblem of the man on a horse being led by another man. She forced her gaze quickly away. Unlike Lord Weirton, Emery had hidden his connection with the Brotherhood cleverly. Jordan had been suspicious of the lad's knowledge, but Emery always attributed that information to gossip and rumors.

She forced her voice to remain even. "Tell Brother James that I will be at the cathedral within the hour."

"He will be pleased to hear that, milady." The monk bowed his head and left.

Shouts came from the cloister, and she went to the window to see what was causing a commotion. Small groups of brothers were talking earnestly together. She heard cheers, but could not discern their words. When Emery offered to see what was happening, she was glad that Jordan urged him to go.

As soon as the door shut, Isabella said, "Emery is a member of the Brotherhood."

"He is too young. It is an organization of men who have sworn allegiance to the king and their chosen successor."

She pulled up her own sleeve and tapped her wrist. "He is wearing the crest. Right here. I saw it, Jordan."

Standing, Jordan cursed lowly, then more loudly. "I should have guessed. The lad acted oddly whenever Weirton was nearby."

"What are you going to do now that you know?"

The door opened before he could answer. Brother James called Isabella's name and urged her to hurry.

She went with the elderly brother into the cloister. Hearing Jordan's footsteps behind them, she hoped he would not tumble off his feet. She hooked her arm through Jordan's as he reached the ground floor. Pleased that he did not lean on her as heavily as he had in their room, she went with him after the monk who set a pace worthy of a man half his age.

"They found more people near the choir," Brother James shouted over his shoulder. "Alive."

"Alive?" she gasped.

"A miracle, isn't it? When the floor gave way, they found a haven in a small catacomb beneath the choir floor."

"Which people?"

"Over there." He pointed to a pallet occupied by a monk with bandages swathing his head. Beside him, two more men were waiting to be tended. One, a second monk, appeared to have several broken limbs, but the other man, who wore lay clothing, was sitting and wolfing down a piece of bread.

Isabella knelt in front of the sitting man. His face and his hands were covered with scratches and scrapes.

"How did you survive?" she asked.

He did not pause in eating, so she had to decipher his words through his mumble. "When the floor broke beneath us, we fell into a catacomb with ancient symbols on the walls. The floor was wet, and water continued to seep, so we never were without water. But we got very hungry."

"Tell me about the catacomb. Was there anything in there in addition to the ancient symbols?"

"There were several caskets, milady."

"What sort?"

"Most were stone reliquaries, but one casket was made of a dull metal. We tried to open them, but they were locked."

She stood and smiled. "You are lucky to be alive. Don't eat anything but bread and milk for the rest of the day. Tomorrow you can have some soup."

"Lent is over, isn't it?" He paused in his eating. "I have been thinking about meat."

"You need to reintroduce your stomach to food after being without for so long. If you do not sicken with the bread and the soup, then you can have meat the next day."

Paying no attention to him bemoaning the evil fate that had befallen him since he went into the cathedral, Isabella hurried with Jordan across the cloister. She faltered when they reached the ruins. Since the earthquake, she had tried to avoid the rubble between the west front and the small section to the east that looked as if it could topple at any time. It reeked of death, and she knew more bodies were beneath the stones.

She considered suggesting that Jordan wait while she clambered over the stones, but he stepped forward. He told her to watch where he went and to put her feet only where he put his.

"Can you tell where the choir was?" she asked, holding out her hands to balance herself when the stones under her feet rocked. If they fell away, she could break a bone, or worse.

"Yes, for I have crawled all over these ruins for the past ten days. The nave was about two hundred feet long, and the choir was near the transept." He shielded his eyes and looked across the ruins. "It should be about twenty feet in front of us where those stones have been shoved aside. Probably when the men were pulled out."

It took longer than Isabella would have guessed to go that short distance. By the time she reached the spot where stones had been piled high, her fingers were torn, and she had bruised both legs from ankle to knee. She did not care when she gazed into the space below them. It was wider than she had expected, and much deeper.

"How do we climb down?" she asked.

"We don't. It is too dangerous because the stones can shift quickly."

"But we must retrieve the metal casket."

"Move back, and let me see what I can discover."

Isabella fought her retort that she could look just as easily and that she was not dizzy from being hit by a stone. She edged down the pile and watched as he got onto his stomach and stretched his arm down into the hole.

"I see the metal casket!" he shouted.

"Can you reach it?" She wanted to scramble up beside him.

"No." He sat and pointed toward the left. "It is beyond my fingers."

"Let me try."

"You? Your arms are shorter than mine."

She uncoiled her whip. "Let me try."

He slid down the stack of stones and motioned for her to climb. He grasped her ankles. If the rocks tumbled, he could keep her from falling to the bottom.

Looking down into the emptiness, she saw water glistening at the bottom. She wondered if there had always been a spring beneath the cathedral or if it had been created during the earthquake. Her smile grew wide when she saw sunlight glint off metal. That must be the casket. She planted her feet against two rocks that seemed solidly jammed against others. Raising the whip, she sent the end flying into the hole.

She gave a cheer as she carefully pulled on the whip. "It is wrapped around something."

Lifting cautiously, she sighed when a board about the size of her forearm emerged. She loosened the whip and tossed it aside. Again she aimed the whip into the hole. When she tugged on it, something clattered in the hole, but she had not wrapped the whip's end around anything.

She waited for Jordan to tell her to step away so he could try again, but he remained silent. When she looked at him, he gave her an encouraging smile and motioned for her to try again. It took her two more attempts before she snagged the casket with the end of the whip.

"I have it," she said, dropping to her knees.

"Do you need help?"

"Just stretch out your hands and grab it as I draw it up. If it catches on anything, it could fall all the way to the bottom of the hole."

Again he stretched out on his stomach and reached down as far as he could. She slowly coiled the whip, wishing someone was holding on to her ankles still, so she did not end up in the water far below.

He grabbed the casket as soon as he was able. Pulling it up and close to his chest, he slid down to sit against a huge stone that had been painted with what appeared to be a cow. He set the casket on the stone, then stood and moved aside.

She drew out the key the abbess had given her. Her fingers trembled as she tried to fit it into the lock. When he put his hand over hers to steady it, she smiled. The key went in and, with a click, turned.

She opened the top and stared at the pages inside the casket. Picking up the top one, she scanned it as he looked over her shoulder. She gasped and shoved it back into the casket.

"No wonder the queen does not want these pages to be found by her husband," he said as he lowered the lid and turned the key. "Richard would be denounced by both the church and the baronage for those crimes. His brother's pillaging of a holy site is a minor crime in comparison to what Richard has done."

She looked at the hole. "Are we serving England to take these pages to the queen and allow Richard to take the throne after his father?"

"You are not sworn to serve England, but to do as the queen asks to prevent another civil war. What Richard has done as prince may be very different from what he does when he wears the crown."

"I hope you are right."

"So do I." Picking up the casket, he said, "If we leave now for St. Jude's Abbey, nobody should miss us for hours. My aunt will know where the queen is so you may deliver the casket into her hands." He smiled. "I mean, we. I recall my vow, too."

"I never doubted that." She took his hand as they picked their way through the ruined cathedral. The road ahead of them was long, but they must reach the queen before father and son could meet face-to-face. Otherwise, all of England might be destroyed as thoroughly as Lincoln Cathedral.

Isabella sat on a rock by the side of the road and tilted her boot upward. A small pebble clattered in the dirt. She smiled at Jordan, admiring how the sun glistened with a blue-black sheen off his hair. "It felt much larger when I was stepping on it."

"I am sure it did." He stroked her leg with the same slow, sensual caress he had delighted her with the previous night when they had found shelter in a byre.

Her fingers curved along the side of his face as she guided his mouth to hers. Closing her eyes, she savored the fiery touch that burned along her lips to reignite the longing within her. Not even in her sweetest fantasies had she imagined she would hunger for a man's touch as she did Jordan's. She longed for his strong hands to slip beneath her clothes and burnish her skin with their eager caress.

He helped her to mount the white stallion, then swung up onto his own horse. "It is still attached to your saddle, still hidden in your sack."

"I did not ask about the casket."

"For once."

She chuckled as they continued down the hill at a steady pace that would not tire the horses so much that they would not be able to continue on the morrow. It was May Day, and the flowers were blooming along the roadside.

"Don't the sisters of St. Jude's Abbey go May-dewing?" Jordan asked as if she had spoken her thoughts aloud. "You were not up with the sun this morning to collect the dew to make your face smooth."

"Did I need to be?"

He laughed. "Always logical."

She turned to look over her shoulder when she heard rapid hoofbeats. Her hand went to her whip as a cloud of dust appeared at the top of hill. Hearing Jordan yell to his horse, she slapped her hand against the stallion. It raced along the road. She leaned low over the saddle, urging it to go even faster.

Risking a glance back, she gasped in horror. Jordan's horse was surrounded by a half dozen riders, and the sunlight reflected off bare steel.

Her horse whinnied a shrill protest as she twisted its head to bring it around. She could not let Jordan fight by himself. If he were killed . . .

Again she hunched down over the saddle and pleaded with the horse to heed her. She rode straight at the men around Jordan. An instant before she reached them, the men glanced at her, horror on their faces. She shouted to the horse to keep going. The men drew in their horses, sending them up on their hind legs as she raced at them. At the last second, she turned the horse and lashed out with her whip. Two men fell to the ground while others shrieked.

Wheeling about, she saw Jordan racing away. She did not hesitate as she saw the men still on their horses giving chase. She yelled St. Jude's name and slapped the horse. She had plowed through the attackers once to help Jordan. She could do it again.

She caught up with the slowest horses. When she tried to pass them, they matched her pace. One dropped behind as she drew even with two more. They slowed, and she had no choice but to do the same because she was surrounded as Jordan had been. With a gasp, she realized she had let them trap her.

As they forced her to come to a stop, she raised her whip. Her wrist was seized. The whip was torn from her fingers. As she turned to see who had taken it, she stared at Lord Weirton's triumphant smile. She tried to free her wrist, but another man's mail-covered fingers dug into it until she mewed with agony. She grasped Lord Weirton's sleeve with her other hand and tore it back to reveal the Brotherhood's crest on his skin. He slapped her hard across the face.

"That is for knocking me from my feet," Lord Weirton growled. "And for interfering with the Brotherhood's punishment of one who tried to thwart us."

"Sir Ryce?"

He did not answer. Instead he struck her a second time, not with the flat of his hand, but with his fist. A flash of pain exploded through her skull, stealing the sunlight and all her senses.

Chapter 23

Murky sunshine surrounded Isabella when she raised her head. Her first thought was amazement that she was alive. The baron had had bloodlust in his eyes. A blistering headache could not daunt her fury. Gritting her teeth, she slowly stretched her fingers to discover she was lying on dirt.

Her hands were bound. Her legs? They were free. That surprised her until she remembered that Lord Weirton had never seen her use her feet against a foe. Pushing herself up to sit, she hit her head. She was in a cramped space with a sloping roof. She glowered at the thatch over the low rafters. Bits of sunlight dripped through the thinning spots to send motes of dust afloat.

The door was less than a foot from her, but she did not move toward it. Lord Weirton would have secured it in some way to prevent her from fleeing. Lord Weirton was vicious, but intelligent. A dangerous combination.

She grimaced, then forced her forehead to smooth again. She would be able to think more clearly if her head would stop aching as if the blacksmith were using her skull for his anvil. The pain pulsed with each heartbeat until she wanted to scream. Keeping silent, she breathed slowly as she struggled to devise a way to escape. Not knowing where she was or where Jordan might be made it more difficult.

The casket? What had happened to the casket and its contents?

As if she had shouted the questions, the door opened. A man she did not know came in. He grabbed her arm and yanked her to her feet. She bit her lower lip as pain resonated through her. Had he pulled her shoulder right away from her body? He bent to pick up her sack. It was bulging, and she guessed the blanket and the casket were still in it, undiscovered by Lord Weirton and his men. Looking at the man, she considered throwing herself to the ground and kicking her feet into the air to strike him in the face. That would gain her nothing because she would still be bound. She had to wait for her opportunity. Her experiments had always worked best when the conditions were perfect. She needed to use that same rational way of thinking to escape Lord Weirton and his companions.

In spite of her determination to remain calm as she was dragged out of the small building, Isabella cried out Jordan's name when she saw him with the baron. The man holding her laughed as he shoved her forward. She fell to her knees between Jordan and Lord Weirton.

Jordan lifted her up gently before the baron could touch her. "Why didn't you keep going?"

"Why didn't *you*?"

He gave her the wry grin that always made her heart flutter like a maddened butterfly.

Lord Weirton ordered, "Leave her bound, le Courtenay, or you will see her die now."

"Afraid of me?" she taunted. "You should be!"

"Isabella," Jordan hissed. Why was she provoking Weirton more? The red mark on her cheek was already swelling. Weirton had bragged about knocking her senseless, hoping to prod Jordan into doing something stupid. Now she was trying the same thing with the baron, and she was risking her life.

"One more word from you, woman," Weirton snarled, "and I shall have you gagged."

Jordan was relieved when she closed her mouth while Weirton went to confer with his men by the abandoned byre where they had imprisoned her. Drawing her down to sit, he asked, "Are you in much pain?"

"Yes, but I am all right." She glanced at Weirton. "At least I am now. What are they planning?"

"They were talking about whether to return us to Lincoln first."

"Then what?"

"I am not sure."

She glanced around, puzzled. "The sunshine looks peculiar. He must have jostled my eyes as well as my teeth."

"Your eyes are not to blame. The sunshine has seemed thin for the past hour or so."

"Hour or so? I was unconscious that long?"

He nodded and stroked her hair while she leaned against him. He did not want to speak of his horror that she had been trapped by Weirton and the other men. He doubted he could find words to express how his fear for her had sent him riding at full speed to surrender in the hope that she would be spared. He had seen the basest emotions of men in Aquitaine when rape was an expected part of a victory celebration. Hating what he saw in others, he had tried to submerge those emotions—and all others—within himself. He had succeeded . . . until Isabella came into his life and refused to let him hide from himself.

"It will be all right," she whispered.

"I know," he lied. All he could think of was how Weirton licked his lips each time he looked at her. Like a beast anticipating the chance to savor his captured prey. Isabella would not die quickly as Jordan would, even if they were both taken back to Lincoln and the torture room beneath the castle's tower, but he knew she would come to long for death.

There had to be some way to distract their guards so she could make her escape. She ran more swiftly than most men, and Weirton's guards appeared too well fed to capture her. She could use her wits to elude them until they gave up the chase.

It was too late, for Weirton was walking toward them. He

motioned for Jordan to stand and move away from her. When Jordan hesitated, the baron put his hand on the hilt of his sword. The unspoken threat was clear.

"Don't do something foolish," Jordan whispered as he obeyed Weirton's silent order, taking two steps away from where she sat.

"Gag her," the baron commanded.

She began, "I did not say—" The rest of her words were muffled as a piece of cloth was stuck in her mouth and another tied around her head. Her gaze fired daggers at the baron, but he laughed.

Jordan was astonished when Weirton, with another silent gesture, sent his companions toward the horses about a hundred yards along the road. The baron moved to stand between Jordan and Isabella, and he smiled.

"They are brothers of lower rank," Weirton said, "so what I have to say is not for their ears."

"So you have ranks within the Brotherhood."

He laughed again. "Of course. We are not like those insipid Templar fools who believe in giving up their worldly goods to their knightly order and being equal even among themselves. I joined them, but left to form the Brotherhood." He tapped the crest on the knife he wore openly at his side. "The Templars' crest shows them riding two men on one horse, all equal in their poverty. We are proudly on our horse as we are served by those inferior to us."

"And that would be?"

"Everyone who is not a member of the Brotherhood."

Jordan made his lips taut so he did not smile when he saw Isabella roll her eyes in disbelief at Weirton's pompous statement.

"So that includes me," he said. "Is that why you had your fellow members ambush us on the way to Lincoln?"

"No! We want you to become a member of the Brotherhood. I had hoped the attack would persuade you that England needs strong leadership. If that idiot had not dropped his sword, you would never have known the truth." He laughed without humor. "He will never make another stupid mistake."

Swallowing hard, Jordan stared at the baron. Weirton was mad, and he had sucked others into believing his insanity was England's salvation.

"The Brotherhood can give you everything you want." Weirton's excitement grew with every word. "Look at me, le Courtenay! I was one baron among many, my lands providing well, my taxes paid on time. Then I founded the Brotherhood with like-minded men, and now I have the respect of my brothers and the expectation that I will be rewarded for serving my king loyally."

"How can you say that when you have vowed to keep Prince Richard from taking his rightful place on his father's throne when King Henry is dead?"

"You have more knowledge of the Brotherhood than I guessed."

"Hiding the entrance to your tunnels in the house where you have guests with curious minds is not a good idea."

Weirton turned and snarled, "I should have guessed you would not halt your meddling, milady."

Isabella raised her eyebrows and shrugged, saying more with her expression than any insult could.

Balancing on his toes, Jordan prepared to halt Weirton from striking her again. He was surprised when the baron faced him and smiled as if Jordan had no more sense than a slow-witted child.

"Le Courtenay, *you* have served both the young king and Prince Richard. *You* have seen both men, sworn to serve their father and the church, rise up against both, destroying what they cannot have. Only John, who has served his father faithfully, deserves to be crowned the next king of England."

Jordan shook his head with a curt laugh. "The Brotherhood does not care what Young Henry or Richard has done. All you care about is gaining more control of England. You want John as king because you believe you can control him. Maybe you are right, but you have forgotten one very important person. The queen."

"She has been imprisoned for years. Any influence she once had is gone."

"Is it? Do you think she cannot raise an army if you try to keep her favorite son from claiming his birthright?" Jordan could not help smiling as he imagined at the head of the queen's army, the ladies of St. Jude's Abbey led by his aunt. No company the Brotherhood put on the field to face those women could be victorious.

"She was defeated twelve years ago, and she has been kept away from the rest of the world for years. Her mind must have slowed. She will present no problem. If she does, she is a woman of advanced years, so nobody will suspect anything out of the ordinary, if she dies."

"You would kill the queen?" Jordan shook his head. "Have you lost every bit of chivalry you possessed? When you swear a vow to King Henry, that vow is for him and his family from that day forward."

"We think of England! And you will join us."

"No."

"No?" He laughed. "Maybe you are right, but *you* have forgotten one very important person. Isabella de Montfort."

Jordan's hands fisted impotently at his sides. "She does not want anything to do with the Brotherhood either."

"Do you think we want a woman among us?" He snickered, holding his sides as if they hurt. "We want *you* with us. That is why we sent Emery to serve as your squire when yours died."

"So he truly is a member of the Brotherhood?"

"Not a true member, for he cannot claim that status until he becomes a knight. He has been eager to show his value to the Brotherhood, and when we wanted to convince you to join us, he was the first step."

"What was the second one?"

Again Weirton chuckled. "Isn't that obvious? We arranged for de Dolan to be killed in the tournament. He wanted a woman that needed to marry one of the Brotherhood, and she had feelings for him. His death served two purposes, for not only did she marry where we wished, but he was your best friend. We left the knife with de Dolan's body, so that the witless prior would refuse him burial within the walls of Kenwick Priory. That brought you to where you could be drawn into our circle."

"Drawn in?" He folded his arms in front of him. "With the help of Gamell, no doubt."

"The man is a fool, but he serves me well."

"So all went according to your plan until . . ." He glanced at where Isabella was fighting her bonds, her eyes flashing with fury.

"How could we have imagined that any de Montfort would care about anything other than who holds their lands?" Weirton smiled as he walked over to tower over Isabella, but looked at Jordan. "Or that you would care so much about her that you would chase after her like a lovesick boy?"

Jordan noticed Isabella trying to catch his eye. What did she think he could do that would not endanger her more? He saw her try to stretch her hands toward him. If she thought he could release her when Weirton stood between them . . . She glanced down at her hands, and he did the same. She was wagging her fingers back and forth against her thumb.

He understood. She wanted him to keep Weirton talking. That was simple. Weirton never tired of what he believed to be his eloquence.

"Or is it you, Weirton," he asked, "who has used the Brotherhood as an excuse to pursue Isabella?"

"Me?" Weirton's laugh sounded forced. "Why would I want this de Montfort woman?"

"Because the Brotherhood could arrange for the rest of the family to slay each other in what appears to be an ongoing feud, and you would possess the lands that belonged to her father." He watched as Isabella slipped one foot behind Weirton's, raising her foot just above his heel.

"You have a vivid imagination, le Courtenay. You will be an asset to the Brotherhood. If— What the—?"

Isabella moved so quickly that her motions were a blur. She put her other foot against Weirton's knee and pushed at the same moment she pulled back on the foot behind his heel. Weirton toppled backward with a shout.

She jumped to her feet and put one boot on Weirton's throat. Jordan stepped around her, so she could not be seen by Weirton's men farther down the road. He reached down to pull Weirton's knife from the sheath on his belt. With two quick slices, he cut away the gag and the rope around her wrists.

"You are amazing, Isabella," Jordan murmured against her tangled hair as he tossed the bonds away.

"I guess I did learn more at the Abbey than I thought."

"And I see I still have a lot to learn." He stroked her shoulder where her gown was torn, then motioned for Weirton to stand.

Isabella slowly withdrew her foot, putting it back toward Weirton's throat when he raised his hands as if to grab it. He put his arms on the ground, and she edged away.

"Get up!" Jordan ordered.

Weirton pushed himself to his feet. "You are making a mistake, le Courtenay. Everything you want for England is exactly what the Brotherhood wants. No more patricidal and fratricidal wars that leave our lands scorched and our tenants starving."

"I swore an oath to obey the king."

"And your oath will be to the new king."

"But not the rightful king!"

Throwing back his head, Weirton shouted, *"Semper minax, nunquam summissus!"*

Isabella drew back her fist and jammed it into his stomach. As he bent over, she slammed both her hands onto his back, knocking him to the ground.

She grabbed her sack and ran toward the trees beyond the byre. Beside her, Jordan was matching her pace. She bent her head to go faster, but almost stumbled into a bush. Stepping back to go around, she bumped into him. He had stopped. Why? Her eyes widened when she saw a phalanx of swords ahead of them. She cursed her shortsightedness.

She should have guessed that Lord Weirton would not leave himself completely unprotected.

Slowly she held up her hands. Her bag was taken, and she pretended not to care, but she kept a clandestine watch on it as they were herded back to Lord Weirton. As they stepped from beneath the trees, she glanced skyward. There were few clouds, but the light was becoming thinner and an odd color. She wished she could see the sun, but it was behind the trees. She could not move while the baron was being helped to his feet.

"If you want her to live past sunset tomorrow," Weirton said, "you will take the Brotherhood's vow. Tell her good-bye and take your oath to join us. Now!"

"I need a few minutes to consider my answer." Jordan folded his arms in front of him.

"What do you need to consider?"

"My answer. Privately with Lady Isabella. You are asking me to put her out of my life. Allow me to bid her farewell."

Isabella held her breath as she waited for Lord Weirton's answer to Jordan's subtle defiance.

The baron glanced at his men and then nodded. "We are reasonable men, making reasonable choices in a very unreasonable time. While we make the necessary preparations for you to take your oath, you may tell her *good-bye*."

She could not keep from flinching at Weirton's threat, but said nothing as Jordan took her arm, plucked her sack from the man who had taken it, and led her a short distance away. She thought Weirton would order his men to halt them. As Weirton shouted orders, she tried not to think what preparations were necessary to take the Brotherhood's oath.

He handed her the bag and whispered, "They will be distracted during the ceremony. Flee, and complete your obligation to the queen."

"I cannot leave you, Jordan."

"You must. You made a pledge, and you must fulfill it. Go while you can."

"He will not let me escape, for I know about the Brotherhood, and there is no oath that can compel me to silence."

"If you vow to *me* that you will never speak of it . . ."

"Weirton will never accept that. I am in the way of his sister becoming your wife, so he can have influence over your lands as well as his own."

He smiled. "How did you become so knowledgeable about the minds of men while cloistered at St. Jude's Abbey?"

"I am a de Montfort. Even though I spent most of my life behind the Abbey's walls, I heard about the battles my brothers fought. I have discovered what lengths someone will go to gain power and wealth while calling it a battle of honor."

When he kept his arm around her shoulders, she pressed closer to him. He would safeguard her for as long as he could. At that thought, her breath burned in a tight knot over her halted heart. She did not want him to sacrifice his life for her. His hand stroking her arm offered sparse comfort when they both could be murdered within seconds.

The sun glinted in her eyes. She looked up and gasped.

"What is it?" Jordan asked.

"The sun is disappearing!"

"What?"

She smiled. "It is an eclipse when the moon and sun move together and share the same spot in the heavens. The earth is darkened. Superstitious fools believe an eclipse is an omen of evil."

Shouts came from Lord Weirton's men. Frightened shouts.

"There are your fools, Isabella," he said.

With a smile, she opened her sack and drew out her whip. She placed it in the grass. The men must have put it in the bag. Pulling out a section of the blanket, she peeked in to see that the casket was undisturbed. She lifted out three pouches and opened them. Two held small containers wrapped in lamb's wool; the other was sooty with charcoal.

"We need to get to the road," she said.

"Why?"

"When I snapped the whip at Gamell, sparks came off some stones. Those sparks could touch off an explosion."

"Have I told you that you are amazing and that is one of the reasons I love you?"

"You love me?" She stared at him. His face was a strange color in the dimming light.

"I thought you knew, Isabella."

"I had hoped you loved me because I love you, but you never said anything. You talked about going to La Tour afterward."

"With you." He pressed his mouth over hers in a swift kiss. "Do you think I would let you go now? You have given my life back to me, daring me to feel again when I was ashamed of what I had seen and done. I want to share that life with you."

"First we have to make sure we both have lives to share from this point forward."

"Tell me what I can do."

She thought for a minute, then smiled. "You are going to act as if I have poisoned myself to escape the Brotherhood. Take me to the road. Pretend you are forcing me to vomit. While I am down on my hands and knees, I can prepare the explosion."

"And then?"

"And then we have to hope it works again." She cursed as she saw some of the men coming toward them. Hoping nobody would notice in the half-light, she looped the whip around her waist as she had in the cathedral what seemed like months ago. Palming the small pouches, she hid them within the whip's strands.

"Lord Weirton said we are ready, milord, for you to take your oath," the man said, bowing his head to Jordan. "If you will come with me . . ."

Jordan hooked his arm through hers and pushed her ahead of him.

The man said, "She cannot—"

With an arrogance that belittled even Weirton's, Jordan snarled, "I do not take orders from you. She goes with me until *I* say otherwise. Do you understand?"

The man cowered back as Jordan walked with her toward

where the other men waited. When they were about ten feet from where Lord Weirton stood, his dagger bare in his hand, she began to wretch. She dropped to her knees and shuddered as she wrapped her arms around her waist. Not only did she appear ill, but she was able to hide that she wore her whip.

"God's blood!" Jordan shouted. "You dolts! You left her sack with her, didn't you?"

Lord Weirton swaggered forward. "What is going on?"

"Don't you realize that she carries poisonous herbs among her medicinal ones?" He pulled her to her feet, dropping the sack to the grass. "Now she has poisoned herself."

"That is her choice," the baron said. "What is yours?"

"To save her life!"

She dragged her feet as Jordan pulled her toward the road. Behind them, Lord Weirton shouted, but Jordan kept going. Several of the men started to follow. Jordan shouted for them to remain where they were until he made certain that what she had swallowed was not dangerous to anyone else. When he had half carried her to the edge of the road, he stopped.

"A bit farther!" she whispered.

He pulled her out into the middle of the road and released her. She fell to her hands and knees. As he berated her for being irresponsible, she bent forward at an awkward angle.

"One quarter sulfur," she murmured to herself. "One quarter charcoal. Nearly twice as much saltpeter as both." She sprinkled the elements onto the ground as she wretched loudly to make the men think she was ill.

"All set?"

"Almost. I am not sure how this will work. If you have to, leave without me."

"They will kill you."

"Promise me that you will get the casket to the queen." She looked up at him. "Promise me, please."

He cupped her cheek and smiled sadly. "I promise."

Blinking back tears, she sprinkled more of the elements onto the road. She was not sure how big an explosion she would need. She was not even sure how big an explosion she would get, if it detonated at all.

"Yell that I just said the vanishing sun may never again shine on England," she said. "Yell so that they will hear you."

"Why?"

"When we were ambushed by the members of the Brotherhood, they believed I was doing magic. Let them think that now. If we can terrorize them, they may lose every *reasonable* thought they have." She grimaced. "Lord Weirton gives logic a bad reputation."

He jumped to his feet and backed away from her. She heard him shouting about how she had regurgitated a toad and was using it to leave the Brotherhood in the dark forever. He went on with more tales, but she stopped listening as she concentrated on mixing the elements together. Her fingers stung from the saltpeter as she looked up to see the sun had vanished almost completely.

It had to be now.

Jumping up, she screamed some nonsense syllables, then shouted, "The cost of your sins is darkness! Darkness and destruction. Pay the price of your sins!"

She snapped the whip against the stones lining the road. One sparked, but too far from the elements. She stepped closer, knowing she was courting injury.

Lord Weirton shouted and ran forward, calling for his men to stop her. She looked across the dark field to Jordan and raised the whip again.

"Pay the price of your sins!" she shouted and lashed out with the whip as the men neared the mixture on the road.

The road exploded with brilliant light. A concussion knocked her off her feet and backward into the grass. Her ears were filled with thuds and shrieks and echoes from the detonation. Stone and dirt pelted her. Someone cried out in agony.

Smoke rose around her. She batted it away as she fought her way to her feet. Someone lurched out of the smoke, and she reached for her whip. It must have been blown out of her hand by the concussion.

"Isabella!" she heard through the ringing in her ears.

Seeing Jordan, she ran past the stunned men lying in the grass. She shrieked a warning when she saw someone move behind him.

He whirled as Lord Weirton leaped toward him. Jordan's hand came up to strike the baron in the stomach. The baron reeled back, clutching the dagger sticking out of him. He started to speak, then toppled backward as his blood darkened his tunic. The knife's haft caught the light from the sunshine that was slowly easing away the half-twilight. It bore the crest of the Brotherhood.

"I hope they bury *you* with that knife!" Jordan spat. "Ryce de Dolan is avenged."

She grabbed her sack and ran with Jordan to where the horses were neighing with fright. He threw her in the saddle. She tied the sack onto the back of her saddle while he freed the other horses. The steeds fled in panic before he mounted and drew his horse close to hers.

"Ready to complete your vow to the queen and to St. Jude's Abbey, Isabella?"

"Yes." She gave him a feigned frown. "You promised to leave without me if you could."

"I know."

"But you did not."

"I could not leave, and didn't you promise the same? I thought a lady of St. Jude's Abbey held her vows to her heart."

She took his hand and pressed it between her breasts. "I would rather hold you to my heart."

"Keep that thought, sweet one." With a shout, he slapped his horse's flank.

She sent the white stallion chasing after him, knowing wherever they went, it would be together.

Epilogue

The queen looked much older than the portrait in the abbess's office. Her age and her imprisonment for almost a dozen years had clawed lines into her face. Even so, nothing could detract from the elegant dignity that had been her birthright as the most eligible woman in Europe who had married two kings and been the mother to one crowned son and who—if her sons did not die from treachery within their family or from defending the Plantagenet lands—might live to see another son crowned.

Sitting in a small chamber in Bayeux across the Channel from England, she was reading the pages that Isabella had found beneath Lincoln Cathedral's ruins. Her expression did not alter, and Isabella doubted Queen Eleanor found anything unexpected in the pages that damned both of her surviving sons for their ambitious dreams.

"The devil runs through all of them," the queen said as she lowered the pages to her lap, "but when I present Richard with this evidence of his foolishness, he is certain to reconsider. After all, he should not have to wait much longer to obtain everything he wishes to possess. Perhaps then he will discover that patience is a virtue no king can expect from those around him."

Isabella tried to swallow her shock. She knew that the king and queen despised each other, but she had not guessed that Queen Eleanor believed her two sons were foes.

"You have served me well, Lady Isabella." The queen smiled,

and time fell away to reveal the beautiful woman she had been. "I understand, Lord le Courtenay, you have asked *my* lady of St. Jude's Abbey to exchange very special vows with you."

Jordan bowed his head to the queen. "With your permission, of course."

Queen Eleanor's smile broadened, and Isabella remembered the stories she had heard of the queen's Court of Love in Poitiers where men and women enjoyed music, poetry, and the arts of flirtation. Seeing Jordan dressed in his finest red tunic that was embroidered with gold threads, she could imagine him amidst that glory.

"You deserve a reward, milord, for your service to me, but it appears that you have been rewarded already if I am to judge by how you look at my Lady Isabella with deep affection. If you wish *my* lady's hand in marriage, you have my permission to have her as *your* Lady Isabella."

"I could imagine no better reward."

The queen stood. "And you, Lady Isabella, deserve a reward as well."

"Serving you and, in doing so, being able to prevent another war has been the greatest reward I could wish for." She smiled at Jordan. "Or almost the greatest."

"As you wish." The queen gestured toward a door at the opposite end of the room from where they had entered. "Please depart that way, so you do not chance encountering the king. He would not be pleased to discover one of my ladies of St. Jude's Abbey here in Bayeux, and I would not subject you to his temper."

Bowing again, Isabella went with Jordan out of the room to the sound of rustling pages as the queen went back to her reading. Isabella reached for his hand. In the antechamber, he whirled her into his arms and captured her mouth.

The sound of a light laugh separated them, and Isabella saw a woman entering the room. Her once golden hair was laced with silver beneath a simple veil. She was tall and slender, standing straight, even though she walked with a cane.

"God's blood!" Jordan gasped.

Isabella could not speak as she stepped forward, some memory from the distant past of her childhood confirming what her eyes showed her. "Mother?"

"Yes." Lady Gemma de Montfort touched Isabella's cheek. "My dear Isabella. It is as if I am looking at my own reflection from the time of your birth."

Isabella fell to her knees and, wrapping her arms around her mother's waist, wept against Lady Gemma's simple gown. "I never thought I would see you again in this world."

"I prayed for this day. I am amazed that the queen would bring us back together after she separated us when you were a child."

"The queen separated us? Why?"

Lady de Montfort smiled. "She arranged for me to live at her favorite abbey at Fontevraud, but she insisted she knew a better place for an intelligent child like you."

"St. Jude's Abbey."

"You are a nun?" Her smile became a troubled frown when she looked from Isabella to Jordan.

"St. Jude's Abbey is not the same as other religious houses. I will explain, but first, this is Jordan le Courtenay."

Jordan bowed over her mother's hand as deeply as he had over the queen's. "Lady de Montfort, this is a great honor. I asked the queen's permission, but I will ask yours as well. I wish to marry your daughter."

"Do you want to marry him?" her mother asked.

"With all my heart, which made a vow to love him forever, and de Montforts do not break their vows."

Lady de Montfort's face relaxed into a smile again. "Ah, that explains what I interrupted." She kissed Isabella on the cheek, then did the same to Jordan. "I will wait outside. I want to hear about your wedding plans, and everything that has happened to you since I last saw you, Isabella."

"It is a long story."

"But with a happy ending?"

Isabella put her arms around Jordan's shoulders as his

arms swept behind her to draw her close. "The very happiest ending ever."

He tilted her chin up to bring her lips to his as he whispered, "Is that a promise?"

"Yes," she answered in the moment before his mouth found hers.

Author's Note

Both the earthquake that destroyed Lincoln Cathedral and the eclipse are true events. The Lincoln earthquake of April 15, 1185, has been estimated by modern scientists to have been between 5.0 and 6.0 on the Richter scale. Because of the design of the cathedral's roof and its location, the whole center was destroyed, while the castle, approximately three hundred meters away on the top of the hill, had much less damage.

The nearly total eclipse of May 1, 1185, darkened much of northern Europe. From the Highlands to as far east as Siberia, it was a complete eclipse, documented with great trepidation in the West and great interest in the East, where scientific thought was far more advanced.

About the Author

Jocelyn Kelley has always had a weakness for strong heroines and dashing heroes. For as long as she can remember, she's been telling stories of great adventures. She has had a few great adventures of her own, including serving as an officer in the U.S. Army and singing with a local group of Up with People. She lives in Massachusetts with her husband, three children and three chubby cats. She's not sure who's the most spoiled.

Learn more about Jocelyn Kelley and her future books at www.jocelynkelley.com.

Look for a new series
from Jocelyn Kelley—The Nethercott Tales.

Lost in Shadows

Released by Signet Eclipse in July 2007.

"It was murder. Murder most foul."

At the whisper, Jade Nethercott glanced up from the book she had taken from a shelf. Her late father had written notes in the margins and underlined sections of text. Reading his comments, which showed he had been outraged at the author's opinions, made her feel as if he were still with her. She had spent many hours with Father and her two sisters in his book room, where the walls were lined with shelves and chairs begged one to curl up in them, as they debated the myriad topics interesting them.

That had ended when her father had died suddenly from a weak heart none of them suspected he had. Neither she nor her sisters had been prepared for the loss, and a year's passage had not eased their grief.

But Father's had been a natural death, not murder. Who was talking about such a heinous crime?

"It was murder. Murder most foul," came the whisper again.

She looked around. "Who said that?"

Instead of an answer, she heard something click loudly in the corridor. As if someone had abruptly unlatched a door.

If this was one of her sisters' idea of a hoax to relieve the boredom of a stormy day, it was not an amusing one. She looked out the door and saw nobody. Maybe it was only the wind playing with ancient eaves where gargoyles spit out the rain coursing down onto the roofs.

She turned a page in the book and continued to read.

"It was murder. Murder most foul." The whisper was followed by the same noise in the hallway.

"Bother," she muttered. Who was whispering such nonsense and making that noise? Mrs. Mathers, the housekeeper, had been at Nethercott Castle for as long as Jade could remember. She oversaw the servants with a strict but fair sense of discipline. Anyone making such a to-do would be turned out by the housekeeper posthaste.

Setting the book on a table, Jade went to the door again. She looked in both directions along the narrow hall at the top of the stairs. Two lamps were lit against the twilight of day's end, creating narrow pools on the wood floor, where it was not covered by a red-and-green runner. The paneled walls swallowed any hint of light, leaving the few paintings in shadow.

Everything looked as it should, and she heard no more clatter. She sighed. Before Father's death, the house had been full of happy voices and laughter. No longer. It was as if after so many months of mourning, they did not know how to be happy again.

She reached to straighten her father's portrait that hung next to his favorite room. In the painting, he looked not much older than she was now. He held a book in one hand and a quill in the other. His gaze was focused on something in the distance, and there was a hint of a smile on his lips. That smile seemed to widen as light spread across the portrait.

What light? There should not be any light coming from the far end of the hall.

But there was. Not from a lamp, for the light shone from a spot about halfway between the floor and the high ceiling. It was a ball; then it stretched toward the floor.

"It was murder. Murder most foul." The voice seemed to be coming from the light. It was, she noticed for the first time, a deep masculine voice.

She blinked once, then another time, but the light grew stronger. What was it? It could not have been anything of this world. Her gaze flicked toward her father's book room and the book she had been holding. A book about restless spirits who walked the earth after death.

No, it was impossible. Her father had spent his life trying to prove that the old castle was haunted, but nothing he had done—séances or attempts to contact the dead directly or special candles or anything else—had turned up a single sign of a phantom clinging to the chilliest spots in the seldom used corridors and chambers. Cold spots in the rooms where the family gathered always could be explained by a drafty window or a piece of furniture blocking the heat from the hearth.

Father had been disappointed, but eventually conceded that Nethercott Castle, in spite of its location on the desolate Yorkshire moors and its generations of inhabitants—first as a priory and then as a castle—was unhaunted.

So what was an otherworldly light doing now, lurking in the corridor outside Father's book room? Fate was so cruel. She bit back an unseemly oath. A laugh tickled the back of her throat. Why was she worried about swearing in the presence of someone who had obviously been cursed? For what other reason would that person still be loitering in the castle?

"It was murder. Murder most foul. It was—" The bass voice in the light halted, then said, "I guess I should be grateful, Miss Nethercott, that you are not screaming or surrendering to a fit of vapors."

A ghost that spoke to her by name? She gasped and pressed her hand over her thudding heart. This was beyond extraordinary. She glanced over her shoulder. If she shouted to her sisters, would the ghost fade back into the woodwork?

Her curiosity overcame her fear. She squinted, and she could see a human shape taking form. The light was still too bright for her to discern what the ghost was wearing.

"I would appreciate the courtesy of an answer," the male voice continued, a hint of annoyance creeping into the words. "It is the least you can offer a guest in your house."

"I am sorry. I am at a loss for words." Jade did not add that such a loss was a most unusual state for her. "You must admit that the common pleasantries are not appropriate. After all, you are a ghost!"

"Obviously." The ghost's tone suggested that he was vexed by his current state. The light around him was easing, and she could see he wore clothing of a very recent style.

But nobody had died in the past few years at Nethercott Castle other than her beloved father. This specter was not Lord Nethercott, for he did not possess the girth her father had acquired along with his many years. Nor did the voice belong to Father. He had seldom scolded her or her sisters, yet she had frequently heard him exasperated with his studies, so she would have recognized that tone.

Deciding there was no reason to waste thought in speculation, she simply asked, "Who are you?"

"I *was* Sir Mitchell Renshaw."

Jade stepped away from the door and peered at the form emerging from the light. The sensation was rather like watching a faded painting regaining its color and texture. She could now see his rust-colored waistcoat and dark breeches draped over his thin form, but his face was a glowing blob beneath his hair that was almost the same shade as his waistcoat. "Why would Sir Mitchell Renshaw haunt Nethercott Castle? He called here only a few times."

"To study with the Professor."

Her breath caught. Even though her father had rightly held the title of Lord Nethercott, twelfth baron, he had preferred to be addressed as "Professor." He had believed it more in keeping with his love for books and philosophy and science. As well, he felt it more of an honor than a title bestowed on a distant relative who had done something to gain favor with a long-dead king.

"You are, I assume, one of the Professor's daughters," the spirit said.

"I am Jade Nethercott."

"Which one are you?"

"The middle one."

The ghost's mouth twisted. Had he been wearing that expression before? His features were beginning to materialize, and they were the ones she recalled belonging to Sir Mitchell Renshaw. Even his fiery, bushy mustache was becoming visible. His waistcoat buttons appeared to be of fine gold, a surprise because burying a man with such affectations was an invitation to robbers to open his grave to relieve him of the riches.

"I thought you were the eldest," he said, drawing her attention away from his amazing metamorphosis from light to the appearance of something solid.

"That is China. And my sister Sian is younger than me by less than a year, Sir Mitchell." She might as well address him as Sir Mitchell, because that was more comfortable than the idea she was carrying on a conversation with a *ghost*.

"I guess you will have to do."

"Do? For what?"

Jocelyn Kelley

A MOONLIT KNIGHT

**In twelfth-century England, St. Jude's Abbey is
no ordinary holy sanctuary: it trains young
women in the knightly arts.**

Summoned in the middle of the night, Mallory de
Saint-Sebastian must leave the Abbey to protect
Queen Eleanor's life as a revolt against King
Henry rages. With a knight's sense of obligation,
she is determined to not only sheild Eleanor but to
find the enemies threatening her. Arriving at St.
Jude's Abbey, Saxon Fitz-Juste is amazed by the
Queen's choice of a female knight as her newest
warrior. A troubadour in Eleanor's royal court,
Saxon is ostensibly loyal to Her Majesty, but his
true mission remains to be seen.

0-451-21827-2

In twelfth-century England, St. Jude's Abbey is n
ordinary sanctuary of prayer and ritual. Establishe
by Eleanor of Aquitaine, it trains young women in th
knightly arts. In times of trouble, these formidable wome
are called upon to protect the royal family and England..

Isabella de Montfort's talents lie not in the knightly arts, b
in science. So she's surprised when Queen Eleanor assign
her the task of retrieving some incriminating papers tha
could destroy the prince and start a brutal war.

To help Isabella on her journey, the abbess of St. Jude
sends along her nephew, Jordan le Courtenay, a knight wh
lost his lust for battle when his best friend was killed in
joust. But soon Isabella inspires in Jordan a passion for th
world around him—and a dangerous longing for her.

PRAISE FOR THE NOVELS OF ST. JUDE'S ABBEY

"Splendid."—Virginia Henley

"Historical romance at its best!"—May McGoldric

www.penguin.com

ISBN-13: 978-0-451-22009-7

$6.99 U.S.
$9.99 CAN.

50699

EAN
S

9 780451 220097